THE CHOIR MISTRESS

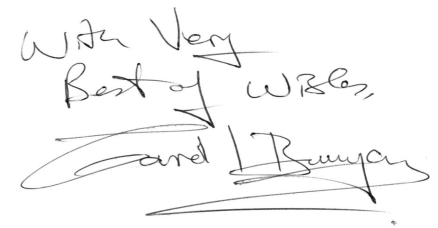

With Very
Best of Wishes,
Carol L Bunyan

Carol Bunyan

Signed 1st.
Edition.
27/11/07.

For Max

Acknowledgements

I should like to thank all my dear friends who have read first drafts, corrected spelling, guided my thoughts and whose help and affection has sustained me and who all, most importantly, believed in me.

My thanks also to Jessica Ruston my editor at The Writers' Workshop for her work on the initial drafts, and Andrew Lucas who helped so much designing the front cover.

I should also like to thank Daniel Cook and his team at New Generation Publishing for all their sterling efforts and advice.

A very special thank you to the members of The Voice Box Choir of Witney for being nothing like the Choir in this novel, but for being the inspiration for the setting of this story. To its accompanist, Keith Harris, for taking the first 't' out of my spelling of Mozart and the Choir Mistress herself, Lesley Morris, who bears absolutely no resemblance whatsoever to the woman in this book, and whose tireless support and encouragement have urged me throughout.

Finally, I want to thank my son, Max, for his patience with my computer skills, his empathy with the journey, but mostly for his love.

Carol Bunyan

Carol Bunyan has written extensively for the Theatre and Television. She worked for BBC TV for twelve years before leaving to be a full time freelance Writer and Director. Her Theatre credits include plays produced at The Royal Court Theatre (London), The Sheffield Crucible, The Courtyard Theatre (London), Battersea Arts Theatre (London), The Haymarket Sherman (Cardiff), Warwick Arts, Manchester, Reading, Liverpool and York Theatres. Her plays have also been produced at the State Theatre Stockholm and in Berlin. Her Television plays include several for BBC-1's "Play for Today", and BBC-2's "Playhouse", a six-part Film Series for BBC-2, and a series of plays for Central Television, ITV and ATV. Her television plays have also been translated and performed in Germany, Sweden and America. Carol is a descendant of John Bunyan, the author of "The Pilgrim's Progress"

"THE CHOIR MISTRESS" is Carol's first novel.

Website: www.carolbunyan.co.uk

Chapter 1

The room is waiting; it is holding its breath. It knows what is to follow, and it waits for the voices and for Anna.

She stands in the doorway and pauses, teasing the moment, as she waits for the room to know that she is there. She knows all its secrets; the moist smell of it, the dampness of anxious armpits and the explanations of uncompleted essays, the walls of the room bannered with the hopefully provocative "What is God? and Where do I find Him?" in a centre circle, with lines shooting outward to several alternative ideologies, careful to include the Muslims - the Head teacher having recently returned from one of those Inclusive Community Week-ends rashly promised at the last Election and beloved of Witsham District Council - the effect rather spoiled by the biro'd addition of Argos Superstore as the most likely residence of the Almighty. The room holds the aching boredom of Geography, and the crushing dread of homework. The wetness of socks balled sweatily into trainers, and a lost fleece that has been lying under the broken chair in the corner since last summer and, under it all, the unmistakeable cheesing of a carpet scuffed with boys' feet.

Anna breathes it in, the dankness, and smells the power, sixteen by twenty feet of control. She draws the curtains; it's a quick snatch at the bright orange squares leafed with impossibly green ivy, and shuts out the compromises and the little splashes of doubt amongst the wet November night.

Anna always gets there early.

She likes to walk into the room and know that it is hers; for two hours this is her place, her arena, and, as she thinks of it when the mirror reflects the careful application of her face…her stage.

This place where her authority is unrivalled and they all look to her. They will look as she raises her baton, and they will wait. They will wait for her signal, her permission for them to sing. She moves the music stand into the centre of the room, positioning it as she does every Monday evening onto the little smear of blue paint that stains the floor - a relic of the doomed Crafts-for-Christmas evening classes that caused all that unpleasantness with the Caretaker. Anna always takes great care to keep on the right side of Reg, the bottle of Baileys at end of Term earning her the freedom of the Staff tea-making facilities and no-questions-asked about ceramic mugs: the ostentatiously marked "Karen's!" in permanent ink being Anna's particular favourite as she takes a small and secret delight in sipping where the School Secretary's coral-apricot mouth has pursed, figuring that anyone who put an exclamation mark after their name on a mug from Didcot Steam Railway deserves all the germs they get.

Outside, sitting in her Volvo, Diane is peering through the smoky wetness, watching the woman inside the schoolroom, and wonders briefly at the violence in that sudden swish of the curtains. Diane has recognised Anna from a dozen Witsham Gazettes: *"Local singer to star in Concert for Disabled Youngsters"* and Anna's elfin sharp little face staring straight into the camera, her arm around the wheelchair's recipient of Rotarian kindness. Anna off to Bergen with the Twinning Society in exchange for eight rather bewildered Norwegians; and always that look, staring out of the photographs, the bright intensity of Anna.

Diane's read about the Choir, Anna's Choir, on the same day that she'd had her last session at the Outpatients. She'd used it as a shield against the usual "Join In and Take Part" mantra, which she took to mean involvement in life in general, but Diane decided that she would start off by joining-in in the particular, the particular being the promise to turn up every Monday and see if she could get away with standing at the back and miming, but watching Anna, and remembering that rather unsettling gaze, doubt nibbles.

Anna is setting out tonight's music along the trestle table by the door.

"Pick up your copies as you come in girls, some lovely new stuff." She tries this out to the room, but shakes her head... "New music for us to learn tonight ladies, take your copies to your seats." Better. More professional. Two new members joining tonight, first impressions were essential.

Trevor, the choir's accompanist, is lingering at the door, unwilling for Anna to realise that he has heard her. She must always be warned of his approach, Anna does not like surprises. He bangs his music case against the door and backs into the room fussing with an invisible obstacle in the hallway beyond.

"Don't lurk, Trevor." And the man allows the injustice of this, determinedly smiling at her. "You got all that lot photocopied all right then?" Anna also suppresses her irritation at the obvious and continues to sort copies of "Adiemus" and "The Rhythm of Life" into little piles.

Trevor is bundling his coat under the piano stool, rolling it into a tight ball so that it won't be in the way. "Only I know what She's like about using the School's printer."

"Oh I think she's getting my measure now after that business with the tea bags."

Trevor's smiling at the memory. "As if you'd use Co-Op Saver Blend."

Anna acknowledges his tribute with a slight nod.

"Only Twinings Assam." Trevor's piling it on too thick now and Anna is wearying of his crawling.

"I'm not a snob Trevor."

"No, no – but you like what you like."

"And I like quality".. and Anna flips the final pile of music down onto the table with a satisfied slap.

"Yes," and Trevor is eager to move onto safer ground. "Did you ask Philip about the drums for Adiemus?"

"He's got another one of his ridiculous Rotary Do's, so it'll have to be Rowena again."

Trevor's face is a picture of genuine dread: "Oh dear."

"Well she did do that Drumming Workshop at the Ethnic Sounds in the Community Festival."

"But that was Tribal wasn't it?" Trevor keeps his alternative side strictly for his Folk on Friday sessions.

Anna is grimacing: "Africa meets Witsham … not a great turnout I seem to remember."

"Well I think you're far too lenient with her, you'll be having to count her in on every bar, remember "Gaudete.""

Anna, who prides herself on a patience not often noticed by her associates, is remembering only too well.

Outside, in her car, Diane is staring at the curtained windows.

She's talking to the windscreen wipers. "Just walk in. It's as simple as that. Just do it." She gets a large travel make-up mirror out of the glove compartment and wonders briefly why it is called that when people never put gloves in it, and stares into the mirror, checking and re-checking the soft peach blusher as she blends it more subtly into her cheeks.

"I'll just wait for a few more to arrive," she tells the mirror.

"Must stop getting everywhere too early," and she's remembering the post Paul dinner parties – driving round streets in the drizzling dark trying to waste that crawling time before she could arrive, the bottle of thank-you Red on the seat beside her. The parking two streets away from that particular lighted window to sit and breathe with pursed lips at the car-fresh little pine tree as it spun with her soft rhythm as she counted the windscreen wipers - thirty wipes a minute, one hundred and fifty for five minutes, and then another thirty before she was allowed to look in the mirror again.

Life is now divided into Before Paul, then that time when she had believed that life was as it should be, that she had joined them, the couples, the how she so casually used "My husband" in conversations about week-ends, the Sundays of Book Fayres and the holidays,
oh the holidays, couples palling up with couples. Paul sussing out who'd be Their Kind of People and then all those evenings spent meeting Ben and Suzy in the bar for drinks before dinner, and then planning to all hire a taxi together the next day to visit the local vineyard. Paul and Ben swapping one-upmanship tales of vintages drunk and that rather special bottle of wine that they'd found in that off-the-beaten-track place in Tuscany; and the wives, smug in their possession, walking a little ahead of the men and smiling in tolerant conspiracy as they listened to the loud barks of male laughter. After the first week the women edging closer to giggled mutterings in the confessional of The Ladies: of the inevitability of holiday-afternoon-sex and sweaty snoring. Their small betrayals understood to be the price for this new shared intimacy, the secret joy of rebellion allowing a raised eyebrow at the male tales of Meetings Attended and Cars Driven. The shared hostages as they swap their little discontents: always having to buy him that smelly organic goat's cheese, and how polyester brings on his rash. The absolute thrill of those tiny traitorous acts. They'll never know, they'll never know we've said this. The power of it, the power of being able to offer each other these gifts of female secrecy.

But no harm is meant, no harm will come of this. Both women know the game that they are playing. It is understood. And when, back in the bedrooms, the men will comment on the other wife. just to test the water: "Wasn't too keen on that top she was wearing tonight..."
Each wife will concur and agree and delight in the preference.
And then the walks along dusty, darkening streets to Their Trattoria, and thinking that it would last forever.

Now life is Post Paul, and she is sitting in a car in a school playground trying to pluck up the courage to go into a room and join a Choir.
Other women are arriving, calling to each other across the car park, "Hope you've brought your pencil this week Grace!" and a screech of laughter at the private joke. And "Jo-Anne's got those photos printed."
"Great, now I'll be proved right about our scarves."

10

Easy in their familiarity: known faces, known routines, the comforting sameness of going through a door that you have gone through many times, that you will sit in a chair that you have sat in and that you can turn to the person beside you and know that she's wearing a new skirt. That you can comment on this, that you belong.

Diane gets out of her car and locks the door with slow carefulness, presses the little button on the key to set the alarm ... safe.
Walks toward the door, drawn to the noise of these women.
She slips slightly, synthetic sole on the smooth wet cement of a step.
Steadies herself and feels a sharp tug at her back. Not now, not now.
Relax. She arches her back against the pain and walks into the room.

Such a small and simple act. Joining the Choir.
How to know? How to feel that slight quickening of future fear.
Did the Room know? The Room that is holding its breath.
Did those shadowy stained walls anticipate the terror?
There will be a Carnival, children dressed as tomatoes, round red balls bobbing and bouncing into each other and the thin and tinkling bell sound of infant giggling. The Women's Institute Belly Dancers trailing cheap gauzy scarves that twinkle brightly against soft over-round flesh. A brass band shrill and strident as steam engines puff and whistle a trivial jollity ...
... and then the Suddenness, the thunder of fear as bright blood trickles thickly into a gutter and the air is sliced open by the terrible screaming.

But the room does not warn her, there is no soft whisper from those curtains that shift in a slight breath of wind, she does not feel any shiver of dread, no pricking of thumbs, for Anna has much to do before that day.
So she looks up and spots Diane as she comes into the room because Anna always knows who exactly is in the room; amid the laughter and the back-chat, her eyes are never still. Her watchfulness the medal gained from years of waiting for the main chance. She's across to Diane – hand held out – bright smile and the eyebrows arched impossibly high into the unlikely dark of lacquered fringe. "Hello ! – Welcome."
Diane's returning the handshake, feeling the slight scratch of the sharply manicured nails: "Diane?" and she introduces her own name as a question as she rushes to explain herself: " I left a message on your ansaphone."

11

Yes. Diane Miles, Anna remembers the stutter over the surname, a dead giveaway; a faded blonde whose roots need a re-touch, soft eyes milky grey with tiredness, probably only the wrong end of thirty but Anna thinks that she looks much older. Of course, that could just be the bewildered Back Out There look of the recently divorced.

Anna herself is in total denial of her own 40 summers and frequently assesses the possible ages of women she passes in the street, these moments never failing to reassure.

"Yes you did ! Well done. Everybody ! This is Diane."
And Diane finds herself returning a dozen smiles.

"A Soprano?" Anna is always keen for sopranos, most of the choir slide tentatively into the Alto-but-higher-if-pushed variety.

Diane is wary of unachievable squeaks and plumps for the middle range and Anna resigns herself to another alto-heavy programme.

The women are arranging themselves in a semi-circle and Diane makes for the lower end of the centre. They're straight into a warm-up before Diane's got her coat off.
"Ah poor dove,
Take thy flight,
Far above the sorrows
Of this dark night"

Then Anna's dividing them into three groups to sit in as a 'round'
This is all too fast and knowing for Diane, who's looking at the woman next to her to see if there are any words she can read.

"You don't need the music sheets for this one, you'll soon pick it up." Anna's targeting Diane's confusion. So, Diane, who doesn't think that she can pick up words and tune in three minutes, is resorting to a general mouth shape that fits all and uttering not a single sound.

Anna is walking along the line of the choir, listening to each voice and Diane can feel that familiar soft wetness, upper lip and chin puddling.

She is saved by Trevor, who has gone onto auto pilot, and is now deep into what he should have said to that Burberry-capped oik in the car park.

Anna's on him, rat on a mole: "Not up the octave yet Trevor, please."
So she nips past Diane to return to her music stand all the better to give Trevor what he thinks of as 'One of her Looks.'

Trevor satisfies himself with rehearsing: "Your car was quite obviously reversing out of your parking space into that lady's pushchair, I merely used my horn to prevent a child's death." He was pleased with that, the understatement of it, and most particularly the use of the word "lady."
He smiles and pushes back into that other place in his head the fact that he had merely muttered "Aah...sorry but .. the pushchair..." and that the Burberry had merely scowled at him and raised a two-fingered salute as he had swung off in his four-wheel-drive monster.
The Jeep, and the spare wheel on the back in a covering emblazoned with a charging rhino, that and the cap and the matching scarf .. Trevor holds these things tight to him in a small closed angry ball. He'd been to school with them. Alan Sharkey would have turned out like that.

Anna's moved on to "La-ing" up and down the scales, and Trevor thumps the keys with hard hate as he remembers. Sharkey at the practice sessions, choosing him to be in goal and then slamming at him, the balls flying in at his head so that he had to duck and squirm away from the hard punch of pain. Then the sneering. If he could have thought it through Trevor would have chosen to take a ball in the face rather than that drawled taunting, but his body always reacted, an instinctive lurch away from the punishment.

Diane's started to actually make a noise now, she's dared a couple of the lower register "La"s encouraged by the noticeable flat sounds coming from Jo-Anne on her left. In her early forties, with a mess of dark curls that had once tried to be a glossy bob, Jo-Anne is an approachable warm woman who smiles too much. She has offered to let Diane share her water bottle, so they're well on their way to coffee-mornings.

All the choir carry water in those "gym" bottles that have a special cap that pops up and down, and Diane makes a mental note to bring one next week. She sees that everybody has these now, even if they're just popping to Waitrose, it's as if we're all anticipating a long dry safari-trek to the well. Just as we all wear trainers when we're not training for anything.
Diane snaps her thoughts back to Anna as everybody is now rummaging in their files for the next piece of music.
"Just share with Jo-Anne for today Diane," Anna's telling her, and Diane's making another note to buy one of those files – Jo-Anne's is

full of "divider" markers and there's a biro'd index at the front. And Diane spots that she's mis-spelt 'Pee-ay Jesu' and is comforted, so that she offers Jo-Anne a Strepsil that's accepted with an unnecessary but satisfying amount of gratitude.

Anna discourages chat between songs, so the rapport between Jo-Anne and Diane is conducted very much upon the lines of the kind of animal interaction learned from David Attenborough's programmes. Lots of eye-brows raised and puckish grins to signal mutual ineptitude at the task in hand, and shoulders shrugged in a pantomime of incomprehension as Anna asks the Altos to: "Really land on that G."

Diane's piano lessons had ended two decades earlier, Wednesday evenings at Mrs. Rice's bungalow; the exquisite torture of having the teacher's cat, Mozart, sit on her lap while she pretended to have practiced "Fur Elise" all week. Mrs. Rice would be in the kitchen, "I can hear you dear," getting Mr. Rice's tea, and Mozart would be doing that claws retracting and digging routine that cats do to the knees of the unwary. Unable to take her hands from the keys and pluck claw from flesh, Diane had perfected the art of turning most pieces into a gallop, a desperate rush to the finish before actual blood was drawn. Well used to children who attended her lessons due entirely to their mother's social aspirations now sadly decades out of date: "You'll always be welcome at parties," a generation soon to be betrayed by the arrival of the record-player, swiftly followed by C.D.s and all things technical, Mrs. Rice had accepted the limits of her calling and concentrated less on "Fur Elise" than on Mr. Rice's seven-thirty return and the preparation of grilled tomatoes on toast. In those innocent days before "Dinner" had filtered down to the lower classes and spaghetti was still something that came chopped up, and soft, in cans, the evening tea was usually something on toast, the achievement of it being "something hot" being all.

So Diane, searching her mind to find "G", and realising that its relevance was in a tangle of the warm stale smells that emanated from Mrs. Rice's kitchen and a particular glint in a feline eye, cannot bring herself to land with any confidence upon this note, and is reassured by Jo-Anne's whispered "God knows."

Anna watches the women in front of her. The new one's pretty hopeless but at least she's keeping Jo-Anne from asking if We Could Just Run This Again Please. With a bit of luck they might pal up and leave.

Anna has Big Plans for the Cheltenham Festival this year and is seriously considering a cull of the more inadequate members. She doesn't want to do this, of course, but she has to be fair to herself, this Choir Reflects Her. She looks across at Trevor, who has appeared to 'float-off' again.

She imagines him, quite literally, floating away on some sort of lake, in a very small boat, still smiling in that vacuous way, with his lips moving to an internal mantra. She looks across at him, only just past his fortieth but he could be a decade older: the wispy-thin greying hair, always just a little greasy, framing a rather podgy face. The softly apprehensive mouth so often with a suggestion of dampness, and always that slightly fretful look behind the grey watery eyes.

She should get rid of him too. She knows that. It was all very well at the beginning, with him being so handy for lifts to and fro, and him never wanting any petrol money. But Cheltenham ! This will be her hour, and loyalty, in the shape of Trevor, may just have to be sacrificed. Anna calls a halt and makes sure that she's the first into the Ladies. They all know that she's in there, so there's nothing but anodyne chat laced with the unlikely "I've been practising all week with the tapes," grovelling, as the rest of them queue up by the wire boxes of footballs and cricket stumps. Anna's negotiating the racks of gym shoes as she squeezes past the others and gets to the mirror. Grace, who's got a long-service medal at Weight-Watchers, and is squashing her size 22 in beside the cricket bat stand, is very much aware that she will have to get past her Choir Mistress: "I don't know why they have to store all this stuff in here," and she's offering Anna a rueful grimace as she gestures to her bulk. "Sorry...sorry," and she's pushing herself hard up against the wall . "It was just like this on the plane and I said to Geoffrey 'we should have had aisle seats.' Grace is acutely aware that this information is as irrelevant as it is uninteresting, and she is flushed with the shame of her size, and the humiliation of having always to explain and confess.

Anna allows the other woman to manoeuvre herself into the cubicle and from inside can be heard Grace's "I talk too much that's my problem...." And the quieter refrain "Geoffrey's always saying.."

Anna is taking the opportunity of a careful look in a long mirror that's been propped up against the far wall. She runs her hands down the side of the fitted grey skirt and looks hard at a body honed rake-thin by an unchecked and unfulfilled ambition. What she sees is a slight wrinkle in the material and she smoothes it straight, long fingers pushing at her thigh and it is almost a caress. She lifts her hands to the angular, rather pointy little face and pushes long scarlet nails into the immaculately layered crop of hair, that perfectly balanced mix of raven and burnt mahogany blended by Justin himself (of "Justin's" – Oxford, not Witsham) and cut with a ruthless regularity into the inflexible helmet that is no stranger to lacquer.

Inside the cubicle, Grace is coughing to cover bottom noises and Anna frowns her distaste as she leaves the room. Not a woman to be comfortable with bodily functions, she has house-rules for the facilities at their home that her husband, Roy, has long since learnt to obey. The en-suite in the master bedroom is strictly reserved for the washing of hands and application of lotions, and Anna is very keen on lotions. Anything of a more radical nature has to be reserved for the bathroom at the end of the corridor. Anna's home is one where the air freshener is much in evidence, especially the plug-in variety that releases regular puffs of "Ocean Glade" into the cool beige rooms. Bowls of potpourri grace occasional tables, and since the lady of the house has discovered the charms of the scented candle in a glass pot, despite her husband's daring insurrection that the sitting room was resembling a religious shrine, the level of fire hazard in Annaroy House increases daily.

The second half of the evening picks up considerably. Anna mentions "Cheltenham" and "Solos", and a delicious fear ripples through the line; there's much "Oh no, not me"-ing from the members, but there's an excitement, a daring, they are each terrified of being chosen, but they want it, it's first-sex with the boy in the upper sixth, it's that first sleep-over and getting drunk on advocaat.

And absolutely no-one is convinced by Linda (lead soprano and Volvo estate in the car park) doing her "Oh please not me again, make somebody else have a go Anna."

Susie, the ballsy alto with attitude, is seconding that :
    "Can't the middle voices have a chance?"

Anna is very slightly wary of Susie who, apart from having far too much glorious red hair, has a husband who has aspirations to the Council and is also the kind of man that Anna feels that she should have met years ago because he looks like a 'Rotary Club and Dinners at the Golf Club' sort of man. Stephen attends the Choir concerts with a video camera and passes, in Witsham, for "media" in that he writes an occasional column in the Hepton Village Gazette and once had a photograph of its Churchyard published in the Guardian.

Anna still tingles with the memory of Susie's "You see it dates back to the Reformation," and the shame of not knowing quite what she meant. Susie votes Liberal, and wears badges that shout "Not In My Name!" that are difficult to ignore. Anna once told her that politics and the Choir were an inappropriate mix, but Susie had said that the Personal was the Political and the badge had stayed.

Susie's pushing it: "We haven't had an Alto solo for months."
Anna flashes one of her bright smiles, brittle as morning ice on grass. "Point taken Susie. Absolutely." But she does not commit to a piece. "Trevor and I are going to discuss the solos after practice."
This is news to Trevor who'd hoped to get back early enough for "The Secret World of the Dolphin" that he'd highlighted in his Radio Times, but Anna is moving swiftly on ..
"I think you'll find we'll come up with something suitable."

There's a moment, as she realises that her knife will have to cut deep as she looks straight at the small woman in front of her. Lindsay, the youngest member of the Choir being still in her twenties, the wedding ring sparkling on her finger still new enough to be frequently touched, is a fey and fragile waif, smiling with sweetly vague unconcern as she packs away her music.
Anna's voice is tin foil, tearing: "Lindsay? Will you be happy to do a solo this time?"
Lindsay, bearing all the enthusiasm of a startled rabbit, is unable to respond immediately. Being usually grateful for her role as the most invisible member of the Choir and the one who, due to her stature, has most regrettably to stand at the very front, she painfully and most obviously stands stock-still throughout all concerts, saucer-eyed with fear. Quite why she attends these events or is indeed a member of the Choir is a mystery to the members. Anna has tried with her "let's all move with the music," sessions, but Lindsay remains paralysed as arms flail and bodies sway around her. But Anna has now Cheltenham to consider, and is beginning her cull. "Every member must be capable of a solo," and she puts her head on one side in a posture of caring concern. "Lindsay?"

The Choir hold their breath. If Lindsay is being asked to sing solo then there is to be no quarter given. Anna has crossed a line and now they are all darting quick anxious glances between themselves.

"This is like Rourke's Drift when the Zulus arrived." Jo-Anne mutters to Diane. Diane's nodding. "Michael Caine."

"Yes All right." Lindsay's baby hamster voice causes several murmurs of shocked congratulation, and Anna can do nothing but smile back. "Excellent. We'll start on these next week girls."

There's general relief that no-one else is to be speared on Anna's sword of ambition, well not until next week, and in the bustle of retrieved coats and handbags Grace calls over to Susie "Drink?" and she's nodding toward the door and the undoubted charms of The Crown and Anchor.

Diane's keen to get out now. She'll do the social "After Choir" stuff another time, she just wants to get home and start breathing again.
She makes a dive for the door and then turns back, wanting to sort of thank Jo-Anne, without actually saying it, but wanting to acknowledge the kindness. Jo-Anne's busy trying to file the new music into her little plastic folders, so Diane goes back over to her. "See you next week then…. Jo-Anne."

"Oh right yes" .. and she's trying to stuff too many pages into the folder and drops the music onto the floor. "Bugger."

"Sorry."

"What?"

"Sorry, I made you drop the…"

"Oh no." Jo-Anne's scrambling to pick up the pages without letting them get out of order…. "I haven't numbered the pages yet you see."

"Oh. Right." Diane's feeling the blouse stick to her back, and calls "Sorry anyway." as she now makes her escape from the room.

Outside in the blessed cool night, Diane takes a ragged breath. She walks toward her car.
She shouldn't have gone back to say goodbye —she'd looked like an idiot.
She fumbles the alarm button on the car key and sets off the alarm. It screams into the night and gets several looks from the other women as they cross the car park, it takes her three panic-quick goes to finally turn the thing off.

Then she's into the car, slamming the door, sweaty fingers slipping on the seat belt clip, and counting twenty until the interior light finally, blessedly, goes out. And she sits there in the darkness, her chest asthma-tight, a raw and jagged little pain on the in-breath squeezed hard up against the seat belt.

Back in the room, Anna is taking one last look, checking that it has returned to that other shape, the schoolroom. She turns out the lights and in the darkness the room sighs. The curtains heave against the cold windows because they know, they know what is to come ..
The fear and the blood, and there will be no avoiding.

Chapter 2

Across the inky wetness of the town, a man hunches his shoulders against the drifting haze of rain that's diamonding under the street lighting. He's hurrying through the large waste of emptiness that parks the daytime supermarket rush: there are only two cars left standing. Lost, rigidly obedient in their marked bays, waiting. A wire trolley drifts, abandoning now its morning movements of sideways crabbing, wheels now free of reluctant stiffness and irritated shoving. It rolls forward smoothly, pushed by ghostly wind.

The man walks past one of the cars and notices that there is a shape behind its wheel, he hurries on in an exaggerated bustle of not noticing, only to look back once he is out of the park. The man who sits in his car in that dark emptiness is leaning back against the seat staring up at the plastic roofing.

The wire trolley clinks against the steel posts holding their little globes of light and the man in the car looks quickly across at the noise. The sound has also disturbed something small and nocturnal that scuttles quickly in amongst the tangled ivy that chokes the attempt at vegetation, little borders of green that divide the serried ranks of white lines, there's a scuttle as a cat that has been waiting long and patiently for this moment pounces swiftly upon the soft fur.

The man in the car watches as the cat begins its torture of the little scrabbling panic amongst the leaves, and he winds down his car window to better view the killing.

"Go on, get it, get the bitch!"
But his urgings startle the cat and it drops its prey.
The man punches the steering wheel in frustration.
"Stupid … stupid," he spits the words at the windscreen.
He lifts his left hand up to his mouth and bites into the soft flesh beneath his thumb, closing his eyes slowly as the redness deepens.

Chapter 3

Anna opens her front door and breathes deeply of 'Jasmine and Peach'

"Roy – are you on your e-mail?"

A thump can be heard from above the open-plan staircase and there's somewhat of a scuffle as Roy appears, his face pink with guilt.

"No, no." It's said too quickly, "No, I was just …"

"Well never mind dear I want to talk to you about Trevor."

"Oh." Roy's voice brims with apathy but he trots willingly downstairs to join Anna in the sitting room, where heavy cream curtains are held back in brocade swags, a cream leather sofa nestles on a thick magnolia carpet; it's the kind of room that would refuse red wine.

"That Susie was stirring it again."

"Not Trevor then?"

"Yes, no well to be fair he doesn't 'stir' as such, but he'll have to go."

"Poor Trevor."

"Don't be silly dear. I've told you."

"Cheltenham." Roy nods, acknowledging the gravity.

"Remember Susie's husband, that Stephen who's always so full of himself, writes those articles about Hepton; ridiculous, used to be just a pub and a churchyard before half the BBC moved in there. Eight barn conversions in a year with inglenook fireplaces and antique beams, just because they're wood-stained 'dark old oak' and they've drilled a few holes in them suddenly they're 'original'. I told you, Ned and his son got the decorating job, broke their hearts when they had to 'distress' the walls. Now it's Hepton Historical Society this and Hepton Newsletter that, and all he ever writes about is Cromwell, well I told you he was 'left'. He even popped up in the Witsham Gazette last week with his "A Village in Perspective."

And then without any sense of contradiction:

"You should do that."

"What?"

"Get articles published. You never put yourself forward." She's looking at him, a slight frown between her eyes as she surveys the corduroy trousers that buckle and fold onto the leather slippers. Roy's lack of height is a constant niggle of irritation to Anna, a woman in a state of denial when purchasing her husband's clothes. "What leg length are those?"

"You always buy them too long, I'm not going to grow into them."

Roy is keen to avert attention from his body lest Anna remembers that she hasn't filled in The Daily Mail's Tums and Bums Chart, which will almost certainly lead to another Salad-for-a-Week malarkey.

But as he looks into those cool grey eyes he is reminded with heart-sinking clarity that Anna can sometimes be uncanny in her ability to read his mind.

"Did you eat that Lean Cuisine meal I left for you?"

"Yes"... it's unconvincing

"You didn't add potatoes to it again did you."

And with great truth, Roy is able to assure her that he had not added extra carbohydrates, figuring that the little box of microwave chips didn't really count, especially since he had hidden the finished box in next door's bin.

He cravenly re-directs her fire.

"So... Trevor..?"

"I'm thinking of approaching Jonathan. I can't be Held Back. Trevor's all well and good for the Day Centre Do's, the oldies love him because he does his Gracie Fields Sing-Along and wears his cap....but you know what he was like when I tried to introduce just a very little taste of Opera into the Christmas Concert."

Roy is rash in an attempt at fair play:

"But they only wanted a quick Carol for turning on the Christmas Lights didn't they, I mean it doesn't last very long – that guy from Emmerdale just said "Hi Everybody," pressed the switch and was back in his car in ten minutes."

"Well that was your lot on the Council's fault. How much did you pay him for that?" Roy transparently remembers the exact fee only too well.

Anna takes a breath of deep longing: "When you're Mayor."

"Oh God." It's almost a wail.

The future Mayoress is relentless: "When you are Mayor, and there is absolutely no reason on earth why you shouldn't be... you're always saying it's only 'Buggins-Turn' and you've been waiting-in-the-wings for eight years now... "

Roy has slumped onto the sofa and is looking at the toes of his slippers. Anna presses on: "When you are Mayor we can really put Music First at these events ... and don't start saying that not everybody likes Puccini. They do. Look at all these Opera Highlights CD's, they're everywhere at Christmas. Anyway..." and then triumphantly clinching it: "Jonathan went to Oxford !"

"He did Geography, didn't he?"

"That's not the point."

"Do you think that Jonathan will really be interested?"

Anna's eyes, grey knives of something uncomfortably close to loathing:

" ... in Just a Small Town Choir?"

"I never actually said that," and it's measured, the words weary with repetition.

"After the Shipbury Concert, to that Committee woman."

"No, I merely ..."

"I heard you !"

"I know, and I've told you. I was being ironic because you'd all done so well and you got three encores for 'Going Up A-Yonder'. I just said..."

"Just a Small Town Choir," and each word is spat at him.

"I said...that you were all pretty fabulous for ..Just a Small Town Choir."

"Ironic? What would you know of ironic. I had to listen to your speech at Eric's Retirement! you are such a..." And she stares at him as the cream leather squeaks at his shifting. He's picked up one of the vanilla cushions and is moving his fingers around the yellow braiding as he turns it in his hands.

"That will stain."

He does not answer her. She is almost shaking as she watches the cushion : "Your hands, the sweat, it will turn that yellow all grey."

He's remembering, it's almost lyrical : "You said it was ochre. I told you it was yellow in the shop, but you insisted... ochre."

"You're doing it to..." and she pulls herself back, and now it's very nearly an appeal "You know I have to have those dry cleaned. I want everything to be nice for Wednesday."

He places the cushion back against the arm of the sofa, pushing a small hole in its centre and pulling the top corners up so that they point like little rabbit's ears.

"There, is that 'nice'?"

Anna stands there, looking at the cushion, feeling that she has lost and feeling suddenly very tired.

There's a long breath of silence in the room. Roy gets up and walks to the door. His slippers shush against the deep pile as if he cannot summon the energy to lift his feet. "I'll make some coffee shall I?"

"Decaf!" she calls after him, and as he leaves the room she turns back to re-adjust the cushion, just a few important inches further into the seat of the sofa, and it's a low murmur: "You always forget... decaf."

Chapter 4

The man in the car park is looking down at his hand, at the jagged weal of teeth marks in his skin. There is a small bubble of blood welling into the deepest place where he has bitten; he gently wipes the blood across the markings, massaging it into the palm of his hand.

He looks at his watch and starts up the car, its headlights punching into the blackness. On the passenger seat lies a folder that's spilling sheets of music onto the floor of the car as it sweeps out into the streets and only the cat watches his leaving.

Chapter 5

Diane is standing in her kitchen, a mug of tea in her hands, she is cradling it against her chest. She is singing softly to herself, 'La-ing' up and down the scales. She has a rich deep voice, and Anna would have been surprised to hear it. It was not the voice of the choir practice. It was a private voice.

* *

Anna is standing in her bedroom, the cup of decaf on a small occasional table by the window. She is looking out, through the swagged muslin, into the street below.

A group of teenagers, stone-kicking bored, are scuffing their trainers against the residents' parking sign. Anna watches them as if they are an alien species and realizes that she cannot ever remember being that young, not that sort of young, that carelessness. Although she is barely forty she has always felt the same. She has always felt a kind of middle age. That was her mother dying of course, that and her having to go and live with Aunt Jo.

Aunt Jo. Anna's mouth twists as she thinks of her mother's elder sister: a spinster, in the old sense of the word, a woman who had never expected nor wanted children, a woman who had fed and clothed the orphan but had not chosen to attend the School Concerts and Speech Days where Anna's light had shone. A woman who had shaken a bemused and weary head at certificates for music, and whose praise had been saved for the tidiness of the child's room.

Anna's teddies were military in the precision of their positioning, and she had seldom played with a doll's house that displayed immaculate settings where the little wooden dolls stood rigidly staring straight ahead, and the small bright blue metal car did not leave the garage.

Anna looks down at the cup of coffee and the dusty brown surface of the cooling liquid. The powdered sweetener has left a swirl of small flecks of white mist, and Anna can taste the tang of the chemicals in her mouth. It wasn't decaff, she was sure of it. Perhaps he didn't want her to sleep? Perhaps he liked her to lie there, night after night, staring at the brass light fittings sheening from the street lamp. Anna sighs, another thing he could have prevented, eight years on the Council and they get a street light slam bang right outside their master bedroom window. Its glare bouncing around the room, finding every shiny surface. Mocking her.

"You don't need a night-light – you're eight now Anna !"

* *

Diane rinses the teacup, wiping the inside with a sponge attached to the end of a hollow stem that has a cap on the end of it; the directions for this appliance were laid on the draining board beside her. 'This Washo-Wand can be filled and re-filled with your favourite washing-up liquid'. Diane was not sure if she had a favourite washing-up liquid and eyed the three-for-one 'green apple' variety with a slight distaste. She had, however, once formed an alliance with 'citrus burst', but obviously so had half of Witsham, and the rash move to another fruit had been an error. Green apples reminded her of that holiday in Kent, and she was weary of this minefield of memories. So that as she filled the wand with the smell of an orchard, Paul's laughing mouth slid like a terrorist into that place in her head that waited for pauses and small hours of the night.

Paul's mouth soft and hot on hers, Paul's mouth.

Diane pushes her body up against the sink and feels the wooden veneer of the cupboard door against her thigh. The cupboard that held two sets of marigold gloves, one 'medium' and one 'large.' Paul's mouth, telling her that he had to just pop into town, again, that his second mobile phone was for tax reasons and that he'd give her the number just as soon as he'd changed his service-provider, again. Paul's mouth telling her that they had to have their own, separate, interests; and then Paul's mouth, drier and cooler as the months of doubts crawled between them, telling her that they needed Space.

Diane decides that she will throw out the 'large' gloves.... tomorrow. She rinses the mug and then dries it with kitchen paper, wiping round and round inside, counting the times that the paper rubs against the rim.

"That's it, that's it".. and she places the mug on the little rack above the draining board. Wipes her hands on the tea towel that hangs on the second hook of the Olives of Provence plaque and looks at the empty hooks that used to hold his Bar-B-Q Apron and the Christmas reindeer oven gloves with the red-nose as the thumb, and she wonders if she will ever be free of this steady drip, drip of him.

Roy is putting the bin out. He too watches the teenagers as they loll against the post, leaning their supple bodies in easy arcs.
One of the boys looks across at the middle-aged man in his leather slippers and yawns at him, a huge slow gape that squashes his nose into the insolent eyes. Roy looks away and rams the lid down onto the waste bin. He thinks that they might knock it over later, and kick it around so that Anna will ask him what the noise is and expect him to do something about it.

Roy closes the door behind him, and hears a bark of young male laughter from the street, and hates them. He imagines going back out there and walking straight up to them. 'You got something to say to me, punk?' and then their faces, uncertain and unsure as he swaggers back to his front door, and then he'd turn again to them: 'And if this bin is touched tonight …' but Roy's imagination falters as he leans his back against the door. They hadn't even spoken to him, they hadn't done anything to him. One of them had just yawned, that's all.

Why did it fill him with such itching impotence, and why did he want to kill them. He threw the bolt on the door with a satisfying amount of noise and then hooked the chain into place, slotting the little nut into its hole and only then did he let go a breath he hadn't realised that he had been holding.

He could hear Anna on the floor above. She was singing. She was always singing. Those bloody choir routines that he had to listen to over and over and then at the Concerts, and he had to smile and smile and applaud until the palms of his hands were pink and stinging with his adoration; because if Anna turned to face the audience and he wasn't in full fan-mode her face would do that slight contracting movement, as if a tooth had caused her a sudden pain, and he'd have to hear all about Aunt Jo again and how nobody had ever appreciated her, and he wondered how many years he had to serve to recompense for another's fault.

* *

Trevor turns off his television, the dolphins hadn't been as good as he hoped. It wasn't a David Attenborough and nobody could do it like him. It was a cheap bought-in foreign job with a commentary that was all "Now we see the mother dolphin…" and Trevor was irritated. "Yes of course we can see, we're watching it aren't we," he'd shouted at his set. He was very good at shouting at his television, witty and urbane remarks that cut into the screen.

He looked at his Radio Times for tomorrow, at what he'd marked up in his highlighter pen, just the News and that Police Pathologist programme he liked; only now there were too many of them. He'd got hooked with "Silent Witness" and that woman who stared into the distance and narrowed her eyes. Intelligent, but didn't flaunt it about. You felt she'd listen if you talked to her, yes he had liked her. But now every police series had a scene in the mortuary and a post-mortem with a cynical bloke who was chewing his lunch to show how unmoved he was at the crisped-up cadaver in front of him that always gave the rookie cop a chance to throw up and the old hands to raise their eyebrows at each other. Why were people always so smug, Trevor rather thought that most likely he'd be the new boy being sick in the corner.

He turned off the main light but left on the standard lamp by the window, the one with the automatic timer attached to the plug. The one that said that somebody was in when they weren't. He looked back at the room, at the armchair that sprouted a foot rest when he tilted back in it, and made a mental note to get that stain removal stuff for the small coffee mark in the shape of Australia. He looked across at his piano, and the table with his recording equipment on it with the stacks of tapes and the piles of music. Tomorrow he'd make the sound tapes for the sopranos, so that they could practice at home. He'd sing along to the tapes to give them an idea of where to take a breath, and he'd mark up the copies of the new music so that they could get a better idea of the timing. He always felt for the ones who couldn't read music, and had developed a system of little biro'd arrows by the notes to help them out. The altos were all right with this piece, they'd got the easy melody line, but the sopranos had a lot of trilling up and down, and they had to land on top F from nowhere so he'd work out something that he could do to help them. Put in an extra chord that Anna wouldn't notice... he chewed his lip at that... he'd have to mention it to her, just casually, just a by-the-way sort of comment next Monday. He'd pop into Smiths and get some more of those coloured felt tips that had gone down so well for "Adiemus", he could even start a system of colour-coding. Blue for the sopranos, Yellow for the Altos, Red for the new Bass members. Another quick look round for fire hazards, at the ash-tray that was just for show because he didn't smoke, and the electric coal-effect fire that he'd turned off on the last ad-break during the dolphins, and he leaves the room, with the light telling the street that he was still up, still busy, still doing something probably quite interesting.

Chapter 6

Witsham at night boasts only two places where Middle-England now feels able to down a civilized pint: The town's Hotel, inspirationally named "The Witsham", a venue mainly reserved for Christmas parties and Office "Do's" and for whenever a Wedding Anniversary demands a little more attention, and "The Crown and Anchor" which is conveniently near to the school and therefore the Choir's main watering hole after practice. Other Pubs now boast "doormen" that look like gladiators, and are full of Young People of the kind that even if they're not on drugs look as if they should be, and emit the kind of music that spark 'Noise and the Environment' articles in the Gazette, and cause such distress at local council meetings.

It is generally understood, in the way that the English understand these things, that the window embrasure is the prerogative of the Choir on Monday evenings after nine. Grace and Susie are onto their second gin and tonic, happily bitching about Anna. Susie had joined the Choir because she and Stephen had wanted to Really Take Part in the country town they'd chosen when they left London. Susie hadn't shone as much as she'd have liked to in Kensington, she just hadn't felt special enough, and she was special. She'd had all those photographs taken after her Make-Over Birthday treat, and Stephen had said that she looked like an absolute star with that crimson lake of wonderful hair. It was jealousy, that's what it was, that blessed "Women in Media Group" who insisted that she had to be 'Published' to join, and that two articles in the Notting Hill News-sheet didn't count, well half of them hadn't even been to Greenham, even on the day's coach trip when they'd taken the 'Support The Wimmin' Packs, and the last straw came when Stephen didn't even get an interview at the Guardian – despite all his work for the Green Party and leafleting half of Holland Park about the squirrels.

It was obvious that he was never going to be appreciated. So they'd chosen the village of Hepton, 'small enough for us to make a real mark' Stephen had said. Just a short Volvo dash from Witsham, a thriving market town on the edge of the Cotswolds. Historically Interesting, which was essential for Stephen, one main high street, and a proper church with a spire and all the right shops apart from a Body Shop but Susie had high hopes for the new shopping precinct. She'd got Grace to join the Choir with her. She'd met her on the "Meet Your Council" Week-end, when Susie had volunteered to represent the Citizens Advice Bureau (she'd been keen to make her mark there as the newest recruit to the Reaching-Out-to-the-Community-Team) She had spotted Grace trying not to eat a second complimentary scone at the coffee break, and had known instantly that here was somebody that Susie knew she could help. Her feminism, though slightly marred by the constant attention to her tresses, often spurs Susie to show other women the route to self-fulfilment. For her part, Grace often feels that the Women's Sunday Encounter Group has frankly a lot to answer for and, although initially grateful for this shining mass of goodwill, has begun to think up excuses for not joining Susie's Gym.

Grace felt that she couldn't actually leave the Choir, not now, not since her husband had made such a deal of it. She felt that, of late, Geoffrey had little cause to be proud of his wife, and joining the choir had earned her a few precious brownie-points at a particularly harrowing lunch with her mother-in-law.

Lindsay is sitting with them, still looking as if she's been hit by a truck.

"You go for it girl." Susie is telling her. Lindsay has never been one to particularly Go For It, and this sadly is not the first time that Susie has said this to her this evening. "Think how pleased Tony will be!"

Lindsay needs no reminding of the pleasure her husband will show upon the news of her solo, which is precisely why she is still sitting here, staring mutely into her lime and soda, when she would normally be back at home sorting out her handbag for the morning. She is only too aware that Tony will greet this news as firm evidence that she is Coming Out Of Herself, and that he will start suggesting all sorts of adventures and challenges to improve her.

The ice has long melted and the soda has lost its bubbles, as she dumbly stirs the mixture with the little glass wand and remembers previous strategies that Tony has devised: The Drama Improvisation Group to make her interact with Others, The Aromatherapy Massage Course to help her to Reach Out and Touch, and realises that, faced with Anna and the Solo, even the white water rafting holiday pales into quite reasonable proportions. At least she'd have a life jacket. At least if she drowned she wouldn't have to stand there and bow for applause.

Susie and Grace have moved onto Hepton Village Politics and the ruckus at last Thursday's Summer Fete Meeting. "Stephen offered to be the Voice On The Mic, and he's a bit nose-out-of-joint because that new couple at The Grange, you know, he used to be in Marketing, she donated one of her felt-with-feeling paintings for the School."

Grace's nodding. "Victorian lamps in the front garden."

"That's them – well they said they'd already sent preliminary feelers out to Radio Oxon, and that the fox from Fox FM might even do the Opening Ceremony."

Grace's not impressed. "Well he's only a man in a furry suit like they have at the football."

"That's what I told Stephen, and how that fox can talk through that big felt head is beyond me."

"We had that funny little man from the Insurance Advert last year didn't we, but I don't think they're any good once you get them off the telly."

Susie's groaning at the memory: "Least said soonest mended, and anyway, that was only because of all that nastiness with Christine Hamilton. I told Stephen, it's not political, she's a Celebrity now."

Susie's taking the opportunity to toss all that burgundy hair, a gesture she uses often to reinforce a point; she's seen it done on Question Time.

"I think there was a lot of bad feeling from the Older Residents.
They said that the Fetes used to be gentle country affairs and that the Newcomers have turned them into Andrew Lloyd-Webber Shows."

"Oh I know, but since we've been there the School has got a
computer room and now the littlies don't have to troop across in all weathers to the Village Hall for Gym."

"I think they miss the Quiet though."

"Think of the safety issues ! – What other village round here has got CCTV in its Children's Playground."

"Caught the dog fouling all right didn't it."

"Mmm. Two hours of that Labrador covering its tracks on the cricket pitch ...shame nobody knew who it belonged to."

"Was that your Stephen who put its photo on all the pylons?"

Susie's nodding. "Yes, Bless him, downloaded it from the CCTV. Still I think the Wanted Dead or Alive was a bit harsh, but it was after that business about the fox being more 'media' and he wasn't in a mood to feel too well disposed to the animal kingdom."

They notice Lindsay.

"Hello, it's The Night Before The Scaffold is it?"

"I wish I drank." Lindsay's staring with great dismay into her lime and soda.

"Have a gin, Grace, get her a gin."

"Oh No! I can't."

Grace's up at the bar now. "Why not? Not another one of your Tony's Rules is it?"

"Oh no, no, no, he's not like that really…" Lindsay is desperate to un-do the harm of previous disclosures. "He only ever wants me to be more confident, to be…" and she's quoting: "More Content In Myself." Susie and Grace share a look.

Lindsay is anxious to dispel the image of the controlling husband.

"No, it's… I'm on tablets."

Grace's cancelling the third gin and tonic.

"They're mainly herbal, Tony saw the advert in the 'Minding your Mind'magazine."

Susie, significantly. "Tony did"

Lindsay's shaking her head .. "No, I know what you're thinking, I know I told you all about that business about wanting a cat. But he was right, you see, it would have been a dreadful "tie" and it would have meant that we could never go on holidays."

Grace's sitting back down with drinks for her and Susie.

"But you never take holidays."

Susie's also pushing it. "Tony doesn't like holidays."

Lindsay is making several vows never to confide in these two again.

"Tony loves his home, that's all, says he doesn't know why we should pay a hotel good money for what's free at home."

Susie, the old-school feminist, has had enough gins to not let this go by: "Oh right! By which he means the free washing-up, the free housework, the free laundry service, the free….."

Lindsay's jumped up. "I've told you. He's not really like that ! I've told you all wrong!"

Grace's round to her: "Sorry, love, we didn't mean to .."

"Yes, I know. Sorry. Look I've got to go. I've got to get Tony's …" and Lindsay stops herself mid-blunder. "Bye then," and she's off before she can betray her marriage any further, before she can let him down again.

They just didn't understand. Tony looked after her. Tony understood what she liked. They were all right if people just didn't ask questions.

Lindsay has left the Pub and is walking hard and fast down the street toward her bus stop, her thoughts in marching rhythm with her feet. People looked too hard at marriages, all those questionnaires in magazines, that one at the dentist's last week "Who's the Boss?" It was all very well for them, those women in jackets with briefcases and College Courses under their lip gloss.

It was all very well to say "Make Him Do His Share", but they weren't there, were they; they weren't there when you'd misjudged the oven timer and you'd forgotten the aubergines. She's breathing hard now, her head shaking in denial as her reflection flits past the plate-glass of the Optician's windows, and her headlong march is mirrored; a small, bustling figure, her handbag swinging out behind her as she rushes into the roadway to avoid a gangling group of youngsters. One of them veers out toward her pushed by his fellows, and Lindsay shies away from him, moving further and more dangerously into the street. A car horn blares and she stops dead in her tracks. Cars swish past and she walks more carefully back onto the pavement. She takes a shudderingly deep breath and looks around her, and realises that she has marched straight past her bus stop.

She turns to walk back, negotiating the group of teenagers without looking at them, keeping her eyes on the ground and a firm grip on her handbag now held to her chest like a shield.

The youngsters ignore her, they had never really seen her, they mill around her for a moment as she passes. They will never remember her, not for the slightest of moments; but she will carry this image, of the threat of it, and the car, and the way she had to go into the road, but she will not tell Tony.
Not tonight. She will tell him about her solo. It will be her gift to him tonight as she gets in and he calls out "Is that You?" and she'll say "Yes, it's the Soloist," and he'll look all amazed and worried for her and then she'll smile and show him how brave she can be and he will be proud of her, and they'll look at the music together and he'll make his little suggestions.

She stands still at that, the very slightest line of a frown between her eyes. She hoped that he wouldn't want to hear her practise her solo. She didn't want nights and nights of that. Of him standing there, listening to her, watching her. Pulling his own shoulders back in a hint that she should straighten up, doing that smiling-while-you're-singing thing with his mouth to show her how to Lighten Up.

She'd tell him that Anna said she should not rehearse at home until they'd all settled on the right key and that Trevor had given her one of his tapes. There. That would do it. And she'd be firm; she wouldn't let him try and get her to do it in the dining room, coming out from behind the curtains in the alcove, that's what had put the mockers on the Drama Club.

Lindsay can see the bus stop in front of her and looks at her watch, ten minutes, only ten minutes to wait. So he didn't like Holidays, it was only natural that he didn't like other men looking at her on the beach. No man wants his wife's body to be ogled at by strangers. She and Tony were fine.
They were all right when they were indoors.

Lindsay has reached her bus stop, and leans thankfully against the cool metal pole. Her breathing calmer now, she looks back along the street. There is no sign of the teenagers; they haven't followed her.

Chapter 7

The man in the car pulls in to park right up tight behind a van; he's on the opposite side of the road to the bus stop, a good hundred yards further down the road. He twists in his seat to watch the woman who stands anxious and alert as she waits for her bus. He watches her as she peers into the drizzle of rain, sharp and stinging against that fretful little face.

He leans forward and looks through the wet mist on his windscreen: "You're late, Lindsay."

Chapter 8

Trevor wakes early and waits for his alarm to tell him to get up.

He looks across at the window and the sun flashing in beneath the hem of the curtains and he can hear the bin men outside in the street; their vehicle whining and clanking between stops, its bleep-bleep warning as it reverses into The Close opposite. He can hear the men shout to each other as they lug the wheelie bins to the back of the lorry, and the clanking as the bins are clamped and raised so that they can be up-ended and the waste pour out in a rush, sudden and violent like vomit. Then the smashing of glass as the bottles from the re-cycling boxes are tipped into the other lorry that follows, its brakes squealing as it huffs and puffs out great irritated gusts of exhaust.

The sudden quiet when the lorries have passed, and Trevor knows that his bin will have been left half way in the middle of the pavement and that it will be all askew.

The machine buzzes beside him and then it automatically tunes to Radio Three. It's some obscure piece by Berio which irritates him enough to make him press the "Snooze/Off" button. Radio Three was going downhill according to Trevor, it was all progressive and atonal stuff now, and never a whisper of a melody, and he didn't like it. You used to know where you were with "*Morning On 3*" but when they started going on about some piece's "chromatic polyphonic reaching the limits of tonality" and its "uncompromising individuality" you knew you'd not be left humming the tune. It nibbled at his confidence and smirked at his musicality. Nowadays when he listened to "*Composer of the Week*" he felt sneered at by these smooth young voices, and he was sure that they were impossibly young, their commentary assuming that he knew their finer academic references, when all that he could hear was cacophony and ugliness. Music had been his salve and he had always trusted it and he had thought that it would never make him feel afraid, but now when confronted by Classical CD covers, all half-naked models standing in water and television-tenors in groups like boy bands, angular and angry, staring out at him, accusing, he feels that some line has been crossed, a line he didn't know about, and that he has been left behind.

This is not a good start. Last year he even gave the bin men a 'Christmas-box' as his mother used to call it, but by February he was back to finding the lid of his re-cycling box over at The Close and last month he'd had to pick up three squashed cigarette boxes and he wouldn't mind but he's never smoked.

He'd mentioned it to the couple next door but they were only ever interested in 'dog fouling'.

Trevor's snooze button re-activates and there's another blast of Berio and he snaps off the machine with a violence he instantly regrets when the digital display blinks at him. He checks that he hasn't broken the alarm, presses the wrong little button and then finds that he has advanced the time, so with crawling patience he presses another little button fifty-nine times to get back to the original time, checks his watch to find that he has spent a minute doing this and that he now has to therefore change the minutes as well. Trevor sometimes feels that he is doomed to a series of repetitious and mind-screaming tasks that other, luckier, undoubtedly more adept people are not heir to. He allows himself several blasphemous expletives that would have so wounded his mother and on his walk to the windows he farts, defiantly and noisily, and is strangely comforted. Pulling back the curtains he confirms his paranoia in the positioning of his wheelie-bin. "Well that's it – you're not getting a tenner next Christmas." Feeling that justice has, momentarily, been returned to his life he gives a satisfied nod to his mirror. "That'll show the .....Buggers" and he rolls that final word around in his mouth, chewing at it, and getting the most out of its flavour.

Chapter 9

Roy is downstairs making the morning tea and has remembered to set out the little plastic dispenser of sweeteners on the tray. He looks down at the tray, at the two Windsor-Rose cups and saucers and remembers how he used to always put a little vase on the tray, with something from the garden in it, a daffodil in spring, a little sprig of grape-hyacinths, then later a summer rose if there was one. One morning, when there wasn't anything much in bloom, he'd got up a collection of herbs; because he thought that they'd smell nice.

He'd taken time to get the colours organized, the purple of the sage and the green of the mint and the yellowy grey of that stuff that was in the pot by the kitchen door, and something he'd thought was thyme.

Roy was not a man to identify smells and had several Christmases of perfume failures to his name so that these days he stuck to Boots vouchers.

But he remembered that morning, and her look, as he placed the tray before her. She'd flicked a contemptuous finger at his herbal collection: "God Almighty Roy that's cat nip and it stinks" and he had never done the vase-thing again.

Roy carries the tray upstairs and pauses outside the bedroom door to get his breathing back. He didn't want another conversation about how he got breathless all the time. If only she'd let go of this weight-thing. He could feel her looking at him and judging, so that these days he wore his dressing gown in the mornings when it had used to be fun to paddle about in his jockey shorts and she'd laugh at his knobbly knees.

Anna's sitting up in bed, a pair of spectacles not seen by Witsham perched on her nose. The contact lenses waited in their solution on the dressing table, along with the Wonder-Life Nude foundation and the rest of her public face.

She's reading the local paper, and looks up briefly as he places the tray beside her. She looks at the little squares of Kitchen Roll that he's put under each saucer and sighs at the lack of napkins. "Have you seen that we might get a Marks & Spencer's Food Outlet?"

"Geoff didn't think so at the last Meeting."

"Well you should push for it, it'd counteract Macdonald's."

"You know I voted against that," he's pouring the tea and she watches it splash into the saucer, not much, but enough to drip on her when she picks up the cup. If only he'd take just a little more care.

She could remember when he used to put flowers on the tray, but that was when she was a size ten and he'd buy her perfume, making a note of her favourite from the TV Adverts. He didn't do that anymore. She'd found the vase at the back of the tupperware cupboard last month when she had a clear-out, and she'd put some of his favourite Madeline daisies in it and put it on the table, but he hadn't noticed.

The vase was really too small for anything much, anyway, so she'd given it to the Fete. When she'd seen it on the white elephant stall she'd nearly bought it back, but then that woman who ran the Energym sessions at the College had picked it up, so Anna had walked away. When she went back after watching the Re-enactment lot doing their Roundheads and Cavaliers business and frightening poor old Mr. Gorringe's horse, she'd got her purse out all ready and remembered that it had been next to the apple-and-orange-on-a-lettuce-leaf-cruet-set … but it had gone.

Anna snaps the Gazette shut and gets out of bed with a bounce that upsets Roy's tea.
"Steady !"
Anna turns to watch Roy pouring the tea from his saucer back into his cup and feels her mouth tightening. She reaches the en-suite and is pleased with her restraint until Roy allows himself a little burp.
"I heard that Roy"
Once the door is shut and the water can be heard to splash into the sink, Roy raises his eyes and his gaze meets the little porcelain angels that line Anna's dressing table. Slowly and with deep loathing he raises a two-fingered salute to their cherubic smiles.

Chapter 10

Trevor is outside the shop that used to be Woolworths, a shop he had always liked. He used to admire its unpretentiousness and the fact that it had still sold kettles and toys and electric fittings and plugs and DIY stuff and sweets. You could always rely on "Wooly's" for sweets. He could remember Christmas as a kid, and buying that cheap no-brand chocolate that tasted of talcum powder but that came in mis-shaped Reindeers and Santas.

But Woolworths has gone now, even shops let Trevor down.

In a long list of disappointments - His Mother, Therapy, Bin Men, The Gas Board's Accounts Department and Radio 3 in particular, Woolworth's ranks as yet another betrayal of something that Trevor had trusted.

He looks up at the temporary sign. Apparently "Everything is 99p" but Trevor doubts it. He pushes open the glass doors and feels a traitor going in.

Inside the shop there seem to be rows and rows of shower gel bottles with the labels bearing European instructions, and Trevor tells himself to avoid any eatables. The "Pick and Mix" sign has gone and all the rows of plastic trays with little plastic shovels for scooping up the pink marshmallow shrimps and the rhubarb and custard sweets. There used to be little jelly milk bottles too, and long wiggly snakes and mini fried eggs that you could suck at for hours.

They used to sell records that were recorded by unknowns and were half the price of the original artists: he'd still got "The Lion Sleeps Tonight" by somebody called Guy Raymond, and a Cliff Richard's hit sung by a Scotsman. 'Cover versions' they used to be called, all his class bought them. Even Alan Sharkey.

He walks along, past the shelves of deodorants and soaps that don't look quite the same as they do in "Boots", and he feels conned. He knows that he is being made a fool of but everything is 99p so how can you lose?

Trevor's spotted a giant pack of mixed little savoury biscuits, and wonders if after a while, when he's been here a few times, when nobody's died from food poisoning and after he's stopped feeling angry, that he'd dare get them for the next Choir party. He'd recce'd a cheese selection in Somerfield earlier that'd go nicely with these. He catches sight of himself in a mirrored wall. His blue anorak bunched over the jacket he wears to the shops, the thinning hair and the glasses that rub little red welts at the side of his nose and despises himself at how quickly he's succumbed. Just like the new Shopping Precinct, he'd signed petitions against that, and then he'd found himself at the opening ceremony, a glass of fizzy wine in his hand, listening to the MP he hadn't voted for welcoming "Café Le Blanc" to Witsham.

He picks up the biscuits and checks the sell-by on the back of the packet, a whole six months to go, so he puts two in his basket. Well, at 99p, as the sign said, you couldn't lose... could you?

They were big boxes, so he reckoned that he'd take along one for the Easter "Do" and one for Anna's Special Social Night. He looked forward to the Choir Parties. The women would all bring along a "plate" and he'd chip-in with one of his crispy-sausage-and-onion pies .. they always went down well. Susie and Grace were all goat's cheese French flans, but he could never see that they weren't just quiches and everybody was sick of those.
No. His plate was always the first to be cleared.

There might just be one up-side to Woolworth's going under, that woman at the check-out that he'd had that little contretemps with a couple of weeks ago, but no, wouldn't you know it, she's been re-hired to continue to persecute Trevor so he tries to change aisles so that he'd pay at the other one, where a nice Indian woman was being very patient with an old dear who'd got 'vouchers', but, just his luck, as soon as he gets to be next with her, a snooty young Under-Manager with plasters on his neck comes up and tells her it's her "Break". "Can you use the other check-out?"
No please, no sorry, usual off-hand manner.
Trevor expects that those plasters hide boils. The man's hormones are obviously in a riot: a sweaty forehead of black-heads, and bum fluff on his upper lip. Trevor is tempted to say something ... something cutting ... something to bring him down to size.
Now the stroppy cashier is joining in. "Over here dear!"
Trevor mutely joins the other queue ...
Don't 'dear' me, you and I have a history, he's rehearsing, but the bored look that stares out of the girl's bland face has no memory of Trevor and he pays for his biscuits saving his rebellion in the proffering of a £20 note. The girl yawns as she hands him his change, her calm unruffled by excess currency, so that Trevor is left with only a demand for a larger bag as revenge.
"Those are the largest bags we've got, unless you're buying electrical."

and she's moving on to the next customer: "You're entitled to three-for-two on those Madam."

Oh it's 'Madam' now is it, and Trevor looks with something close to hate at an inoffensive middle-aged woman in dark glasses, and then realises that she might be blind, and then feels like a shit. He turns to look back at the Under Manager: "When one has queued up for eight minutes at one check-out it is extraordinarily irritating to be told to use another."

He hasn't said it loud enough for this barb to reach its target so that the younger man just looks blankly at Trevor as he strides out of the shop.

The girl on the check-out raises her eyebrows at the woman in dark glasses and they share a "Men!" sneer.

Outside the shop, Trevor is repeating his comment to himself, adding an extra "or possibly ten," after the eight minutes, and an "as such," at the end. He is pleased with these additions.

The "blind" woman leaves the shop, getting a biro out of her handbag, and Trevor walks away so that he won't have to watch her checking her shopping list.

He is glad that Anna doesn't do that dark-glasses-indoors nonsense, and believes that it's only done by people pretending to be actresses. Anna doesn't wear glasses although when they were doing that September-Years Gig, she'd got into a bit of a pother with something in her eye in the changing room and had made him nip out to the car to get her eye-drops. Since he had had no idea where her eye-drops were, and hadn't liked to ask because she was in one of her waving-her-arms-about-moments, he'd rushed out into the car park, hung about a bit, tried to stand up by the door to avoid the teeming rain, and hoped that the moment had passed before he had to go back in.

When he had rejoined her she was in full lip-gloss application mode and had made no comment regarding the rain dripping steadily from his hair, and, so as not to draw attention to the wetness, Trevor had just dabbed surreptitiously with the paper towels he always kept in his music case.

Neither of them had ever referred to this incident.

Trevor is humming "The Rhythm of Life" as he trots along the high street, unconsciously twiddling his fingers as he goes through the piece, nodding his head during the fast syncopated chords; these mental rehearsals took him away, away from the put-downs and the Under

Managers that seemed to dog his life, twisting and pulling him into the hamster-wheel of justification where he trod daily, round and round in a cycle of wearying dispute. Doomed always to be prey to the casual cruelties of check-out girls and almost anybody in the Post Office.

When asked if he had ever married, Trevor was fond of saying
"My piano is my wife and my life" and this simple truth had sustained him through forty-one years of determined bachelorhood. The advent of the computer had only recently tempted Trevor to stray from this calling. One evening, feeling more than usually wounded after a particular dressing down from Anna, Trevor had paddled in the dangerous waters of the Chat Room and with Anna's voice in his head and her stinging "You really are such a wet sponge Trevor!" he had further roamed the delights of the Lonely-hearts pages. He had absolutely no intention of following up his tentative contact with 'Hazel – Libran loves music and line-dancing' but felt that he had somehow Joined In, and Trevor had never really Joined In.

School had been a nightmare (Alan Sharkey could still bring Trevor's palms into sticky pools of remembered fear) University had been a bit of a let-down; dreaming of Oxford spires he'd had to settle for Plymouth and his mother's disappointed face. Only recently, and with the Choir, had he found his niche. Monday nights were his Moment; a culmination of a week-end spent recording tapes and practising the numbers that Anna would require. On Tuesday he would go over the previous night's pieces, practising long into the evening. By Wednesday, a certain flatness would descend until he could begin the Friday night's preparation for Monday, lovely Monday.

Anna and Trevor did private "Gigs" for several assorted W.I.'s and local charities, and his preparations for these Concerts were a special treat: supper round at Anna's. Sitting around their kitchen table, one of the family, wanted, needed, accepted....He'd ring the doorbell and hear her calling to Roy "Oh that's just Trevor, let him in" and he would smile to himself... Just Trevor... he belonged.
Roy would sometimes bring him in a can of beer and raise his eyebrows to Trevor when Anna complained about him putting it on the piano, men's stuff, the masculine exchange of reactions to women's ways. Trevor loved those evenings. Anna would be wearing just a T-shirt and trousers, Roy would be in his slippers, absolutely no formality at all: it would be like he'd been with Mother, but without the criticism.

Anna had to be more formal at Choir practice of course, he understood that, and it made those other times so special; when she kicked off her shoes and sat beside him on the piano stool and Roy would call through from the kitchen "Is it time for coffee and biscuits?"

Trevor didn't want to think of that time before the Choir, before Anna, that business with the Redundancy and the nastiness that had gone before. Well he'd got Mother's money now, and he'd always have the house, he didn't need to work again. That Doctor had said - what was it? - that some people just cannot cope with the hurly burly of the workplace, that was it. Hurly burly, and the Gas Board Accounts Department had been very hurly burly. Well he was off those pills now and Mother had been right about the cognitive therapy after all.

All Was Well. It was.

Trevor is smiling as he passes the coffee shop, pushing deep into "The Rhythm of Life" to prevent the Gas Board from taking hold, and so does not see Anna sitting at a table to the rear of the café, a young and nattily suited man leaning across to hear her soft conspiracy.

Trevor crosses the road to take a look at the market stalls; he's on the hunt for some better scarves for the Choir. It was the Farmers' Market day today too, and he might just treat himself to some of that lime chutney. The 'home-made' preserves have attracted some members of the Choir, and Trevor is pleased to be able to salute Lindsay, who jumps with startled guilt.

"Oh ! I thought you might be... no...right."

"Only me." It's Trevor's habitual refrain.

"I think these jams are marvellous, don't you." Lindsay is holding the Country Strawberry, turning it round and round in her hands, considering..

"Do you think anybody would know that it wasn't actually Home Made?"

Trevor is happy to re-assure her, wondering briefly at the rather haunted look as she scrutinises the label.

"I think this would peel off..." and she's trying it.

"Do you want that love?" The stallholder's watching her.

"Yes – can I have six?"

Lindsay is looking around her, eyes flicking sparrow-wary as she hastens to pay for the jams.

"Could you put them in those thicker brown paper bags please, only I have a long way to go with them."

Trevor does not comment on this strange lie, women were always having secrets it seemed to him, his mother had whole areas of her life that kept their mystery although he seemed to remember that most of those had been bathroom-orientated.

Lindsay scuttles off, a mouse back to its hole, and Trevor is left to wander around the stalls just in case he could find a different chutney to go with his cheese. He could smell the cheese stall but would save that purchase for the last; his music case, that permanent adjunct to his right hand, housed purchases as well as his sheet music, and Anna could detect country cheddar a week after it had neighboured his Gershwin Melodies. Trevor always carried his music with him. A half of beer in the pub later would need the company of the music spread out on the table before him. It bespoke activity and denied the loneliness.

Lindsay is sitting on the bus, the brown parcel held close to her stomach. She's rehearsing a speech that she will say to her husband. Her lips move and eyes appeal as she goes through the motions of a perfectly reasonable conversation that she will be unable to have.

Chapter 11

Diane opens her front door to Jo-Anne.

"Oh !" Diane had not expected her and is not one to like surprises. Totally thrown by this arrival, she is almost panicking to retrieve her sense of composure, her control of this situation. She hasn't done her make-up, the kitchen is all plates and smells, and she can't remember if she'd put away that bra.

"Sorry. Is it inconvenient? Only I was up this end of town and I just thought…"

"No, no. Sorry." But Diane still just stands there at the door, trying to think why she is so afraid.

"Only you said you wanted copies of all the music we've done so far since the Christmas Concert, and I was able to photocopy them at work and…."

"That is so kind… please, come in."

Diane is beating herself up for being like this, this reticence. Why couldn't she fling wide her door and let people in? This anxiety was maiming, she would change, she would.

Jo-Anne is wise enough to praise the kitchen units and tell Diane that if she had dropped in on *her* unannounced, Diane would have had to wade through a sink of breakfast crockery and several mucky cat litter trays; so that by the time the women are sitting around the table over coffee and bourbons, they have achieved that easy camaraderie that women reach once a few domestic inadequacies have been exchanged.

"Oh I'm never likely to get a solo, I don't mind, in fact I dread it. I'm happy just to blend in….." Jo-Anne is blissfully ignorant of her infinite capacity to hit a flat note on most occasions. "…I've been in the Choir since Anna started it, oh three years back now, it's become part of my life I suppose. We have lots of Social Do's too, parties at Anna's and we always go for a pizza after a Concert."

Diane's nodding: "Yes, it was the social aspect that I joined for, I've got this silly deep voice, I'm OK with Nina Simone numbers in the bath, but I hoped to not be noticed musically, it was really just a way to get to meet people."

"That's all most of us are in for I think, although Linda and Susie are a bit aspiring."

Jo-Anne feels that they've negotiated the preliminaries and is emboldened to get to the meat. "So you've not been moved in long then. I watched these flats go up, well we all did, it's fascinating how one minute it's all breeze blocks and girders and everybody saying as how they're being built on a flood plane and then before you know where you are it's all Show Flats and stainless steel coffee tables."

"Oh." Diane's a bit thrown by swirling water lapping at foundations. "Was it a sort of swamp before then?"

"No! – sorry I shouldn't have said that – only there was ever such a to-do in the local paper and Susie's Stephen took lots of photographs of wet bricks and then did one of his 'Grave Fears' articles in the Hepton Gazette."

This is not comforting.

Diane's is actually peering down at the skirting boards under her kitchen table. "I had a very thorough Survey, only you never know, do you, it's like when you take the car in, all that teeth sucking and nodding that men do when they want to scare you into paying more."

"Oh I'm sure it's alright now." Jo-Anne's wishing she hadn't started this, she's not cold hearted but is not particularly interested in discussing Diane's survey. Having once had an affair with a Structural Engineer and feels that she has had her life times fill of Building Regulations and Subsidence. She waves a careless arm at the greying window. "Anyway, it hasn't rained for weeks."

Diane's eyes are still roaming the walls for 'Damp' and Jo-Anne is anxious to get down to the essential business of Diane's Life.

"So you moved here from ….?"

Diane takes a short stab of a breath: "We had a house up on Craft Street.. It was.. bigger.." and she's looking around at the narrow worktop and the cupboards that are too small for cereal packets.

"He moved to one of those Riverview Flats, he was supposed to move away you see, I thought he'd go to Cornwall. He said he would. But then his .. . well his …Girlfriend .. fancied Brighton, but he wasn't sure of that because of all the gays."

"Right" Jo-Anne's trying to put the pieces together "So… you're on your own as it were …?" and she laughs. "I'm not very subtle am I?"

Diane grins back at her, it is difficult to refuse such candour. "I'm divorced."

There, she's said it. The first time she said it was to the removal men and they'd all chorused back "Absolutely right love," just as if they had known Paul, just as if it was obvious that everybody should get divorced. Diane had supposed that they must have to remove lots of wives from their homes into smaller flats, they must be used to the Last Look Round and the Tears.

They must have to do the husbands too, although Paul had moved out by stealth, bit by little bit carried out to the brand new estate car he'd bought just after his Solicitor had sent her that letter. She had stood in a kind of stunned amazement as he'd carried the set of heavy French saucepans through the hallway, and then the box of photo albums ..."But they are photographs of me," she'd said and she had thought of all the nights she'd spread the prints out on the dining room table and sorted them into date and holiday order.

"What copies do you want then?" He'd asked, and she couldn't think what to say. Those albums were the record of the last eight years of her life, of their life. She didn't understand why he wanted the pictures if he didn't want her.

"Diane, I cannot just ignore these last years can I? It would mean that they were a total waste of time."

And Diane had reached out and picked up the one she had labelled 'France – IV. Friends and Camping', as she had labelled them all, using those peel-off sticky letters from Smiths. She used to stick in odd mementoes too, train tickets and postcards, and menus from restaurants. Paul had never been interested in the photos before, had never bothered to look through when she'd finished another album. She could hear herself saying "Another one done! I'm up to last Easter now," and he'd laugh at her and tell her that while she was parcelling up their past he was living their present.

Oh yes, he was living the present, only it wasn't Their present.
It was the present with the Receptionist from the Health Centre.

"So you want that one then," he'd asked, juggling the box of albums on his hip, their Best Man waiting outside in his van, too embarrassed to come in case she made a scene. In case she started crying again. In case he had to say all that "Beth and I are really sorry about all this, Diane, but you must move on," routine. Beth had rung her up and asked her for her Flan Dish back the morning Diane got the "Nisi" document. Apparently that meant "unless". Unless what? Unless Paul started to love her again, unless he had got bored of the younger, smoother skin already. Beth had told her that this could be a Brand New Opportunity for Diane to Start Again. But Diane didn't feel Brand New and she didn't want to start anything again. Beth had told her that she'd noticed that Diane had given up having her hair highlighted and that she had been surprised that she'd let her Pilates classes go. So that Diane had told her to fuck off and that she could whistle for her bloody Flan Dish.

Jo-Anne is smiling at her with that all-understanding-smile that the happily married use when confronted by the recently divorced. "Oh I know."

No you don't, Diane's trying not to say it, trying not to push away this woman who could be a new friend. They think they understand, they've read articles in Cosmopolitan and seen it in Coronation Street: they've cried along with their favourite Soap character and felt that they know that particular pain.

But really they're thinking that if only these people Worked At their marriages then all would be well, and they're congratulating themselves on working at *their* marriage, so that now Jo-Anne's trotting out the next Good Marriage Guide homily: "Mike and I have gone through some hard times I can tell you."
No, no this doesn't help!

"Do you think I didn't try ? ..I….." ..and she's feeling for the word, a word that would hold the way it had been …

"I... *treasured* my marriage. Do you know I used to play a little game, at night when the lights from the house would all be shining out, I'd go out the back, into the little garden we had then, and I'd stand there in the middle of the lawn in the dark and I'd look back at the house, at the kitchen. The blind was always rolled up because we weren't overlooked, and I'd stand there and stare into the lighted kitchen, all yellow and warm because we'd done the walls in Buttercup-Sunshine, and I'd look all round the room, at the bowl
we'd bought from Nice with all the oranges in it, and the wine in the terracotta bricks and the red silk poppies in the vase by the window and I'd pretend that I didn't know who lived there, and that I was a passer-by who was looking in at.. at an 'Ideal.'."

Diane's back there, standing out in the cold in a garden, and Jo-Anne's picking a biscuit crumb off the inside of her coffee cup, dragging it up to the rim with her finger and reminding herself that bourbon's don't really 'dunk'.

Diane's gaze focuses onto Jo-Anne's finger as she rubs the smudge of biscuit against her thumb. "I miss the garden."

"Oh well then!… I could help you turn that into a patio." Jo-Anne's pointing out at the small concrete square beyond the kitchen door.

"It would look marvellous with a few pots and tubs, we could put up some hanging baskets….." and she's all enthusiasm and healing, and Diane listens to her and feels washed with tiredness.

Chapter 12

Lindsay is standing at the work surface in her kitchen; the six jars of 'Country Strawberry' stand in front of her, lined up, her troops in a small war. She's looking at them with great intent. One of the labels has been attacked with a knife in an attempt to remove it, and the woman now fills the sink with warm water, placing each jar of jam up to its neck. A garage door slams outside and she freezes, staring down at the sink, her eyes saucer with a genuine dread. There's the sound of a key in a lock. Lindsay cannot think, she's a hedgehog frozen in the headlights turning itself into a little ball against the wheels of the truck.

Tony walks into the kitchen and throws his newspaper onto the work surface. " What a Farce! I told him I wouldn't have that Report finished by Friday and now he's told everybody it's late!" He's jabbing a finger into the newsprint. Lindsay is looking at the newspaper. "In the paper?"

"Of course it's not in the paper, don't be ridiculous! ...He told everybody at the *office !* What's the matter with you?! You've got that frazzled look again, you're not going wobbly again are you?... It's this Solo isn't it, it's going to be too much isn't it, it'll be The Boxing Day Buffet all over again!"

"No, no Tony it won't honestly. That will never happen again, I've told you. I've promised you."

He's looking at her, waiting for proof.

So Lindsay is pushed to rashness: "The Solo's going really well, I've been practising to the tapes this morning, I feel really good about it."

Patently unconvinced, Tony pushes his tongue up under his front teeth "Mmm, I've got an idea about that."

His eyes fall to the sink, and the jars ..."What're they?"

Lindsay holding her hands over the jams, moving them backwards and forwards across the surface of the lids as if she could cover their very existence with these fluttering movements

"You're not supposed to be home yet," it's a small sound, a justification.

Tony watches her hands and the fingers splaying out to increase the hiding. He reaches slowly into the sink and removes one of the jars of jam. He holds it up so that the light from the window shines into the dark red fruit. He does not say anything. Lindsay does not say anything.

Very slowly he turns the jar so that the label faces her. Its corner is hanging off, beginning to peel away from the glass. If he had come home just a few minutes later she would have been saved.

With infinite slowness and care he places the jar of jam on the working surface, and pushes the corner of the label back into place.

Then he leaves the kitchen, sighing with immense sadness.

Lindsay picks the jars out of the sink and puts each one, very carefully, into the small pedal bin. They fill it, and the lid won't go back down, it yawns accusingly at her.

Tony, upstairs now, is standing by the bedroom window looking out at his week-end's gardening; at the pleasing symmetry of the angular little chips of wood bark he'd raked over the earth between the Lobelias and the Amelanchier Lamarckii, its oval leaves silkily unfurling, and he worries his fingers across his upper lip, smearing the fine beads of sweat that had pearled there, as he traces his fingers around the tight mouth. The Gardener's Year Book had warned him that this shrub could develop into a tree but he had been seduced by the "clouds of starry white flowers and the autumnal breathtaking red foliage". He should have planted it further away; he couldn't have a tree, not an actual tree that near to the house, there was always the fear of the roots, roots seeking water, the foundations...

His finger has pushed its way between his lips and he tastes the stale salt, he bites down hard until the nail flattens and gives him a small dull pain.

He continues the pressure. It soothes him. They have always soothed him, these little pains; as a child he would rub his fingers up against the pebble-dashed walls, feeling the prickling roughness of the surface, and his mother would be calling him:

"Tony, you are to come here now ! I know what you've done, I've found it.. you disgusting boy !"

And the child would rub harder at the sharp little stones and sometimes, just sometimes, if he was clever enough with the angles of his finger tips against the stone, there would be blood.

Chapter 13

Anna is tapping an immaculate fingernail along the carefully indexed CD rack. She removes her favourite and smiles at her choice, a smile of secret congratulation. She places the silver disc into the stereo system and waits until Bach's Violin Concerto in D minor fills the room. She jabs at the fast forward button, selecting the second movement, and conducts the Largo, her hands making soft arcs in the air as one solo violin emulates the other, following… so each hand follows the other and rolls over and around, her white long fingers flexing with the dialogue between the strings. Her body sways with the sheer satisfaction of that sustained beauty.

The telephone rings and Anna's head snaps round to look at it. She turns back to the stereo, to turn the music off before she answers… a moment while she considers… then she picks up the phone. Anna likes it to be heard that she listens to Music. She is rewarded.
"Jonathan! – let me just turn this off will you."
And she holds the telephone near to the speaker for Jonathan to hear her choice before she snaps Bach into silence.
"Did you think any more about what I said? .." and a frown as she has to remind him "..The Choir!…"
She listens to him and her face softens as he purrs flattery.
"Well that's very nice of you, but…. yes well I suppose I do really."
And Anna is twirling a strand of hair through fingers that had moved to Bach and now are flexing to a lesser tune.
"Lunch at Orsino's? – that's rather grand isn't it?….Of course I think I'm worth it, it's just….. well shall I bring the new Pieces?"
and again she has to remind him.. "For the Choir, for Cheltenham!"
"Right, tomorrow then…right," and she listens to the dialling tone after he has hung up, looking at the telephone, speculating. She replaces the receiver slowly, her fine teeth gnawing gently at the inside of her mouth as she carefully removes the CD from the stereo and slides its case back into position. She looks at the row of CDs, her head tilted to one side as she reads the labels and decides to change the exact order of her collection, the Violins now to the right of the Oboe Concertos for stricter alphabetical accuracy.

Anna wants this, it's a physical ache that gnaws at her, if she could just have Jonathan, if she could have Cheltenham she would be happy, she would.

So much has disappointed, there have just been too many little stabs, too many slivers of ice that have cut and stung. She'd got over them not getting the Time-Share, she had, but Roy not becoming mayor had been an acute blow, she'd anticipated it, she'd even written it into her "Our Year" letter that she puts in their Christmas cards. So now there's all that "Whatever happened to you being Mayoress?" from the ex-neighbours they'd been trying to get rid of since they left Southall. But if her Choir won Cheltenham, well that would show them. Never mind not having children because this would show everybody that her Career was the thing. This would prove that she was happy. That Aunt Jo had been wrong, she had amounted to something. She'd created that Choir from nothing, bullied Trevor into leafleting half the town and now look at her - hardly ever out of the Witsham Gazette advertising the Concerts. Three last year if she counted the Easter Bunnies gig, and she'd got three paragraphs after the Crematorium Open Day. But they had to 'Up' their game, she had to improve and perfect them, get rid of the dead-legs, and Jonathan was the key. With him on board there'd be no stopping her, and this was only the beginning.

She has such Plans, she and Jonathan could be a proper classical Duo. Light Opera beckons, herself in a long satin gown, a deep scarlet, she thinks, her hand resting on the piano....

Anna watches the talent shows on the television obliquely; she always has a copy of music on her lap, marking up the breathing points, careful to not be seen to be wanting it. Careful not to stare at the screen, and the young, and they are always so young, those slips of girls singing as if they are divas.

The interviews before their auditions, and all that "This is My Dream" stuff, and how they "Deserve It." And they're not twenty, half of them.

Anna had been deserving it for years but she had never had their chances, the singing lessons, the money spent. Aunt Jo had said that Anna couldn't have the school trip to Holland *and* singing lessons, but she hadn't wanted Amsterdam. Nobody had wanted to sit next to her on the coach and she hadn't got the right clothing, Anna had shivered her way round all those flaming canals, and then the clogs she'd bought had got stuck because her feet had swollen up with all the walking round those churches looking at little phials of 'Christ's Blood'. Even at twelve, Anna had sussed that Christ must have had a lot more than his eight pints if these were all genuine.

Pricilla Larner laughing at her feet when Miss Etch had tried to put some elastoplasts on the back of her ankles where the wood had rubbed the skin raw, and then having to paddle in the freezing sea at Brunnen to try and shrink her feet to get the clogs off. Miss Etch had thought to bring her little hacksaw, she was a resourceful Teacher, she'd even packed the three-in-one oil and a tube of expandable wood filler apparently, although nobody had actually had much use for those. But on a previous trip there'd been quite a call for an adjustable spanner, and Miss Etch had vowed never to be caught short again.

Anna had had quite a crush on Miss Etch, a woman who had quite an amazing posture so that in the school photos she had a military bearing that attracted the young girl.

There had been that terrible day when Miss Etch had been in the music room, a rare occasion, History, particularly military History being the subject closer to her heart. Hardly a lesson went by without some battle being drawn on the blackboard; Roundheads and Cavaliers, and all that Tudor sword waving, it didn't seem to matter as long as different coloured chalks could be employed illustrating the "right flank of the attack" and the "main thrust of the cavalry."

So that Anna couldn't help thinking that her Darling had been a bit of a loss to the Women's Auxiliary Forces. But she'd been standing there, looking at the new piano and muttering about Resources and Anna had walked in and had heard herself ask the teacher to hear her sing. So Miss Etch had stood there, ramrod-straight listening to Anna breathily delivering "Greensleeves" (she'd chosen it especially because of the Tudor connection) and then that awful wait, at the end of the song, as the teacher had smiled rather vaguely at her and had asked her if she'd handed in the Wars of the Roses essay that had been due last week. She had been supposed to realize, like the auditions on X-Factor, when the judges suddenly recognise genuine talent, Miss Etch was going to know, to see Anna at last and to understand. But that had been just another one of those little shards, glass pricking the skin. The only moment that Anna could hold on to now was when the Teacher had knelt down beside her and peeled the backing of the elastoplast, but the moment was blurred and spoiled by the smudge of blood that stopped the plaster from sticking to the raw flesh.

Anna shakes her head and sees that she has left a little puddle of sweat on the Plastic CD cover. She'll have to get a piece of kitchen roll for that now.

If she wins Cheltenham she'll write to Miss Etch, suggest coffee, anything would be possible.

Chapter 14

Roy sits at a desk behind a small wooden plaque emblazoned with "Accounts" in fine golden lettering; a present from Anna, who had had the engraving done in town when it had originally read "Accountant".

But Roy had yet to pass those final unreachable exams, and Anna could not bring herself to take this back to her local shop and had travelled into Oxford for the correction to the merely departmental "Accounts"; these small disappointing adjustments have formed the fabric of their marriage, and although Roy can only see the back of the little wooden sign, and he daily moves his pen holder to obscure the view, it rebukes him. As he rises from his desk he notices that the middle button of his shirt has gaped open again. He breathes in and re-fastens the button, and remembers that tonight is one of Anna's "Salad-and vegetable crouton dip" evenings. Roy looks down at the straining cotton and thinks how he must remember to change this shirt when he gets in before Anna can do that thing she does with her mouth whenever she looks at his stomach these days. Roy picks up the briefcase that stands beside his desk, those three sections of leather that hold his morning paper and a biro with R.H.M along its barrel; Roy has Christmases of initialled office equipment, so that the briefcase is always positioned with its monogrammed side facing the desk, so that the others will not see Anna's aspirations. He holds the gold lettering to the side of his leg and thinks softly of the Pizza-Slice-Take-Away that he will pass on his way to the car park. Maria smells of pepperoni and tomatoes and gently baked dough, Roy watches her through the window of the little shop, he watches as her smooth white arms move in gentle rhythm, cutting the pizza into slices, the cutting disc sinking deeply into the mozzarella. Maria looks up and sees him and smiles.
And that is enough.
That is enough to stop it mattering; the little wooden sign on his desk, the buttons that gape, and the fact that he carries deep in his guts when he sits aching on the toilet seat in the middle of the night; the fact that he will never be Mayor.

Maria is not Italian, the wide generous mouth, the supple olive skin and thick black hair were born in Clapham. There must have been a grandmother with a secret and a holiday in Rimini somewhere in the family past and its legacy is Maria.

Roy goes into the shop and for a little while he tastes a different world of possibilities.

Chapter 15

Trevor is trying on several different cardigans and frowning hard at himself in the mirror. What had he been thinking of? That "Lonelyheart Chat Room" had been a severe error of judgement. Supposing Anna found out; and he has to sit down on his bed and breathe deeply through that one.

Hazel, the musical Libran with an unfortunate penchant for line-dancing .. he hadn't realised that he'd clicked on "Contact", he'd meant to consign her to "Saved Favourites" where all his other Possibles lurked; Jenny (Mozart and Backgammon, 'curvy' so the wrong side of a size 20, and Basingstoke so a bit of a schlep) Rachel (Meditation Workshops and Self-Awareness, but at least she was local) and the rather unlikely Morwenna who'd underlined Alternative, described herself as a Mystic and said that she only wore black, also not one to raise the spirits from her picture – sort of Gothic meets Coven if the chicken was anything to go by.

So, a little slip of a finger on his computer mouse, and he's got himself meeting Hazel in an off-the-beaten-track pub off that roundabout he hates just outside Oxford. He can't be seen by Witsham, so he'll just have to Indicate and Go, get into the left hand lane and just stick at it until he gets to the third turning off; it doesn't matter if he goes round twice, nobody would know. If they know he's going round twice then they must be going round twice, it stands to reason doesn't it. "Indicate and Go" – yes Mother, I know.

Mother had never driven a yard in her life but was an expert on negotiating traffic. "All you have to be is Resolute." Yes – well it was all very well being resolute, but if you had an articulated lorry up your bum and a bald tattoo in a white van on your left, there really wasn't much of anywhere to go, never mind what your little yellow flashing indicator was pleading.

He'd take his music case, so at least if she didn't turn up he would go over next week's pieces. He was thinking of giving the basses a bit of a break and putting in their line on the "Easter Hymn". All very well for Anna to say that they'd get there eventually, but there were only two of them and it didn't hurt to give them a few hints with their bottom C's to D flat. They had to hold that against the soprano melody and were all too easily seduced up into their singing the tune-but-an-octave-lower routine. He could hear them, the basses stood right next to the piano. Anna had managed to poach the two new male members from the Witsham Warblers and Trevor knew from past experience that men tended to drift off, the call of the Parochial Church Council is a strong one, and there always seemed to be the demands of The Wife.

So, Trevor would keep these two, the Choir needed them, he'd tell them to listen out for the musical clues he would give them, a sort of male-bonding.

Trevor is pleased with this thought and settles with almost content upon the brown with mauve flecks that his mother had *not* knitted. He turns sideways to the mirror and refuses to look at the belt area, concentrating on the set of the shoulders now that he has thought to pull them back.

He'd always thought that Music was enough. Enough for him.
It was that just lately ... the faithful dog that had greeted and accompanied his days had turned and nibbled at him, had shown teeth, and had unsettled his certainty. Trevor faces a ridiculous truth, that Radio Three was pushing him into matrimony.

Downstairs now, and one last coffee, and then the inevitable last visit to the loo before Trevor finally closes his front door, leaning back against it to double-check that it is locked, pushing against the wood to confirm safety.

Chapter 16

Anna is sitting before her dressing table and looking at the face she has created in the mirror. Her make-up is immaculate, if a little heavy for midday. But lunch is to be at Orsino's. Well, he's an Oxford Man. And she pictures Jonathan waiting for her, having ordered a rather good crisp white wine. It will be resting in its cooler as she enters, and he will rise to greet her.

In the mirror she rehearses the smile that she will give him as she walks to the table, and changes it; not too broad, perhaps even a little cautious.

Anna often practises smiling.

Downstairs, she pours herself a glass of water from the filter jug in the fridge, and notices that Roy has forgotten to refill it again. She pauses as she lifts the glass to her mouth, remembering the faultless lipstick, and tips the water into the sink.

Chapter 17

Trevor is driving with unnecessary caution, it occurs to him that if he were to speed past the police car in front then he would be pulled over, like on those 'Police Chase' programmes on Channel 5, he'd probably be told to "spread" by some gun toting redneck cop as he was forced to lean against the side of his car, feet wide apart, hands on the roof... but this is not L.A. and Trevor has never been 'pulled over' in his life, has never even got caught on a speed trap camera, an omission he feels keenly; everybody he knows moans about that and he joins in, just as if he was one of those people who speed about and to hell with the rules, just as if he was normal.

It hasn't counted, all this obeying the rules and never parking on double yellow lines, even when Mother was taken in to A&E that last time, God Almighty he'd even parked in the Hospital car park and paid the correct parking fee, fumbling the coins and putting them in too quickly so that he had to press the Return button and start all over again. Even then Trevor had obeyed the rules. Even at Mother's Funeral, he'd moved his car because Cousin-Bloody-Edward had wanted a quick getaway after the Internment and Trevor's little Skoda was in his way. He should have told Edward to shove it.

Well, 'Hazel line-dancing' had better watch out, that's all. He wasn't going to be messed about, she'd probably have him taxi-ing her all over the place. Well he'd done that; Taking Mother Out. Tuesday was her bridge night (all that way to Reading so that by the time he'd got back there wasn't enough time to start up his keyboard before he had to set off again to pick her up) Just because she'd had that row with Joyce and couldn't go local. Wednesdays was Diamond Years Club, then every other Thursday was Witsham Ladies.

Don't do this... all that therapy, all those sessions with Zenata, don't get back on this merry-go-round. Think of Mondays, blessed Mondays, sitting behind the piano, watching Anna for the 'off' . But the waste of it, every week-end at the Garden Centre because of the Nice Disabled Toilets, standing there with the wire trolley, waiting for her to choose another pot of lobelias, counting the minutes and the hours of it all. Stop it, stop it now, let it go. Well it was all very well for Zenata; with her dream-catcher wind chimes and that Buddha poster on the wall. He'd seen her in Sainsbury's with *her* mother.. couldn't have been sixty, all executive cropped hair and one of those big ethnic shawls round her shoulders on top of her coat (he could never see the point of that)…

Just wait till she's eighty and on a walking frame and telling you she won't eat chicken – just try all that 'shared wisdom and mutual enrichment' stuff then.

The roundabout is just ahead and Trevor is now in full Agincourt mode, he crashes down the gears and goes straight into the left hand lane and he's round and off at the third turning before he can be daunted by the blaring of horns. He pulls into the car park of the Stag at Bay and is confronted by dozens of cars. There's obviously some sort of "Do" at the Pub.

Great, he'd chosen this venue because of the large car park and no hassle, and the fact that it was usually pretty empty at lunchtime. He could hear the revellers inside even with his window wound up. Great, Hazel was supposed to spot him, sitting by the window at the far side of the bar with his music case on the table.. nice touch that, he'd thought, subtle, not pushing the professional accompanist bit but letting her know.. Now he'd be lucky to get any kind of seat at all, and he'll look a right pillock putting a case on a table surrounded by the kind of oiks he can hear that are inside, he's reckoning that it's an Office Thing, all the young bloods from IT showing the secretaries how much lager they can drink.

He's locking his car and setting the alarm, looking in at the little red light on the dashboard to make sure that it's flashing to confirm that the alarm is on. He counts the flashes, one, two, three. Yes, that's safe.

He opens the door to the Public Bar and is hit by a wall of smoke and testosterone. He was right about the IT lads, half of them were in some sort of fancy dress, the theme of which escaped him; there were several gladiators, and a couple dressed as chickens. Trevor looked over at the intended point of rendezvous and noted that his intended seat was occupied by a short man with black flippers and a padded white front.

Oh great, Hazel would have a date with a penguin.

Chapter 18

Anna is pondering the dismal truth that nothing ever turns out how one imagines: Jonathan has just texted her: *"Running late, order what you like. Soz. J."* She assumes that soz means sorry, or not, actually.

Please let this not be another splinter, another Miss Etch moment to be there always pricking under the skin.

She sits at a very small table, too near to the door to the kitchens, and reads the menu, again. The ice is melting in her Diet Coke. The waiter had handed her the wine list but she wasn't going to be thwarted; she wanted Jonathan to choose the wine, she wanted him to look all knowing and suave and order just the absolutely right bottle. She'll wait until he arrives. She wants to try and re-capture the image she had of this lunch. It wasn't a date, oh no, no. She wanted Jonathan but not like that, if she thought of him like that it spoilt everything. No, she wanted Jonathan behind the piano.

He was here, oh dear and he was angry, striding over to her and registering the table. "Bloody traffic!... why are you sitting here?... this is no good..waiter!" and Jonathan is commandeering another table, one by the window, the one she had asked for and had been told that it was reserved. Anna is torn between anger at Jonathan, and humiliation at getting this wrong, for not being the kind of woman who would insist upon a better table. Because she *is* that kind of woman, a Joan Crawford kind of woman, but she had been 'thrown' because he was late, and because it wasn't how she had imagined.

Jonathan is all charm and smiles now that he has got the table of his choice, and Anna is impressed with how he is dealing with the waiter, and the way that he flicks his jacket off his shoulders and has draped it around the chair, the waiter is pulling the other chair out for her and murmuring something about a misunderstanding, and Jonathan's soothing: "No problem Mario" assures Anna that Orsino's is a regular haunt.

Jonathan staring hard at her, it's a long and practised look.
"Are you very, very cross with me?"
"No of course not, don't be silly."
"It was the bloody Woodstock Road."
"Forget it."
His smile is of congratulation upon her forbearance.
"I'll order us a...." and he scans the wine list. "Ah yes, I think you'll like this Anna."
So she lets her shoulders relax into the scenario she had planned.

Chapter 19

Trevor is being attacked by a spider. It is six foot tall and has a
"Comic Relief" tin on the end of one of its legs, there are eight of them,
the more solid variety ending in its feet and the other six are waving
about in Trevor's face. Obviously only two of the legs are practical in
that there are arms inside them, and they are not to be ignored.

"It's for Charity mate!" The spider is shouting at Trevor.

Oh well that's all right then isn't it, it's for *Charity,* you can do what
you like for Charity, you can push people into bowls of custard in the
middle of the high street if it's for *Charity,* and of course it's even
better if you dress up in the most unlikely and deeply unhumorous
costume imaginable.

Trevor stands there, biting his teeth together and says nothing.

He fumbles in his pockets for change. The insect is shouting at him
again: "Dig deep, people are starving."

Oh yes, we're all Bob Geldofs now aren't we.

Hazel is looking at him from across the room, well he assumes it's
Hazel because she's the only other person in the pub dressed as a
human being.

So Trevor's getting his wallet out now, and praying he's got a fiver
in there and that he won't have to give the arachnid a twenty pound
note.

He's trying to squeeze the note into the slit in the tin, but he's folded
it so that it's too thick for the opening, and he and the hairy black arm
are having to both push and shove.

"Careful! – we're doing this in our own time you know!"

"Well nobody asked you to, did they" Trevor's hissing under his
breath, smiling so that Hazel can see the goodwill.

The black antennae – long wires with little black balls on the end are
bobbing up and down: "The starving did, and Paul McCartney last
night on Famine Watch."

Trevor's still trying to shove the note in: "Well perhaps he could
give them a couple of his billions and give the rest of us a break."

"That's right, kick a man when he's down. Macca's had another
tough year."

Trevor's staring at the black bulging plastic eyes:

"*He*'s had a tough year? – He's just got married again hasn't he?"

The spider's nodding, antennae waving their solidarity with his idol

"Well I know ... we're all very pleased for him now that he's found his new wife..." The spider is smiling, assured in the cosy familiarity he obviously feels with the celebrity.

Trevor is shaking in his exasperation: "You don't *know* him! ... Just because you watched his wedding on the News doesn't mean that he'll let you pop round for a cup of tea!"

"You must be Trevor." Hazel is standing behind the spider. One last shove and the note's in the tin. The spider backs into Hazel, spins round to see what it's done and hits her with one of its non-functional legs.

Trevor reaches over to steady her.

"Watch what you're doing!"

The insect turns back, its appendages shaking magnificently in its anger: "It's people like you who should be starving."

Trevor takes a deep breath, remembering Zenata's nasal-snatch technique, and gives Hazel the smile he has hitherto reserved for particular blunders at Concerts. "Shall we go somewhere else?"

"Oh, where?" Hazel is remembering the strictures of first-dates, *somewhere safe, somewhere open, somewhere known.*

The insect is now telling the gladiators and the chicken about Trevor and this motley crew are making their way over to him. Trevor holds Hazel gently by the elbow and is leading her to the door.

"Let's discuss this outside, shall we."

The bright yellow fowl is waving its wings at Trevor: "Oi You! Just a minute!"

The ignominy of being chased out of a pub by a chicken is making Trevor bold, and he is scuttling Hazel over to his car. Hazel is sniffing abduction, and realising that 'The Office' had been right. "Would you please let go of my arm."

Trevor's looking back for signs of pursuit and when he turns back he has steered them straight into a banana.

"Are you all right love?" The banana is talking to Hazel.

"Would you mind escorting me to my car please."

"Oh God," is torn from deep inside Trevor's soul.

Hazel seems to have no concern about trusting her safety to a seven foot high banana with large yellow Wellingtons. The banana is holding its Charity tin on the end of its green leaf, and Trevor can think of nothing to say but to correct the obvious error. "You never see a banana with leaves."

As Hazel gets into her car, she presses a donation into the banana's tin, gazing up at it with smiling gratitude.

Trevor waves over to her. "I'll ring.... shall I?"

Chapter 20

Jonathan is draining the last of the wine into Anna's glass.

"Will you be serious." Anna is giggling.

"I am being perfectly serious," and Jonathan is reaching across the table to still Anna's fluttering fingers.

"I have always been serious where you are concerned, Anna."
He pronounces her name Un-na. "You make me sound ... Russian."
Jonathan stretches his arms wide. "I feel Russian!"
Anna is delighted with him and throws back her head, her mouth wide.
He's staring at her, an opaque feline gaze, a look he has practised in the mirror, and it is almost a purr. "You don't do that enough."

"Laugh?"

"Are you happy, Un-na?"

This is too much for the waiter, who has arrived to ask again if the couple want their bill. Mario has heard these tired words so many times, has seen the women melt and confess their limits of happiness to men that are promising so much more. He returns to the kitchen, to another cup of coffee. He will wait until the lying has stopped.

Chapter 21

Trevor is driving back home the long way round. He can't face
the Roundabout again, not now, not today. The Ring Road will take
him to the other side of Oxford, but he can always pop in to the sheet
music shop, he was going to do that tomorrow anyway. Well not
actually tomorrow, but it was on his "To Do" List. He liked the shop,
the bloke in there was always so helpful.

He'd think about ringing Hazel once he'd got home. No, tomorrow.
Let her sleep on it, things always looked better the next day. Yes, that's
it, he'd think about it tomorrow.

The frontage of Orsino's is all trailing ivy and those trees with
impossibly round little balls of foliage on sticks. The greenery an
inheritance from the restaurant's previous days as "The Arbour" the
pretension of whose miniscule portions of unidentifiable exotica had
not been a success. Orsino's kept the décor and the prices, but serves
recognisable food in portions more suited to the burghers of Oxford.
Mario stands outside the porch, a cigarette hidden in the palm of his
hand, allowing himself deep and hasty drags when he is certain that the
Manager is busy with Anna and Jonathan as he takes unctuous account
of their bill. Mario had suggested that his Manager pursue this task as
he had proved unequal to Jonathan's staying power in pursuit of his
prey.

The Manager is ushering Jonathan and Anna out of the door and
Mario nips smartly around the back of the building to return to his
kitchen.

It is the flash of Mario's white jacket that alerts Trevor. That quick
movement against the dark green ivy, and he watches the man, thinking
of Police-5 Videos and inappropriate behaviour.

Trevor often watches people if they are darting about, always
vigilant for the chance to be the One Who Saw It. So it is not the well-
dressed couple who catch his eye, not until he has to slow down while
some idiot has to manoeuvre out of the bus lane. If he weren't such a
good driver, always careful to let people out, even if they're not
indicating, if he wasn't so conscientious and that Ford Fiesta hadn't got
stuck behind the number 34 bus, he would never have seen them.
Trevor thought afterwards about that, about the chances of that. "What
were the chances?" he'd have said to Mother, "What were the chances

that I'd be there, right there at that moment, that I would have seen them."

Anna does not look across at the man in the car, she is looking up at Jonathan. It is that look that tells Trevor everything. He does not know it yet, but later he will say that that was the moment that he knew he would be betrayed.

Trevor drives on, and forgets to call at the sheet music shop, and forgets to pick up his Radio Times so that he misses his Badger-Watch programme because the newspaper only lists 'London', and the 'Regions' are in a little list at the bottom of the page and Trevor seems to have a bit of a headache. It's not actually a headache, but there is a dull, sore ache somewhere behind his eyes so that he wants to close them.

Chapter 22

Monday, blessed Monday, and Trevor is the first to arrive. He has decided to get there before Anna. Let her see him at the piano, rehearsing tonight's pieces. Let her see how he had already set out all the chairs, with the new copies of the music that he's laid out on each seat.

Jonathan would never do this, he's too 'big' for this, he wouldn't sit up last night until eleven forty-five marking up the revised lines with highlighter pens: red for bass, yellow for alto, blue for soprano… Jonathan wouldn't even want this, this smallness.

Trevor is looking around the room, he knows that it is just a schoolroom – not even in the main building – just an extra two-room block that was added a couple of years ago from the Parent Teachers Association. All those Fetes and Jumble Sales so that the Year Seven overflow could have a real classroom instead of the Pre-fab. Jonathan was an Oxford Man; if the building didn't have a couple of turrets and a quadrangle he wouldn't even regard it as a school. No, Witsham Comprehensive was way below his touch.

Trevor looks up as he hears a car arriving and he snatches a peep out of the window; a rabbit-quick scan of the car park. He doesn't recognise the car, he doesn't want any of the choir members to arrive before Anna, he wants a few moments with her. He looks at his watch, it is not like Anna to be late, she's never late. Why would she be late tonight of all nights, he just wants a moment, that's all, just a quick moment for her to realise….

Outside in the car park Diane turns off the engine. On the seat beside her is a plastic-covered file filled with little plastic wallets ready for the music. Her handbag bulges with a sports-cap bottle of mineral water and a box of Strepsils. She'll wait for Jo-Anne and go in with her. She looks at the windows of the choir room, they are watching her just sitting here. She opens the file on her lap and looks down at it, as if she is reading the music, frowning in concentration at the empty plastic pages.

Anna is standing outside the Estate Agent's window; it's the nearest building to the school. She is reading through the details of the houses in the town. She is waiting for another car to drive into the school car park. She knows that Trevor is in there, she saw him arrive. She doesn't want to be alone with him, she doesn't want to hear him tell her how much he's prepared for tonight. He'll tell her about his highlighter pens again, and she doesn't want to look at his small soft mouth worrying the words.

She notes that The Old Vicarage is trying it on at £575,000 and reminds herself to slip that into the conversation at next week's Hunger Relief Lunch (All the great and the good of Witsham sitting around eating soup and a hunk of rustic bread and discussing school fees) She lets her thoughts slide into wondering if she would have sent her children to a Private School; well, what with Roy's Little Problem and her Tubes it never really came up.

They'd discussed 'names' once, that month when she was a week late and she'd actually allowed herself to walk into Mothercare...

Anna shakes her head; it's a brisk flick of the lacquered hair to brush away the memories. The Choir – that's her baby. She's a real Career Woman, whatever Aunt Jo or Miss Etch had thought. She is a singer, and a Choir Mistress.

Susie's four-wheel drive passes Anna, its cattle-bars gleaming a warning to any cows that might linger thoughtlessly in the school entrance. Grace is in the passenger seat, waving her arms about in that irritating way, probably telling Susie some 'humorous' tale concerning her bulk, about her getting stuck in Sainsbury's doorway. Anna has no patience with fat people. Watching the Range-Rover turn out of sight, Anna begins to stroll slowly in its wake, thinking that she can time it so that they all arrive at the same time.

Trevor is sitting at the piano, staring at the keys as he hears the laughter from the car park and the slamming of car doors. He stares at the music that's propped up in front of him with the brightly coloured markings and starts to play one of the rounds that Anna likes to use as a warming-up piece, and he notices that his fingers are trembling, just slightly, so that he has to concentrate rather too much for this simple tune.

Diane has spotted Jo-Anne and gets out of her car. The women wave to each other, and Diane's face is a bright beam of smiling relief.

Susie and Grace, heading for the classroom, call over to her, pointing to the new file under her arm and giving her the thumbs up.

She is beginning to belong.

Another car has arrived. Tony is at the wheel, and he is smiling, all calm assurance as he positions the BMW exactly within the two white lines of the marked bay. He opens his door to confirm the precise five inches between the gleaming bodywork and the line, and is satisfied.

Lindsay is sitting in the passenger seat looking down at hands that are resting on her choir file. A fine film of sweat under her fingers mists out onto the green plastic. Tony turns off the engine and Lindsay looks over at the black driving gloves resting on the wheel, at the circular holes that reveal the back of his hands and the fine film of black hair. She is willing him not to remove them.

Tony is slowly unbuckling the little plastic studs that hold the gloves onto his wrists.

"There's no need for you to come in," it's torn from her.

"I told you, I want to talk to your choir mistress."

"But you can't just turn up." Her hands are slippery, small hot puddles collecting under her palms.

Tony turns to her, infinite in his smiling patience: "I'm going to offer to do the Drumming. You agreed with me yourself after the last Concert. That dreadful Rowena woman ruining it."

"It was because she did it a bit too, well, ethnic really."

"She made it sound like an African war dance."

Lindsay's defending: "Gaudete isn't English, I think she was trying for a European feel."

Tony clinches it: "Her drum had giraffes all round it."

"Tony, I just feel that we should have rung Anna first, she's not very good with surprises..." and it's a dreadful memory: "I'll never forget that birthday party we sprang on her."

Tony is folding the driving gloves together, re-sealing the wrist studs.

"I don't know why you're so negative, I thought you liked me to support you." He turns an aggrieved face toward her. "You bewilder me, Lindsay, I try and encourage you, I try to be interested in everything that you do, I...."

"Yes, I know! It's just that it's sometimes too... too much?" and she falters, so that it's a question.

"Never." He reaches out to take her hands in his. "Nothing is too much for you, kitten."

He's turning her hands over in his, looking down at the fine film of sweat.

"You see how you get? .. I just want to look after you."

69

Tony is looking at her, there is no guile in this look, it is the genuine and heartfelt stare of a man who knows he is right.

But it is just very slightly too intent. "I love you so much."

And she is lost.

Inside the classroom Rowena, innocently assured of her role, is quietly tapping a rhythm on the goatskin drum. Anna is watching her "A little less tribal, I think, more sprightly." She flicks her long fingers in the air.

Rowena nods solemnly and continues to pound her darker rhythms. Her status as the percussionist and, in her late twenties, as one of the younger members of the choir, has convinced Rowena that she is an important member of this group. Her attendance is regular and she feels that she has made many sacrifices. Her husband's Wine Circle Dinners have often had to be missed because Anna needed the constant beat of her little drum. She smoothes back the fringe of soft brown hair from tortoiseshell glasses that frame small round eyes, brown little puddles of constant surprise in an oval dish of a face.

Trevor is hovering around Anna, a puppy waiting for its ball to be thrown. "Did you see that I'd...... " "Yes, thank you Trevor, I saw the highlighting," and she moves over to her music stand.. "Now come along everyone, we must make a start!"

The choir shuffle and bustle into position. Paulette, the Choir's Treasurer and Secretary, is volunteering again, because she always volunteers. "Anna, shall I type out those words-only copies of that Greek thing, only several of us could do with a phonetic version?"

Trevor looks up at that, wishing he'd thought of it.

"Hands up all those who want just the words then." Anna's counting the several women who are raising their hands, more to support Paulette's mission to Be Useful than for any real vocal help.

Paulette, a woman whose clothes are liberally covered with spaniel hairs and who is surrounded by the aroma of dog, has anxious eyes and long wispy blonde hair that trails into her mouth where it is chewed with a constant and fretful unease.

Lindsay comes into the room; she's nipped ahead of Tony and goes straight up to Anna. It's a breathless gabble: "I hope it's all right, only my husband used to be a drummer, when he was at University, he was in a Band."

Anna is always alert to the word University; it unsettles her and puts her on her guard. Anna notices that Tony is giving her what she describes to herself as that Male-Smug-Boss-Smile.

"Hello, it's lovely to meet you. I do so enjoy the Concerts."
Not that easily won, Anna is sorting out the music on her stand and avoiding the 'shaking hands' moment.

Tony recognises something not unlike competition, and keeps his hand at his side. "I am here to offer my services," and he shares a humble look with the room. "If I may be so bold."

Rowena has picked up on the threat and moves her drum between her legs.

Lindsay is not sure whether to take her place in the choir or to stand beside Tony. She moves her weight from foot to foot, holding her file to her chest.

Susie and Grace are sharing a look, and watching Tony; they're remembering the talk in the pub last week. Susie's shoulders are flexing. "He can't just walk in here."

Grace's nodding. "He's not a member," and Jo-Anne's leaning over to add her grievance. "Nobody else brings their husbands along. My Mike would love to come and listen."

Since My-Mike has yet to put in an appearance at any of the choir's concerts this is welcomed as support but ignored as a matter of actual fact.

The choir are feeling a sense of threat. It's undefined but they can smell the faint scent of it and Trevor, over at his piano, watches Tony, and recognises an Alan Sharkey. The School Playground has furnished Trevor with a sharp antenna for bullies.

Anna smiles her sweetest 'professional' smile at Tony. He is standing four-square in front of her and she recognises the inflexibility and the determination. She does not want this challenge, she could not possibly lose this, not in front of the Choir, she must not show her full mettle to this man. She will compromise and save her sword for another day.

"Do please take a seat. It's Terry? is it?" She'd read that in Cosmopolitan, it's a real put down that, not being bothered to remember the name.

"Tony," he's caught her gaze, he knows this game. He's all smiles and genial affability as he takes the chair at the side of the room, the chair to which Anna has gestured with a condescending flick of her hand.

"If you'd just like to watch, and then maybe Rowena?"

Rowena is trying not to meet Anna's gaze.

" ... Rowena could lend you her drum later in the session...?"
Rowena has clamped her not inconsiderable thighs around the little painted giraffes and is glaring balefully at Tony.

"Oh, it will be marvellous just to watch this evening. If you like I could bring my drum kit in next week."
Now Anna is impressed with "drum-kit". It sounds professional, it sounds Jonathan and Cheltenham.
Susie, always ready for a crusade, is stirring it. "Well I think Rowena's drum fits the ethos of the Choir."
Grace's loyally nodding and there are a couple of murmured assents from the group. Anna is keen to regain her control, dissent must be thwarted:
"Now I think we can leave this for the moment. We have been here twenty minutes and haven't even opened our files. Come along now! We'll warm up with the Greek song."

Jo-Anne is holding out her music for Diane to share. Diane's taking a fortifying swig of water from her bottle. "Oh dear, it's actually *in* Greek."
"Don't worry, none of us have got it yet.".. Paulette is leaning across to whisper her helpfulness.. "I'm typing out the words this week for us."
Anna, ears like a bat, is onto her. "Yes thank you Paulette, but let's just give it a try shall we," and she waves at Trevor to begin the introduction.

Anna can feel a pulse throbbing in her temples. She is watching Trevor as he fumbles to find the right sheet of music, and Jo-Anne and Diane as they brace themselves for the unachievable. She hadn't thought it would be like this, this compromise. She didn't dare remember her dreams for this Choir: The Royal Albert Hall, BBC Radio guest spots, this lot will be hard pressed to get Cheltenham under their belts.
She looks again across at Trevor whose unkind God has allowed him to knock the music sideways across the piano's music stand, the sheets are falling down onto the keys and floating softly onto the floor. Paulette's there, swooping down to scramble beneath the piano stool, helping to pick up the music.
Anna can feel Tony's eyes upon her. She does not deserve this, this inadequacy.

Jo-Anne's taking advantage of this to help Diane with the Greek words.

"*Anamesa Tsirigo* .. you sing that three times… then the chorus is *Kerkira ke Kefallonia* ..just think sort of Captain Corelli's Mandollin .."

Diane's doubtful: "I only saw the film, I found the book a bit heavy goi…"

"Thankyou!" Anna is becoming a little terrible and the choir shivers in anticipation.

"Lindsay, I think we should hear your solo straight after the warm up."

Now that the sacrifice has been chosen, the Choir are at liberty to send the little lamb small nods of sympathetic encouragement. Lindsay can feel Tony looking at her. Lindsay is psyching herself up.. *it was all right in the bathroom this morning, in fact it was actually quite, well, it was all right. Take a deep breath, it doesn't matter. It doesn't matter that Tony is here.*

Trevor is trying not to hate himself.

So he knocked the music over, so what. If Anna hadn't been late, if he'd been able to have those few words he wouldn't have got himself in such a stew. He could hear Mother telling him to "Stop getting in a state." He could hear Zenata telling him to "Connect with his inner calmness." Problem was, Trevor had never had any of that, his inner had always been a sort of simmering, that quivering of water in the pan before the veg goes in. It was an unsettled shaking, waiting for the carrots.

He was going through the warm-up now. The choir, under the lash of Anna's venom, were almost in key. It would be fine. He'd talk to Anna at the end of the session; maybe they could go for a drink. Trevor's imagination failed at that point and he forced himself to concentrate on his playing.

Tony watches Lindsay. He is giving her an encouraging smile and nodding at her and Lindsay looks across at him and just for one slight moment she imagines him dead, falling forward in the little wooden chair onto the floor. Heart attack, hardly any pain at all. Just Gone. It is a narrow sliver of a thought, it lasts merely seconds, but it has the clarity of fine glass.

At the end of the warm up Lindsay remains standing while the other members scramble about in their files for the next music. Anna's trying to actually look at Lindsay, she is trying to quell the slight feeling that this might not actually be fair, so she's bracingly loud: "It's 'Down to the River to Pray' everybody, now we've done this before, and Lindsay's been practising in the week, haven't you dear...you got the tape I popped through your door...good ... thank you Trevor."

Trevor is looking across at Lindsay, for her to give him a sign that she is ready, Lindsay is staring straight ahead so Trevor launches into the introduction with what he hopes is an encouraging volume.

Lindsay opens her mouth, and starts to cough. Tony looks down at the hands he has clasped on his lap. Lindsay looks across at Trevor and nods for him to start again. She can feel the sweat trickling down her arms, her whole body feels a wetness and she wonders if she might actually melt, right here, in front of everybody, like on a sci-fi film when the aliens dissolve. She thinks that it might be rather nice to dissolve.

Lindsay does not dissolve. She sings the solo. It's not terrible, not Oh-my-god-that's-appalling, but nothing ever is, is it. It's just not very good. Like most things. She cracks on the middle A, and forgets to give two beats on the second line, and when the rest of the choir join in for the chorus she finds that she has stopped singing altogether.

Grace is leaning forward and mouths: "That wasn't that bad"

and Susie, standing behind her, is rubbing her shoulder in an irritating women-together-against-the-odds sort of way. Anna is managing to look aggrieved and irritated all at once. Trevor is nodding at her, his lips compressed into a line of determined optimism.

Lindsay cannot look across at Tony. She can feel him; she can taste his disappointment in the thickness of the air between them.

The overhead strip lighting is flickering and Lindsay watches it, looking up at the stuttering blue-white light as if there is some meaning to this.

There are general groans of "Oh Not Again!" from the choir, and Trevor is getting up from the piano: "I'll go and get the Caretaker, he should be around somewhere," and he darts out of the room.

Anna is leaning on her music stand in an attitude of deep martyrdom. She is directing her remarks to Tony, but not looking at him.

"I have complained about that light twice this Term, good grief we pay enough for the hire of this place."

Paulette's offering her services. "Shall I go and help Trevor find Reg?" Anna's shaking her head, but Paulette is determined to explain just how she could be of use. "Only I could go the opposite way and look in the Science Block..?"

"No, Paulette! – we don't want half the choir chasing around the school – let's just try to ignore it, it's not *that* distracting..." but as Anna looks at her Choir she finds that most faces are upturned to the light fittings as the fault now includes another fluorescent tube.

Susie's voice betrays just a small tremor of glee. "The light next to it is on the blink now too..."

Tony has not taken his eyes off Lindsay, but she will not lower her eyes from the ceiling. He gets to his feet and, with apparent great reluctance, he walks over to her.

"We can work on it. Lindsay?" He's standing right in front of her as her eyes follow the flickering above her. It is as if she cannot bring herself to look away from the faulty lighting, as if the flashing will wipe out this moment and save her.

Outside in the corridor, Trevor has found Reg sitting in the Games Cupboard, his presence betrayed by the thin trail of cigarette smoke that drifts around the door that is left just slightly ajar.

The Caretaker often sits here; the cupboard is a deep one and a small wooden stool and an ashtray on one of the shelves attest to this regular bolthole. It's where he can escape from the School Secretary's "Lists": those limitless tasks that usually are heralded by the dreaded words *"Reg, could you just...?"* and that usually involve something unpleasant to be done involving chewing gum or an equally irremovable substance in the Boys' Loos.

"Reg, sorry to bother you old chap, but it's the lights again..."

Trevor is standing outside the door, as if he is talking to someone on the lavatory, not actually looking round the door to look at the Caretaker, as if this particular privacy cannot be invaded. There is silence from inside.

Trevor actually knocks on the door of the cupboard. "Hello?"

Reg is maintaining his asylum and does not reply so that Trevor, imagining Anna's fury at the length of time that this is taking, dares to peer around the cupboard door; he is greeted by a particularly well aimed gust of smoke from inside the sanctuary. This would not happen to Jonathan. Jonathan would not have bothered to try and find the Caretaker in the first place.

Reg is grinding his cigarette out, it's a slow and grudging gesture.
"Yes?". This, with great weariness, from inside the cupboard.
"The lighting – it's flickering again."
"I've reported it. It's on the Maintenance List."
Trevor is trying for man-to-man empathy: "Look, you know what Anna's like…"
"I certainly do, mate, I remember the Yoghurt Incident."
Trevor's mouth tightens. "Well there you are, so if you could just…"
Trevor is almost bowled over as the cupboard door swings open against him and Reg comes out of his Retreat.
"I'll take a look, just to shut her up, but there's nothing I can do, I've told you, it's on the List.."
"Yes, yes." Trevor is gratefully sheep-dogging the Caretaker along the corridor, trotting on ahead and then nipping back to Reg's side in an effort to speed the caretaker's laborious lope. Trevor is trying to sound casual, it's how he thinks that men talk to each other: "Just look at them, wiggle a few switches, keep her quiet, you know the sort of thing."
Reg knows the sort of thing all right, he performs such teeth-sucking fiddling-about motions on a regular basis.

Trevor is dodging in front of him so that he is the first to enter the choir room
"Here's Reg!" Trevor gestures to the Caretaker, a soldier returning from the wars with his captive.
Anna's look would wither a less sensitive soul but Trevor is emboldened by his success. Reg is seldom found and has only rarely offered actual assistance.

Grace's calling out "Good old Trevor saves the day!" and Trevor looks across at Anna and shrugs a deprecating shoulder that he hopes will impress upon her how totally indispensable he is. He's saying *"Jonathan wouldn't do this"* over and over in his head, trying to imprint these words on her mind.
Anna wonders why Trevor is looking at her in that peculiarly intense way, it's how he looks at her in their little Concerts when he thinks she's forgotten the words.

The Caretaker is dutifully turning the light switches on and off and shaking his head at the strip lighting.

"Told you, these have been on the Maintenance List since January.."

"But that's months ago..." Anna is raising her immaculate eyebrows.

"No – January *last* year." Reg is indicating the passage of years by pointing out of the window, and he adds, as if it were obvious:

"These are all pre-New Block supply you see."

Anna, used to the vagaries of plumbers and decorators, is not to be thwarted... "Will you please report this, once and for all, to the Head Teacher."

"Won't do any good you know... School Secretary will just tell him that it's on the..."

"The List, yes, I heard you. I shall talk to Karen myself."

Anna hopes that this use of the Secretary's name will impress her rank upon Reg, and that he does not know of the antipathy that exists between herself and the implacable Karen. She turns away from Reg, dismissing him, and picks up her baton: "We'll just turn the lights off for now. Trevor ! I really want to Get On."

Tony still stands up close to Lindsay and watches as she remains steadfast in her attention to the flickering. He gives her a tolerant smile, father to child:

"It's not Fireworks, Lindsay," and he walks in a measured slowness to return to sit on the other side of the room.

"Let's press on... with..." Anna's leafing though her music, trying to salvage this Session. "Yes, I think 'Rhythm of Life' will buck us all up a bit."

So Trevor launches into the rousing introduction and the choir sing bravely on into the gloom.

Chapter 23

The Session ends early.

Trevor packs his music away in a haste that will have to be paid for later; his usual correct filing of the sheets into his case is sacrificed tonight as he scrambles to engage Anna before she can leave. She seems to be rushing, which is unusual. Anna likes to have little words with her favourites, little hints are given, advice passed on in small parcels of magnanimity. Thus are solos sought and granted in these precious minutes when the members can have "Just a few words" with their Mistress. Rowena is first up beside Anna: "About the drumming...Anna, I'm sorry, but Lindsay's husband is not in the choir, and I really feel..."

Anna watches Rowena's mouth, she watches her twisting it around the words, justifying, pleading, explaining. The aggrieved tones whining and wheedling their way around the tale of loyalty betrayed and drumming workshops attended. Anna is bored; she is weary of this woman with her inadequate skill and her goatskin drum. She does not want Rowena's African rhythms to compromise Cheltenham. She looks across at Tony, who seems to be supporting Lindsay out of the room. She should have said something to Lindsay about her solo. She should have had a word with Tony about the drum kit. And now Trevor is hovering about, wanting a word. They all want a part of her. Tonight had gone all wrong and she was made to look foolish. Lindsay should have asked her if her husband could come. And those bloody lights, it looks unprofessional and Anna prides herself on being the ultimate professional.

Rowena is still talking, her mouth now turned into a small and puckered cat's-arse of aggrievance.

"........I mean, I've never minded bringing my drum along, even when I haven't had the car when Colin has to have it for Rotary, even when it was icy and I had to bring it in a pillow-case..."

Trevor is imagining impaling Rowena on a pike, like the ones the Roundheads used in the Re-enactment Society that Mother had wanted him to join. Trevor was not a violent man, and he has always prided himself on his behaviour towards women, but it had been a bit of a week – what with the 99p-Shop incident and that business with the Spider at the Pub – and all he wanted was a word, just a word with Anna, to smooth things out, just to get them back on their even keel. He was watching Anna's face, at the hardening of her eyes as Rowena went on and on, and he knew that he had 'blown it'.

Jonathan would not be standing here, like some supplicant waiting in line for a favour. Jonathan would know how to get rid of Rowena.

Trevor had stuffed his music into his case any old how, and he'd be up half the night sorting it all out now, and all for nothing because of flaming Rowena and her stupid little drum with the giraffes on it. Trevor looks at the drum, at Rowena's feet, and thinks about giving it a kick, just a small kick, enough to get the thing rolling over to the other side of the room, so that Rowena would have to chase it, and Stop Talking To Anna.

Trevor is staring at the drum, working out the distance between it and his foot, and the trajectory of the kick. It's reminding him of football lessons and those diagrams that Mr. Skelton would draw on the blackboard, all those arcs with arrows showing the direction of the ball into the net.

Trevor looks up. Rowena is picking up her drum and holds it huffily to her chest as she walks away. Anna has turned back to Paulette who is offering to Do Something Useful, and they walk together toward the door, heads bent in conversation, excluding interruption.

Outside in the car park Tony is holding Lindsay's hand in a careful grip of deep kindness.

"Come on...come on, Kitten," he's shaking her hand up and down in his, laughing, softly chiding, as she squirms away from him.

"It was just... you were there, and I felt..."

A look of sharp hurt crosses Tony's face as he lets her hand drop back into her lap. She knows that she has offended him and a heavy thud of dread settles in her chest as Tony drives them out of the car park.

Diane had watched them from her car, seen the way Tony leant into Lindsay, seen the laughter in his face and the handholding. She could not remember that she and Paul had ever had that, but perhaps they had, perhaps they had and she'd forgotten. Wouldn't that be terrible; that they'd had that, and there must have been some, but that now it was lost amongst all the walking out of rooms and the slamming of doors.

Trevor walks past, he too is watching Tony's car, but it is Lindsay's shuttered tight face that he is watching and he has a picture of himself, sitting in the changing rooms with his gym kit in the draw-string bag Mother had made out of the kitchen curtains. He can see himself, eight-and-a-half and looking at his hands, and knowing that he won't be able to hold onto the rope and that his feet won't go round the end of it and lock on so that he can push himself up the rope to the wall bars. That Knowing that he was going to slide all the way down the rope, his hands burning against the knotted hemp.

Lindsay looks out of the car window and Trevor catches her eyes for one moment. He knows.

Anna and Paulette are still deeply engrossed. Anna slicks a wary eye over at Trevor and allows the other woman to monopolise her across the car park.
Paulette is in full Useful flow: "You see I don't have an actual job at the moment, so I'm pretty available all round really, so I'd be only too pleased to do more. Chris is in Puerto Rico, you see."

Anna, brimming with apathy at the whereabouts of 'Chris' is aware of Trevor now approaching.

"What is it that Chris actually does...?" "He builds the pipe lines, so he has to be out there to supervise the Engineers. He was in Egypt last year. I get wonderful postcards."
The women have reached Paulette's car.

"I wonder, could you drop me off.. I walked tonight, but.."

"Oh Yes!" Paulette is opening the car door for Anna, her delight a little painful to watch, but Anna can't talk to Trevor tonight, not tonight, and has no pity to spare.

Paulette is the doting owner of an ancient spaniel and her car has the distinctly clinging smell of wet dog. Anna wrinkles her fine nose but her escape from Trevor's pleading eyes overrides her usual avoidance of all things animal. She remembers too late that Paulette's garments are often sprinkled liberally with long shaggy hairs and that there is a staleness about the woman that remembers a wet nose and dribbling mouth. Anna does not like smells.

Trevor watches Anna positively leap into Paulette's car, she's making a great performance of buckling the seat belt. "This is different to mine, Paulette, where's the thing to click it in?"

Trevor is standing beside the car and motions to Anna to wind the window down. Anna mouths through the closed window; she's holding her right hand up to her ear to imitate a phone: "I'll call you!" through the glass, before she twists away to search again for the clip, Paulette is helping her to fix the seat belt. Anna does not turn back to look at Trevor, and he stands back as the car drives away.

* *

At the other side of the town, in the smart new housing development of Executive Dwellings (each house angled so that it does not look into the windows of its neighbour, ferociously mown lawns fronting the bright new yellow of the unlikely 'Cotswold' stone) Tony is driving his car up the crunching gravel of his drive that is just long enough for his BMW to be off-road. He turns off the engine and leans back against the seat, and Lindsay watches him slowly unbuckling the driving gloves, watching the hairs curling back as he pulls the soft leather off his hands.

* *

'Annaroy House' is in the older part of town with its wider streets and gardens each fenced off from the other in private separateness. Anna gets out of Paulette's car and waves her away having resisted the only too obvious hints of coming in for coffee. She's had enough, and Paulette's loneliness can wait for another week. So Anna opens her front door and inhales 'Jasmine and Vanilla' and wishes that she had changed the plug-in to 'Relaxing Lavender'.

Chapter 24

Searing, screaming pain. The agony is blazing, hot and intense as her hand sends shooting darts tearing along her arm. The pain has stopped her breathing; she is trying to inhale against the blackness that threatens to engulf her.

She's hit by a wave of nausea and she's choking against the vomit.

Her hand is against the rim of the car door, the fingers are already red and swelling thick with the damage. There's a thin crack that's opening along the knuckles, blood is seeping quite slowly down the back of her hand.

Lindsay can't think, can't understand what has happened.

She takes her hand away from the door frame and looks at it.

The shock and the pain have made her stupid.

"Tony?... Tony, my hand."

Tony is walking with slow carefulness towards their front door; he does not turn at her voice.

There's a fog around her, the slow and sluggish bewilderment of a dream. But the shattering pain is no dream.

She doesn't understand. She is so full of the pain and the blood that is smearing onto her blouse and the blood that pounds in her head that she cannot comprehend what has happened.

She leans out of the car and vomits onto the driveway.

Tony has slammed the car door on her hand.

She tries to stand and her knees buckle.

She's holding out the hand, trying to show Tony what has happened.

He has gone inside the house, he's calling back to her: "Come on Kitten." His voice sounds rather high pitched, it's almost a singing "Come...on..."

Lindsay tries to stand up, she holds her hand out before her like a gift as she makes her way to the door...

"Tony...you don't understand...Tony," she's calling after him.

Tony has gone upstairs "I'm just going to have half an hour in my den....sort out stuff. I should have done it this evening, but I came with you... it's put me all behind and I need to catch up for tomorrow," there's self-pity in the words and he sounds just a little aggrieved at the wasted evening and the work that this has caused.

The words do not make any sense to Lindsay, she's standing at the bottom of the stairs, calling to him: "Tony! – my hand, you must have shut the car door on my hand!"

"Don't be silly," and it's from far off.

"I'm bleeding!"

With weary patience: "Just put it under the tap, it'll be fine."

"Tony .. it's bad!"

"You're not going to make a fuss are you?" It's said softly, but there is just enough of a warning in it.

Lindsay staggers into the kitchen and holds her hand out under the tap, she turns on the cold water and makes little tearing cries as she tries to keep the hand under the splashing cold. Her hand is shaking with the deep throbbing and she has to lean against the sink to stop herself from fainting.

She stands there a long time, listening to Tony in the room above.
She hears the musical tones of his computer as he turns it on, she hears him walking backwards and forwards across the room that he calls his Den, and she thinks that she can hear him whistling under his breath.

Chapter 25

Diane has stopped off at the Kebab Van on her way home.

Paul had always said that kebabs were drunks-on-their-way-home food, but Diane had always liked the comfort in the taste of the fat and the greed of it; the large pittta with the salad stuffed inside and the chilli sauce oozing out along the gaping mouth of the bread. It was the kind of food that insisted on fingers being licked and mouths wiped with the back of a hand.

She has stopped here many times in the last months, and the young Greek is smiling down at her as she stands beside his van.

"With just a little chilli and extra cheese!" he's slapping the pitta onto the hot plate. "Your usual."

"Yes, thank you. Do you remember *all* your customers?" and she is foolishly aware that she's begging the compliment.

He knows the game: "I remember *you*."

She's smiling back at him knowing that they both know their lines.

It's easy, this speaking of words that mean nothing and they both slip into their roles. The young man has said this many times, the words hardly vary. Nothing is expected from this, nothing will happen.

He double-wraps the kebab "So that you don't get the chilli juice on your coat," and she leans against the van and tells him he is very kind.

She hands him the money and he pretends not to want it. The movements of this little dance are foretold, and this little dance is one of many little dances.

She holds the kebab, feeling its soft warmth through the paper that is already oozing greasily onto her hands.

"Have a good night," the young man has already turned to slice the meat from the large skewer, he wields the knife in practised arcs through the brown meat that trickles its wetness into the metal tray beneath. He looks at the slivers of brown with the white fat speckling the meat and he is thinking of dry brown earth speckled with white blossom on a path that leads to a turquoise harbour and small boats rocking gently in an Aegean breeze. Diane has laid the kebab on the seat beside her and knows that the car will smell of it in the morning. She buckles her seat belt and flicks the windscreen wipers to clear the soft drizzle of rain that has begun to fall.

Through the smearing she can see the young man, he is smiling, so she smiles back at him and raises her hand to wave a goodbye. But he is looking straight ahead, out of the van, and is far away from the greyness.

Chapter 26

Tony is staring at his computer screen; his tongue seeks out the crevices in his teeth, exploring possible areas for new fillings. He can hear the water running into the sink in the kitchen below, but he cannot hear Lindsay any more. That whimpering has stopped.

He taps his mouse-button to close the page and the rows of figures disappear into the dark blue of his Desktop. The screen-saver that he has chosen is of a palm tree fringed beach with white frothed waves. Tony frowns at it and spends several minutes trying to access the icon that will change this image. Scottish tartan does not appeal and he is mildly irritated to have to settle on the same pattern that he remembers from a Christmas-tie that his mother had bought him.
What a fuss she'd made that year, all the business about how she didn't expect her son to ring *every* day but he knew she was ill and surely it wasn't too much to ask....

Tony takes a quick hard breath. Everything had always been such a fuss. If his mother had had a headache it was a migraine, if her legs were sore it was Veins, she didn't have eyes she had cataracts, and then there was the vertigo and the palpitations and the tablets, oh god the tablets... all in that plastic box labelled with the days of the week, and then her getting confused and missing a day and trying to Catch Up.. He'd say: "You can't catch up, Mother, you just have to move on to the next day, otherwise you'll always be a day behind." But she never got it.
Father was even worse, getting their tablet boxes muddled up and refusing to take his painkillers because of some damned documentary he'd seen about side-effects, and always the fuss, the bloody fuss...
And now Lindsay, she'd banged her hand on the car and now he was supposed to go down and Sympathise and make cups of tea and tell her how sorry he was. She was always so slow getting out of the car, and he'd wasted the whole evening trying to support her and encourage her. He'd had to just sit there, facing all those women; sniggering at him and watching him, watching Lindsay and that bloody solo, and she hadn't even *tried*, that's what got him. She hadn't even tried to get it right. Just four lines! Just four lines of a piss-easy tune before the rest of the mob joined in and she couldn't even do that. What was the point of all his ferrying her about in the car, buying her that new plastic folder in Smiths and she couldn't even be bothered to...

There's a crash from the floor below.

Tony gets up and stands stock-still, waiting, holding his breath for the next noise. He has closed his eyes, his head on one side, straining his ears for what will follow.

The computer screen has gone onto "stand-by" but Tony doesn't want to turn it off – it will make that jingly music tone if he turns it off, and she will hear it, she will know that he's coming back down. Not yet, not yet.

Lindsay, he'd chosen her because she wasn't like the others, he'd encouraged her to join that Choir, he'd seen it advertised in the paper, reckoned it was a bunch of middle-aged women that'd be older than Lindsay. Keep her occupied and stop all that silly thinking and saying that she should Do Something with her life.

But that had turned out to be a mistake, like so much else, now she was always going to rehearsals and it was "Anna says" and "Anna thinks."

Anna had told her to smarten up because she stood at the front being so small, and Anna had suggested that his wife cut her hair, his wife!

He'd told Lindsay that a woman's hair is her glory, he'd even pointed out their wedding photos and how he'd insisted that she have it hanging loose around her shoulders instead of having it pinned up in that ridiculous scroll that the hairdresser had suggested "because then the veil could be pinned into the coil of hair." Insanity! Well he'd told her, he'd told that woman that she was supposed to be dressing a bride for her wedding, not an Executive in an Office.

Anna had even showed Lindsay pictures of all these cropped hairstyles from some bloody magazine. Tony hated those magazines, all that "How to" stuff for the bedroom, and "What Women Wanted". He knew what women wanted, he knew what his wife wanted.

"I know what you want, my Lad,".. no, no that wasn't it. That was Dad, and he hadn't wanted it. "You'll get what you deserve Anthony," that was always the next thing. Well he'd changed his name hadn't he; he'd left Anthony among the Christmas crackers that he hadn't been allowed to pull because he'd left his sprouts, and the belt that hung in the kitchen with the buckle shaped like a hand.

There hasn't been another sound from downstairs since that crash.
Tony creeps across the room to stand at the door and cranes his head

out into the landing. He takes long steps along to the stairs, walking on the balls of his feet so as not to make a sound; his face is a contorted rictus in the effort of silence.

He peers down the stairs and waits. There is no sound from below. He stands there in the silence, frowning in concentration. He looks at the stairs and tries to remember which is the one that creaks, and then begins his descent. He moves in slow motion until he is betrayed by the third stair and a loud protest from the wood breaks his silence. Tony takes the rest of the stairs noisily and looks into the kitchen.

He had a hamster once, and it had hurt itself on its wheel. His father had said that it would be all right in the morning and that you didn't take hamsters to vets because they were too small.

Tony had sat by the cage and watched the small ball of fur as it sat on its little bed of straw and trembled. He hadn't wanted a hamster, he'd wanted a dog, but his father had said that dogs were "a tie" and that you couldn't have holidays if you had a dog. So he'd been given this cage on his ninth birthday, with the bedding and the bag of food. The mixed grains and nuts that would go in the little dish marked "Hammy" but the little animal didn't seem to know the rules and there'd always be a pile of hamster poo in with the grains, Tony still couldn't eat muesli to this day, and he remembered that morning, when he'd crept downstairs, holding his breath, creeping up to the cage to see if the thing was dead.

Lindsay is sitting at the kitchen table, her hand is wrapped in a tea cloth and a packet of frozen peas lies across the top. She is just sitting there, staring at the little puddle of water that is seeping into the wood under her hand.
Tony takes a gulp at the air. "There you are !" and he says it as if he has been looking everywhere for her. There's the lid of a saucepan quivering on the ceramic floor tiles that had caused the noise, and Tony looks down at it and regrets his emphatic denial of vinyl flooring.

Lindsay is very pale. "My hand…" it's a hoarse, dazed whisper.
"You must be more careful, Kitten." He's shaking his head in amused bewilderment at her. "What would you do without me, eh?"
She's looking at the packet of vegetables defrosting on her hand:
"These were those cheap ones you didn't like"

"That's fine! – don't be silly – that's a good idea, stop any possible bruising." Tony is bustling about, filling the kettle.

He's facing the sink, not looking at her : "Nice cup of tea?"
Lindsay looks over at him, at the square shape of his back, and at the way his shoulders curve slightly over as if he's hunching, expecting a blow.

She is trying to make sense of this, trying to shake off the fogged bewilderment, trying to focus, but all she can see is the soft black hair curling over at the back of his neck, brushing his collar, and all she can think of is that he needs a haircut.

Chapter 27

Anna is taking off her make-up. Sitting before her mirror with the little film-star light bulbs all around it, she wipes the cleansing lotion off with a large wad of cotton wool and stares at her reflection. It's a shiny and rather greasy Anna, the eyelashes bare of mascara, the lips pale. When they were first married, Anna would wear her make-up to bed, afraid that Roy would see this plainness. Years of the sourness of regret and disappointment, combined with Roy's bottom-noises, have put paid to such romantic delicacy.

Anna's high-street silk scanties now lie in their yellowing tissue paper in the drawer along with the French knickers and the low-cut nightwear, and she tells herself that the lacy frills around the necklines used to scratch her, and that everybody wears cotton these days.

Roy is downstairs, she can hear him bumping into the furniture and knocking himself against drawers that he has opened and then forgotten to close. Anna closes her eyes and remembers how Jonathan had tossed his jacket over the back of the restaurant chair. Roy is calling upstairs: "Do you want a camomile tea?"

Anna does, but cannot bring herself to ask for it. "No thank you, I'm going straight to bed." She knows that this doesn't actually negate the desire for tea, and her mouth waters slightly at the thought of the warm liquid. She frowns into the mirror, peering hard for any evidence of laughter lines. He'd forget to put in her sweetener anyway, so what was the point.

Chapter 28

Jonathan is sitting in his favourite wine bar. Lots of young men in suits you couldn't buy in a chain store, and girls – he always thought of them as girls – in smart skirts and those weirdly ugly handbags that cost a month's wages. Plenty of chrome, glass tables, and an abundance of mirrors that afford him excellent angles of the back of his haircut and the exquisite layering of his highlights.

He's toying with a tall glass, the ice cubes rattle around the dregs of his gin. There's a girl by the bar he's seen before, she had looked over at him, just once, and then let her eyes scan the room behind him allowing him a long look as she stretched her neck back to shake out the mane of streaked blonde hair. Jonathan is an expert on hair colouring and he admires the expensive; this wasn't a cap and pull the hair through the holes job, no, this was foil layering, and several colours; two, at least two shades of blonde, he reckoned 'ash' and 'honey' and then two more light brown to blend. This wasn't done in Witsham. Oxford or probably London, and three figures.
The girl was leaning down to touch her shoe, letting the hairdressers expertise swoop over her face.

Jonathan wanders over to her, he's holding his glass toward her.
"I'm just ordering another, can I get you one?"
The girl raises surprised eyes as she straightens up.
"Oh …I.."
"I hate to drink alone, don't you?"
The girl laughs, expensive dentistry too. "Well thank you. Just until my friend arrives."
Jonathan turns to the barman. Behind his suave smile he's calculating: *Oh it's the friend about to arrive is it, well we'll see.*
Within a few minutes Jonathan has bought the drinks and negotiated the move away from the bar: "Let's sit down over here shall we, a bit quieter, away from the…" and he gives a disparaging look around them "….crowd."
She has to agree with that, or appear to enjoy the elbow-jostling from the other suits and skirts. He's marked them out as special, not just part of the 'crowd' and they now sit at a corner table, the seating nicely arranged so that Jonathan looks straight into a mirror behind the girls face. He's watching himself run long white fingers through the soft curve of hair that flops endearingly over his eyes.

"I want to know everything about you," he's leaning forward, touching her glass.

"I work for *B.G.W. & Carling.* I'm on the Export side....."

He's watching her mouth and those fine sharp little teeth, very white, with the dark red lipstick that's been outlined with a thin brown line.

She's fluttering her hands as she describes her life, Jonathan picks up odd words, he has an acute radar for this.

"Business Class Flights.....my secretary.... the Board Meetings..."

He knows that half of it is bullshit and that doesn't matter at all, she's downing her scotch with practised ease, she knows the game.

She opens that mouth wide again and Jonathan spots the lipstick smear on a tooth.

"Keep still," and he's leaning toward her.. "There's just..." and he wipes the little red stain off with his finger.

She has not moved away, her mouth remains open for him.

The Game is on.

Back at his flat an hour later Jonathan is making coffee.

"Brazilian or Columbian?"

"Oh, whatever you've got .. this is a lovely flat."

Jonathan knows that he has a lovely flat and doesn't want to get into the estate-agent-show-round routine. This sitting room, with its mahogany tables and ample leather sofas, is perfect. A couple of catalogues for antiques auctions, and lots of sheet music in 'casual' piles. The bedroom is also fine, it always is, just in case; but he doesn't want her in the kitchen with last night's take-away and a sink full of three days of cereal bowls.

"Oh, you've got a piano!"

God she's bright. The Steinway stands in pole position at the far end of the room, lit by a carefully placed spotlight, and there's a rather complicated piece by Berio on the stand.

The girl walks over to it and is pressing some of the keys in the jangled order of the unmusical; Jonathan controls the urge to rush over and slam down the lid, having never fancied himself as James Mason, he gestures to the deep squashy leather.. "Do sit down, won't you?"

"Why don't you play me something?"

Oh God no, not that, she'd have him at it for hours and then probably start singing along to something inappropriate.

"I'd rather talk to you."

So she's flattered, and sinks into the shiny leather that squeaks slightly as she leans back against the deep cushioning. "I didn't know leather came in this colour?"

"I didn't know eyes came in your colour." Sometimes even Jonathan cringes at the words he has to say, but it's the Game.

The girl knows what she's doing here, and he's more than aware of the hard thud of lust that's twisting his designer underpants up into his groin.

"Perhaps we'd be more comfortable…?"

"No, I'm fine here. Is the coffee ready? I'd really love some … in my office we've had a real issue over freshly ground, and Gavin says….."

Jonathan slips into the kitchen to avoid Gavin's pronouncements, he's had rather too many of these in the last hour, and while pouring the coffee into his Chinese mugs – white porcelain, and a shape that's not that easy to drink out of – he takes the opportunity to jiggle his nether region into its correct order. He has often thought that women have no idea how complicated it gets down there, and the sorting out can be quite painful.

The girl has followed him into the kitchen, and Jonathan is caught with his hand on his crotch. She stands behind him and puts her arms around his waist.

Why do they do that, it's completely impractical, he can't do anything *to* her like that. So Jonathan turns round and pulls her to him. Oh well, if she's going to come on to him by the sink…and so her skirt is pushed up without too much ceremony, and the no-panty-line thong is yanked aside, and he's inside her.

Pushing hard and fast, his head buried at the side of her face in amongst that hair, that bloody wonderful hair. He can smell the expensive shampoo and his face is slippery against the gloss of it.

The girl is looking over Jonathan's shoulder at the Tandoori Palace takeaway bag; it's surrounded by tin foil boxes smeared with thick red sauce lumpy with slivers of half eaten chicken. The tandoori sauce has dribbled onto the table and the girl thinks that the stain will probably never come off.

Chapter 29

Lindsay wakes to the sound of Tony shaving. When she was first married Lindsay would lie and listen to this. She would hear Tony whistling through his teeth, and the way that the note of this changed when he negotiated a difficult angle. She had used to think that the whistling meant that he was pleased with her, that the sex had been good.

Before her marriage, she had never heard anyone shave. Her father, a small and private man, had managed to conduct all bathroom activities in almost complete silence, a situation she had not questioned. Lindsay was an only child, and only children do not have a yardstick to measure abnormality, they accept that their home life is how everything should be, although sometimes there is that nagging little itch of a fear that nobody else is like their parents, that they are abnormal in some small but significant way. Her mother did not change out of her nightclothes until the afternoon, her underclothes laid over the back of the kitchen chair 'to air'. Her father abhorred 'casual' clothes and would even mow the back lawn in his suit.

Lindsay had not liked to bring school friends home for tea – that dreadful rite of passage in order to belong – she had not wanted to explain the rows of little bottles of pills set out by her mother's plate, and the Dr.Scholl's appliances for feet: brownish pink pads of foam cut into strips to be stuffed between toes. She was sure that Hannah Bentley's mother didn't have twisted toes that scrambled to lie on top of each other if not held down by the assistance of foam and rubber.

Mother washed these aids, and the sink bobbed with the pink pads that were 'In to Soak', a process that seemed to have no limit to the time that these items would foam and bubble with the washing-up liquid.

Lindsay had also to be diligent in the detection of her mother's undergarments, and their casual placing around the house, just in case there was that slight stain on the back of her mother's slip, that yellowing.

Although none of this had struck Lindsay as particularly unusual, she had become used to adjusting to others' deformity. Marriage to Tony had meant a passport to what everybody else was like. Tony always knew how to go about things, which house to buy, and then which furniture and where to put it. She had always felt confident with his choices: the meals, her clothes. If he had chosen an outfit she knew that he wouldn't be able to criticise it, so it was easier really. It was easy to take his advice and know that she was pleasing him. It just meant that there wouldn't be a great discussion, just as they were about to go out, and she wouldn't have to go back upstairs and change into another outfit because her choice had been so unsuitable. Tony said that it was her mother's fault, that she had never guided her daughter, and so Tony told Lindsay what to wear and she was grateful for the guidance.

Lindsay looks down at the bedclothes, her right arm is hidden under the duvet and with a careful look towards the en-suite door she pulls back the bedding to look at her hand. The bruising is quite dreadful and the knuckles are so swollen that she can barely flex her fingers. The cuts where the skin has split along the finger joints have sealed over with deep red scabs and her nails look as if they are just lying on top of the skin, as if they might come off if she touched them.

She listens to Tony's whistling and the confusion and bewilderment of last night settles like a heavy cold in her head. She even shakes her head to clear her thoughts.

It was an accident. He didn't realise what he had done, then he felt guilty, that was it. He felt guilty and so couldn't really accept how bad the injury was. Just like a man. They can never be wrong, and Lindsay even smiles to herself at this generalising of gender. You see it all the time on the television, the situation comedies where the woman just sighs and raises her eyebrows at the husband's foolishness. It didn't do to make too much of things, that was it. There was just no point in making him feel bad over this, he'd just get all offended and then she'd have to spend weeks walking on egg-shells and coaxing him back. She'd pop into the Health Centre after he'd gone to work, get some arnica from Boots. That's it, that's what she'd do.

When Tony came out of the bathroom Lindsay's hand was back under the duvet and she smiled up at him. He blew her a kiss: "That's my Kitten."

Lindsay listened to him as he almost ran down the stairs, she heard him turn on the radio. Tony always liked to leave the radio set on Channel 4, for the news and the serious morning discussion programmes. Lindsay had left it on Radio 2, and she held herself still, her lips pressed tight together as she waited for his reaction. There was a moment, but he did not re-tune the radio and he even started to sing along with the banal little song.

Lindsay let out the breath she did not know she had been holding.

It was going to be all right.

Chapter 30

Trevor hadn't slept well; it was all very well Zenata saying 'Let it Go' but once Trevor had got into what he *would* have said to Anna, and what he *should* have said, if only she'd given him the chance, then there was no going back at all.

He was a mouse on a wheel, round and round within the cage of his mind. Zenata had given him that "Don't let the Small Stuff get into the In Tray" book on his last session, well that was all very well, but Trevor didn't actually deal in the Big Stuff. He was happy to leave that to the U.N. and The Musicians Union. Nobody was going to ask him to negotiate truces. No, his war was very much on the home front; his own little areas of conflict had always been Small Stuff, what Mother had called his "silly insecurities". It had been just the same at the Gas Board what with all that nastiness over Mr. Gillespie's expenses.
(He had *not* said that he was lying, he merely mentioned that £41.98p was rather a lot for a one-way mileage claim to Abingdon; good grief you could do that journey in half an hour, and he knew because Mother liked their branch of Sainsbury's better than Witcham because they had a better assortment of crispbreads... apparently.)

The whole thing had got totally out of control with Mrs. Warner maintaining that the gas explosion at the Leisure Centre was down to him because he was so involved with working out the possible routes and mileage involved that he hadn't passed on the gas leak query. Well – nobody had actually died, had they? Anyway there was that special number people were supposed to dial, it was on the side of all the vans "Smell a Leak? Don't delay, Dial Now" and the number in fluorescent writing. He'd even authorised that, the bright red graphics.

It wasn't his fault that the work experience kid had called the main office. Mr. Gillespie had seen his chance, diversion tactics all round, sending e-mails about fourteen fire-fighting appliances and the Golden Years Group having to stand in the car park in their swimming costumes. It was always the same.

And now – now Hazel was on his ansaphone, she'd rung last night so he had that to listen to when he'd got back from Choir.

A load of nonsense about having to report him to the Agency because It Could Happen To Other Women. Trevor didn't think that the Internet went very much on public relations and health and safety, he thought that it was all a bit buyer-beware. He was forever getting offers from porn sites and having to un-subscribe at the bottom of the page, so surely they wouldn't pursue a small contretemps in a car park. Would they?

The blessed banana had rescued her, hadn't he, so what was she going on about? He wasn't going to worry about it. He really wasn't. It wasn't as if he could ask for anybody's advice either, he didn't see himself ringing Mother's solicitor and explaining about Spiders and Chickens and on-line dating. He should never have got involved in it.

Last night he had thought he might write in to one of those "Margie Helps" pages in women's magazines until he'd realised that they'd probably publish his letter, due to the fancy dress element, and then of course everybody would know, and Hazel would probably sue him, not to mention Famine Relief getting on the bus, and then he'd be persona-non-grata and Anna would say that it besmirched all their charity concerts and that it was his fault now that Roy would never be Mayor.

Trevor has been staring into the mirror over the sink; the toothpaste that he'd put on his brush twenty minutes ago has bled down the plastic handle and is dribbling onto his hand. He often stands like this, in his bathroom. The mirror reflects the leaping dolphin tiles around the bath – a hangover from the last occupants who were very big on fish judging from the kitchen wallpaper. Mother had wanted floral but tiling wasn't exactly Trevor's forte so he hasn't bothered to change them; anyway, he likes dolphins.

Mother's leg ointment is still in the white plastic wall cupboard (Trevor is better with rawlplugs) along with the last packet of his pills, empty, but he'd kept the packet to remind him of the name of the tablets, just in case.

"I'll ring Anna." Trevor's talking to the mirror as he brushes his teeth.

"I'll ring her today – suggest coffee – nothing outlandish in that."

"I've got to know where I stand. If she's smooching up to Jonathan there's only one explanation."

He's brushing with great vigour and bares his teeth to inspect the gleaming.

"Nip it in the bud."

His gaze remains fixed on his mouth as he runs his tongue along the front molars, sucking the remaining toothpaste off and smacking his lips; he does not raise his eyes to meet his own gaze, he knows what he will see reflected there and is determined to ignore the uncertainty.

Chapter 31

Jonathan can smell the dank moisture. He's lying face down into the dark navy cotton and the pillowcase is damp where he has softly dribbled during the night. Jonathan is aware of his wet mouth and has tried many remedies: not drinking water during the night, sleeping with a small square of towelling under his face, but every morning he awakes to this wetness. He lifts his face from the pillow and looks down at the darker stain. He'd thought that navy blue wouldn't notice so much, but he can still see the damp outline.

He wipes his mouth with the back of his hand, hating this humanity.

Walking into his en-suite he takes a look back at the hot chaos of his bed. He'd slept heavy after the Girl had gone. She'd said that she'd got a Meeting in the morning and blah-blah, and Jonathan was only too pleased to get rid of her. He thinks that it will be best to avoid the Wine Bar for a week.

Why were they always so predictable and easy, too easy.

That is why Anna itched at him, because she wasn't easy.

As Jonathan inhales the torpid air, he's glad that they hadn't made it to the bedroom; there's an old coffee cup on his bedside table - half full, the milk clotted into a sour yoghurty thickness - and Jonathan can smell his sheets.

Standing in the shower he lets his piss mingle with the warm water, letting the yellow stream trail down his legs. He tries to angle himself so that his urine hits every one of the soap bubbles, squirting the shower gel onto his stomach and shaking the soapy mass onto the porcelain between his feet. He does not allow himself to hold his penis; the trick is to swing his hips to aim his flow.

He's grinning at his expertise. Such are the pleasures of men.

Anna is standing in her kitchen and surveying the precise order of the room. The tea-towels hang in neat rectangles; this week it's the red and yellow combination, both of them a squared pattern on crisp cotton. Roy has learned not to combine these with the blue and white set. The sink sparkles, the four pine chairs are angled exactly around the table, upon which a vase of silk red poppies spray in pretty drooping order; the tall ones at the back, the shorter ones nestling around the neck of the vase, their faces luckily turned upward for better effect.

Anna breathes in the coolness of the order. Disorder unsettles her, it actually shakes her, microwaving her stomach into a fluttering, fearfulness.

Aunt Jo had always praised Anna's sense of order. The school uniform always hung up on its matching little plastic hangers, the underwear drawers with their rows of knickers arranged in regimental precision. Socks balled into pairs and stored in the shoe boxes that Anna had labelled.. "Socks".

Anna, standing outside their sitting room door, would listen to her Aunt talking about her to their neighbours: "She's such a neat child!" and Anna would hug herself, bending double with the joy of it.

Anna places an apple-shaped coaster at the corner of the table, and stands a little back to confirm that the poppies happily pick up the red of the fruit.

The telephone rings. It's Jonathan.

"Lunch again!" Anna's delighted but feigns uncertainty: "Let me just get my diary."

The diary is in the kitchen table drawer but she does not need to open it to know that she will meet him. She opens the drawer and looks down at the leather-bound book. Smiling, she feels deliciously in control.

"Y-e-e-s that would be fine. One o'clock. The Riverside Pub? That's a long way out, are you frightened of being seen with me?"

She laughs flirtingly into the phone, examining the cuticles of her left hand; she's seen women do this in films, women who are powerful, shoulder-pads-women in some clever business deal.

"All right. I'll be there."

Anna puts the phone back onto its hook and gives a little skip as she leaves the kitchen. She practically cannons into Roy who's just toddled down from bed. He's wearing his dressing gown and his feet are bare.

Roy's feet are not his finest asset. There's the suspicion of a bunion on the left foot and several of his toes are adorned with corn plasters; those circular pads with holes in the centre so that they form a row of small pink 'O's. They've been on his feet all night and a couple of them are curling at the edges.

"Roy! You're going to leave great sweaty footprints all over the quarry tiles."

Roy looks down at his feet. He's wiggling his toes in a slight defiance.

"Who was that on the phone?"

"The phone?"

"Yes, just now."

Anna is still looking at Roy's feet. They are waving at her.

"Oh, just Trevor." She does not know why she is lying; perhaps it is something to do with those corn plasters.

"I thought you were avoiding him."

"I was, but I'll have to tell him soon." She's drumming her fingers on the back of one of the chairs.

"What am I supposed to say, if I see him?"

"Why would you see him?"

"Well I might bump into him in town."

"You don't say anything, why should you?" Anna's voice is becoming a little shrill.

"Well it seems a bit rough."

"Roy, will you stop wiggling your toes at me!"

Roy's shrugging: "You know best."

"Yes I do, actually. I know *exactly* what I am doing," and with such certainty, Anna brushes past him to go upstairs to change for lunch.

* *

Jonathan's kitchen is still littered with the debris of the Indian food.

A fly is sitting on the tandoori sauce and Jonathan is remembering a documentary about how flies ingest food; they vomit on it first, apparently. He watches the fly. He pulls the waste bin out from under the sink and an empty milk carton falls off the top of the pile of rubbish. He pushes the waste down into the bin with his hands to make room for the take-away, and the tandoori sauce smears onto his hands as he throws the tin foil containers on top of the rest. He kicks the bin back under the sink and rinses his hands under the tap. He sniffs his fingers. He looks at his watch, he's got an hour before he has to leave to meet Anna..... Anna. He liked it so much that she was difficult.

Jonathan rubs a thoughtful finger along his bottom lip and smiles softly.

The fly has escaped death in the bin and is buzzing lazily against the window. It's dozy in the splash of sunshine that's filtering through the blinds. Jonathan tears a piece of kitchen-roll from the holder on the wall, slowly so as not to disturb the insect, he folds the paper into a wad and then – with a quick and sure movement – squashes the fly against the window pane.

* * * * * * * * * * * * * * * * * * * *

Anna is looking into the drawer of forgotten silk underwear.

She has showered, again, with a perfumed thoroughness, and listens for Roy's departure as she looks at the delicate sheets of tissue that divide the cream lace confection from the rather saucier black.

Roy's car is growling out of their drive, and Anna winces instinctively as she hears him crash the gears into second.

She takes the cream camisole out of the drawer and tells herself that she will feel better if she is wearing this underneath the perfectly respectable blouse. Jonathan won't know. Nobody will know.

She really does not want any sort of Involvement with Jonathan apart from the music.

She needs him for Cheltenham.

She needs him to make everything all right, to wipe out all those Miss Etch moments and that pitiless dismissal when Anna had sung for her.

She's letting the silk slip against her fingers; this is her secret, that's all, her naughty little secret. She could handle Jonathan. She'll have him sitting at her choir piano within the week.

Chapter 32

Lindsay enters the Health Centre and is confused by the New System.

The Receptionists are behind a screen with a grille placed just low enough so that patients have to bend to speak into it; there's also a yellow line on the floor in front of the screens and a notice that asks patients to queue behind the line until they are called to the screen. It's an unfortunate cross between an airport check-in and the post office, and she expects that this has got something to do with the coleslaw-throwing incident that had been all over the Witsham Gazette last month.

She approaches the desk. There is no-one else queuing and she stands on the yellow line. The Receptionist is four feet away.

Lindsay looks at the woman behind the screen who apparently cannot see her because she is continuing a conversation with another receptionist who stands beside her:

"I told him, I'm not touching them."

"Don't! don't you go anywhere near them."

"I told him, I said, we need special rubber gloves here on the Desk."

"In one of those dispensers."

"The Diabetic Nurse has got one."

"Oh she's got everything, she's even put in for her own set of In Trays."

"Excuse me?" Lindsay is emboldened by the throbbing in her hand. The seated Receptionist looks up at her. "Can you wait *behind* the line please," she's indicating the printed notice. "It does say so very clearly."

Lindsay moves backwards the two required inches.

The receptionists are continuing their discussion.

"I've told the Practice Manager, we're at the end of our tethers."

"You should do another one of your memos."

"Oh that'll only start Dr. Warris on one of his paper-saving missions."

"He'll have us re-cycling the prescription pads again."

"Well I know for a fact that Dr.Patel takes them home for his wife's shopping lists."

"I'm sorry, but I really do think I should be seen." Lindsay is holding her hand up to show the women the wad of make-shift bandaging.

The receptionists share a look and the seated one bends to shout through the plastic grille.

"Next please."

Lindsay steps forward.

"Name?"

Lindsay's reply does not pierce the screen and the receptionist indicates that she should bend down and talk through the little holes. Lindsay complies and she and the receptionist shout to each other through the waist-level grille.

There's a row of patients sitting on the new plastic chairs (each one bolted to the floor to deter any furniture hurling) Frustration figures largely at this Practice, and Patients are further cowed by another large printed sign that warns: *'Any disorderly conduct will be dealt with by the strongest of measures, our staff will not tolerate shouting, spitting or the throwing of articles (including Forms)"*

The waiting Patients have the appearance of people who have been sitting on their seats for many hours. They stare in mute obedience at the Health and Safety notices, their mouths occasionally moving to the words of the "Tetanus Kills!" poster with its rather alarmingly sized rusty nail.

A young pregnant woman is watching her toddler climb in and out of a large plastic stacking tray, a helpful present from the local supermarket, and an elderly man is quite obviously asleep. Lindsay hopes fervently that it *is* sleep and not a more permanent relaxation.

Lindsay has been told to sit in this Waiting Area, and joins the row of silent endurance. Occasionally a tannoy will announce that a Doctor is available to see his next patient, but, in the nature of all such equipment, the voice is transmitted as strangulated and indecipherable so that: *"Doctor Plannicey will sar Mrs. Warblahfont"*...

The patients look along the line at each other and no-one seems to own the lucky name, also from the wooden plaque detailing "G.P.'s on Duty" Lindsay can see no such Doctor.

Lindsay is distracting herself from her pain by imagining Dr. Plannicey sitting alone in his surgery, forever doomed to solitude. Somebody else has arrived at the Check-In, and the patients lean forward to listen to the shouted exchanges of private symptoms. It's Diane, from Choir, and Lindsay is torn between the terror of explaining her hand and the solace of such company.

Diane is being grilled as to the precise nature of her complaint, and the receptionist's strident query of: "…and what is the exact colour of the discharge..?" being greeted with the fascinated interest of the Waiting Room.

All such symptoms are greeted with transparent disbelief by the receptionist who has been put on this earth to deter all possible patients from disturbing the peace of her doctors.

Finally and grudgingly, Diane is gestured to join the waiting dead.
She smiles over at Lindsay and there follows a complicated scuffle as Lindsay tries to move to another seat in order to be next to Diane.

This involves the requested move of a very thin woman with a basket on her lap. The basket appears to be moving of its own volition, and she hands it to Diane to hold while she gets up.

"I think I've stuck to this seat Dear."
The basket jumps alarmingly in Diane's arms.

"Oh don't worry, Dear, that's only Monty," the woman's explaining.

"He hasn't been to the toilet you see, and I've been here since eight thirty."

Diane holds the basket out away from herself as she hands it back to the woman, and both of them look at the basket as it judders. A small hole has been cut into the side, and something very like a claw can be seen to protrude. The claw is thick and yellow and at least two inches long.

The woman is peering into the basket: "Bless him, he wants his lunch."

Diane does not want to imagine how large 'lunch' will have to be to satisfy that claw.

Lindsay's right hand is hanging down at the side of her chair and she has made sure that Diane sits on her left. Lowering the hand has increased the dull throbbing and Lindsay closes her eyes against the pain.

Diane is full of the injustice received at check-in: "It isn't as if you'd come here unless you had to. I used to be with the Health Centre across the road."
She looks warily over her shoulder at the brick wall behind her, as if her defection could be seen.

"Oh." Lindsay is fighting the vomit that is rising in her throat.

"I didn't want to move, but there were, well, personal reasons"
Lindsay is keen to be distracted from her pain: "What, er, what were they then?"
Diane takes a moment. She looks at Lindsay, deciding.

"It was my husband. Kept popping down to the doctor's, said it was for repeat prescriptions... I thought it was strange, those tubes of rash cream last weeks don't they, you're only supposed to 'Use Sparingly' and they were steroid too ..well it turned out that he was obsessed with the Receptionist."

Lindsay raises her eyes to the Keepers of the Gate behind the screen and looks her doubt.

"Oh she's nothing like those," and then, as if it were obvious: "No, you see Paul and I moved here from Croydon. We should never have left. Everything would have been all right if we'd stayed there."

Lindsay, befuddled by the screaming in her hand, cannot follow this at all: "I'm sorry, I don't...."

Diane takes a deep breath.. "Right. Paul and I moved here two years ago, we bought a house on Craft Street. It was lovely really, a garden and.... well that's not where I live now, I live in one of those new flats by the Leisure Centre. It's very nice really. I could make it better if I put my mind to it. It's just; well it's been a bit of a jolt really. I only moved in two months ago you see, joining the Choir was part of the New Start."

She's ground to a halt, staring down at the table of magazines that's in front of the seats. There's a Country Life that's seen several months, and a copy of Cosmopolitan with half its front page torn off.

"Probably a special offer."

"Sorry?" Lindsay thinks that she will start screaming if the Doctor doesn't call her name.

"A coupon, you know." Diane is looking around the waiting area; the story of her divorce has died in her mouth.

"Mr. Wovvam tar say Doctor Nall plee."

The patients do not even bother to look at each other this time. They just sit in mute resignation to their fate.

Lindsay is beginning to regret coming here and wishes she'd thought to go somewhere she would not be known, somewhere away from Diane's stream of words, but she didn't know whether she was allowed to go straight to a hospital, and Lindsay is always anxious to obey the rules.

Diane looks at Lindsay and, mistaking the expression she sees there for pique, she battles on, explaining: "I shouldn't have brought things from the house .. they've just brought the memories with them. You know those Plaques you buy in France, the ones with the olives on... well I didn't think *that* would hurt."

Lindsay stands up quickly, and just as quickly has to sit back down.

"I'm sorry, I..."

The Receptionist has spotted 'Trouble'

"Are you going to be sick, Dear?" It's a strident bellow through the grille.

"You'd better get your friend to collect the Toilet key."

The toilet key is being passed under the screen; the key is attached to a large flat piece of wood with the words "Toilet. Patients use only" but the wood is too thick to pass under the narrow gap at the bottom of the screen. Diane has obligingly gone over to the desk and is pulling at the key while the wood remains loyally stuck on the receptionist's side of the desk.

"We haven't had to use this since the Alterations," the receptionist is trying to wiggle the large rectangle of wood under the grill.

Lindsay is walking towards the door marked "Treatment Room"

The receptionist has spotted her: "You can't go in there!"

Just sometimes there does seem to be a slight sliver of evidence as to the existence of a God; a nurse comes out of the room, sees Lindsay's face that is now the colour of pale khaki, and bustles her into the Treatment room.

The receptionist has given up fighting with the toilet key that seems doomed to remain stuck in its present position, jammed under the screen, the metal key tantalisingly obtainable on the patient's side.

Diane returns to her seat and mentally crosses Lindsay off her possible-friends list. Lindsay hadn't been interested. She wishes she hadn't talked about Paul.

It was just sitting here, in a Health Centre, it had brought it all into focus. Why was everything a reminder? And why did everything point to the loss of it. She's looking around the room and is grimly satisfied to confirm her fear. There's a sign up on the notice board: *"Could YOU Be Pregnant?"*

Well no, actually. Paul had been adamant. He didn't want children. They had each other, wasn't that enough for her? He'd had four younger brothers and had spent most of his adolescent years babysitting; he'd done his bit. He was never changing another nappy.

In the way of women, foolish in their love, Diane had believed that he would change, that after a few years of watching their friends having babies, he'd soften. He was so kind, and he loved dogs – though as he pointed out they couldn't just go off on the spur of the moment for their Week-ends if they had one of their own – but he cried buckets over that film they'd rented about the dogs finding their way home all across America when their owners had moved.

Diane had taken folic acid tablets and read all about Preparing your Body for Pregnancy and had waited, waited for him to change.

Inside the Treatment Room, Lindsay is explaining just how she managed to shut her own hand in a car door.

The Nurse, a gentle Irishwoman with a voice that promises lush green hills and warm Guinness, is looking at the swollen mess of pain, and knows better.

Outside in the Waiting Room Diane is leafing through Cosmopolitan and learning how to apply the perfect fake tan, while at the Health Centre across the road, the Receptionist, a pert and darkly pretty woman in her twenties, is smiling dreamily, her hands cradling her swollen belly.

Chapter 33

The Riverside Pub tables are set out on a patio leading down to slow running water that pushes soft, gently rotting foliage to lie thickly against the sloping banks. Willow trees sway lushly, trailing lazy leaves into the water; this hazy sensuality has governed Jonathan's choice for this meeting. It's too obvious, but Anna lacks the experience of seduction. Anna is watching the willow leaves dipping into the water. She has closed her eyes.

"You look... sleepy." Jonathan is stirring his drink with his finger, pushing the wedge of lemon against the side of the glass, squeezing its juice into the gin.
Anna smiles at him: "It is so marvellous to relax."
"You look so good when you can just be yourself, when you are away from all that."
"You mean away from Roy."
"Not just him, away from everything. When you are just Anna." and again, as in the restaurant, he calls her 'Un-na'.
She warms to this, this exotic otherness.
He's pushing it further: "Roy doesn't appreciate you."
"Oh, well in his way, I think..."
"No." Jonathan is determined in this. "He doesn't really... know you. Not the you that I see. He does not see Un-na."
There is a heaviness in the air between them. Anna can feel it, she can feel the languor and she tries to focus up on the point of this, she actually gives her head a little shake; a dog coming out of deep water.
"You have no idea how stressful Choir has become."
Jonathan is watching her. He can almost smell this, her softening.
The Girl last night was easy and he is sick of easy.
Anna is a challenge, she doesn't want the sex and he is intrigued; how does this immaculate woman get into a bed? and lie down? and be naked? could he make her wet, or would she be dry and tight...with him – what would she be like with him? He can feel the heaviness settling between his thighs, and reaches out to touch her hand, it's a light touch, a stroking along the back of her fingers that trails down to her wrist. Anna thinks that this is the right moment: "Would you be my Accompanist?"
"Oh dear." Jonathan's pouting a sulky mouth at her, still trailing his fingers on her wrist. "And I thought you were going to ask for something else."

Anna pulls her hand away, not too quickly; it's a slow teasing gesture, a beckoning.

"Now, Jonathan, we have known each other too long..."

"And I have always wanted you." There, he's said it. He looks straight at her and pushes the look deeper. He's done this before, this intensity. This is The Game.

"And I want you...as.."

He interrupts her :"...as your Accompanist," and it's a groan.

"Yes!" She's laughing at him, he's such a boy, an adorable boy.

It's such fun that he wants her; she hasn't felt wanted – not like this – for years, and she knows how to play him.

He sees her face change and he shuts his eyes quickly, raising a hand to his mouth. He looks suddenly hurt and maybe even a little angry.

Anna instantly reaches out and takes the hand that is playing with his mouth ... "Oh Jonathan, please don't...I didn't mean..."

"You don't want me." He's trying not to sound sulky, childish, and only partly succeeds.

" What I need right now is you sitting behind that piano in my choir room."

"And what about what I need?"

"Oh .. Darling." The word is foreign in her mouth; she holds it there, tasting it.

So Anna, cool controlled Anna, is slipping into another country and does not feel the journey.

Chapter 34

Tony is parked in a lay-by. He likes to think of it as *his* lay-by; it's too small to be a night-stop for lorries and too near to the town for the vans that sell snacks and hot drinks, so Tony believes that there's no reason for anyone else to pull in here. It had taken him months to choose this particular spot for his lunch. This way he avoids all that sniggering in the staff canteen, and he can eat his sandwiches in the way his mother was used to call 'ugly'; he could open his mouth as wide as he liked here, there was no-one to see, and he could chew with his mouth open. His thermos is on the seat beside him, and as he reaches across for it he spills some mayonnaise from between crusty bread cut extra thick so that it would fill his mouth. Tony watches the creamy whiteness as it oozes across his leg and knows that the fat will leave a stain.

He pushes the remains of his lunch into the plastic bag at his feet, and squashes down hard onto the soft bundle with his shoe.

Today his BMW is at a slight angle, and not parallel to the kerb. Another day he would have re-positioned the car and it has unsettled him, that slight wobbling deep inside his gut. He sits in the driving seat, staring ahead at the windscreen, and whistles softly into the silence of the car. His hands tap an irregular rhythm on the steering wheel.

A couple of motorbikes pull off the road, they swerve and sway around his car, parking a few feet in front of him.

"You stupid bastards!" Tony's anger sprays out at them, small drops of spittle landing on his windscreen.

The young men on the bikes pay no attention to Tony. They are shouting to each other over the roar of their machines, they do not turn off their engines and are actually revving them up; the snarling screams are building with each flick of their wrists, the leather-gauntlets massive on the handlebars.

Tony is watching them. He is beating a tattoo on his steering wheel. The youths are still shouting at each other, they are not angry; they are simply planning their route. They do not see Tony, he is not part of their world. Their world is the noise that fills the air, thick with the metallic squealing.

Tony gets out of his car, he is juddering with fury. He walks stiffly up to the nearest biker, his legs moving in short, staccato little jumps.

"Turn your fucking engine off!" He's shouting into the helmeted face.

The helmet turns to look at him, its unseen eyes behind the dark visor.

The helmet does not speak.

Tony is holding his arms out, fingers stretching, to stop the noise that is pushing against him.

"Turn it off! Turn it off!"

The biker kicks at the ground and puts his foot back onto the pedal as he coasts away. The other biker follows him, swerving his machine into a circle behind Tony before he swings out of the lay-by.

The Helmets are shouting back at Tony: "Wan-ker!"

Tony stands in the dust watching the bikes roar off into the road and listens as the wall of noise recedes jerkily into the distance.

He holds his arms around his stomach, rocking himself, and he decides right there, at that moment, that he will buy a gun.

He knows how to do it. Gerry's in the T.A. and he's always bragging about his friends in the Regular Army. The Territorials went on these Exercises; Gerry was only saying last week that the Regular's couldn't do without the part timers these days. If you wanted anything it was all about contacts and networking, well, Gerry was a contact, wasn't he?

Tony was remembering all the stupid evenings he'd had to sit and listen to Gerry and his mates bragging on and on about how they could be rung up at any moment and have to be Operational. Gerry kept his uniform in his garage, all hung up on the life-size dummy his mother had bought for her Dressmaking Course (only Gerry had stained it with khaki and green patches and taken the stuffing out of the tits to flatten them under his flak jacket). Gerry had strung his belt and water bottle round its middle and the rifle – Tony had seen the rifle – was propped up over its shoulder. The whole macho effect was slightly spoiled by the metal stand with "Lady-Form" printed on its base, although Gerry had tried to scrape that off initially, lately he had made do with standing his kit-bag over the words.

A gun, that was it…. He was sick of being pushed around, and nobody ever gave him an inch. That cow, that Choirmistress, winding him up with her: *"Sit over there"*, all regal condescension and sneering at him.

Well he'd show her. If she hadn't made him sit in the corner like some bloody little kid, it wouldn't have happened, all that silly business later.

110

That Birthday Party, the only one when he'd been allowed to invite the rest of the class, and Father making him sit on his own by the fireplace all because he'd got over-excited and jumped up and knocked over his glass of squash. His Mother had bought a "Birthday Boy" paper tablecloth from the newsagents on the corner; he'd helped her lay the table that morning. The tablecloth was red and there were little blue boats all round the edge of it, and toy drums with sticks crossed on top of them, and he'd helped to lay out all the matching paper plates round the edges and put the iced-gems and the jammie-dodgers biscuits into the bowls in the centre … he'd been reaching over to get one of those, that's all, and his sleeve had caught his plastic beaker … that's all.

Father had raised his hand and shouted: *"That's it!"* and Tony had had to sit away from the table, on his own, for the rest of the tea.

When Mother had brought in the cake, in the shape of a drum because he'd just started the drumming lessons, Tony hadn't been able to blow out the candles because his breath was all caught up in his chest and when he blew, it came out all jagged. Father had told the little kid, the one that Tony had only invited because he lived next door, to help Tony blow the candles out, and the kid had done a great big huff at the cake and blown all seven out all at once. Tony hadn't even got to blow out one of them, not one; because of the breathing and the way he couldn't really see the candles through the blurring.

Tony is over by his car. He has opened the passenger door and runs his hand down along the metal rim of its frame, testing the bright shiny edge for its sharpness. *"Sit in that chair, over by the fireplace…..* stupid cow, stupid stuck-up cow. I'll drum for you all right and you'll love it, you'll beg for it."

Chapter 35

"…..You must remember that Roy and I were together at College; we were doing evening classes, he was doing his Corporate Accountancy Course and I was doing that Aromatherapy Massage, just to get another string to my bow at the time. He had such aspirations to be a financial wizz-kid and I like a fool believed him. I'd taken a bit of a break from the singing, that audition for the Welsh National Opera knocked me back quite a bit I can tell you….."

Anna is leaning back into Jonathan's deep leather sofa and this is his own particular idea of hell. Why do women think that if you ask them to tell you about themselves that you mean it? When you ask people in the street *"How are you?"*, especially if they are men, they do not tell you that they have just come out of Hospital having something done below the waist, something hidden and possibly festering. He has often heard women talking together, usually in supermarket checkout queues, as they swap tales of Procedures Undergone with a general casualness that belies the details of the fluids drained and the exact sizing of "lumps". Women seem continually to have to endure Tests and Smears, and always there is that wetness, that secret between their thighs, something darkly oozing.

Their marriages are examined in similarly clinical exactness, not a stray comment is forgotten, not a slight disregarded. All are hoarded up to be told to some poor sap who's paid for a lunch to be helped down with a couple of bottles of Something Special. That's where he went wrong of course, Anna had kept saying that she didn't usually drink at lunchtime, but he'd kept pouring and she'd been swigging back the stuff, but he should have known, once she started getting maudlin about Roy's Exams and the fading likelihood of his becoming Mayor.

Jonathan attempts to halt the flow, it's drowning him, and he is sick of looking at Anna's mouth and the way the disappointment in the words has turned her lips down at the corners so that the lipstick there bleeds into the fine lines that trail away to her chin. He had not noticed these lines before, nor the slight frailness of the skin around the side of her face.

"Would you be more comfortable in the bedroom?"

"No, I'm fine. This is a lovely sofa.. I was only saying to Roy the other week that ….."

And she's off again, Christalmighty she had actually thought that he was suggesting a room change for *comfort !*

Jonathan gets up: "Another coffee I think," and he walks quickly into the kitchen. Please God she will not follow him. Please God he can get it back, when they left the Riverside Pub she'd been all warm smiles and acquiescent softening, but the journey had involved waiting at those bloody road works and he'd let himself have a little rant about how long it took to lay a gas pipe and the Council Tax and he'd blown it. By the time they'd got to his flat "Just so that I can show you that new piece I was telling you about – the Brahms," she'd got back on line about the Choir. So he'd played the "Roy doesn't see the real you" theme again and he'd thought, just for one wonderful moment when they'd sunk into the leather and she had allowed him to glimpse a trail of lace at the low neck of her blouse, he'd thought .. she's wearing her best undies, and he'd thought that he was There.

Now he didn't think he'd ever be There – not today.

He's poured two more coffees and takes them back into the sitting room in time to hear: ".... if only Roy would just *attempt* more, you know ....You know, Jonathan, I mean, you've achieved so much.."

"Please don't let us talk about me."

"You're so sweet, but I do want to talk about you. About you and I joining forces – just think what a Team we would be!"

Jonathan reaches down and holds Anna's hands, lifting her from the sofa; it's worth one more go, it's got to be, this has gone on all day. He pulls her to him.

"Together. You and I," and he bends to kiss that mouth, to stop the words coming out of it.

The first kiss, as first kisses are, is mismanaged. The angle of the mouths is all wrong and in trying to adjust the positioning, there's the inevitable smearing of saliva across lips that will not part.

Anna is not fond of wet kisses, she has actually been known to turn away from the television once that 'Open-mouthed-stuff' starts.

She is not quite revolted by Jonathan's advance, but she pushes at his chest and holds him away from her.

"Aw come on Un-na ... don't be a spoilsport."

"I think I had better go," she's smiling up at him, her manner is fond and deeply maternal.

She's shaking her head and actually tutting at him and she can have no idea just how screamingly irritating this is. She taps a finely manicured nail against his cheek.

"You are a naughty little boy. I'm not cross, but you must not step over the line, and you have, you know, just a little."

She picks up her handbag, placing a final patronising little kiss on his cheek as she leaves.

And Jonathan has a terrible feeling, sneaking around at the back of his mind, that in Anna he might – just might – have met his match.

Chapter 36

Diane is walking slowly past the Estate Agents, the Bangles-n-Beads, and the Country Elite Clothing that is Witsham high street. The Arcade houses the real shopping, the supermarket and the private butchers (hanging on by the skin of his teeth) which leaves the high street free to cater to women who shop in high heels. There's a whole shop devoted to the art of the Candle, and one that sells ethnic jewellery and little polished stones that are *'known for their healing properties'* .. ...The stones are in rows of boxes in the window, the black hepatite recommended for brain disorders and the turquoise will apparently cure cancer. The need for belief in a god-less world negating all logic so that worried souls are soothed by the presence of a brightly coloured pebble. From inside the shop she can see the dream-catcher mobiles and the 'lucky' pendants, and she stares and thinks of an ancient witchery.

By the time that Diane had come out of the doctor's surgery, Lindsay had apparently left. Diane had asked at the Reception Desk only to be told that Patient Confidentiality ruled that Lindsay's whereabouts could not be betrayed. The Receptionist had warmed to this theme, her delight at having the law on her side increasing the pleasure in her righteousness. By the time that Diane had unbent from speaking through the security screen's waist level grille, the Receptionist had managed to attain the human manifestation of 'Justice', and Diane was reminded of a painting in the Town Hall of a woman with a sword in her hand and a very large metal helmet on her head. The Receptionist was surely wasted in this Health Centre; she was needed at some bloodier War.

Diane can see herself reflected in the shop window, and unclenches the angry face that she has surprised there. She also feels niggled by an itching guilt that she should have asked Lindsay why she had been in that waiting room; she'd looked ashen, and Diane is only too aware that she had been too busy going on about herself - she does that too much - trapped in a hamster wheel of pointless explanations.

She turns toward the road and sees... Paul. Is it Paul?
It is Paul !... God no, not now.
He's standing on the other side of the road; he's just come out of the Bank. He's busy fiddling with his wallet, looking down, he hasn't seen her. Diane dives into the ethnic shop, peering around the dangling Indian Feathers and wood chimes to watch him.

She knocks her head against something metal and mystic that clanks.

A woman who is old enough to know better is dressed in trailing black 'Gothic' weeds and jingles with an excess of jewellery, she is approaching Diane:

"Can I help you?"

"No I was just…"

"…Looking. Yes. Please do. I can explain everything." The woman waves black draped arms to include her wares and Diane thinks of a spider; the ones with those long thin floaty legs that cling to walls.

"Yes. Thank you."… Yes, I bet you can. Perhaps you can also explain why my ex-husband is across the road and why he left me for a Receptionist. Oh God a Receptionist…

If only we'd registered with the other Health Centre then he'd have had Boadicea to contend with, he wouldn't have kept going back to *her* for his repeat prescriptions. It wouldn't have happened. If only I'd thought to research the options, if only I'd visited both Health Centres before we'd…."

"Can I show you these 'healing stones'? There's a little book here that explains how they have helped since Ancient Times." A wispy black trail of lace is lying on Diane's arm as the book is held out to her.

Diane looks up at the suitably witchy face and notices that the woman has the faint bruising and the fine tracery of a scar that reveals a recent eyelift and is oddly comforted by this treachery; obviously ancient remedies are for the commercial rather than the personal.

When she looks back at the window, Diane cannot see Paul, and the black spidery woman has wandered away to bewitch another lost soul who has wandered into her web of lies.

Diane's walking back down the high street, she keeps tight in against the shop windows to be less visible. She's getting good at this, being unseen.

Why didn't they move away? Why hadn't Paul taken his Receptionist to Cornwall? He had been banging on about Cornwall ever since they'd married. When they'd moved from Croydon she'd reminded him about it but he said that they should Save That. Save that for what?

Perhaps if they'd moved to that little harbour in Port Thing then he'd never have met whatserface.

Diane has reached the crossroads that leads down to the two Health Centres, they're situated opposite each other and Diane wonders if the doctors stand outside and look across at each other, in a sort of High Noon stand off, each waiting for the other to reach for their stethoscope.

She looks down the street and teases herself to walk down there, past the building where the woman works, just to take a look. She's never even seen a picture of her. Just walk past, the woman won't know that it's her. But perhaps Paul has shown her one of their photograph albums and the woman has seen that photo of Diane coming out of the shower with a towel on her head and her face all red and puffy. Diane is filled with an acute shame; she's trying to remember which album Paul took away with him and what pictures of her are in it. Have they laughed together over those shots of the holiday in Lanzarote and of Diane sitting on that stone lion – her legs splayed out and her squealing because she's about to fall off. She was wearing that fat pink sun-suit too, wasn't she… was she?

Diane stops. She's half way down the road. When she'd come down here earlier this morning she had practically scuttled into her own doctor's surgery in case she was seen. She'd had her umbrella up and was walking with it tilted against the other side of the road. Her umbrella .. it was still in the waiting room. Well then she's got to go down this street, hasn't she.
She lives in this town; she has a right to be here. Hasn't she?

So Diane walks with a deliberately casual stride down toward the Health Centres. There is no going back now, the umbrella has sealed her fate, she'll pop in, get it back, and then just cross the road. Cross the road and just happen to look up at the long windows and see her. She'll be sitting there at a desk, won't she.

Diane's level with the buildings now and she takes a quick, darting glance at the long windows; vertical blinds hang against the panes, their crisp cotton panels closed tight, hiding all against the curious.
Diane looks back at her own Health Centre and cannot face Boadicea again today; it was only a cheap umbrella and anyway, she's used to losing things.
She walks on, not wishing to be seen to reverse her steps; she walks round the back of the street into the older part of town and wonders if perhaps *she* should have moved to Cornwall.

Chapter 37

Anna is standing looking out of her window and watches Diane walking along her street. She wonders briefly why some women hunch their shoulders up when it's not really cold at all, and resolves to mention this at choir during one of her loosening up and breathing exercises.

Anna is waiting for Trevor to arrive; they are to rehearse their Old Time Music Hall numbers for the Drop-In Centre's Open Day.
It's not until next month, but Anna wants this rehearsal over before she has to broach the Jonathan situation. The Open Day clashes with the Witsham Annual Carnival Parade so she doesn't expect that anyone of any significance will attend, it'll be just the usual suspects; the bewildered with their care workers in tow and somebody lumbered with buggins-turn from the Mental Health Team. Still it doesn't do to let standards slip, you never know.

She'd got Roy to alert the local press but they will be all tied up with the Carnival and would be snapping away at small children being dressed as tomatoes and Rotarian Men in tights, so she didn't hold out much hope of any cameras being focused on her in her Edwardian number and Trevor in his cap.

She spots Trevor walking toward her house, and muses that the words "hang-dog" were written for Trevor's walk. Jonathan *strode,* and she smiles a pussy-cat smile of pure pleasure as she remembers how he had kissed her at his flat. It was … nice. Yes, it was nice to have some attention. All perfectly innocent of course, he'd just had a little too much wine, silly boy. She straightens the curtains and looks at their deep cream folds and she is almost purring.

Trevor knocks on Anna's door and does not call out his usual refrain of *"It's only me."* Something has changed, just shifted slightly, so that he's thrown into being less casual today. Anna opens the door and Trevor thinks that she looks particularly feral, her eyes slanted with a smile that reminds him to be wary.
"I thought that we could just run through the Programme, I know it's a bit in advance." Anna is leading the way to her music room.
"We do have four weeks yet.." Trevor trots behind her, he is confused by this sudden rehearsal and senses danger.

"Yes Trevor, I do know that, but it won't hurt to spot anything that we need to polish up."

"But we always do the same programme." Trevor is trying not to sound as if he is complaining so he adds a compliment "Well you know that I do so enjoy our little sessions, whatever the reason, it's an absolute joy to accompany a singer who…"

"Yes all right Trevor." It's too shrill. Guilt is weighing heavy on Anna's shoulders and his grovelling is not helping, so her mind seeks out a genuine complaint to explain the snapping. "Look – about the Basses, they never come to choir these days. I spent hours nurturing that Kevin – I don't usually go to that baker in the Arcade, as you know, but I went there three weeks running and had to compromise over the stone-ground so that I could persuade him to join – so he turns up twice last month and now nothing, and I'm sorry Trevor but I do think that you are to blame."

"Me?" and there's genuine disbelief in Trevor's face.

"Yes! – think about it. Men want other men to be involved, otherwise they feel threatened."
Trevor's baffled. "But I'm there, I'm always there."

"But you're not very…" and Anna is trying to find a word that will not hurt that much. "Well you're not really that testeroney are you? "

Trevor sits down on the piano stool, facing away from Anna; he's staring at the keys.

"Oh dear – I don't want to be rude Trevor but you know what you're like. Don't get me wrong, I think it's marvellous that you are so… sensitive.. in touch with your feminine side…"

"Are you saying that I'm a homosexual?"

"No, no – of course not – good Lord you're a musician, you're bound to be well.. less…" and she's trying not to say the word 'male'..

Trevor hadn't expect this, he's trying to rally his thoughts to defend himself: "You know what the men are like, we've seen it all before, they've always got PTA Governors' meetings and Wives…"

Anna realises that she has gone too far. She really hadn't meant to say any of this. It was just that he'd looked so pathetic and she didn't really understand why she was so angry with him. He was in the way, that was it. He was in the way of Jonathan and Cheltenham. If Trevor wasn't there she knows that she could persuade Jonathan to join the choir. At his flat he'd gone on about how loyal Trevor was, and how he couldn't possibly invade such faithfulness, and Anna had wanted to scream, but then Jonathan had wanted to know all about her and Roy and the moment had passed.

Once Trevor was out of the picture Jonathan wouldn't have any reason to refuse, especially as he was growing so fond of her. She would have to keep that in check of course, but she could handle him.

Trevor was still looking down at the piano, running silent fingers across the keys. Anna's on a bit of a roll now. "Well what about Adam – the other Bass. Just the same, came twice, just enough to get all the copies of the music that we'd be doing for the next term and then we never see him again."

So Trevor, feeling pushed to explain the ways of men, tries a little reason. "Kevin brought him, didn't he. They'd been mates at school or something. Stands to reason that Adam's not going to come without Kevin."

But Anna is exasperated by the mind-set of men.

"Oh why are men so hopeless! You don't see the women only coming if their friend's going to be there."

"Women always go to the toilet together..." Trevor's sulkily pressing middle C... "You see them in the pub, it's *'Oh I'll come with you'* and off they go for three quarters of an hour."

"Trevor when do you ever go to the Pub with women?"

"It has been known, particularly when there are no Chickens or Bananas about."

Anna wonders briefly if she has pushed Trevor too far and that he is beginning to ramble. She's seen it at the Day Centre, one day they're fine and then the next time you see them it's all *"who are you Dear and where's my potato?"*

She goes over to Trevor and lays a comforting hand on his shoulder:

"I'm sorry. I didn't mean to get into all that. I'm just worried about the choir, that's all." Now Anna is not often known to apologise and the words sound a little stiff in her mouth, and although this is due to their unfamiliarity, Trevor hears them as heartfelt, this was obviously a difficult thing for Anna to admit and he is mollified. He plays a little running trill on the piano to signify his acceptance of the apology, and he and Anna then get down to the gritty realism of Music Hall Melodies.

After two choruses of "When Father Papered the Parlour" they have almost attained their usual harmony, the familiarity of this rehearsal returning them to a previous accord.

Trevor will not mention that he had seen her with Jonathan, Mother would have told him not to look for trouble or he'd be bound to find it.

Mother had plenty of these sayings, and Trevor wishes that his mind was more like his computer and that he could put these little homilies into the recycle bin, in fact, thinking about it – and listening to Anna's rather breathy soprano - he rather wishes that he could put Mother into the recycle bin. Perhaps he wouldn't have been such a 'sensitive' soul if he hadn't had to look after her for all those years. Perhaps the meals on trays in her room and all the washing-up had worn away at the maleness.

Anna is not going to say anything else about the choir. Not now.
She's registered a slight discontent so that's all quite useful now that she thinks about it. She'll let him do choir next Monday, and then she'll find a moment. He'll still have the Charity Do's, she's letting him do this one next month after all. He'll have that to look forward to.

The rehearsal finishes and Trevor is painstakingly packing away his music into his case, sorting out each piece. Anna's watching him and his pedantry is itching at her.

"Well I'll let you see yourself out, only I've got to go and change for tonight," .. and she runs upstairs.

Trevor is a little startled at this quick departure, and worry niggles again until he hears her calling down to him.

"See you on Monday!" and he breathes again.

Chapter 38

Tony is sitting in his Den. The evening is darkening the room but he has not turned on the light. He can hear Lindsay downstairs, there's the comforting clink of saucepans that tells him that she is preparing their meal.

Earlier, when he got home, he had noticed that there was a professional-looking bandage on her hand but he didn't say anything. She, too, hasn't said anything. She's probably embarrassed. She knows he doesn't like people to make a huge fuss and she's probably regretting that she hadn't just dealt with it herself. That frozen packet of peas had been a good idea; she should have stuck to that.

Tony closes his address book – he has rung Gerry. Gerry will come up trumps or he'd look a fool for having bragged about all those guns and how easy it was to get hold of one. Tony didn't actually think that it was as easy as Gerry boasted, but he was surer of the other man's ego and he knew that the gun would be obtained.

Tony sits in the darkness and fingers the large wooden box that's on his desk.
It will live in here, when he gets it.
The box used to house the cutlery set that they got as a wedding present, and there's lots of those little foam pads to separate the knives from the forks.
The cutlery's in the kitchen now, but he had kept the box; he had liked the dark red grain to the wood and the little brass clip at the front.
Gerry has promised him he will get it by the weekend, so Tony is preparing for it.
It will need to be kept somewhere special.

When he gets it he'll wrap it in one of those soft cloths that Lindsay uses to polish her best glassware and then he'll lay the gun amongst the padding to prevent damage.

Lindsay is managing quite well with just the one hand. Straining the broccoli through the colander will be a challenge, and she's worried about the boiling water. She could ask Tony to hold the saucepan, but she doesn't want to draw attention. He'd think that she was doing it on purpose, just to make a point, and she didn't want that.

She can hear him coming downstairs and she finds that she is counting the steps, and she's reaching to pour herself a glass of water because her mouth is dry. Lindsay thinks she must be getting a cold.

She is standing by the sink with her back to the door and she cannot tell if he is standing there.

"Tony?"

"What's for supper, Kitten?"

She turns and sees the rather rumpled dark curls flopping over his eyes, he's wearing the shirt she gave him for his birthday, and there is a slow sense of release somewhere in her chest and she lets herself sag slightly against the working surface.

"I'll lay the table, shall I?" He's going over to the cutlery drawer.

"Yes, thanks love."

She watches him as he carefully picks out the knives and forks.

She's keeping her right hand just a little behind her back; she's embarrassed by the amount of bandaging that the nurse had applied, it makes too much of it, and she mustn't spoil everything.

Everything was going to be all right.

Chapter 39

In Oxford, the lights from the Pizza-Slice beam out into the dark grey street. Roy is leaning against the serving hatch looking deep into the soft caress that is Maria's cleavage.

"You're gonna look like a pepperoni soon." Maria's Clapham vowels clack across the room but Roy hears pure Italian.

"When do you get off?"

"Are you askin' me forra date?"

"No, I just wondered if you fancied a cup of coffee, well, after standing here all day on your feet. You've given me a slice of pizza every night this week, and I just wanted to say.. well, thank you really."

Roy cannot believe that he has done this. Oh he's said the words often enough, in the morning when he's doing his teeth, into the little shaving mirror. He'd just mouthed the words, of course, like they used to on Top of the Pops before he stopped watching it. It was all because of the extra onions; Roy had asked for extra onions, because he liked them so much, Roy had watched her smooth white hands pushing the onion mixture into the yielding dough and had gone into rather a dream before realising that he'd probably have to breathe later on, when he got home, so then he'd cancelled them.

Maria had then had to scoop off the onions, and she hadn't snapped at him or said *"Oh Roy Really !"* and he had been so overcome with a deep gratitude that he'd asked for extra pepperoni and then, well then he'd just blurted it out.

Well what harm could it do, a coffee. They were friends, after all.

He spoke to her every evening, which is more than he did to most people come to think of it.

Maria is looking at the rather short man with the very large briefcase and smiling her tender smile. She's sick of the Waynes and the Tyrones who came in after a night on the piss and make fat-girl jokes, this guy's sweet. He's bound to be married, of course, they always are but.. well, just a coffee.

Chapter 40

Tony is pouring Lindsay another glass of wine as they sit over their meal. She's lit candles, just two, and the darkness is consoling.

Lindsay wants to refuse the wine, the nurse had said to keep off alcohol while she was on the painkillers, but it's more important to get things back, so she smiles at him across the table as he pours the soft and fruity red into her glass.

"Oh Kitten, that Choirmistress eh?"

"Anna?"

"Yes – she's a real trouble maker that one."

Lindsay would like to agree but is a little confused.

Tony's explaining it to her. "She made you do that solo far too soon, really set you up, you know. Then having me sitting in that chair.." Tony's hand is gripping his wine glass just a little too tightly.

"Oh, yes, I needed more time to rehearse at home. Tony, I've been thinking, perhaps I should leave the Choir?"

"No!" and he's adamant. "We're not letting Her do that to us."

"Only I just meant…" Lindsay's looking at him through the gloom, trying to see if he's angry.

There's a moment.

Tony puts the wine glass down and then gives a playful laugh.

It's a giggling conspiracy, he and Lindsay against Anna:

"Ha!… we'll show her, I'll take along my drum kit next week, that'll make her jump, eh?"

Lindsay's relief is palpable, she's joining the giggles. "When she hears how you can play.. well!"

"Just like at the Office Barbeque, remember?"

"When you made everybody go silent, listening to your solo."

"They all took notice then, didn't they!"

And they are laughing together.

Tony leans across to hold her hand, the left one.

"I love you, Kitten, you do know that don't you."

"Yes, of course,".. and she's a little breathless.

"We're all right when we're on our own, aren't we."

"Yes, just the two of us."

Tony is watching her, he's not sure that she understands:

"It's just.. it's just that I always want you to be your best, the best you can be. Your mother, she never.. guided you, she didn't support you, did she?"

"Tony, I…"

But he wants to convince her, he wants her to know what he means:

"Kitten, I will always be there for you, I will always support you, that's how you know I love you."

"Yes, Tony, it's OK, it really is. I understand."

He's nodding. "We're all right."

He looks around the room, at the flickering candlelight playing on the shelves that are full of their thimble collections and the miniature ceramic animals.

"You love this home don't you Kitten, all your little bits and pieces. I knew you'd love this house, remember when I met you after I'd first seen it? How I told you.... 'I've found our house'... remember me saying that?"

"I know, I remember."

"This is all for you, you know."

"I know. Tony, I do appreciate it."

Tony leans across the table to kiss Lindsay, who half stands to receive his mouth. He kisses her on the forehead. It's almost a blessing.

Lindsay closes her eyes and moves her right hand further back behind her so that it will not rub against the edge of the table.

Chapter 41

"What I'm saying is that we must Up our Profile. If we did something at the Carnival it would put this Choir on the map." Susie is holding forth, as always the flash of her ruby mane punctuating what-Susie-wants.

Her friend Grace sits opposite her. They're in The Crown and Anchor and, it not being a Monday night, they are reduced to sitting at the bar.

"Stephen says that we could have the Float that the Liberals used for the Election – you know, when they did that 'Looking Again at Drugs' with the daffodils."

"Well I can't see Anna going for a Float – you know what she's like."

"She should loosen up. Trevor's keyboard could be strapped onto the front."

"…where they had that giant hypodermic needle…"

"Exactly, that didn't fall off, well not until the yobbos on the estate had a go at it but that was after the procession."

"Are we going to be actually Singing though?" Grace's still doubtful.

Susie's waving her gin around in an expansive confidence: "We'll have to discuss that with Trevor. He's very au-fait with microphones."

"I think we should get several of the members 'on board' as it were before we raise it on Monday though…." Grace wants support for this. She doesn't want the cannon-fodder to be just her and Susie.

"… and I can't see Lindsay going for it."

"Her husband would, he'd have his drum kit up there, banging away for all to see," and the women are laughing.

Suddenly Grace has a terrible thought. "We're not going to be dressed as something Amusing are we?"

Susie's realistic. "No, I know that we might just get her up on a float, but I can't see Anna in stockings and suspenders"
"Eh?"

"You know, like the W.I. did last year. Mind you, they've gone potty since that Naked Calendar business."
Grace gulps at her drink: "Well I'm not doing that, it's all right for you but I'm not waving my size 22 around."

"No, no, but you see what I'm saying, they raised their profile. They got a feature film made all about them too."

"Just don't mention the W.I. to the Choir. That Linda is very ambitious, she'll do anything for a solo and she's forever going on about how she loves to go topless in Marbella."

"Stop fussing Grace, I know how it should be, we'll do it along the lines of St. Margaret's School."

"I am not wearing a gym-slip!" Grace's digging her heels in again.

"Oh Grace, It wouldn't be that revealing.. your legs are…."

"No!" Grace's hands are begin to puddle with an anxious sweat, she's been here before, thin people always think that it doesn't matter, that it'll be fun – it won't be fun, it was never fun. At Witsham Technical College they'd had that Victorian day and she'd looked like Pavarotti in a tent. There's only one wedding photo that she allows to be on show and that's the one with her going into church and looking backwards over her shoulder and it's only of her head and shoulders because she'd made a big point with the photographer about not seeing the Whole Thing all in one go – but he had been just as bad, telling her she looked "lovely" and Grace knows that she has never looked lovely.

She's twisting her hands, one over the other, trying to dry the wetness.

Susie is anticipating a 'Fat Moment' and is keen to placate.

"No – I meant we could point up the religious element. We could sing Panis Angelicus in long skirts, that'll be dignified enough for Anna."

"That's not very jolly for a Carnival…." Grace's remembering "…I seem to remember it was even a bit of a 'downer' at the Crematorium Open Day."

"Just back me up on Monday, right? .. the Carnival's the biggest thing Witsham does, and we should be in on it." The women are downing their drinks.

Grace's inching herself off the barstool, only too aware of her bulk.

There are two men at the bar and they are watching her progress as she hitches one buttock off the stool and reaches her hand out to the bar to steady herself before attempting an ungainly hop to the floor.

Susie does not help her; this is not because she is unkind, it is simply a thinner woman's inability to comprehend the awkward stiffness of muscles that carry too much weight. The men share a look between themselves and one of them can be heard to snigger.

"Dear me!"

Grace's face is clenched tight with her shame. She straightens out the skirt; a black tent with the inevitable elasticated waist, and pulls down the voluminous top that has risen up alarmingly during the descent from the stool. She is yanking at the clothes in a hot and embarrassed scramble, wanting to be gone, wanting to be invisible. Susie's picked up on the hurt in her friend's face.

"Grace, you should maybe think about wearing sort of...."
and she tails off, the challenge of Grace's flab is beyond her.

" .. less floaty clothes? That's what Geoffrey says."

"We-e-ll, less material maybe."

"Geoffrey says that if I go back to weight-watchers again, and he has to watch all that weighing of portions in the little plastic scales, and the writing up of the food points in the book, and then have to go through all the recriminations and regrets when I get back after the weigh-in sessions... well he says he can't go through all that again."

"That's a bit mean."

"Well, I've done it eight times now you see.. once after Sally was born, once before that holiday in Greece for the bikini, twice before two Christmases in a row so that I could get right down and then be able to enjoy the turkey, once before my sister's wedding so that I could get into that Laura Ashley jacket we bought in the sale, once before Geoffrey's Presentation Dinner so that I could wear an off-the-shoulder, once..."
Susie stops her. "Yes, I get the picture."
Grace looks doomed. "I do try."

"I know."

"I didn't have dessert last week, did you notice, after the pizza. I'm always denying myself."

The women leave the pub, Susie's put her arm around Grace and is rubbing her back to soften the anguish.
Grace's grimacing. "You see I'm not really a Gym person ... am I?
and Susie replies, with great truth, "No."

Chapter 42

Roy is stirring his cappuccino, watching the chocolate sprinkles dissolve into the white foam, he spoons a little of the froth into his mouth and smiles across at the woman opposite him. Maria's smooth white arm is resting on the table. Her skin is supple, pliable; he thinks that if he reaches out and touches it the softness will yield gently to his fingers. He wants to bury himself in her.

"You probably meet a lot of men like me." He's hoping that it isn't true, he wants her to tell him that he's different.

She just smiles her tender smile and he reads a world into it.

"You like your pizza dontya," and this acute observation is enough for Roy.

"I've been a bit of a disappointment you see, to my wife that is. I'm married…"

"Yeah. I saw the ring."

"Bit of a giveaway, isn't it?" Roy's making a joke.

She laughs and he is grateful. Anna doesn't laugh at his jokes any more.

"I've never been slim enough you see, nor tall enough, nor posh enough."

"I like litt-tawl men." And he laughs at how she says 'little.'

"I used to think you were Italian, because of the pizza, you know, and the name… Maria" He says it liltingly.

"Oh that woz me Dad, he said that Grandma had this picture of Italy on her wall and she used to look at it and say 'hea-ven, hea-ven' and as a kid he used to fink it was where God lived."

"We could go there."

"Wot?"

"Why not?" the blood is pounding in Roy's ears, suddenly everything seems so simple.

"You're 'avin' a laugh."

"No – I don't think I've ever thought of anything so sensible in my life.
... Just do it. Just go."

Maria's looking at his eyes and at the light that is shining there.

"We don'even know each uver."

"We don't have to. Don't you see?"

Roy reaches across and takes her hand and is encouraged by the way that it just lies there in his.

"Look, I don't fink…"

"Don't fink…er think. That's the problem, everybody thinks too much, weighs up the odds, checks the columns of figures and none of it is worth a damn. I've been careful all my life, I'm even scared to put my own bins out."

Maria gently takes her hand out of his rather damp clasp.

"Look, yora lovely bloke, really, but I'm just the girl who gives you a slice of pizza evry night, that's all."

Maria had expected him to make a pass, but this is different, and the earnest appeal in his face is unsettling her.

"I'd betta go. I'll see you tomorra right?" and she's getting up, picking up her handbag, going over to the door of the café.

"I didn't mean any harm." Roy's getting up.

"It'salright, " and she gives him one of her tender smiles as she walks away, her wide hips swaying in Mediterranean rhythm, and the faint aroma of onions and cheese floats off with her into the high street.

Roy sits down again and looks into his brown froth. He can't think what had possessed him; what was he thinking of? What would Anna say if she knew? and it is this thought that propels him to grab his coat and briefcase and scuttle toward the door.

"Oi mate!" Roy is being hailed by a waiter.

"Sorry, sorry," as he fumbles in his wallet, leaving far too much on the table, the pound coins rolling off onto the floor.

Roy bends to pick up the coins, the waiter is standing over him, Roy looks up at him. "I'm sorry, my mind was… elsewhere."

Elsewhere. Roy walks into the street. Elsewhere, anywhere but here.

Walking towards the car park, Roy thinks about a picture of Italy on a wall and an old woman with a memory and a heavenly dream.

As he reaches his car he sees the catalogue for lawn mowers lying on the back seat, and remembers that he was supposed to have ordered a new one, and if he doesn't, Anna will make him go round that bloody Garden Centre again. Anna wants a new shed too, at the back of the Utility Room, so that's going to mean another week-end of weighing up the odds between the un-treated wooden ones and the expensive mahogany-looking ones that Anna really wants. He knows that it'll end up with him sloshing that wood treatment stuff on the cheaper model, and it never being good enough, nothing's ever good enough. So Roy drives home to his cooler place, and Italy fades amid the smell of wood preserver.

Chapter 43

Anna stands in the Choir Room, she has been surprised to see an expensive looking drum kit standing in the corner of the room. She's rattled that she has been denied her moments alone in the room, That precious time, that preparing. Tony must have got in here earlier, probably got the spare keys from Reg. She walks around her room, trying to reclaim the feelings that Monday evenings give her, but something is lost, her power is diminished by the presence of those drums.

Tony has challenged her authority within this place. Trevor hasn't even arrived yet. The drums are filling the corner, it's where she usually puts her music bag, it's where Trevor sometimes keeps his guitar. This place is hers, for two hours every Monday it is her arena and now this Tony, this husband of the worst singer in the choir, has taken it over.

Anna walks over to the drums, and flicks the cymbals. The noise, tin hitting tin, is pinging around the room, bouncing off the far wall and reverberating against her.

"Hope it was O.K.?" .. There's a call from the doorway.
"Only I thought I ought to get them set up before the others arrived. That Caretaker chappie said that I could pop them in here."
Tony is employing his disarming smile. Anna is considering her tactics; she must not let this man know that he has bested her.
"Good idea! I just do wish you'd asked me about the positioning; I'm sure that my accompanist would rather the instruments were together."
She's pointing over at the piano, on the other side of the room.
"Oh, only the Caretaker said…."
"Reg doesn't have too much of an idea about music, you see."
She lets that sink in, lets it bite. "Never mind, I'm sure that it will be fine .. just for tonight."
Tony is watching her. "I'm in your hands dear lady." He's holding out his arms in a gesture of submission that is anything but.
"Let me hear you play, it's 'Tony' isn't it?"
Christ, she's going to make him do an audition, for this piddle piss of a small town choir, the cow is going to make him beg for it.

Tony walks over to his drum kit and sits down. He picks up the sticks and holds them, pointing them toward Anna, it's almost a fencing gesture.

"What would you like to hear?"

"Whatever you'd like to play," and she turns away from him to unpack her music bag and make ready for the session. Tony looks across the room, at the back that she has turned toward him, and he flicks the drumsticks up at her.

The drum solo he plays is an accomplished, if violent piece; there's fury in his drumming and the noise is deafening.

Anna is remembering how Miss Etch had listened to her, all those years ago, and she straightens her back into the military posture of her teacher.

Lindsay is standing out in the hallway; she has let Tony go in alone to talk to Anna. She is standing, looking at the school photographs that adorn the walls; trips taken to worthy places, rows of children lining up for their presence at Ironbridge to be recorded for posterity, anorak hoods up as they huddle beside the coach to avoid the pouring rain.

She looks along the rows of little faces and listens to Tony's drumming and she is trying not to flinch.

Diane is coming down the hall and spots Lindsay.

"Oh good, look I wanted to apologise.." and she spots the large bandage: "What's up with your hand? ..was that why you were at the Doctor's? .. Oh I'm so sorry, I should have asked you, I was just too busy going on and on about my stupid divorce, and my stupid…"

"No – that's fine. It's nothing."

"It doesn't look like nothing."

"The nurse at the surgery put this huge bandage on it, that's all."

Lindsay is walking away into the choir room,

Diane dodging behind her, "But what happened?"

"It was just so silly, I just caught it in a door, that's all."

"But…"

"Please, please don't mention it."

Diane isn't convinced but it's obvious that Lindsay doesn't want to talk about it. "O.K."

Lindsay goes into the choir room just as Tony is finishing his 'audition'and he smashes the cymbals for the last time. Anna stands in the centre of the room, buffeted by the noise as it crashes all around her.

The room buzzes with silence as Tony lays down the drumsticks, and the walls seem to heave against the sudden stillness.

Anna is still sorting her music, she does not look up: "Thank you Tony, that was fine." Tony is looking at the immaculate coiffure that is bending over her music case ...fine, so she thinks that that was 'fine'; that was electric, that was passion, and this cow thinks it's 'fine'.

Lindsay is looking across at him and he is struck by the bandaged hand, the whiteness of it, it's so obvious. He walks over to her and turns her away from the room, so that they are both facing the drums, they guard their secrets – talking in low murmurs together: "I thought you were going to wear some black gloves?"
"I can't get them on over the bandage."
"It'll just cause a whole lot of questions .. is that what you want? Perhaps that's what you want?"
"No, no. Tony..."
"You have a silly accident and you want people to poke and pry into our lives?"
"No!"

Other members of the choir are entering the room. Diane is watching Tony and Lindsay; Anna sees her look and also watches the pair.
Trevor bumbles into the room; he looks as if he has been dragged through a war zone, his jacket is pulled down off from one shoulder, his tie is askew and he's holding his music case like a shield. Anna looks up at him.
Trevor, explaining. "That dog at number three."
Anna nods with a casual interest and little sympathy "Oh, the black Labrador; well it never goes for me."
Trevor is making his way over to his piano, and it's muttered darkly "It wouldn't dare."
"Sorry?"
"I think it's a Doberman actually, and they're supposed to wear muzzles these days aren't they?"

Anna is looking at her watch. Trevor's fidgeting at his piano, he wants to justify himself: "Thing is he always spots me getting out of my car, so I have to do a detour round the war memorial to get on the other side of market street; but oh no, he's spotted that, so he back-tracks round the side of the floral clock to meet me head on by the funeral directors, so I'm standing in their doorway – pretending to look at the flower display in that big urn – and the blessed thing thinks he's cornered me, he's all chuffed and growling, and don't tell me to just Walk On Past, if I'd walked on past I'd be eaten.. "

The choir are all looking at him now, listening to the tale, and Trevor finishes lamely: "So ..so I had to leg it to the school gates."

"Don't tell me you've shut them? How's everybody else supposed to get in?"

The blaring of horns can be heard quite clearly now, and the choir go over to the window to see Susie in her cattle-beater stuck behind the gates. A large black dog sits patiently behind the gates, its tail is quite patently wagging.

"Oh yes – it looks friendly enough now – just you try going out there and opening the gates," and Trevor watches as Susie climbs down from her four-wheel giant and pulls the gates open. The dog watches her with a mild interest, receives a pat as she passes him, then trots happily after her car into the car park.

Trevor is incandescent: "Well it obviously doesn't bite women! probably highly trained."

Diane feels that somebody ought to defend Trevor. "Well, that's right, it probably thought you were a burglar." Anna's casting a jaundiced eye over her accompanist. "Oh yes, they're known to wear jackets and ties, burglars."

The choir move back over to their chairs. Lindsay is managing to hold her right hand down between her legs, with her music folder on her lap as further cover. Tony has gone back to sit behind his drums, he's feathering his wire brush across the top of the snare drum; it's an irritating buzzing.

Rowena stares across at him and his array of shining metal, she's holding her goatskin drum with the giraffes round it, and she walks over to her chair, a picture of wounded dignity.

Diane and Jo-Anne are bending earnest heads over their music, comparing the notes that they made after last week's session, checking with Linda and Paulette that they've got the same corrections and additions to the Greek number.

Susie and Grace come in, followed by the dog, who looks around the room with polite interest, the black fan of a tail waving cheerily behind him.

Trevor is trying very hard not to actually hide behind his piano.

Anna has not seen the dog, she is busy handing Tony a piece of music:

"I've added the percussion, as you see. Perhaps you could just give it a try along these lines."

She's behind him, over him, her sharp citrus perfume cutting through the air between them. Tony inhales it and closes his mouth tight against the odour.

"Right, let's begin. As you can see Tony has very kindly brought along his drum kit, so I think we'll go straight into 'Gaudete' to see how it feels with this extra rhythmic drive." Anna walks over to her music stand.

"Still no male basses this week?" and she casts Trevor an accusing look.

Trevor, his misery compounded, is too busy looking at the dog to react to this injustice. The dog is sitting in the sopranos section, giving a front paw a thorough wash. Nobody pays him any particular mind and he seems quite happy to have joined the town's choir. As the piano is situated at the other, lower voices end of the room, Trevor is warily content to leave sleeping dogs to lie, even if they're just sitting and washing.

'Gaudete' goes rather well, Tony has moderated his style to fit the squeaky sopranos and the wobbly reverbs from the alto section.

Linda, pushing to be chosen for the solo verses, sings throatily, willing Anna to look at her, and the dog cocks his ears at Trevor, he has not forgotten his prey, he is just biding his time until Trevor tries to leave the room.

At the break, Susie gives Grace a significant nod and makes her announcement. "Anna – several of us have been thinking..." Anna is used to 'several of us' being dragooned into Susie's thoughts and braces herself for more Concert Costumes suggestions. "The Carnival. We were wondering about having a Float." There are interested murmurs from the other members: "You mean we all stand on a lorry and get wheeled round Witsham High Street.." Jo-Anne is obviously not keen, and Diane's shaking her head too, but Linda's all for it. "Oh it'll be a laugh" and there's a jumble of voices:

"Advertise the Choir!"

"Attract more members."

"Attract some men!"

Paulette's keen: "I could decorate the Float with giant sheets of music…"

Linda's nodding: "..with cut-out notes and treble clefs .."

Anna wants to nip this in the bud: "I'm afraid that this is out of the question, you see Trevor and I have one of our Charity Concerts on that Saturday."

Anna turns back to her music-stand in the manner of 'subject closed', but Susie's not that easily deterred: "But that's the morning isn't it? The Grand Parade's in the afternoon"

"I'm sorry but I firmly believe that this compromises the dignity of the choir … what say you Trevor?"

Trevor knows only too well what is expected of him: "Yes, I have to agree with Anna. Anyway it's totally impractical, if we sang we couldn't be heard, and the piano would be a health-and-safety issue."

Anna actually smiles at him, and even the dog looks impressed.

Susie's not letting go that easily: "It's about Raising Profiles Anna, if we're seen to be part of the Town…"

Anna's thinking about the Christmas Lights, and the Turning On Ceremony, and that the Witsham Warblers had put in a bid for next year's open-air Carols Service in the Market. Bloody silly idea, of course, everybody freezing, children sobbing and the W.I. passing round that muck they call 'Punch' but still …A Float, maybe she shouldn't dismiss it totally, not yet.

Not until she's had a chance to think about it; Anna likes to ponder changes in her life, rolling new ideas around in her mouth to taste them, to see if they are really 'Her'. Would Jonathan think it common? That's the point.

She'll run it past him next week, after she's got rid of Trevor.

Anna looks across at Trevor, preening himself for being a good boy and she is sickened by his cloying loyalty.

"Can we leave this until next week? I'll make some enquiries."

Trevor is surprised and looks his question at Anna.

"Well sometimes one must embrace a new venture; move with the times Trevor. Some changes are for the best, you know."

A cool breeze of dissent shivers Trevor's shoulders; he's picked up on 'changes'.

The dog yawns loudly and lies down, his head resting on his front paws as he gazes up at Anna.

"Trevor, did that thing follow you in here?"

"It's not <u>my</u> fault, it came in with Susie and Grace."

Grace's talking to the dog. "You wanted to sing didn't you?" and now Paulette's cooing at it. "He's lovely, he's been sitting there ever so sweetly, he's just like my Harvey – only he's a spaniel of course –"

Trevor can feel his hands beginning to dampen with dread; Oh God, the women have adopted the thing, now Anna will expect him to do something about it. His doomed fears are soon justified. "Trevor just get rid of it."

The dog gets up, pushing his paws out in front of him in a long languorous stretch, and he looks over at the man who is to get rid of him.

Trevor looks across at the yawning mouth and the fine set of extraordinarily long yellowing teeth, and he can see 'fancy-your-chances' written all over them.

From behind his piano, Trevor manages to sound perfectly reasonable: "I'm not very good with dogs" He looks at Anna and in his head he can hear her telling him that he's not very good at anything, that Jonathan would be very good with dogs, that Jonathan wouldn't be chased into the choir room by a mutt.

Tony, unexpectedly, comes to the rescue. He walks over to the dog and clicks his fingers. The stupid animal obeys him and waddles over to the door. Trevor has often heard of the sixth sense that animals have about people and he has also often been witness to the total nonsense of this theory. His Uncle Harry had been an appalling drunk and thoroughly bad egg, but his dog Maurice had adored him. Harry would often give the dog a wallop if the mood took him, but the animal had just stuck to his heels and, with pure illogic, had growled with great menace at everybody else. Trevor's fear of dogs had started with Maurice, and a very unpleasant afternoon spent in Uncle Harry's shed, while the dog patrolled outside.

His Father had finally come round and let him out and given him a cuff for being such a coward, and the dog – as dog's do – had sat there all sweet as pie and let him walk past it as if it had never attempted to chew his leg off at all.

So, now, there's that Tony, another nasty piece of work if Trevor's not mistaken, and another bloody silly dog getting people wrong.

Trevor thinks that it stands to reason that if one is afraid of dogs that one is not going to hurt them, so why don't they save all that growling and chasing routine for their enemies?

".....Trevor!" Anna is saying something to him.

"Now that the dog's gone perhaps we can move on to the Bach."

Trevor obediently dives into his case for the music, ignoring Tony's smug look as he passes the piano to go back to his drums.

But the dog hasn't gone, has it. It's standing outside in the corridor, isn't it, and it's waiting for him. He'll have to try and wangle it so that he goes out with Susie and Grace, perhaps it won't go for him if he's with them. Anyway, Susie looks like the kind of woman who pushes horses aside when she's climbing over stiles (something Trevor has never perfected) so she'll probably be useful in hanging onto the thing's collar while he legs it to his car. It is with these consoling thoughts that Trevor faces the rest of the session with a lesser panic.

Lindsay is thanking her God. He is usually not that interested in how she feels, and Lindsay thinks this is absolutely right and proper and would much rather He be doing things in Africa anyway. Today, though, he has sent a dog, which has distracted everybody wonderfully. When Diane started on at her in the corridor Lindsay had thought that she should never have come to this session. Tony had even hinted as such, asking her if she would not rather rest, but she had been worried that Tony would then be pestered with enquires about where she was and that it would look distinctly odd for her not to be there when he was to take part. Now everybody was beginning to pack up, choir was over for this week and she had got away with it. Tony was looking pleased; Paulette had offered her services and was helping him to dismantle the drum kit, so Lindsay might even get out of being seen to carry one of the drums one-handed. On top of that, Anna hadn't even asked her to do her solo.

In fact Anna was realising that if Tony was to be her new rhythm section then she couldn't really get rid of Lindsay, and that her Cheltenham Cull had stalled before it had started. Jonathan. She must get Jonathan on board.

Anna looks at Trevor, who seems to be hanging around Susie and Grace, which isn't like him at all; the very evening she wants to talk to him and he's busy shepherding those two trouble makers out of the room.

Linda is hovering: "Anna, might I have a quick word?"

"Yes of course," ever the professional, but Anna is also watching the door behind Linda's back, and watching Trevor leave the room; he has managed to wedge himself in between Susie and her fat friend and seems to be actually linking his arms through theirs so that the three of them look like a chorus line.

"You remember that I mentioned Singing Lessons?"

"Yes."

"I really feel that I'm ready for them now, I mean it would be a marvellous opportunity to prepare for any solo work…" Anna looks into ambitious eyes. She understands Linda, the woman wants something better.

"I have a space on Wednesday afternoons …?"

"Yes. Great."

"Right then, two-o'clock? .. You've read my handout on Fees and Cancellations?"

"Oh yes, thank you Anna, I won't let you down."

Anna was quite sure that she wouldn't, which would make a nice change from the sulky teenagers with mothers who liked to think of themselves as musical.

Trevor is standing in the car park. The dog has gone. Susie and Grace had got him through the corridor outside the choir room; he'd had to pretend to be changing his mind about the Carnival and got into a very surreal discussion about the choir dressing up as 'crotchets' but then Grace had got all huffy about the fatter members having to be 'minims', but by that time he'd swivelled his head round so many times to make sure that the animal wasn't lying in wait for him that he'd got quite dizzy. Grace is clambering up into Susie's tank, never an easy manoeuvre, and after he's made quite sure that the dog had obviously gone off to intimidate somebody else, Trevor decides to go back into the choir room. He has to talk to Anna. He watches Tony and Paulette manhandling the drums out of the room and doesn't offer to help. Lindsay is carrying the cymbals out to their car and Trevor notices the bandaged hand, and he looks back at the husband and wonders.

Linda's calling over to him: "Bye Trevor, see you next week."
Anna is still in the choir room, she's writing in her diary.

"Ah! I thought you'd gone. Linda's having singing lessons, you never know, if I work on her she might be able to carry the solos. Heaven knows, there's nobody else."

"Anna, I wanted to have a word..."

"Yes. So do I." Anna snaps the diary shut and turns to face him.

"There's no easy way to say this, Trevor, but the thing is I am planning Big Changes for the choir. Bringing Linda on is just part of it. Getting Tony on board, that's another move in the right direction.."

Trevor can feel a leaden weight somewhere in the area of his chest; it's pushing at him, there also seems to be something dry and hard in his throat and he wants to cough to clear it. Anna's talking on ... something about a Time for Change, New Approaches and Moving On.

"What are you saying, Anna?"

"I'm saying that I think we've come to a point where *both* of us have to move on."

"Where am I supposed to be going?"

Anna ignores that . "The Choir needs a new direction, I think that's obvious. After a while there just has to be new blood or things become stale, I'm sure that you can see that."

"You don't want me as accompanist."

"Of course I do! You're doing the charity concert with me next month, you can't have forgotten that ... it's just the choir, that's all."

"But the Choir is ....all."

Anna's picking up her music case. "Please don't make this any more difficult than it has to be; we've had some marvellous years, and I value you as a friend, Trevor, I really do. I don't want to lose that. It's the friendship that's important, isn't it, in the long run."

"So ...it's Jonathan."

"Well ... possibly. That's not the point. The point is that we both need to move in different directions. You'll thank me, you know, in the long run.. You need to be *pushed* Trevor, you always have, and I think that right now what you need is to be pushed..."

"...Pushed out."

"If you must put it like that, yes."

Anna is keen to be gone now, she doesn't want to look at his face any more, it's gone squashy; high red spots of colour flame under his eyes amid a grey paleness. She collects her bag and makes off toward the door.

"I've got to go, Roy wants to have another discussion about his blessed lawn mower" and she actually laughs, the old conspiracy of them knowing Roy's funny little ways. "You know what he's like."

Trevor sits down heavily on one of the little wooden school chairs, it's child-sized and the arm rests bite into his thighs. He's winded, he's taken a blow to his stomach and he bends over double, dragging in breaths against that stone in his chest.

Outside in the car park he can hear Anna calling out:
"Well done Paulette! – you've got a 'roady' there now Tony!"
and then the unmistakeable barking of a dog.

Trevor gets out of the little chair and picks up his briefcase and then walks out into the corridor, the dog's barking is louder now, and there's the bottom note of a growl in it. The corridor is long and Trevor walks past the official school photos and the pin board that heralds the School Fete and notices about the Cricket Club and the Self Defence Classes. Trevor wonders what his life would have been like if he had done self defence classes; perhaps the entire class of 5A wouldn't have tied his gym shorts to the top of the climbing rope and perhaps Alan Sharkey, a name that he would flinch to hear on the day he died, perhaps Alan Sharkey wouldn't have waited for him every day, every bloody day at the school gates and he wouldn't have had to hand over that shilling. Just a shilling, the smallness of that was the shame. Sharkey didn't want the money, but he'd stand there and make Trevor give it to him every day.
One day Sharkey had thrown the coin up into the air, just to show that it wasn't the money, and the other kids had scrambled for it.   It was the ritual that was important, the power and the humiliation, that was the game. Trevor had always had to play that particular game; the whistling when he walked down a dark street and tried not to look round and then, so much later, when he had thought to be free of it, perhaps Mr. Gillespie wouldn't have met him round the back of the Gas Board office and threatened to kick his head in if Trevor didn't verify his expenses.
That shilling, the crawling shame of that shilling;   when decimalisation came in Trevor had rejoiced to know that he would no longer have to handle that coin, because it would no longer hold that history.

And now there is a dog standing at the end of a corridor, and it is waiting for him, as they have always waited for him.

Trevor reaches the door and looks into the eyes of the bully.

"No." Trevor tests the word into the quiet of the corridor, then louder: "No.... No, bloody No!" The dog barks back at him. "No! No! No!" Trevor is advancing upon the dog, who – more in surprise than fear – is actually backing away from him. "You want a shilling do you! .. well you're not bloody getting it! Not any more..."

Trevor is marching in a straight line towards the dog.

"Bugger off! Go on. Get out of here!" and he waves his arms at the animal who turns round and runs, out of the car park and out of the gates, its tail a black banner flying behind the skidding, scampering paws.

Trevor stands in the car park and watches it run away.
He looks back at the Choir room and there is just the slightest lift of a chin. "I'm not doing it, I'm not playing the game, not any more...."

Chapter 44

Tony's locking up the car. "I'm going to leave the drum kit in there". He's throwing a blanket over it. "Nobody will know what's under that."

Lindsay is standing by their front door. She's looking back at the car, at the passenger door and trying to remember last Monday, and she's trying to remember how it happened.

Tony is whistling, that hissing flat sound that seems lately to be his companion. "Come on Kitten, you're dreaming again," and he ushers her into their house. "I thought that went rather well .. the drumming." He's buoyant, practically bouncing on the soles of his feet as he goes into the kitchen.

Lindsay watches him as he puts the kettle on and busies himself with mugs from the little row of ceramic hooks that they'd bought in Clovelly, and she's trying to bring back those days they'd spent so casually, hours of ordinary smiles watching the donkeys trotting along cobbled streets.

Tony's shoulders are feeling her gaze and he half turns his head toward her, he's concentrating too much on pouring milk into mugs, the business of making their drinks a shield against her thinking.

"Tony...."

He jumps in on her words stopping whatever it is she is going to say:

"We should try semi-skimmed you know, apparently if you use it for a week you don't notice the difference."

Lindsay's face is a small tight smile. "You do, you just pretend you don't"

Tony's holding the kettle over the mugs, the steam curling hotly out of the spout. Lindsay looks at the kettle.

Tony quickly sloshes water into mugs, and frowns at the coffee granules that have risen to the top.

"I loathe 'Instant' but I just thought that this once...."

"Well it's quick isn't it."

"Why is it in that cupboard anyway? Why do we have any?"

"It was left over from when we had the plumber."

"Oh yes."

"Tony, why did you marry me?"

He's stirring the mugs, the metal clinking against the china.

The stirring goes on and on. They're both watching the little brown pieces of coffee bleed into the liquid as they dissolve.

"That's a silly question, isn't it Lindsay?"

"Yes. Probably."

Tony's picking up his mug and taking it with him. "I'm just going to have a couple of hours in the Den." and he's up the stairs, two at a time.

Lindsay sips at her coffee, it's foul, and she tips it down the sink.

She's looking at the brown stain around the plughole and, on automatic, she reaches into the cupboard for the Cif cream and the little brush on a stick.

As she cleans the sink she can hear Tony pacing about in the room above.

Why did he marry *her?* She certainly hadn't been the prettiest nor the most interesting of his girlfriends. Tony was handsome in a rather obvious clean-cut tall and dark sort of way, and Lindsay had thought him an Ideal.

He'd been like a white knight, rescuing her from the moderate abnormality of her family. Tony had taken her away from underclothes airing on the back of chairs and Mother's foot appliances in the sink. Tony had been strong and capable; he'd built her a wooden cabinet for her collections, with rows of little alcoves to house the miniatures. It was just .. it was just that there had been those moments, those little moments when he'd pushed her, or grabbed her arm. He hadn't meant to hurt her, it was just that sometimes she had felt a slight tightness at the control of him. That heaviness that reminded her of how she had felt at school, when the Headmaster had walked into the classroom.

But that had been nothing, not really, because the main thing had been that He'd Understood. She'd sent him a thank-you card once, after he'd bought her all those ceramic thimbles, and she'd written: *'to my Mister-Under-Stand-Me Man'* She had thought that no one else would. No-one else would be bothered with her awkwardness and her silly little fears in the middle of the night; Tony would hold her and call her Kitten and sometimes wouldn't even want the sex.

It was Anna's fault – making him sit on that chair in the corner last week and now this week making him *audition.* He'd been angry about that in the car, once they'd got rid of Paulette and her endless 'Is there anything else that I can do', he'd got cross at the traffic lights on the way home just thinking about it, she never auditioned the choir, well Lindsay wouldn't have got in if she had, it was outrageous, Tony was right. People wound him up, they didn't understand how hurt he could get. Well that was all over now, he was their official drummer, she had seen how impressed Anna had been after 'Gaudete'. It was a shame about Rowena, but, as Tony says, the weak sometimes have to go to the wall. Everything would settle down now, like before. Perhaps she would suggest they go to Clovelly again.

Upstairs in his den, Tony is leafing through a catalogue. This whole new world of names that he has never heard: there's pages of Heckler & Koch, and an article on the 'Glock 18', but Tony is rather taken by the American 'Berettas' and of course the standard 'Colt '1911'. He's rubbing at his mouth as he reads about the 'blow-back system with tip up barrel' of the 'Beretta 3032 Tomcat', and the words sink into him; the cowboy words, the gangster words, bad-boys games words: *traditional double action, ambidextrous, safety-decock lever and external hammer'* The pictures of the blue-black metal, the snub noses, the black ridged handles … oh yes, this is Big-Boys' games.

He was to meet Gerry again tomorrow at a pub out of town, Tony liked the subterfuge of this, it fitted with these new and dangerous words.

Tony picks up the wooden box that waits for his gun and lays the catalogue in it, just for now. Soon. Soon it would be there, lying amid the foam padding.

He'd never been allowed to have a toy gun, not a proper silver one like the kid next door had, that bloody kid who'd got to blow the candles out on Tony's birthday cake. Tony had used to stand in his little garden looking over the fence at cowboy games, watching the way the other boy held the gleaming metal, and he'd point it at Tony and laugh. "Look, I've got a gun."

Well now look. Tony is squeezing his hands between his thighs in a pure tight clench of joy. Look at me. I deserve this, I should have always had this.

I will have a gun.

He turns the key on the little brass lock and puts the key into a small ceramic box that Lindsay had bought him; it was supposed to be for his paperclips, and had a penguin painted on the top.

Why had he married her? Women were always asking these sorts of questions, what was the point. When he met Lindsay he'd just finished with that tart Claire – she of the ball-breaking feminism and the - 'I can change my own tyre thank you.' - He liked to be appreciated, needed even. Men do, and he'd had enough of her bad language too, and all those demands in bed. Claire turned foreplay into an Olympic Challenge. But Lindsay.. Lindsay had been different; she was such a gentle little thing and she used to blush when there was sex on the TV and look down in her lap, he'd liked to see that, that sweetness.

He liked it that she always asked him what he thought; she'd never just go off and buy a sofa on her own without referring to him. He liked the way that she agreed with him about homemade produce; that jam business had been a bit of a shock, but it was probably one of those women at the choir that had put her up to that nonsense.

He liked it that she'd knock on the door of his den if she wanted to come in; not that she actually came in, but if she was asking him if he wanted a cup of tea or to let him know that she was going out. That was another thing he liked about Lindsay, he always knew where she was, she'd let him know if she was popping out to the shops and how long she expected to be. Then in the evenings he'd ask her about her day and who she'd met, and they'd laugh together about them, and he'd tell her how stupid other people were. Yes, he knew where he was with Lindsay.

She would never think of rooting about in this room, she'd never look in that box; she wasn't that sort of person. Lindsay was an innocent and Tony would never spoil that; he liked to keep her naïve, there was a purity in her and you didn't get much of that these days, not in women. He was old fashioned, that was it, and women had changed too much. He protected Lindsay, so he wasn't going to say anything about the gun, it would only worry her, and besides these things were men's things.

Chapter 45

Trevor's television is flickering Newsnight into the room, but that new woman is being caustic again, so Trevor's got the set on mute. He's sitting with the Radio Times on his lap, marking up the next week's viewing with his highlighter pen. He's got as far as next Wednesday, but he's stopped, pen poised over another episode of 'Bear Week' and a particularly anticipated one about the 'Spectacled Bears'. Trevor has seen them before, the bears have got black rings round their eyes and, when they're not accidentally sitting on them, the mothers are especially kind to their cubs.

Trevor looks up to see some grease-eyed Politician swivel in his chair, evading the finger wagging. At least Jeremy Paxman didn't flick his hair about, and then Trevor notices that the New Woman wears the same shade of lipstick as Anna. Well that figures. What is he going to do about Anna?

Jonathan is totally wrong for the choir, he hasn't got the patience to put up with the Paulettes and the Dianes, and there's Lindsay. Trevor has been thinking a lot about Lindsay; that bandage has stuck in his head, and the way she had looked in the car park, that bleakness.

Trevor has decided to fight for it: the choir and his life. He sees it as simply as that. The choir has *been* his life. He'd beaten the dog. He'd beat Jonathan.

Trevor knew his limitations; he would fight this *his* way. Spectacled Bears fought for their territory, well not actually fought, there just seemed to be a lot of pissing up against trees and making little scratches on the barks to show the other bears that this was their territory. Marking it out. Then they climbed up the trees; the mother-bears were rather clumsy at this, and last week one of them had unknowingly knocked her cub off his branch because she'd turned round and bashed him with her bottom. The commentary had laughed at that, especially as the mother bear had climbed down to see what had happened to her cub – cuffed it soundly – and then hugged it. So they weren't particularly clever, these bears, and they bumbled about making mistakes, but they held their territory.

It would take some thought. Trevor was going to get on his computer and type out a list of Options and Possible Strategies. He'd already made notes round the edges of the Radio Times: *Meet Jonathan, tell him how irritating the choir-women can be.* That was a definite possible, Trevor was pretty sure that Jonathan had little time for the Dithering Female and he didn't see him coaching solos out of the inadequate. No point warning him about Anna's Little Ways; he might come a cropper there, because (although the very idea sent little shivers of pure fear into Trevor's spine) he had a fair idea that Jonathan was rather attracted to Anna's little ways - Snake attracted by the Tiger sort of thing – no, best to stress the level of boredom involved and the lack of challenge, that was the way to put Jonathan off.

* *

Jonathan of course is ignorant of the schemes and the plotting. His own plans involve little more than some light seduction of a woman who appears to not welcome his advances, always a turn-on where Jonathan is concerned. So he too sits, watching Newsnight, television joining these men across a few miles of inky streets.

Jonathan, predictably, rather likes the New Woman interviewing the Member for Gravesend. He had used to fancy Edwina Currie until he found out about John Major; she had disappointed him there.

So Jonathan watches the interviewer's mouth and thinks of Anna and lets his imagination foul her lips and her tongue so that he has to unzip his trousers against the swelling.

* *

Trevor's pleasures are of a less licentious kind, and he highlights the Spectacled Bears programme with a green circle. But there is resolution in his eyes as he watches that same mouth with Anna's immaculate smear of deep colour. Trevor is not going to allow that mouth to hurt him; he has had enough of that familiar feeling in his stomach, that shame. He gets up and turns off the set, watching the mouth fade to blackness, and tonight he turns the light off by his piano and to hell with what the neighbours think.

149

Chapter 46

Diane, pressed by guilt and not a little boredom, has decided that she has to invite Lindsay out for a coffee.. or something. After all she had joined the choir to Meet New Friends and she and Jo-Anne were progressing well, it was just that married women always had to liaise with husbands, and Jo-Anne and Mike had his parents over for the week which left Diane at a bit of a loose end. She had the perfect "in" – following up her concern about Lindsay's accident – so it didn't look *too* clingy.

Diane's looking down the typed list of Choir Contacts and finds the telephone number: "Hello? .. Lindsay? It's Diane. Diane from the choir." There's not much of a reaction, so Diane rushes on. "I was just popping into town and wondered if you'd like to meet for a quick cup of something..?"
There's a rather off-putting "Oh" from Lindsay, so Diane piles on the excuses: "It's just that you've been in the choir longer than me and I was wondering if you could give me some advice..?"
She cradles the phone in her neck and listens to Lindsay.
Diane's frowning at the response: "Well if you're not feeling too well maybe I could come round, I've got that Echinacea stuff which is brilliant for colds.."

Diane puts down the receiver and wishes she hadn't rung. Lindsay had sounded flustered and she could hear that husband of hers in the background asking who was on the phone. Then she'd said that she'd call her back 'another time' so that Diane didn't know whether she meant next week or next year. Shit. This was the wrong one to pursue, she should have rung that ballsy one, Susie, but then that sort always want 'interesting' people as friends and Diane didn't feel particularly interesting these days.
She should get a job, that or move to Cornwall. Stupid to stay in the same town as Paul.

The phone rings, it's Lindsay. "It's all right, Tony's gone out for a lunch meeting. Yes, do come round."
Diane shrugs, newly single, but she is beginning to be cynical about wives fitting around husbands, and wearily unsurprised at the quick about-face once the man's not around.

* * * * * * * * * * * * * * * * * * * *

150

Meanwhile, over on the modern estate of Executive Dwellings, Lindsay is hovering anxiously in her hallway. Tony had said that he was about to go out, and had got as far as the car, so she'd rung Diane back, guilty at sounding rude and pushing the other woman away. Now Tony had remembered something he needed from his den and had come back in and gone upstairs. And Diane was on her way. Lindsay calls up the stairs: "Tony?! – I thought you were going out?"

Tony is in his den, taking a last look at that catalogue, writing down some notes about the model that he prefers. He doesn't want to take the catalogue in the car, doesn't think "Hand Guns Monthly" will look too good on the driver's seat, but he doesn't want Gerry passing him off with any old rubbish.

Lindsay is coming up the stairs. Tony can hear her. What's she nagging him about? He wants to write down these details for Gerry but he doesn't want her seeing this catalogue. Why couldn't she just leave him alone?

He scrambles the catalogue into the top drawer of his desk as Lindsay reaches his door.

"Tony?"

"What !"

"I thought you said…."

"Yes, I'm going out. Don't hassle me Lindsay. I have to copy some notes up for this Meeting!"

"Sorry, it's just…."

"Anyway, why are you so keen to get me out of the house? What's all the rush?"

"Nothing" - it's a quick gasp.

There's the sound of a car approaching. Lindsay would wring her hands if it weren't for the bandage. Suddenly it seems desperately important that Tony doesn't realise that she's invited Diane round; she hadn't told him this morning, and Diane was bound to give it away that they'd just talked on the phone.

Tony hates that kind of subterfuge, that 'women gossiping with women against men'. He had often told her about it happening at his office.

Now he'd think that *she* did it; arranged little tête-à-têtes behind his back, and she didn't!

The car has stopped outside the immaculately mown lawn, a door slams and there's footsteps. Lindsay is almost beside herself. "Tony I thought you were going out..."

The doorbell rings.

Tony looks at Lindsay; they are standing at the top of the stairs and can see the dark shape of Diane against the glass of the front door.

"Who is that?"

"I don't know."

"Yes you do, that's why you wanted me out of the way."

"No.... I ..."

"What's going on Lindsay?" It's said calmly. Tony reaches out to take her hand, the bandaged hand.

"I thought you were going out.."

"So you said."

"I thought it wouldn't matter."

"What wouldn't matter?"

"It's only Diane ... Tony, my hand ! Please! Don't squeeze my hand!"

"I'm not hurting you. I just want to know what's going on."

The doorbell rings again. Lindsay pulls her hand out of Tony's grip and scuttles down the stairs to open the door, she flings it wide, like a magician revealing a trick: "Look! It's Diane. It's only Diane from the choir."

Tony stands at the top of the stairs and looks down at the women as Diane steps into the hallway and into the crackling tension of the house.

"I'm sorry, I thought you said it was fine to come round, if it's not convenient, I'll..."

Tony walks down the stairs, holding his hand out to Diane, he's smiling a huge welcome: "It's Diane isn't it. Yes, we met at choir; I was the idiot on the drums." He's laughing and shrugging his shoulders, all deprecating charm.

"Lindsay you should have told me Diane was coming round, we could have had a lunch in the garden."Lindsay is so shocked at this unlikely event that she cannot respond.

So Diane's demurring. "Oh please no, I didn't mean to cause any..."

"Came round for a girly heart to heart did you?" and there's just the slightest edge of metal in Tony's voice.

Diane is looking from one to the other, Lindsay is just standing there with her mouth open, she looks as if she isn't actually breathing.

Tony pushes past the women. "Well got to dash", and to Diane: "One of the lunchtime Meetings so beloved of Middle-bloody-Management," and he's grinning at her, and Diane is reminded of the monkeys that used to grin in tea adverts and that they were really grimacing with fear.

She's surprised at the "bloody" too, Tony doesn't seem the type to swear, well not at lunchtime. Lindsay still looks as if she's been turned to stone, so Diane actually says 'goodbye' to Tony in a rather wifely way and waves at him as he gets into his car.

Lindsay closes the front door and seems to sag back against it.
"Are you alright?" which Diane realises immediately is a ridiculous question to a woman who is transparently very near to collapse.
Lindsay looks at the other woman, seems to remember herself, and gives her head a little shake. "Sorry."
Diane's looking rueful. "Did I interrupt a bit of a 'domestic'?"
"Yes!" Lindsay's relieved at Diane's reducing of this to the normal, the usual married tiffs: "You know what it's like ... sometimes."
"Oh yes, I've just come through a divorce, remember."
Lindsay didn't actually know anything of the kind, but the fact that Diane had been mauled in the marriage market was some kind of salve to her shattered mind.

They go into the kitchen.
"You sit down, that cold has obviously knocked you for six. I'll make us a brew shall I?"
Lindsay had forgotten the 'cold' lie from earlier, and is grateful for its cover now as she sinks into a chair and watches Diane busy about.
"I just don't know what's wrong with me these days, I seem to be so, well, nervous about everything. It's probably menstrual."
Diane doesn't think it's menstrual. "Look, I've just been dumped for a Receptionist, so you don't have to feel awkward with me about marriage problems."
"I'm just a bit... confused, these days. I think it's that solo. I get jittery about things you see, it was the same with the yearly Displays at my Ballet School."
"Oh, you were a dancer!"
"Oh no, it was only a Saturday mornings thing. My mother thought it would help with my deportment; people don't bother with all that now, do they...?

"No, well, every year we'd get all dressed up in costumes and put on a display for the parents. I hated it, we had to get our mothers to make the costumes you see ..Mrs. Young, that was our teacher, would hand out these cut-out paper patterns and the mothers were supposed to buy the material, pin it to the paper shapes and then cut them out and sew them up," and Lindsay is screwing her nose up into a tight little frown. "I seem to remember that they were usually fairies, the wings were a right palaver."

Diane's watching the other woman's colour creep back into her cheeks and is glad that Lindsay seems to be coming back.

"My mother wasn't terribly good at needlework, well we were all buying ready-made stuff by then, weren't we, so she used to ask Grandma to help with the costumes … anyway, the point is that Grandma had cataracts, and by the time the night before the Display came round I'd still be at the pinned-together stage and I can remember getting in a dreadful stew about it all…"

"Yes, I can see that you would." Diane's trying not to smile.

"Dancing with pins isn't really ideal."

"Sounds like that terrible fairy story – when they make the girl dance on hot stones and every step is agony – I could never understand why stories for little children had to have all that pain."

Lindsay's nodding. "Like Cinderella's ugly sister cutting a piece off of her foot to fit the silver slipper…"

"Yes…Prepares you for Life… I suppose that was the idea behind it."

The women are contemplating Life; Lindsay is the first to come out of the reverie: "So you see I've always been like this really. I take things too much to heart I think, yes, and I *think* about things too much, turn them over in my mind. Blow them out of all proportion."

Lindsay is genuinely smiling by now, and Diane is glad that she came round, she's making another friend, she's Moving On.

Chapter 47

Gerry, a wiry, almost thin man in his late thirties sits at a table by the window in a smoke filled bar. He has the sharp features of the permanently wary, and flicks regular glances toward the door. He's smoking a roll-up with the intensity of a man who has another twenty to get through before nightfall, but the studied hard-man image is slightly dented by the khaki and brown jacket that is not the genuine military attire that it pretends to be.

The bar, born out of the necessity of the No-Smoking Laws, is part of a "Gentleman's Club" in the way that Soho strip clubs are given that epithet to exclude the women and to show that there is nothing gentle about the doings inside those walls.

Tony enters the bar and looks around. Gerry doesn't signal to him but just sits staring at the other man until Tony spots him and walks over to the table.

Gerry nods, a barely discernable gesture. "I didn't want to draw attention.." This man really has seen far too many bad movies. Tony sits down, more than willing to become a member of this undercover scene.

"Get some drinks in then."

"Oh right, yes." Tony jumps up again. "What are you having?"

Gerry just looks at him.

Tony fidgets with his wallet. "Beer? Right?"

Again that smallest of nods.

While Tony is at the bar, Gerry runs a thin hand through his cropped fuzz of ginger hair, it's a brutal crew cut and the hairs spring back like wire away from the nicotine-stained fingers. He watches Tony as he brings the drinks back, the beer sloshing at the top of the glasses.

Gerry takes his from Tony quickly to prevent more spillage and downs half the pint in one open throated gulp. Tony is watching Gerry and approves this maleness; he's also a little in awe of him.

"So … how's it going?"

"It takes time."

"Yes, yes, of course."

"It's not like going into a shop."

"No, right, I wasn't meaning to hassle you."

"When's your FDD?"

"What?"

Gerry's rolling another smoke, he looks up at Tony and sighs his boredom at the other man's ignorance. "Final delivery date"

"Oh! right, well, soon as you can really."

"You'll have the cash, sterling, not dollars."

"Absolutely" and Tony's nodding in the manner of a man used to not dealing in dollars.

"Sterling's safer eh?" Tony's rubbing his hands between his thighs, he hasn't felt this good for months.

"Dollars would attract attention"

"Certainly". The sheer nonsense of this exchange escapes Tony, he is too excited by it.

"My, shall we say, friend-of-a-friend prefers it in T's."

"T's?"

And again, the weary patience, as Gerry explains .. "Tens"

"Right, right."

Gerry takes another long pull at his beer. Tony is keen to reclaim their friendship. "You're getting to look like your Dad."

Gerry's looking at him through the bottom of his glass.

Tony rushes on, keen to establish the remembered 'friendship': "Remember him taking us through the fields when we were at St. Vincent's, showing us the signs of the rabbit's burrows?"

"Yeah" - it's not particularly encouraging, but Tony presses on:

"He was great your Dad, real farmer type, he taught you to shoot didn't he? Was that when it started? The interest?"

Gerry puts down his empty glass: "I remember the other kids sneering because he used to pick me up at the gates in all his mud."

Tony can remember this too. "No! – No – I think we all thought it really cool that you had all those animals" .. but it lacks conviction.

"They stopped sniggering when I told them how Dad slaughtered the pigs though, remember that?"

Tony can remember that little "Talk"; Mrs. Garner had asked the boys what they'd done that week-end and Gerry had stood up and delivered a talk of blood and severed-trotter to the Class.

"They stopped calling me shit-shoes after that."

"Yes."

"Our yard was mud up to y'ankles after rain. Nothing you could do about it."

"Of course not."

Gerry looks to sink into remembered umbrage, so Tony reaches across the table and taps his glass. "We should do that again sometime ... go over the fields with a couple of rifles."

Gerry looks across at Tony with thinly veiled contempt. "I don't do that any more. I've got bigger rabbits now."

"Right. How's all that going then?"

"Sorry, can't talk about it."

"No – of course not – shouldn't have asked."

"Mind you, got to keep myself on stand-by, what with all that's going on."

"Absolutely !"

"Have to have all the kit ready, you know…"

"Right."

"… my rifle's under strict lock and key – regulations, you know." Tony's nodding, he doesn't know anything of the sort, but he's keen to be army-savvy.

".. have to clean it regularly, special stuff for it. Can't just use any old cloth…."

Gerry's leaning across the table, a quick look around them to ensure that no eavesdroppers can pick up the information.

"… has to be lint-free, because of the bits of material. Even a microscopic bit of material could foul up the firing mechanism …"

Tony's leaning forward, they're practically nose-to-nose.

"….'Course .. I can't talk about the Other Equipment."

"No. Obviously."

"Let's just say that my garage would surprise you."

"I bet it would."

"Oh yeah – there's more in there than a pair of jump leads, I can tell you."

Gerry leans back, he lights up his roll-up, drawing deeply on the thin and twisted paper. He sucks at the smoke that spirals out of his mouth, squinting his eyes against the stinging haze.

"Yeah – this lot …" he's gesturing to the rest of the pub with a contemptuous flick of ash .. "…this lot would shit themselves if they could have a look in my garage …" and his eyes are filled with a deep pleasure.

"Another drink Gerry?"

"Yeah."

"I've got a Meeting" Tony's looking at his watch in what he believes is a busy executive manner.. "But sod-em, they can wait another twenty minutes."

"What's your ETA?"

Tony's got up to go back to the bar, and just waves a dismissive hand at that; he feels that he's levelling the ground a bit now and so he doesn't like to ask for another translation of Gerry's initial-speak.

Chapter 48

Anna is wearing her silk underwear again, the slippery softness of it rubs against her as she walks. Jonathan is waiting for her at the school gates; she wants to show him her Choir room. It's early evening, only Reg the Caretaker will be around. She can feel a fluttering in her stomach, she hasn't told him why she wants to meet him, he'd been flirty on the phone and told her to wear 'that sexy underwear' again … she'd demurred, but she's wearing it.

Jonathan is sitting in his car looking out at the concrete blocks and the snot-smeared windows of Comprehensive greyness. Anna had been all honey-voiced and suggestive on the phone, and she'd actually giggled when he'd mentioned her knickers, this is not a woman who giggles on a regular basis and he's encouraged; this little game has gone on long enough and just the thought of her stretched out over one of those class-room desks has got him tingling with a sharp lust.

Anna sees his car and waves to him, he watches her; she's wearing one of those pencil skirts that hold her thighs tight, rubbing against each other and he thinks they'll be hot and a little damp. While Anna watches Jonathan's lazy smile and imagines it looking back at her from over the top of the piano.

"Hello Darling," she calls him darling all the time now, it's slightly showbiz, reminding him of their shared talent.

Jonathan hears the word and thinks of bed.

"Now just why do you want me here?"

"I want to show you something", and she's leading him through the gates.

They walk across the car park, there's just a couple of teenagers scuffing sulky trainers against the tarmac as they trail off home from a spell of detention. Reg is coming out of the main school building.

"I was just going to lock the gates now I've winkled those two out, this building's supposed to be cleared by seven."

"That's all right Reg, we haven't brought our cars in. We'll let ourselves out the side gate."

"It's not Monday !"

"No - it's not choir - Karen O.K.'d it."

Reg couldn't really care less, and his loathing for the school secretary was at a record high this week so he could use this as 'Another example of non-communication resulting in possible Fire Hazard' in his weekly whinge to the Head… Stands to reason, if that snotty choir woman lit up a fag and it wasn't a Monday and he wasn't informed, well, there you go!

The idea of Anna indulging in a crafty smoke appeals to Reg who is undeterred by its improbability. Reg is giving Jonathan the once-over and has assigned him to the suited masses of Estate Agents and Insurance Salesmen who are too far above themselves to bother to check that smokes have been extinguished in ashtrays, so the Caretaker trots happily off to his home content in the belief that the school will be burnt out rubble by the morning.

Anna opens the door to the choir room with slow deliberation.
"Here we are," she's slightly breathless.
Jonathan's really hoping that this is not what he thinks.
"This…" and he takes in the NHS curtains, the broken chairs and the overpowering smell of feet ..".. this is your choir room."
Anna can see the place that is hers, totally hers, for those precious hours and she can see only power. Jonathan strolls over to the school piano that has seen years of spilt drinks and casual kickings, there's even a biro smudge on one of the keys: "And this…this is the piano?"
Anna is standing in front of him, she's running her hands up his arms.
"Things can always be improved, once we've got Cheltenham under our belt, there's always Lottery Grants."
Jonathan has slipped his arms around her waist.
"Did you?"
"What?"
"Wear them."
Anna's smirking playfully up at him. "Wear what exactly?"
Jonathan's bending his head to nuzzle her neck. "You know, you witch.."
"Perhaps I don't.."
Jonathan has worked his mouth inside her blouse, and he gives a gurgled "Ye-e-s" of triumph as he bites at the lace of her underwear.
"I always wear these."
"Li-i-a-r," and it's a throaty caress.
Anna is leaning back against the piano to evade him, but Jonathan presses into her, bending her and pushing her ever further.
"Jonathan, I want to talk to you…" she's trying to squirm sideways away from the hot, wet mouth. She's not really alarmed, but this is too quick and too much. He's pushed aside the silk and his lips seek her nipple, his tongue smearing a trail of wet saliva across her breast.

159

Anna does not like the stickiness; her mind slicks to how she will have to soak this camisole tonight, she's thinking about the bubbles of soap that she will squeeze out of the garment.

She's still holding him off, still in control, almost letting this much happen just to be able to call a justifiable halt. Jonathan can feel her control, her assurance that she is setting this pace and he moves quickly to hold her waist hard against him as the other hand reaches up her skirt. Anna is laughing softly but it is the sound that women make when they are cajoling to refuse.

"No.. come on, Jonathan... no ..."

His hand has reached the silk panties, his fingers yanking at the narrow gusset, pulling it aside. Anna's eyes widen with a jolt of panic.

"No!" and she's pulling hard away from him.

Jonathan lets her go, and she falls back against the piano keys, her elbows hit the notes in a discordant clash.

Anna's face reclaims the smile that his hand had wiped away; she doesn't want to lose this, so she reaches out a conciliatory hand to touch his shoulder and is once again the ruthless professional: "Not here...Darling ..."

... putting it off, not actually refusing, not forever, just for now.

Jonathan's face is mottled with hungry red blotches, he's panting and a trail of sweat trickles from his hairline to puddle over an eyebrow.

"Tease..." it's said lightly, but his face betrays his anger.

"Look, Jonathan, I don't play these games" and it's true, Anna has never played this particular game before; she's playing with a fire she doesn't totally understand. She's frazzled by this, but determined to get what she wants.

"Women always say that. I thought you were different, Un-na".

He's got enough self-control to remember to use his special name for her, the game is still on.

Anna is straightening up, the edge of the piano has pressed hard into the small of her back and there'll be a bruise to remind her.

"I am different. I just don't like... sordid"

Jonathan is leaning into her again. "You should try it sometime"

Anna moves swiftly away from him to stand in the middle of the room, where she stands to command the choir, her position, and where she quite literally calls the tune.

"This is the choir room, I know it's not really your style Jonathan, but think of it as a stepping stone."

He's shaking his head, laughing – whether at her or himself is unclear.

"You're priceless, you know that."

She takes it as a compliment.

"I've fired Trevor."

"Oh, that's a surprise", and it is: ".. I didn't realise you'd gone that far."

"But I told you..."

"Yes, but I just thought that, well that it was something you were planning to do in the future," Jonathan's walking round the room, straightening his clothes, pulling his anger back inside.

"I told him on Monday."

"Poor sap."

"He knows that it's you that's taking over."

"I didn't say that I would."

"Please... Darling" and she moves back over to him, she's twisting her fingers around the buttons of his shirt. "Think of it, us two together, there's no limit to what we could achieve."

Jonathan reaches for her again, and she allows him to maul his hands across her breasts. He raises his hands and places them lightly around her neck.

"I could throttle you," he's grinning down at her, teasing.

"What a waste.." she's playing at the game again, smiling with pussy-cat eyes into his, they're cooler and darker still with the anger at her rejection, but the chase is still interesting him, for now.

Jonathan is looking at her, weighing up options and desire, and compromises and opportunities; and the pull of her, the pull of the sex wins.

"I'll do it just once, this Monday, just to see how it goes."

Anna is trying very hard not to look her triumph.

"Good. that's .... that's a good idea. See how you feel."

"Seal it then, seal it with a kiss."

He's standing back, making her come to him, making her begin the embrace.

She almost saunters over to put her arms around his neck; she pulls his face down onto hers.

The kiss is long and deep; Jonathan's tongue sliding around inside her mouth and Anna thinks of the spearmint mouthwash that stands on the white marble-effect sink unit in her en-suite, of the turquoise liquid rinsing all this away.

161

Jonathan finally ends the kiss. Anna can still taste his spittle on her lips and wills herself not to swallow until she can wipe it away.

"A deal then."

"A deal." She's still holding her mouth open and he puts a finger onto her lip, moving it along the length of her mouth, rubbing in the wetness.

Anna does not move away, she's still smiling at him.

Jonathan moves away, keen now to be gone.

"Right - Monday then. I'd better go."

"Yes."

He's taking a final look around the room.

"Well, I'll know where to come," and he's gone.

Anna only then allows her hand to reach up to her mouth.

Her lips have dried but she rubs at them. She moves back over to the piano and catches her reflection in the laminated wood. She looks at the face she sees there and there's an uncomfortable niggling awareness that she has paid a Price for this, a sensation that's creeping into her that she has paid a high and certain price, and as she walks slowly to the door and looks back into the choir room, she's not sure that it's the right price.

Anna reaches her home and looks up at the lighted windows with the curtains looped back with their brocade ties. The front door hushes against the deep carpet as she enters the hallway, and she is welcomed by this week's favourite air-scent, the sweet vapour of peach and jasmine.

"Roy!" she's calling upstairs, and there's the sound of her husband dropping something and the subsequent muffled exclamation.

"Roy, what are you doing?"

"Nothing," said quickly, too quickly. "Coming !"

"No – I'm coming up." Anna is keen to get to her bathroom, to the freshness of that turquoise liquid.

Roy and Anna cannon into each other at the top of the stairs. Roy's breathing rather heavily.

"Roy! – your breath smells of onions!"

"Does it?" He's closed his mouth and is breathing through his nose, dragging in the air with noisy catarrhal gusts. Anna has placed her nose to his mouth.

"Breathe."

"I am," through rather clenched teeth.

"Breathe, Roy!"

Roy opens his mouth and a blast of Mediterranean tomatoes and onions floats warmly into Anna's discerning nostrils. Anna just looks at him.

"Oh Roy."

"Sorry."

"No you're not. I try and try to help you. All those snippets I cut out of the Sunday supplements, all those slimming meals in the fridge. The low-fat spreads, the 'lite' mayonnaise … and what do you do ..?"

Roy's nodding.

"You don't help yourself, that's the problem."

"I know Dear."

Anna goes into the en-suite and Roy stands and listens to hear her nagging him and gargling with mouthwash, it's a watery jumble of complaint interspersed with an occasional spitting:

"I recorded that video for you about 'Digging your Grave with your Teaspoon'…*(gargle)*.. that got you off sugar, didn't it…*(spit)*.. And you like that new sweetener that doesn't have the acid after taste…*(gargle)* ..well now you're at the pizza again, and don't tell me it was the low-fat one I got from Sainsbury's ..*(spit)*.... you haven't touched their 'Looking after yourself' range, I know because I checked the freezer……"

Anna is feeling better, on safer ground berating Roy for his secret eating, rinsing Jonathan out of her mouth. Washing him out of her mind for now; she'll think about all that tomorrow, but tonight she's back with the comfortable and familiar attrition of her marriage.

Roy's standing there, letting the flow of it wash over him, and he's miles away; under an olive tree with a girl with black hair that curls all over her face and the taste of soft buttery cheese in his mouth.

Chapter 49

Trevor is on the phone, in front of him, balanced on his piano's music stand, is the Choir Contacts List.

"It's just that I think that the Choir, as a whole, should be making this decision."

On the other end of the line is Susie, gloriously bolshie red-haired Susie, she's full of republican zeal and power-to-the-people, as opposed to Anna's autocratic behaviour – Susie is very big on Anna's 'Nazi Tendencies' – which Trevor, always trying to be fair minded where Anna is concerned, finds a little harsh. Never mind, he's found his Champion.

His second phone call is to Rowena and is equally satisfying:

"I'm sorry, Trevor, but I just cannot forgive her traitorous behaviour vis-à-vis the drumming."

"So you'd come along to my special meeting then?"

"Absolutely .. Anna won't be actually there in person will she?"

"No, no. I'm sorry it's got to be in the 'Corn Café' but my house isn't really suitable for larger gatherings."

Trevor is ticking off the Contacts List, Susie will bring Grace, and Paulette's always offering to do extra duties so he'll ask her to do the 'Minutes' – best to make this official.

Trevor looks round at his sitting room. Pity he couldn't have had the meeting here, really, but the thought of all those women sitting around and looking at his furniture is too daunting a prospect. Anyway, he's telling himself that he doesn't have enough mugs and he's not getting out Mothers 'Crown Derby' tea set.... Trevor only just stops himself from following this line; with all the memories of asking the Church League how many sugars they wanted, and trying to remember who wanted milk, and his getting it wrong, and Mother's face....No, let it lie.

The Corn Café will do nicely; he knows that Anna thinks it rather a common little place where that builder with all the tattoos goes; she prefers the new stainless steel and mirrors cappuccino bar in the high street, so she's unlikely to drop in and catch them all.

Paulette is in a moral quandary; she's just put the phone down after talking to Trevor. Her dog, a runny-eyed spaniel called Harvey, is gazing up at her.

He's on the cadge for biscuits, simply because this is the animal's chosen career and a fact that should be very well known to his owner. Unfortunately Paulette in common with most devoted owners believes that the animal is emotionally involved with her every mood and reads empathy in those blood-shot eyes.

"I know, Harvey, I know. This is when we wish that Chris was here, don't we?" Believing these words to herald the arrival of a digestive, Harvey wags an understanding tail.

"Oh, bless you. Should I ring Linda? – Well I've told you how she's the main one – solo wise – so she should be in-on-the-know with this shouldn't she?" Harvey's salivating and licks his lips.

"Yes! – clever dog!" and, much to Harvey's profound disappointment, Paulette returns to her telephone.

Harvey yawns hugely and tries staring particularly hard at his owner's face, he's also employing his head-on-one-side technique that has proved successful in the past, but to no avail, the woman's talking, but she's not talking to him.

"Linda? It's Paulette.. has Trevor rung you?"
Paulette's nodding as the other woman speaks.

"It's just, well, frankly I feel this is all a bit under-hand, don't you? and it smells of Plotting to me... Oh? ...... She's agreed to give you singing lessons? – well there you are, we're piggy in the middle aren't we, caught in the cross-fire."

Paulette has now sat down on the little stool by the telephone, and Harvey has seen this all this before. He'll have to give up biscuit-begging, just for now, anyway there's an interesting smell behind the sofa he should attend to.

The result of this heart-searching is that half an hour later Paulette, accompanied by a reluctant Harvey, is standing at Anna's front door.

Anna has peered through her spy-hole and seen Paulette's anxious little face and is anticipating more offers of unnecessary help when she opens the door.

Harvey, safely below the level of the eyehole, is an unwelcome surprise to Anna who has instantly recognised in the hound a tendency to dribble.

Paulette's straight in with her excuse. "Sorry, but I always take Harvey on this route for his walks.." This is news to Harvey, who is not actually terribly fond of 'walks', preferring sitting or sleeping should he be given the choice.

Paulette's registered Anna's look at Harvey. "Oh his paws are very clean …"

Anna is reluctant to admit the dubiously spotless paws onto her cream carpets, so compromises with a gesture toward her kitchen.

"Come and have a coffee Paulette" and she leads her visitors through onto the 'genuine' quarry tiles.

Paulette sits down at the kitchen table; she holds her hand toward her dog, palm-facing him, then slowly lowers the hand to the horizontal.

"Sit, Harvey!"

Harvey allows his tongue to loll out of the side of his mouth which could be interpreted as a smile, and remains resolutely standing.

"He's not very obedient is he?" Anna's looking at the dog.

"Oh Dear – I'm afraid we had to interrupt his puppy training regime at the Centre, he had a snuffly nose you see, and he's never really regained the lost ground."

"You should be firmer with him." Anna's frowning, noticing a fine trail of drool appearing from the animal's jaws. Harvey's not that fond of Anna either and treats her to a yawn of spectacular boredom.

Paulette's shifting uneasily on the antique-effect pine chair.

"The thing is, Anna, Linda and I are rather uneasy about the latest development choir-wise."

Anna's all ears now, her back prickling with unease. "The addition of a new drummer should…"

"Oh no – not that – well, I suppose there *is* that, in that it's part and parcel of the 'Changes' that we feel are happening, and now that Trevor has called this special meeting…"

Anna has spun round at that, startling Harvey who is betrayed into something very like a bark. Harvey does not bark, as a rule, finding the effort never really worth the result in that Barking does not ever result in Biscuits.

"Is that dog savage?" Anna's jumped at the noise.
Paulette is as surprised as Anna. "He never barks normally"
Harvey, however, is quite pleased to be thought of as savage and is pondering taking up this barking thing more often.

Anna's passing Paulette her mug of coffee, keeping a wary leg away from the animal's biting end.

Harvey is enjoying this new sensation of being dangerous, and follows Anna's ankle with his muzzle.

"What special meeting?"

"Oh dear, I really don't want to cause any friction, I'm very fond of Trevor as you know, well, we all are, but ..."

"Yes, yes I know, but what's this about a meeting?"

"But as Linda pointed out, our loyalty is being torn asunder!"

"What Meeting !?"

Anna's almost shouting, and Harvey's considering practising his barking again. Paulette takes a deep breath and blurts it all out in a rush. "Trevor's called one, it's about him being fired as the accompanist, he thinks it should be a Choir decision, that we should have been consulted and that there should have been a Vote."

"Oh does he, does he really."

It's not a question, and Paulette should have heard the danger in Anna's voice.

"Oh yes, really, Anna."

"And when and where is this Rebellion to take place?"

"I don't know. I think some of the others know; only I said that I couldn't make Wednesday because of Harvey's vaccination," and she's 'mouthing' the word vaccination so as to avoid distressing her pet.

"So it's Wednesday."

Anna turns back to look out of her kitchen window, she's thinking strategies.

Paulette is so guilty at having given away the day that she launches into a self-justifying tirade.

"The thing is I would normally have talked this all over with Chris. That's the big thing about having a husband who works away; you don't get all the what-did-you-do-today stuff. You see by the time I'm standing at Heathrow waiting for him to come through customs all I can think about is will he notice that I've lost the weight and I mustn't start telling him about how the dishwasher's on the blink, well not until we've got past the M25, but most of all I'm standing there thinking will he actually come through that door at all because I'm always convinced he'll have had a heart attack on the plane.

"I never really worry about him when he's out there, Puerto Rico you know, but I always think that he'll be Almost Here...only a half an hour away from saying hello, and that that's when he'll die. The last minute irony of it; I can imagine it in the Witsham Gazette: the - 'local man dies just as he was about to fall into his wife's greeting arms' – headline. Chris says I'm morbid, well, that's why we got the dog you see. But then, that's why I can't go out there all the time and be with him."

Paulette reaches down to fondle Harvey as an apology for blaming him for tearing her and Chris apart. Harvey is unconcerned by marital separations and believes the affection to herald the possibility of a bourbon. Anna looks the kind of woman who has those chocolate cream biscuits in her barrel and he is smug in his confidence that Paulette will procure one for him.

Anna wants rid of them both, she can't think with that woman wittering on, and that animal has started moving about, and there's another trail of dribble beginning its journey to Anna's floors. She'll have to have a mop round with the Dettol as it is.

"Paulette, I'm really sorry about your husband's heart condition, but ...." she's looking at her watch.

Paulette's getting up and getting even more flustered.

"No, well not yet he hasn't, I'm sure he hasn't really, I was just saying that when you live alone you tend to run things over more in your mind. I don't want you to think that I'm one of those interfering busy-bodies.."

"No, no not at all" .. and Anna, looking at the fretful eyes and the trails of hair that are wet with chewing, realises that Paulette could be quite useful as her spy. "I'm just so glad that you felt able to come and talk to me about this. Now if ever you feel that you are uncomfortable with anything that's taking place in the choir that I may not be aware of ... you see I can't have my ear to the ground all the time, and it's so important for me to know the 'pulse' of the group..."

So Paulette has employment at last.

"Yes ! – I could be your ears and eyes within the choir .. in a strictly positive way of course."

"Of course."

"I could let you know the mood of the others, especially regarding any new pieces that are not proving popular, or maybe a member who'd like to have a solo but is too nervous to actually ask for one..."

"That's the ticket," Anna's leading her visitors to the door.

"Chris is forever saying that I should get a job."

Anna's opening the door, aware that Harvey's blood-rimmed eyes have not left her ankle. "Has he ever actually bitten anybody?"

"No! Not my Harvey!"

Harvey smirks at this testimonial but thinks that people who have bourbons to spare and don't offer this hospitality deserve all the teeth marks they get.

"Don't forget, Paulette, I need to be kept up to speed about this meeting of Trevor's, who goes to it and what's said ... I'm sure that Harvey's vaccination could be done at another time."

Harvey has heard that word, that word usually goes along with the Vet's word and a lot of unpleasantness standing on a table.

He's not having any of that, so as Anna closes the door none too gently on her guests, he treats himself to an extensive, hot and steamy piss against her porch.

Paulette's too excited about her new assignment to pull him away and Harvey is particularly pleased with the length of the yellow stream that runs down the path and is now pooling in the gutter.

On the other side of the door, Anna's face is working with fury.
She cannot believe that Trevor has dared to do this.
It is Her Choir. She started it, she got Roy to put all those adverts in the paper that got the whole thing going, she did all the negotiating with the school for the room, she chooses all the music. All Trevor ever did was to hand out a few leaflets. This choir is everything, it's her passport to Festivals, to Competitions, to Concerts with their local MP in the audience…. And Cheltenham!

Why don't they understand, they can't do Cheltenham with Trevor! She's been coaching them and bringing them up to standard for years. *They* cannot do this, ganging up against her.

Everybody lets her down, they always have, and now Trevor.
Roy has always let her down; it has been her efforts that have dragged them up to their position in this town. He's not even trying for Mayor now, spends his time mooning about upstairs in his little office smelling of onions.
It's always been the same, everything she has achieved she has had to do for herself, it is all down to her that the choir now has Jonathan.
A classical pianist, an Oxford pianist, he will give the choir class and she is doing this for the Choir – her choir. She has to raise standards and that's why she has had to get Jonathan on board.
A vote on it – they want a vote on it !
They don't know the difference that Jonathan will make.

She can't show Aunt Jo that she's a success, she can't prove to Miss Etch that she was wrong - that she should have listened to her that day - she can't heal all those sharp little cuts without Jonathan.

Anna is pacing up and down her hallway, she is quite demented with anger. Her ambition has carried her all her life, it has borne her along, keeping her hopes high; ambition has promised her everything just as long as she keeps on pushing and planning. Without this hunger, this hunger for more, for better, without this she cannot Be Anna, and if she once turns round and looks at the shadows behind her she will be lost.

That Choir holds her ambition and her hunger; she cannot lose control of the Choir. They know nothing; they don't know what she's done for them.

They don't know what she would do for them, and she is thinking about Jonathan, and the Price.

Chapter 50

Lindsay is preparing lunch for herself, washing a lettuce in the sink.

Her bandage is getting soaked and she unwraps it, taking it off. She doesn't need that anymore; the line of scabs across her finger joints have hardened crisply red, and the bruising is at last beginning to fade.

Tony has another one of his Lunch Meetings today, he'd seemed very excited about it, and Lindsay was glad that he was getting on better at work; all that silly business of the other men talking behind his back seems to be over, he hadn't mentioned it for a couple of weeks now. She didn't understand Office Politics, he'd told her that it was all cut and thrust and favouritism. Lindsay's knowledge of office work is limited to the eighteen months she'd worked at Electro-Sell before she met Tony. She'd never really got on top of it; the woman who'd had the job before hadn't left any information as to how things had been done or where anything had been filed and the computer had been wiped clean of any templates or examples of letters that had been sent.

Lindsay had been told that the previous occupant of her typist's chair had left under 'somewhat of a cloud' (excessive quantities of stationery being taken home apparently) and it was clear that the woman's revenge had been to ensure that her successor's role would be to show just how indispensable the woman had been; in this she succeeded beyond her dreams, Lindsay, never the boldest of souls, had been totally overwhelmed by the impossibility of ever completing her daily tasks. No-one in the office seemed willing or able to help her, whether out of a misplaced loyalty to her predecessor or simply that they would themselves shine in comparison to the newcomer, was never really clear. Lindsay had not managed to endear herself to the other women – her rather stilted shyness being taken for snobbery.

Tony had saved her from all that, that evening when he had come round to her parents house and found her typing the office letters at home in a vain attempt to catch up. So he had encouraged her to leave the world of letters that detailed electronic widgets and memos that complained of delivery dates, and all that she had misunderstood or misheard and that had caused such a fiasco in the delivery yard. Lindsay still shudders at the memory of her inept muddling, and even today will find detours so as not to pass Electro-Sell's office. So she had backed away from the world of work, feeling safer at home with Tony. He'd told her she didn't need to work, and she had believed him. He'd told her she was too sensitive to be a hard-nosed career woman, and she was too pleased to be taken care of to question this. She had proved, hadn't she, that she couldn't cope in an office; and her qualifications, such as they were, were geared to that world and did not encourage any thoughts of an alternative.

She had assumed that she'd get pregnant soon, anyway, so what was the point of getting started at something else. The looked-for pregnancy did not come. Tony had been marvellous about it, telling her that they were fine as they were and that he did not blame her. Sometimes she had wondered about the sort of sex they had and whether the endless stroking should lead to something more.

Tony always said he didn't want to hurt her, and just lately all he wanted her to do was rub at him, but when she watched that milky flow dribble out onto the sheets she did sometimes wish that it could have a more profitable home.

The front door slams and Lindsay finds that she is holding her breath.

"Lindsay!" it's Tony and he's shouting.

Lindsay bundles up the discarded bandaging and puts it into the bin, then she pushes it down under the rubbish, placing the discarded outer leaves of the lettuce on the top.

Tony comes into the kitchen: "Oh you're here, didn't you hear me?"

"I thought you had a Meeting?"

"Bastard didn't turn up did he."

"Oh – do you want some lunch? I was just preparing a ..."

"I drive all the way there, I've organised everything my end and he doesn't show. Thirty-three minutes I've sat in that filthy pub."

Tony's pouring himself a glass of water, leaning across her to get to the tap.

Lindsay's still at the sink, she's breaking the lettuce into quarters.

Tony leaves the tap on, it's pouring full blast into the sink and the water is splashing all over Lindsay.

"Tony!"

"What?" He's gulping at the water, pouring it down his throat in a quick and desperate need.

"You were thirsty"

"Yes" and he's panting.

Lindsay's placing the lettuce onto a plate on the working surface.

"Shall I get you another plate?"

"Er, well just do me a sandwich, I've got to get back to work."

"Tony .. why do they have work meetings in a pub?"

"What?"

"You said it was a filthy pub."

Tony looks across at her.

"This isn't like you."

"What do you mean?"

"Questioning me."

"I just wondered, that's all, only you're always going on about that new meeting room they've got with the bottles of mineral water and the free biros…"

"Look I only brought those home for you, a souvenir, because they'd got the Department's name down the side."

"Perhaps you shouldn't have – people get fired for taking biros home."

"What's got into you? Don't tell me how to behave in my Office, you don't know anything about it."

Lindsay has moved around the other side of the working surface, she's getting another plate out of a cupboard and is telling herself that is why she has wanted to move away. He's watching her: "Have you had one of those choir women round, that .. Daphne wasn't it?"

"Diane. No. I'm just here on my own. That's it really. Tony, I've been thinking, and, well, I think…" but then she catches his eye … "Do *you* think that I should get a job?"

"Where the hell's *this* come from?"

"Well everybody else has jobs, don't they. Susie works at Citizens Advice, Grace works at the Council Offices, Linda …"

"Who are all these people?"

"Just the Choir."

She's buttering bread for his sandwich. "Do you want ham or cheese?"

"What?"

"Your sandwich."

Tony's distracted; today has not gone to plan and now this.

"Ham … no, cheese. Look, what's all this about?"

"Nothing really, I was just thinking, that's all."

Lindsay's about to place some of the lettuce onto his sandwich, and Tony reaches across her to snatch it out of her hand.

"Not lettuce ! – not with cheese, I like pickle with cheese, you know that."

Lindsay looks up at him, still holding the lettuce over his sandwich.

"Well, you sometimes…."

Tony, suddenly and viciously, knocks her arm away and the lettuce flies out of her hand and onto the floor.

"You hit me." Lindsay's voice is a dry, flat sound.

"No I didn't, I just knocked your arm." He's irritated but weary casual.

"You hit me." It's as if she is trying out the words.

He's carefully enunciating. "I did not hit you Lindsay, I pushed away your arm because you were about to put lettuce on my sandwich."

"You... hit... my... arm." she's trying to place the words into reality.

Tony is round the work-surface, he's almost running, and he's up beside her.

"No.... *That's* a hit !" and he slaps her across her shoulders.

He runs out of the kitchen and into the hallway, he's ranting as he goes:

"All the questions, questions ..."

Then he's impersonating her in a whining squeaky voice ".. *'Why am I having Meetings? Where am I having Meetings?'* and then it's *'I'm going to get a Job.' .."*

Lindsay can only seem to focus upon the injustice of his mimicry:

"I don't speak like that."

The door slams in response.

He has done it; he has actually hit her. This time it is real, his hand has touched her body. Now she knows.

This was not a mistake. This was not a car door, this was not an accident.

There is no way back from this, she can no longer pretend.

He has hit her.

Chapter 51

Diane walks through the Health Centre doors, it's not *her* Health Centre, it's where that woman works. Paul's woman. The woman he has left her for.

Diane is not really sure what she is doing here; she had woken up with an absolute intention of putting Paul and his new woman out of her mind and her life, she had decided to move to Cornwall. She'd even rung the Tourist Board and sent for their "Welcome to the South West" package, and she had come into the town to go to the travel agents because they probably had leaflets or a brochure she could look through in the meantime. She couldn't live with this permanent sore, this enduring and painful scratching at her; everywhere she looked, every day. She wanted to exorcise him and That Woman.

Standing outside the Travel Agents she'd read the sign in the window "Run Away to Paradise" and it was a picture of white sand and blue sea and palm trees. Run Away, that was it, that was what she was doing, what he was making her do. She'd turned round and had walked straight along the high street and turned into the road leading here, without consciously intending it, only her feet had known and they had brought her right up to the Receptionist's Desk.

This Desk didn't have the airport check-in and plastic barriers, this Health Centre had opted for the Hi-Tech touch-screen approach.

There was a large sign above the computer screen: *"Please tap the screen and follow the instructions."*

Diane didn't really feel that they'd have instructions for "coming to have a snoop at my ex-husbands new girlfriend", but there seemed to be no alternative to this procedure.

The screen displays two lozenges: *"Male"* or *"Female"*

Diane obediently taps the screen over the Female, the screen flashes at her and then demands that she type in her date of birth. There was a panel of numbers beneath the screen, so Diane puts in her date of birth, feeling more and more foolish.

The Receptionist's Desk is deserted, but a small room can be glimpsed behind the desk. Three women are sitting looking at computer screens and catching Diane's eye, the elder one (who cannot possibly be That Woman) points to the screen and 'mouths' hugely: "You have to use the screen dear, you can't get to the desk until you've filled in your particulars."

The particulars being demanded of the screen now are Diane's postcode and National Insurance Number.

Who the hell knows their National Insurance Number?

There is no graphic to tap to indicate that Diane does not know this number and, when she presses the "Next" button to move onto the next graphic, the screen tells her that she has not filled in her correct National Insurance Number. Diane has, of course, not filled in *any* number.

She's beginning to feel hot, and her chest is tightening; but she doesn't want to stand here and use her inhaler, not now. God Almighty she just wanted to pop in, see The Woman and go. There is a small queue building up behind Diane, the man right behind her is leaning forward to read the screen: "You need to put your National Insurance Number in love."

"Yes, thank you, I know."

He's watching her, and she's just standing there, practising breathing.

"You press those buttons, like at the Bank."

"I know .. I don't know my number."

"Oh well, there you are,"... and he turns back to the woman behind him to helpfully pass on the news. "She doesn't know her number you see."

The woman behind the man in the queue reaches across to Diane to poke her none too gently in the back. "I keep mine in my glasses case now, we all have to be vigilant don't we, they were telling us last night that we can't go back to being 'Complacent' yet, we're still on 'Threat Level : Severe' .."

The man is joining in again: "Is that higher than 'Threat Level: Critical'? "

The woman's putting him right.

"No it's like the difference between an attack being 'Imminent' rather than 'Highly Likely' – it was on 'NationWatch' – they went live to the Joint Terrorism Analysis Centre."

The man's nodding: "JTAC."

"I think it's marvellous that we're so informed."

Diane is quietly losing the will to live.

The entire queue are now happily exchanging Terror Scares and Airport Searches amongst themselves, so Diane steps away from the screen and moves over to the rack of 'Are You Diabetic?' leaflets.

Her breathing has eased, that feeling of being strangled from inside now cooling to a throaty rasp on the in-breath.

A door opens further along the corridor and a young woman comes out into the reception area. She's carrying a pile of folders and they are resting on the top of her stomach. The woman is behind the desk, shielded by that great wooden façade that protects the staff from the patients and Diane cannot see the pregnancy, that gently curving oval carried with smiling unconcern, she just sees the dark curls bouncing prettily around the young face...yes, young.... probably not much more than twenty.

A telephone is ringing somewhere in another room.
It's answered, and another voice is calling: "Sarah .... Sarah."
The woman turns, and Diane does not need to be told that this is the one. She does not need to hear the confirmation ringing across reception.
"Sarah ... Paul's on the phone."

Diane is out on the street, her feet have taken over again and she is walking stiffly away; but she has to stop a couple of times, just to bend over, doubling at the waist, just to vomit into the grass verge beside the gutter.

Chapter 52

The Corn Café is in the rougher part of the town. The older residents like it: The coffee isn't nearly all froth but comes in cups and saucers and is dark brown with a little metal jug on the side if you fancy more milk; there are china cruet sets with flowers on them, and lardy cake on the menu. The walls are lined with paintings of kittens and bowls of fruit by local artists, and the waitresses have been there for years and call you 'dear' and wear aprons with a frill round the edge.

Trevor is sitting with his back to the windows and has commandeered a large table. It's six o'clock, the Café stays open until seven to catch the builders wanting a quick fry-up before they head for the boozer; they've got an hour. Susie and Grace are going to come straight from work, Linda he's not sure of, he'd had to listen to rather a long preamble on the phone comprising mainly of 'loyalty to Anna', singing lessons, and not wanting to take sides.

Trevor had watched Linda wangle herself all the solos last year, and heard her "Oh yes Anna"s whenever her choir mistress had asked the choir if they'd enjoyed a certain piece, so he was not hopeful. He's surprised that Diane's the first to arrive, she's usually sitting in the car park or revving herself up in the corridor for twenty minutes before she puts in any appearance. Diane practically stomps into the Café, throws her handbag down on the floor and hurls herself into the seat opposite Trevor. He looks at her, at the flushed face and the bursting-with-it attitude. Oh God, some female problem, please may this precious hour not be women telling other women about what-the-doctor-said and how shit men are.

"She's Twenty!"

"Oh." .. He was right.

"Can you believe it, all those years of sniggering at menopausal men opting for the Mark Two Younger Wife, all that 'We share a common history' bollocks."

Trevor's nodding, looking over at the door, praying for rescue.

"It's just the lying, you know," and Diane gets up again and marches off to the door.

"Diane." – Trevor's holding her handbag up to show her that she's left it behind.

Diane opens the Café door .."I'm coming back!" .. and slams it behind her.

"Right-oh." Trevor's talking to the cruet set. This table has got the poppies and barley stalks for the salt and the bluebell spray for the pepper. Trevor looks across at the next table. The salt next door is the bluebells, and there's a poppies and barley pepper on the table by the window; Trevor gets up and swaps all the cruet sets around to complete matching sets. The waitress, a lady of some sixty summers and one who had thought that she had seen it all, is watching him. There are little stainless-steel baskets on the tables housing the other condiments; Trevor's picking up the tomato ketchup dispenser that's alongside the vinegar and the mustard. The waitress foresees more interfering: "The vinegar's aren't meant to match." Thus stilled in his fussing, Trevor is reduced to looking at the paintings round the walls and wondering why all the puppies-and-children ones have the most ornate brass frames.

"Has she gone then?"

"No she'll be back. There's others coming too."

The waitress shrugs: "So you say."

Trevor is trying to work out if this is an insult or a statement of fact when the door opens and Lindsay comes in. Trevor's heart sinks as he looks at her. Oh God, she looks even worse. Lindsay comes over to the table and sits down. The waitress swoops, scenting an 'order' at last.

"I thought we'd just have a couple of pots of tea and lots of cups, if that's all right?" Trevor's smiling at the waitress.

"How many for then?"

"Let's start with one pot and four cups, shall we?"

The waitress sighs heavily and he feels that he has let her down.

"Am I the first?" Lindsay's clasping and unclasping the clip on the handbag that's on her lap.

"Diane popped in, and then out again, said she was coming back though."

"Oh .. good."

Trevor, confronted by the white face and the restless hands, feels that he has to say it: "Are you all right?"

Lindsay smiles at him with her mouth, her eyes are just blank.

"Oh .. yes…thank you Trevor."

It's the 'thank you' that gets him.

"Only you look…" He shrugs, unable to tell her "… and the other week, in the car park after choir, I thought that you were… upset." He's aware that the word is inadequate, and she smiles at him, a sad and weary ghost of a smile.

He doesn't mean to do it, but he reaches out to touch the fingers that are gripping the handbag so tightly.

"I'm sorry," .. he says it with great tenderness "I'm really sorry."

179

Susie and Grace are entering the Café, spot the moment and give each other a Look. "Sorry if we're late, it was my fault, there's always some Wally coming in at five-thirty with a whole life-story of intimidation."

Grace's staunch in her support: "You should just say 'Tomorrow' before they start on the he-said, she-said routine. We do it all the time at the Council, you've got to be firm or they walk all over you."

They've both now joined the table.

Lindsay is rummaging in her handbag for something and Trevor's trying very hard not to look at her.

Jo-Anne arrives at the table, all breathless and on-the-chase:

"Has Diane been in? "

"Yes, but she went off again."

"Oh No – I've got to find her!"

The waitress has returned with the teas and almost collides with Jo-Anne as she goes out again.

"They come and they go, don't they," she's looking accusingly at Trevor.

Rowena arrives with Diane behind her, and there's a jumble of 'hello's as the women sit down.

Diane's looking round the group: "Has Jo-Anne been in?"

The waitress turns to her. "I think she's just left dear."

Trevor glares at the waitress as Diane goes back to look out of the Café window. "I think I know where she's gone, she thinks I'm there you see because of my text .. I'll just go and get her." and Diane goes out again.

This is giving the waitress unending pleasure and she treats herself by giving Trevor a quizzical look.

Trevor attempts to gain control of this meeting. "Thank you everybody for turning up, I've had a list of apologies from other members of the choir."

Susie's sneering: "Cowards" and there's general agreement from the others.

"I know that I have explained on the phone the situation, thing is I just felt that this was a matter for the choir as a whole."

Susie, the self-appointed chorus is chiming in again: "And not just Anna being power mad."

Grace's nodding "Absolutely. Trevor, we think it's awful you being just booted out like this, after all you've done for us."

Rowena's nodding. "So what's your plan?"

Trevor had rather hoped that this *was* the plan, the meeting, but sees that more is expected of him.

"Aah. Before I tell you my ideas I wondered if you had any thoughts at all ..?" Trevor is pleased with this; it's what Mr. Gillespie used to do at all those Departmental Meetings for 'Efficiency in Communication Skills Across Specialisms.'

Susie's rising to the challenge. "We should go on strike!"

Grace's nodding. "That'll show Her."

Rowena is adding her own personal grievance into the mix. "And we should boycott that Tony and his Pop-Group drumming. It's totally inappropriate."

Trevor watches how Lindsay's eyes seek the windows of the café, and he thinks of a sparrow trapped in a room looking toward the light of escape.

He's quick to protect her. "Rowena I really do think we should keep this action to the main issue, and it is rather unfair on Lindsay isn't it"

"I'm sorry, Lindsay, but it's how I feel" ... Rowena leans back, her shoulders giving a self-justified wiggle... "Anyway, this is the main issue as far as I'm concerned. I'm being fired too you know."

Susie's passing her the milk jug. "Hardly."

Trevor doesn't want to lose a supporter "Look, if I can get back into the Choir then I'll have a word about the drumming." He catches Lindsay's quick glance. "Do you want Tony in the Choir?"

The women all turn to look at Lindsay.

"No" and she takes a shuddering breath "No, I don't."

"Good girl!" Susie's clapping Lindsay on the back "The Choir's *your* thing, you don't want him muscling in on it."

Trevor watches the indecision and doubt flicker across Lindsay's face, she looks across at him and the uncertainty and trepidation in his own face meets and melds with hers, and there is a comfort in this exchange, and for both of them a Recognition.

Susie and Grace are well into Greenham Common tactics; there is much talk of lying down in front of the entrance to the choir room and Banners. Trevor is beginning to feel that the carpet is slipping slowly away from his feet and is relieved to see Diane and Jo-Anne come back into the café, their arms linked in that women-together-against-the-odds sort of way that both irritates him and ignites a kind of jealousy.

Jo-Anne is settling Diane into a chair and pouring her a cup of tea with a possessive consideration that demands the respect and attention of the rest of the group. Diane is slightly uncomfortable with this, but grateful for the care.

There are concerned murmurs from the others around the table: "Are you all right, Diane? "

Jo-Anne, the self-nominated carer, replies for her: "She's had a terrible shock."

Susie is ever practical. "Shall I drive her home?"

"She wants to attend this meeting" Jo-Anne's self-importance is growing as she bends to peer into Diane's face "Don't you, dear?"

"Please, please ignore me. I'm fine."

Trevor thinks there is fat chance of this as he watches Jo-Anne straighten up, and wait for the group's full attention before announcing:

"It's Paul" and she mouths 'Paul' to prevent it being overheard by unseen watchers.

There are nods of total comprehension from the table.

Lindsay gives Trevor a small, rueful smile.

Trevor leans over to her "Well at least it's stopped the Militant Two"

Jo-Anne is not letting go of her moment. "Diane doesn't want to talk about it, she's told me Everything of course, but I don't think it's going to help her for this to be *common* knowledge."

The word *common* seems to involve all but herself, and manages of course, at one stroke, to alienate the entire sympathy of the table.

Diane wants to divert this attention. "Trevor, what is it that you want us to do?"

"We could all offer to leave!" Rowena's mind is still firmly fixed.. "Unless Anna re-instates Trevor and fires Tony."

"Why don't we just all write to Anna, expressing our concern and distress at losing Trevor."

The blinding sense of Lindsay's suggestion stills the table into silence.

"What a very good idea." Trevor's beaming at her.

This seems to signal the end of the meeting, Trevor is trying to remember how Gillespie ended the Gas Board Awayday's:

"Thank you everybody, I think we've tossed around some

Ideas in Action and Shared Knowledge and that we can all Take-Away some Innovative Information Sharing."

Lindsay's got out her purse and is uncertain of the bill-paying protocol at meetings.

"No, no, this is on me. I called this meeting." Trevor's peeling a note from his small leather purse. "I think we've established a Core Purpose today."

Lindsay is looking at the purse, and remembering what Tony says about men with purses; she looks at Trevor's soft, bumbling fingers as they fiddle with the little zip and at the way that the notes have been neatly folded in order of monetary value, and she feels that perhaps there is a safety in such a man.

As they leave, Susie is still regretting the loss of Direct Action.
"I still think a small demonstration outside the school gates would hammer the point home; Stephen's got loads of placards we could use." Grace's agreeing: "...and we could have looped chains around the piano ... Music in Manacles."
"Could have got it into the Witsham Gazette with that."
"I could have brought my drum, we did the 'Beat of Revolution' at that drumming workshop."
Susie's not convinced. "I think that's more Africa, Rowena."

Jo-Anne wants to prolong her best-friend evening and is keen to get Diane back to her house: "It's all right, Mike's taking his parents back to Huddersfield, he won't be back till after eleven; his mother always wants him to stay so that they can have a proper de-brief about what a terrible wife I am, I tell you, I shall be paying for that burnt quiche when I'm sixty."

Diane is beginning to question the benefits of this friendship but is too shattered by the day's events to resist the temptation to Tell-All to a sympathetic ear. She doesn't think that she can face her flat, even though she has left Radio-2 on so that she won't walk in to silence.

Trevor's paid the bill and endured the waitress's witty comments regarding the varying number of his 'harem' and then he's so caught up folding away the fiver that he's got in his change that he misses Lindsay leave the café.
He watches her as she flits past the window and thinks again of sparrows.

Chapter 53

Lindsay puts her key in her front door and pauses; she's just standing there, with her hand on her keys, looking up at the lock. She has come home because she does not know where else to go. She had gone to that meeting because it was somewhere else to be, a justifiable absence from this home that now feels so different.

The front door looks the same, the geraniums that Tony had planted in the pots by the door are the same... and then she notices that he has watered them; the wetness still stains the stone and there are drops on the leaves; small round shiny pearls against the feathery green. He has watered the plants.

He has come back from wherever he had run to, and he has watered the plants.

She opens the front door. Everything looks the same, and nothing is the same.

She can hear the metallic clink of saucepans and the sound of water running into the kitchen sink; ordinary noises, their normality should be comforting...It is not. Lindsay stands at the kitchen door and looks into the room, Tony is chopping the stalks off the broccoli spears; neat and precise little movements with the small vegetable knife. He is taking enormous care, fanning out the little green trees on the wooden board, slitting the thick fibrous ends to tenderise them.

"Do you remember this?" he's indicating the chopping board, it's shaped like a tomato. "We got it in that gift shop at Blenheim didn't we?"

"I don't know." She's shaking her head; she does not want this conversation.

"Oh come on, you must remember, I wanted the celery-shaped one – because it was longer – better for French bread sticks, and you wanted the tomato."

"I don't remember."

".. and so! we got the tomato!"

"Tony, what are you doing? "

He pulls a 'funny face', an 'it's obvious but I'll humour her' face: "Making supper?"

"No, I mean what are you _doing_?"

He holds his hands out. "I give in. What am I doing?"

"We can't just ignore... what happened."

He almost raises his eyebrows "Oh come on… come on kitten." and he comes round the working surface, over to her, takes her elbows in his hands, and leads her gently over to the kitchen table. He lowers her very slowly into a chair. She does not flinch at his touch; there is a numbness about her.

He sits down opposite her and holds his hands out on the kitchen table, palms up, appealing.
"Give me your hands … come on." He's an adult coaxing a child, and he is almost laughing, a gentle world-weary shaking of his head, as he rocks her hands in his: "Come on …don't be silly …. all couples have rows. Do you realise that was out first real row! – we should celebrate! – we've had our first row."
"Celebrate" and the dull flatness of her voice echoes the word.
"Yes ! – I mean it – it's a milestone. Like Anniversaries, you know, what is it? – paper, leather, for the early ones, then silver, gold and diamond – just think of it, our Diamond Anniversary!"

Lindsay is trying to hold onto the reality of what has happened, but it is slipping away from her, his words are slithering in between the sore place on her shoulder that rubs against her blouse, and the truth of how she had felt when he had hit her… and he _had_ hit her … but it was sliding away now getting lost among the softness of his voice and the chopping board and the broccoli and the Anniversary names.

His steady fall of words continue their blurring.
"The thing is that we mustn't over-react, neither of us; it's all too easy for these things to get out of hand. We both said things that we regret…" and he raises a hand, it's a fencing gesture of an acknowledged fault… "I know, I'm just as much to blame. If you want to get a job then we should discuss it properly."
Her stunned silence encourages him: "Now Lindsay you know what it's like, I'd just that minute walked in the door and you were on to me, if you'd just waited until I'd got my jacket off… eh?… you see?"
He's smiling, the reasonable adult dealing with an unreasonable child.
Lindsay is trying to focus on him but she keeps seeing the dark wetness on the stone pots by the door.
"You watered the geraniums."
He seems to think that she is thanking him "I did!"
"You hit me and then you watered the geraniums."

185

Tony gets up, shaking his head; his infinite patience is being sorely tested, and he is deeply weary: "Here we go....here we go"

"Tony, you're always saying that women over-react to trivia, like they do in your office, but this is not like that. This is me, this is our home and you hit me."

"Oh Lindsay, don't start ... "

"I don't 'start' " .. I don't do that, I don't 'go on'..."

He's placing his hands on the back of his chair, and leaning onto them, sighing with the effort: "It was a silly row about nothing. These things happen in marriage; the test is that we move on. Forget it and move on."

He's walked over to the working surface and has picked up the chopping board; he's holding it out to her....

"Look, I wanted the celery, you wanted the tomato... it's give and take isn't it, sometimes it's me, sometimes it's you..."

Lindsay feels a great tiredness wash over her, there is a madness to this conversation and she knows that she cannot win, not tonight.
She wants to go to bed, she wants to sleep.
She looks up at him, at his reasonable, smiling, face and at the broccoli lying broken on a tomato chopping board.

"I'm going to bed Tony."

"That's it Kitten, you have a good long sleep, you'll feel better in the morning."

Lindsay walks slowly up the stairs, she's pulling herself up by the banister, breathing hard against the effort of the climbing.

Chapter 54

Diane is trying not to notice the muddled cosy domesticity of Jo-Anne's house: the daughter's schoolbooks jumbled on the kitchen table and the husbandly Classic Cars magazine beside Jo-Anne's hairbrush.

Three sets of walking boots by the door, three sizes, like the three bloody bears. Diane looks away and tries to find an area that she can look at that does not mock her.

"I know just how you feel, you know, I do really." Jo-Anne's pouring red wine into two glasses.

Diane seriously doubts that the other woman knows anything of the sort and takes a gulp at the wine.

"Oh yes – they're all the same."

Diane is noting the "To My Dear Wife" birthday card on the Welsh Dresser.

Jo-Anne follows her look. "Oh that's just words isn't it .. thing is, right now he'll be slagging me off to his ruddy mother, really enjoying having a good old moan about 'Instant Meals' ... I've told him, if I finish at six thirty on a Wednesday I have to file away all the Not In My Back Yard Applications and I'm never back until after eight, well if he wants a Mother-Meal with cheese dumplings all squishy on top of his casserole then he can do it himself."

There's a thump from upstairs, and Jo-Anne goes to the bottom of the stairs to holler up to her daughter "Faye! no kick-boxing in the bedroom, those joists won't stand it, I've told you!"

Diane can feel a headache, thick and solid as black coal, pushing up the back of her neck into her hairline.

She should have known that it would be a competition; the wifely moaning about trivia to prove that Jo-Anne's pain is comparable to that of Diane's being dumped and betrayed.

Why do they do that, these Wives? These smugly contented spouses with their doggedly faithful husbands, why do they always want to claim the supposed hurt of the single woman. Perhaps they feel that they have been denied an experience, all that watching "Jeremy Kyle" of a morning and nodding in shared misery as overweight white trash spill their grief and their agony into middle-class sitting rooms.

Jo-Anne pours herself more wine and holds the bottle over Diane's glass. "Come on, get that down you."

"You've always said that Mike's really sweet, Jo-Anne."

"He's really boring!"

"Oh I think I could do with a bit of 'boring' right now."

Jo-Anne's shaking her head "No, people say that but it's not true you know. Anyway, he's never ever come to one of our Concerts."

"Never?"

"Not once." Jo-Anne's proudly triumphant. She has a wound and she's going to make the most of it. "Every time I get him a ticket and every time I stand up there watching his empty seat, and every time I wait for him to arrive."

Diane leans forward, knowing her role in this. "And …?"

"And he never arrives!" Jo-Anne's flourishing her glass.

"Even when we sang the Chorus of the Hebrew Slaves last year and I'd bought that CD to learn the words. Mike said if he had to hear Russell Watson singing "Va pensiero" one more time he'd go demented. I told him we had to be word perfect, you know what Anna's like about not having the music 'on stage' even when we're not on a stage, she went ballistic that time I pinned the words to Grace's back…"

Diane's confused. "Sorry …?"

"I stand _behind_ Grace, don't I, anyway, thing is that when we all filed off the platform Grace turned round to talk to Susie and everybody saw the bit of paper. Well it could have been _anything_, couldn't it?"

The pain in Diane's head is moving slowly to the front, winding itself around her forehead to push in against her eyes.

"I really think I should go, Jo-Anne, thanks so much for all your help today but …" Jo-Anne not ungently pushes Diane back into her chair.

"Oh not yet, we haven't finished the wine! I wanted to have a really good talk, get it all off your chest, you know."

There is a steady thumping of thick-soled boots coming downstairs, and a shout from the hallway:

"I bloody told 'im, din'I? I bloody told 'im."

Jo-Anne's daughter clomps into the kitchen, totally ignoring her mother and Diane, she is screaming into her mobile phone:

"I'm not goin', it's crap innit."

Jo-Anne seems to sink lower into herself as she looks at her daughter.

"Faye could you not shout in here please" it's wearily said and expects no result.

"Well tell'im then, you bloody tell'im !" Faye punches a button on the mobile to end the call.

The girl is eighteen-with-attitude, the massive boots would serve quite adequately for a yeti; they're trimmed with long shaggy fur-like substance and the soles are thick enough to withstand impacted ice. Stick thin legs lead up to a denim mini-skirt, artfully frayed to illustrate poverty and age, the cropped top is similarly 'distressed', displaying the naked belly button with regulation septic piercing oozing pinkly around its metal stud.

"Faye, have you eaten anything?"

The girl turns round to look at her mother as if she cannot imagine why she is there, or even who she is.

"Did you have the supper I left in the fridge? , I left you a note."

Faye shrugs, very slightly.

Diane feels she should introduce herself. "Hi – I'm Diane – I'm in the choir with your Mum."

Faye looks at Diane as if she is insane. Jo-Anne smiles an apology at Diane. This mother is far too accustomed to her daughter's behaviour to expect anything else, after five years of teenage tantrums she has been eroded into this, this drained acceptance. It is only just occasionally, as now, when she sees the look in Diane's eyes, that she even attempts any control.

"Faye, love, Diane and I are having a little chat, so if you haven't eaten ..."

"Pizza."

"What?"

"Pizza."

"You mean you want a pizza or you've had a pizza?"

"I said din'I!"

Diane is looking at the girl's sulky mouth as she begrudges each word directed at her mother. There is a metal stud through the lower lip that ends in the soft valley above the chin; a livid red circle of allergy surrounds it. She watches the small metal ball move irritably against the lip that is stained a dark purple, the lipstick bleeding at the corners of the mean little mouth.

"Faye, did you have a pizza in town?" Jo-Anne's talking very slowly and calmly, it's the sort of calm that holds down years of temper.

The girl's mobile rings. She punches at it and shouts into the mouthpiece:

"Well, wot d'he say? I'm not goin' I said .... it's crap innit!"

"Faye?" Jo-Anne reaches out to touch the girl's arm and Faye flinches away from her mother with exaggerated disgust.

189

She shouts "I'll see ya there then" into the mobile and marches out of the room, at the doorway she turns back to her mother and yells at her, as if it is obvious: "Pizza!"

"Faye... are you going out? When will you be ...."

The slamming of the front door is her answer.

Jo-Anne shrugs at Diane and gives her a self-deprecating little smile.

"Kids eh?"

"Why is she so.. angry?" Diane's pushing her fingers into her temples.

Jo-Anne's sinking into her chair "God knows, she's been angry since she was thirteen and everything I do is wrong. We have discussions, we lay down rules, we make ultimatums, but then everything goes back to square one. What can I do? I can't throw her out of the house, I can't hit her – we've never approved of physical violence to children – she's not *really* terrible, I mean, she's not on drugs or anything ...."

Jo-Anne's biting her lip, a doubt niggles "We've been very firm on that, No Drugs." She gives a resolute nod of her head to emphasise this, but her eyes are less sure. "I mean – it's not as if you can send them to their rooms, not these days, she's got her television, Sky box, computer, music centre, double bed, en-suite shower ....I sometimes wish she'd send *me* to *her* room."

Diane's at a bit of a loss, she's trying to remember herself at eighteen; listening to records in school-friends rooms, generally mooning about, she couldn't remember the anger. Perhaps that was the trouble, she should have been angrier earlier, got in some practice.

Jo-Anne's sloshing more wine into her glass. "You see half of me wants to kick her up her smart little arse and the other half is terrified that she'll just walk out that door and never come back, and then one day I'll trip over her sitting outside Boots – you know, in that little alcove where some of them sit on the ground among the MacDonald's cartons and the stains of dog pee. You see them sitting there, don't you, usually with a mongrel on a piece of string."

Diane privately thinks that Mummy's-little-Princess would be hard to shift from her en-suite facilities and electronic haven: "I'm sure she wouldn't do that; she's still studying isn't she?"

Jo-Anne's not convinced: "Sitting her A-levels this year but I've yet to see her open a book. I bought her all those Study Guides from Smiths, but they just lay there under all the CDs."

"What does she want to do career-wise?"

"No idea! The School are pushing University, but they try and get everybody to do that these days because it looks good on their Brochures, you know, '75% of students went onto further education' and never mind if it's suitable or they'll stick at it and they don't give the kids any real preparation for how it will be. Most of my friend's children have dropped out after the first year.

When she was little she used to want to be a Vicar"

Diane coughs at her wine. "Really!"

"I think the training's putting her off though, that and Dawn French. It's so easy when they're little; oh it's exhausting, and there's all that running them about to school and friends but, when I look back, I do wish that I'd *enjoyed* it more. I wish that I had stood still and just *watched* her. I can remember going into her Primary School once, to help out, and I'd walked into the school room and she was making a picture of a garden and sticking on bits of dried pasta that she'd painted, then one of the other mother's called me into the staff room to show her how to use the photocopier and by the time I got back everything had been packed away, there was just these little bits of rigatoni on the floor.

"I'd missed it, you see, I'd missed the moment. I could imagine her little pixie face all twisted up in concentration, sticking the pasta onto the cardboard, and I'd missed it. By the time half term came round and the kids brought home all their pieces of work, the picture had got lost in a drawer somehow and Faye couldn't even remember doing it. It's so fragile, it goes so quickly, and we look away and it's gone forever."

She gulps down another glass of the red.

"Meeting them after school used to be good; there's just that brief moment when they see you standing there and they run up to you and they're handing over their school bags and the gym kits and it's all a jumble of them telling you about their day, and how they don't like 'colouring-in' and what they had for lunch ....You see, they actually seem to *like* you then.

"I just can't remember when the hate started."

Diane had expected to feel miserable tonight, but there is a strange kind of comfort in this, a mean and secret ease; whenever she had tried to ask Paul about children he'd gone on about how they only needed each other, and how he'd been a baby-sitting slave to his dozens of brothers and sisters ... and how it should be a joint decision, and *he* had to *want* it too, and it wasn't just about *her* needs, when she had wanted to be pregnant she had thought of babies and chubby toddlers trotting alongside her, reaching a small warm hand into hers; she hadn't thought

191

of a Faye and of the disappointment. When Faye had flinched away from her mother's touch, Diane had seen a kind of loathing in the girl's eyes that had flashed out under the cruelly pierced eyebrows. All that hurt.

"What about Mike? – what does he say?"

"Not much, blames me for spoiling her; his flaming ruddy Mother blames me – goes on and on about how I drove all the way to Swindon one Christmas because Faye wanted the "Skating Barbie" and I'd rung round half of Oxfordshire trying to get one. But what can you do? You love them, you want to make them happy? Is that so wrong?"

Jo-Anne's got up from the table. "Shall we open another bottle?"

Diane's had her fill of maudlin tales of lost childhood for tonight, and she gets up and makes towards the doorway.

"I'm sorry, I really do have to go," she's looking at her watch.

"Oh not yet!"

"I'm sorry Jo-Anne, it's just that – I've got an Interview first thing." Diane has no idea where that came from, she just wanted out and she's always offered a little lie to wiggle her out of social situations, it never seemed to matter much and she could never understand how other people did it, that truth-despite-the-pain thing.

"Oh.. a job?"

Oh Lord, now she'd have to make up a whole career for herself.

"Just local, you know."

"What as?" Jo-Anne's following her to the front door.

"I thought I'd have a stab at the Health Centre." No ! No. Why had she said that? .. not that, she'd be telling the woman she was going to be a Receptionist next.

"That's marvellous Diane, really, just what you need." Yeah, right. Diane's opened the door.

"I really do hope that .. well, you know.. the issues with Faye…"

"Oh yes, I'm sure we'll all be laughing about it when she's thirty."

Jo-Anne's trying for the light and airy goodbye, and failing; her face is flushed a podgy red from the wine, her hair has fallen out of its clip and the wisps stray greasily around her face.

"Good luck tomorrow morning – tell me all about it at Choir."

"Right." Diane is trying not to look too doomed as she waves herself off and walks quickly away down the street.

Jo-Anne's leaning against her doorway, watching Diane.

She winds a strand of hair back under the clip at the back of her head and looks out into the night. There's a shout of young laughter from the end of the road and the mother peers into the darkness.

"Faye?"

Chapter 55

Two heads are bent low over a table in the corner of Witsham's "Gentleman's Club". Gerry's, that wiry fuzz of ginger is inches from that of a bald pate. There's a tattoo at its nape, two daggers cross with a flaming sword - so not much room for interpretation really. This second man is thick-set, in his late thirties and he wears a white T-shirt that's emblazoned with the logo "Whatever" but the "W" is four daggers crossed over each other, and there's a gap between that and the rest of the word so that the message reads: W HATE-EVER – with an extra 'e' thrown in just in case one might miss the information. The subtlety of this is matched by the bull neck with its cleverly matching dagger theme so that he is, in fact, a stereotype of the man you wouldn't want to meet on a dark night. Gerry's snatching long, urgent pulls at the roll up that's clenched between his thin lips. His eyes scan the pub in a constant sweep across the bar that's puddled with spilt beer and sodden squares of stained towelling, and, against the far wall, the row of slot-machines that clash and clatter as young men in vests punch their 'hold' buttons and yank at the metal handles to spin their luck. Smoke swirls thickly around the rather superfluous sign that hangs over the bar:

"Smoking IS allowed in this Bar! Take it or Leave it!"

The Club had used to be a Pub - sweetly misnamed "The Golden Angel" - a name that might have tempted the unwary to enter these dark portals, since illumination is another scorned advance; the light bulbs, such as there are, are limited to a dimness of wattage aided by the fact that the glass shades are so mired with a greasy nicotine yellowing that little of the electricity can pierce the surrounding gloom. The strictly adhered to dress code appears to be vests and muscles or faux military.
On one wall there is a massive flat-screen television surrounded by England flags, and a large union jack hangs dustily beside several framed photographs of footballers and boxers, the suggested fascism of the décor seeming not to exclude the many black faces of pugilists.
Gerry and his friend are looking into the near empty pints of beer.

"He'll be 'ere in a minute, let 'im get'm in." Gerry's looking at his watch, a device that enables him to tell him the time were he to be forty metres underwater or to fall from a seven-storey building. His friend grunts his approval.

"You told him to bring it in sterling?... not dollars!"

"Told 'im."

"See he does then."

The men are nodding in grim agreement.

"I'm not 'avin' dollars."

"It's sorted, I told 'im."

"No way." Gerry's friend is shifting his bulk on the wooden seat that creaks and cracks as he moves.

"I gotta be careful, Gerry."

"I know."

"I'm only doing this for you, you know that."

"I know that."

"Because of Basingstoke."

"Right" and Gerry leans over to punch the fist that lies on the table between them.

"I won't forget that, Gerry."

"Anytime, mate."

"I know that," and the fist slams the table in recognition of the debt. There's a moment as the men remember Basingstoke, before Gerry's friend can pull himself back from that moment to ask. "How d'you know this Tony then?"

"He's kosher, I told you. We've been through some Stuff, you know."

"Army?"

"No, no .. when we were younger, just kid's stuff."

"Wot then, Juvenile? Has he got a Record?"

"No, nothing on paper." Gerry is trying not to say that he and Tony were at School. Playground bullying doesn't really hack it in his friend's world.

"Young Offenders stuff then is it?"

Gerry is relieved not to answer as he sees Tony enter the Bar.

"Here he is!"

Tony comes over to the table. Tony looks pleased: Gerry's friend looks like a person who has guns; in fact Tony thinks he looks like a person who has whole shed-loads of munitions and probably an army in tow.

The friend is muttering to Gerry. "Looks like a ponce."

Gerry pulls Tony down to sit at the table.

"We don't want to draw attention."

A quick glance round the club assures Tony that the entire clientele look as if they're dealing in arms.

"This is Tony." Gerry's thumbing a nicotine digit between the other two men.. "Tony this is...."

"No names!" the friend slams his hand on the table. "I told you, Gerry, we gotta be careful."

"Right." Gerry's pointing at his friend, then at Tony.

"You got that Tony?"

"Yes, Absolutely." Tony is enjoying this, but nods grimly to convince the other men that he understands the gravitas of this moment.

"You 'aven't brought dollars?" the bald head is leaning in to Tony's soft curls.

"No, of course not."

"There's no 'of course' about it, is there?"

"No, well probably not."

"I told you, I told 'im" .. Gerry's nudging Tony .. "Didn't I Tony?"

"Yes – I haven't brought dollars."

"Right."

"Right."

The Hate-Ever T-shirt leans back against the protesting wood of his chair, he reaches with deliberate slowness under the table, pushing a canvas rucksack over towards Tony's feet. Tony makes to look under the table.

"Don't look!"

"Right" Tony straightens up, he's seen the bag though and is disappointed, it looks like one of those free-with-over-five-gallons-of-petrol ones that don't last because the straps always break.

"So? ...your bag?"

Tony hasn't brought a bag. The money is in a large padded envelope and he reaches into the inside of his jacket to get it. Gerry and his friend immediately react as if Tony's reaching for a weapon. Gerry actually flinches back to lean almost behind the wooden pillar beside the table, his friend ducks his bulk over the table. Tony almost laughs, but checks this instantly as he sees the look in the other men's eyes.

"I'm just getting the money" Tony feels stupid saying this, and pulls the large envelope very slowly from out of his jacket inside pocket.
The other men cover their foolishness with blustering anger.

"Never do that!"

"Not to a military man."

"You could have lost an eye doin' that!"

"Never forget our training.." Gerry's flicking his head over at his friend "He's got reactions like lightning."

"Under the table!" the bald head is jabbing at Tony.

"What?"

"Pass the envelope under the table."

Tony holds the envelope and Gerry leans down with exaggerated casualness to reach under the table to take the money. Tony can feel the canvas bag pressed against his legs, he's aware of the slight hard weight of it pressing against his shin. In that bag there is a gun, a real gun, a gun that can kill.

He looks around him, at the hard-men at the bar with their thick boots and jeans shiny with grease, at thumbs hooked into the torn back pockets, the hands mired with dirt that's worn into the cracks and creases, thick fingers splayed wide across stained buttocks. This is a man's world, a cowboy world, and he breathes in the smell of it; the smoke and the stale sweat and the slight acid tang from the door to the Gents.

What would they think if they knew? Here he is, this respectable man in a jacket; they probably think that he's just some wanker from an office. Tony rubs his foot slightly against the bag and feels the comfort of it, he moves his foot away to tease it, only to move it back again and press hard against that power.

He smiles at the secrecy of it and he's fifteen in the garden shed with a mouse in a jar and the big kitchen knife that his mother has lost.

Nobody knows, nobody knows what he can do, what he will do, and nobody can stop him. Mother's in the kitchen making macaroni cheese and she knows that he hates macaroni cheese, that slimy yellowness and the way he has to count to three to make himself swallow the worms of pasta.

She'll make him eat it, she always does, then he'll have to do the washing-up and scrape all the thick yellow muck out of the pan, she makes it too thick and it smells like pus.

Gerry and his friend are muttering to each other, and Gerry's still darting those sharp looks around them. There is an air of the comic about these two, a sense of playing in a big-boys game, in the almost ludicrous precautions – no-one in the pub is remotely interested in the transactions at this table, they are all far too involved in their own nefarious deeds – but this is not a game, and it is not a toy lying in the bag under the table.

Gerry's nudging Tony.

"So that's all right then? Told you I'd get it."

"Yes, great. Thanks." Tony looks across at the Hateful T-shirt: "Thanks."

The man sees his look and pulls the garment out flat so that Tony can read the logo.

"Stops people asking questions."

"Yes, I can see that it would."

Tony realises that there are questions he has to ask, about the gun, but he doesn't want to ask if there are any 'Instructions' with it..

"I suppose it works like er.... the usual ... it's just that I'm not used to this particular model you see."

Tony can feel Gerry's eyes on him, he's mumbling under his breath.

"You've used a Beretta before, haven't you?"

"Oh yes .. but I was just wondering in case there's some new gismo?"

Tony knows that this sounds lame, he's desperately trying to remember that catalogue, he's read it so many times and he takes a chance, so he whispers across the table.

"The blow-back system is it, with the tip up barrel?"

Gerry's friend nods and Tony leans back in his chair to feel the sweat congealing cold along the middle of his back.

He puts his hand over his mouth to conceal the words.

"And the ammo?"

The bald head tilts to one side, the back of his giant paw rubs across the thick lips: "You could blow away half of Witsham with that lot."

"Oh" and Tony seems to find this information soothing, he smiles and his eyes slide away to the window, to look through the smeary panes out into the night..."Oh, Good."

Gerry actually seems discomfited and he leans towards Tony to murmur at him: "A man needs ... something these days."

He's warned by this friend's quickly raised paw not to say the word 'gun'.

Gerry's eyes sweep the room.

"Don't say the word, Tony."

"It's good to be handy these days" baldy's breathing into Tony's face, it's a smell of dead animals and fat.

Tony feels that it is expected of him to justify this purchase.

"I need to protect myself."

"'Course you do."

"My family, my wife, there's all sorts hanging about the streets these days."

"Naturally" this from the man who is the epitome of the sort that inspires the urban fear. Tony leans back, secure in the other men's agreement. "There's just no respect is there, that's what really gets at me, nobody gives you an inch, they walk all over you, treating you like shit on the bottom of their shoe.."

Gerry's rolling his knuckles into the palm of the other hand.

"All the old standards have gone ...yobs all over the streets, bits of

197

kids not twenty, you 'ave to get off the pavement for. Just standin' there, lollin' about and it's you that has to step into the gutter to get past...

"No respect for someone who's fought for their country"

Gerry is undeterred by the fact that fighting for his country has got him no further than Salisbury Plain and a week-end's lying about in the rain; that this resulted in a particularly lingering head cold has qualified him to feel brotherhood with most of the regular army and enables him to cheer in a comradely way at television news coverage involving any form of uniformed conflict. Gerry's regular cheers of "Come on lads!" have moved easily from the football pitch to dusty plains of desert soil, his bonding with the men dodging bullets a total marriage of his fantasy and passion.

He knows all the names of all the Battalions, and refers to them with an easy familiarity: 'The Staffs. are going out there now, they'll show'em', and he has been known to give the thumbs up sign to any military vehicle that happens to pass through Witsham, this rare occasion not denting his enthusiasm.

Baldy is nodding his respect to Gerry. Tony is not actually sure what conflict it is that Gerry has recently been involved in, so plays safe.

"You've certainly done your bit, Gerry."

Gerry is feeling generous in this warm bath of approval and leans over to include both men in a heartfelt moment.

"Tony, this man..." he's pointing a pedantic finger at his friend, "this man was there for me, put himself on the line."

The bald head is shaking in becoming modesty.

"No – I'm not forgetting it! I'm not forgetting it, Dave!"

All three men register that Gerry has said baldy's name.

Tony is quick to feign deafness.

"Sorry, what was that? – not forgetting what? – I missed that."

He's rather over-egged the pudding, but Gerry's too relieved to doubt it: "Nothing. Forget it. Forget it, right?"

"Right."

Gerry has not looked over at Dave and is keen to divert any possible anger, he's drumming his fingers onto the table.

"Right, right ... the women are the worst y' know. They think they can do anything, sounding off all the time, got bloody mouths on them like navvies."

"You married, Gerry?" and there's an edge to Dave's voice.

"Not bloody likely," and he realises: "... you know that."

"Yeah. I know." Dave looks straight at Gerry, a point has been scored and small revenge for betraying his name.

"I've had my share of women, don't you worry !" and the hollowness echoes in the men's ears.

"Who wears the trousers in your house, Tony?" Dave's turned towards Tony, leaving Gerry to stare into the emptiness of his beer glass.

"No problem. We both have our roles. It's about give and take really, but my wife realises that when it comes down to it, there can only be one boss in a house."

"What's her name?"

"Sorry."

"What's her name ... your wife?"

Tony does not want to give his wife's name to this man.

"She's a very private person, my wife, old fashioned really, shy y'know.

"I have to bring her out of herself or she'd spend all day in doors.

"Not her fault, she had a rotten mother"

Dave's nodding; rotten mothers are a currency that pays for later sins.

Gerry's watching the other men in sulky jealousy. "It's Lindsay."

Tony and Dave turn to look at him.

"His wife's name's Lindsay.... Well, isn't it.?"

Dave smirks at him. "You're good with names, aren't you Gerry."

Tony can feel a small patch of heat somewhere at the back of his head as he looks at Gerry.

"Well? – that is her name, it's Lindsay."

Tony stands up and talks loudly over his wife's name. "I'll have to be off. It was good to meet you..." and he falters, he's holding out his hand to shake Dave's, like at a meeting; executives being polite to each other.

Dave looks at the hand and gives it a sort of slap.

"Take care man."

Tony is anxious to be gone, this is all getting too edgy, and he wants to get home and unpack his toy.

Tony picks up the canvas bag and he's aware of its weight, he passes it to his other hand to experience again the heaviness, and he feels like he does on a Sunday, after the roast, that fullness.

He moves through the bar, past the shaven heads and the camouflage jackets. If only they knew! If only they knew!

His hand grips the canvas straps and his fingers are rubbing against their rough sewn edges, he's rubbing harder and harder until he can feel a soreness beginning.

Out into the street and he allows himself to look down at the bag, at the way that it swings beside him. There's a knot in the thread along the hemming on the strap and it's biting into his fingers. Tony is breathing faster and a hot, livid flush is staining his neck.

He's a kid on Christmas morning – only Christmases weren't like that, not with Father. It didn't do to be too excited, you had to pretend that you didn't really want it. They'd sit around the table by the Christmas Tree, and there'd be all the presents laid out in three little piles; with Tony's crayoned labels "Mum" and "Dad" on the badly wrapped ones, and then there'd be his pile, with "Tony" on the labels made from last year's Christmas cards; Mum would have used her "pinking shears" from the sewing basket so that the edges would be cut in a zig-zag pattern and look like shop-bought.

His mother would be making the tea, and taking an age to let it brew, and his father would be fiddling with the radio to find the Carol Service from St.Paul's, and he'd be looking at those parcels on the table and knowing that he had to be calm and quiet and not be greedy. He'd actually look away from the table and pretend to be interested in the Radio Times. That was what had started the row that year, he wasn't really looking at the television section, he'd just opened the magazine to prove that he wasn't pleading to open his presents; but his father had caught him looking at the article about the Morecambe and Wise Show.

"That's right, rub it in." His father couldn't find Radio-3 and was starting to wind himself up into one of what Tony and his mother called His Do's.

"I was only just looking…"

"Only just looking…. Mother! he's only just looking at the *television* listings isn't he… we're not good enough for him you see, just having a radio …oh no…."

Tony had been so desperate to placate his father:

"No, really, Dad, really, I was just flicking through the pictures."

"Yes! pictures .. not sound, sound's not good enough .. it has to be vision now doesn't it …" His father had been lashing himself into a deeper temper, and Tony had wanted so much to stop this, to go back to five minutes before, before he'd picked up the Radio Times, before that anger had started to build.

"Please, Dad, don't Dad…I'm sorry"

"Why don't you go next door, they've got a massive telly, twenty-two inches isn't it Mother?"

"Tea's ready, now where's that Carol Service Dad?"

Mother was trying to ignore the raging, it was what she always did, and it never worked, Tony had never understood why she didn't realise that it never worked. It made Dad worse.

"He's whining about us not having a telly."

"I'm not, honest I'm not."

"Don't you argue with me, my lad!"

His father still couldn't find the right channel for the Christmas music, the radio was old and the little black markings for the wavelengths were worn; they didn't usually listen to Radio-3 and his father wasn't used to finding it on the dial.

"Where's the bloody thing ... it's somewhere along from the old Light Programme isn't it...Tony! – make yourself useful for once, find the Carol Service. We're not opening presents without the Carols."

So Tony had tried to help, his fingers slipping sweatily on the plastic knob as he twiddled it along the wavelengths, backwards and forwards listening to the crackle and then a sudden blare of pop music as he hit a wrong channel.

"Can't we have... something else Dad?"

"Something else ! It's bloody Christmas and you want Something Else, some of that crap that's on the tele-vis-sion I suppose, you'd rather have that wouldn't you... eh? ... eh?!"

Tony had felt pushed and pushed towards it:

"I don't want a bloody telly!" He had shouted it, in a desperation born of the panic that Christmas was going to be ruined because he'd read the wrong section of Radio Times. And his father had looked almost triumphant, as if he had succeeded in something.

... "Right that's it !" ..

Oh that dreaded "That's It!" that meant an end to anything and everything, when his father would stop his world.

"You can forget those presents, lad, you're not having those until you've learned some manners."

And he'd had to wait until Boxing Day, and watch his mother move the parcels from the table and put them onto the floor while they ate their dinner, and he fretted that his father would tread on them as he went to and fro to the kitchen for more gravy.

And there was that crawling with a kind of shame that he had to pretend that it was perfectly all right and that he didn't want his presents anyway.

Tony is walking faster and faster down the street; the redness is creeping up his neck and onto his face as he rubs his fingers over and over the knot on the canvas; he's slamming the bag into the side of his leg and there's blood on the straps.

Chapter 56

Anna is sitting at her kitchen table, a sheaf of letters in her hand.

Roy peeps cautiously around the doorway, he's in his dressing gown and was on a fridge raid; he'd been looking forward to the chocolate mousse he'd hidden behind the salad container.

"Oh – you're in here." He's shifting his weight from one slippered foot to the other. Anna's looking at the letters, chewing at her lower lip.

"Anna? – you all right? It's gone eleven."

"It's letters from the Choir…. they're revolting."

"Well I've always thought that."

"Roy, you don't make jokes."

Roy's making his way past Anna to the fridge working out how to get his treat without her noticing.

"Trevor's been winding them all up, meetings and now letters; they're upset that I've sacked him and ….Roy! what are you doing?!"

Roy's twisting himself so that he has his back to her, the fridge door is open and he's managed to get his little pot of chocolate heaven into his dressing gown pocket. "Nothing". It's the instinctive lie of a child.

Anna looks at him, at the rumpled purple sash around his waist, it's the cord from his last dressing gown and it doesn't match this one.

"Why have you got that old one..?" She's tugging at it and then sees the bulge in his pocket. Roy sees her look.

"Crème caramel?"

"Chocolate mousse."

She nods.

"I like this sash". Roy's fingering it. "You said I looked like a Roman Emperor in that dressing gown, the purple silky one.."

"Yes, I remember."

"And then I put it on 'Cottons' in the Bio Wash and that was that, but the sash is still OK .. so that's why I wear it, it reminds me of what you said …"

Anna's looking at him, a sad and empty little smile shadows her face.

"A Roman Emperor."

"You used to think that, you know. Can you remember?"

"Oh … yes."

"You used to like the flowers I brought you every morning.."

"In that little vase."

"You gave it to the Jumble Sale."

"I tried to buy it back."

"I bought it back."

"Did you?"

"I hid it in the shed, under the Black-and-Decker Boxes."

"Why?"

He shrugs. "I don't really know, I think I was sort of embarrassed. I thought you'd ...well, laugh I suppose."

"Why did you stop.. the flowers?"

"It was the cat nip – don't you remember – you said it stank."

"No. No I didn't. I remember putting your favourite Madeleine Daisies in it and putting it on the dinner table and you didn't notice. You never noticed when I did anything like that."

"I don't remember."

"No."

"They're not my favourites – the daisies – they were your Aunt Jo's favourites."

"Were they?" Anna's trying to remember.

Roy's shaking his head. "I've never liked white flowers, I like the bright colours, the yellows and the bright reds, like you see in Italy."

"You've never been to Italy."

"No." Roy's glumly shaking his head.

"I thought you liked France, you always said you loved our touring trips."

"I hate the driving, I always hated the driving; they never give you a chance, the French, it's a quick blast of the horn and they're in there, coming in from the right when you're in the fast lane of the motorway.."

"You never said." Anna's turned round to look at him.

"Yes I did, I always said I dreaded that Route Circulaire."

"I thought you were just doing your traffic moaning thing."

"I used to hate it that I didn't understand the signs properly."

"But you took French, you got your O-level."

"Yes – and that's what you kept telling everybody – all the butchers and the bakers in all those little towns we stopped at; they used to snigger at us you know, after I'd done my "encore du pain" routine."

"You didn't say anything."

"No."

"I don't remember it like that at all, I always thought that they were our well ... our good times."

"Oh Christ." He's put his head in his hands.

Anna looks across at him, at the thinning hair and the sagging chin, and the way that his pyjama jacket collar always folds itself over into a roll round his neck.

"I have tried, Anna. The job, the Council, I tried to give you what you wanted; it just never seems to be enough. The thing is I'm not as bright as you think I am, and these days I don't really want it anyway."

"What?"

"Any of it."

She's laid the letters down onto the table, and they both sit and listen as the silence of the room is punctured by the fridge, its harsh electric whirring filling their emptiness.

They're both sadly far away in the memories and the mistakes and the missed moments of their marriage.

Anna gets up from the table and goes over to the sink to collect the empty milk bottles.

"I'll put the bottles out, you're not dressed."

Roy shakes his head. "I don't think any of the neighbours are waiting to catch me in my dressing gown."

She walks into the hall and opens the front door, taking a deep breath of the night air as she bends to put the bottles beside her porch. The stain of Harvey's pee still darkens the cement, and Anna's nose flinches at the lingering acrid smell.

"That dog! Paulette's savage mutt!"

And she turns to shout back into the house.

"Roy – bring me the Dettol!"

But her sometime Roman Emperor has already climbed the stairs to his bed.

Chapter 57

Trevor's up early, there's a little pile of letters on his table, they're copies of the ones that the choir members have sent to Anna; that's the beauty of computers, in the old days you'd have to pop into the newsagents and fiddle about with the 10p-a-copy machine by the door with everyone seeing what you were doing; Trevor could remember with a cold clarity the day he'd left the Choir Contacts Sheet in the machine after running off all those copies for Anna, and him not remembering until he'd got way down the street past Morrisons, and then that panicked run back just knowing that somebody else would be using the photocopier and find his original. All those private numbers and personal e-mail addresses, and he'd got a stitch in his side with the running as he'd raced back into the shop to find the Manager waving the sheet at him:

"You left this in the machine, you know!"

Yes of course he bloody knew, why else was he standing there in the doorway, leaning on the ice-cream sign and clutching his side in breathless pain. No, computers had saved all that, all the choir had to do was ' mouse down to print' and there it was, and it was good of them to send them to him too.. Trevor felt emboldened with the words.

" .. our most valuable asset .." (He smiles at Grace's support)

"Quite simply, the Choir will be lost without Trevor!" (this from Susie, good old ballsy Susie, no compromise there !)

Rowena had written *" .. saddened by these catastrophic changes... ...and the ethos of the Choir destroyed by additions of commercial expertise rather than grass-roots loyalty ."* Which Trevor thought harked more onto her own personal grievance and he itched at the 'commercial expertise' knowing that Anna would translate that as Trevor's bumbling amateurism vs Jonathan's career professionalism.

Jo-Anne had put it simpler *"Trevor IS the Choir "* which he thought was probably his favourite. He'd read Diane's twice but it seemed to be full of far too many *"I know I have only just joined ..."* and *"I am sure that the others feel ..."* for his liking, and then there was a whole paragraph about Betrayal which seemed to be about something else entirely. He had been keen to get a copy of Lindsay's letter, but something told him that she probably didn't use a computer. He'd been thinking about her all last night, about that look and the sort of fluttering. He walked over to his piano, and ran his fingers along the music stand; he could almost see his face in the dark reflecting wood. "Mustn't get involved" he told the little brass hinges that held the pages down. "She's married after all, and I've got enough on my plate."

Thus Lindsay's Knight sheathes his sword.

Trevor looks outside into the street, across the road at the old barn with the yellow planning permission signs pinned to the door; the notices had been slid into plastic covers but the rain had dribbled in and watered the print into an unreadable blur. He had meant to write to the council and register his objections, but this business with Anna had wiped away his usual concerns - and then he noticed it, the dog, that black dog, it was there again. Roaming around the barn. It was waiting for him to go out, Trevor was sure of it. It knows where he lives. It used to just hang about in town, by the War Memorial, now it's tracked him down here where he thought he was safe. Trevor marches into his hallway and opens his front door.

"Trevor IS the Choir." He's shouting across at the black Labrador.

"So you can bugger off!"

The dog looks across at him and even waves his tail in an agreeable enough way, but Trevor is not convinced; he's been here before with dogs, get within tooth distance and it'll be all that low growling stuff.

The dog has no intention of moving away, there's a really good smell just by the side of the barn and the possibility of a rat. The man opposite is standing in his doorway, but he doesn't have a stick to throw so the black nose bends again to its task and hoovers along the cracks in the old wood and breathes in that glorious rotting.

Trevor is watching the animal and remembers when he'd shooed the dog away after choir, after Anna had told him to 'Move On', and he remembers that feeling of almost change, that slight shifting.

He closes the front door and picks up the small leather address book that's on his hall table; it lies on top of a square of faded material that his mother had embroidered with tall pink lupins. He picks it up and runs his fingers over the little lazy-daisy stitches that form the flowers and knows that he should get rid of these old-lady touches to his home. He crumples the material in his hands and thinks of throwing it into the bin, and then opens his hand; the lupins unfold and smile back at him in their familiarity, and he smoothes out the material, rubbing his fingers over the creases as he lays it back onto the hall table. It is not easy to throw away a past.

Jonathan's telephone number is listed under "P" for Pratt. Trevor hugs this little joke to himself, a joke that nobody would ever know, and dials the number. Jonathan takes an age to answer and Trevor is beginning to regret that he hadn't dialled in the 'withhold caller number' because he doesn't want Jonathan to wrong foot him by knowing that he's been desperate to get him, but just as the pratt's incredibly pompous ansaphone kicks in, Jonathan picks up, so Trevor has to listen to the other man's shouted "I'm bloody here, don't hang up," at the same time as the recorded "*Jonathan Charles here, I'm almost certainly at Rehearsal right now, so do leave a message if it's urgent or work-based..*" played to a background of some Mozart-ish piece that Trevor's not sure of.

"It's Trevor."

"Who?" ...Well that was inevitable.

"We met at Anna's ...I'm her accompanist when we do our Charity ....."

"Oh yes – the Choir."

Oh thank God, he hasn't got to explain everything and have to squirm around the 'used to be her choir accompanist' bit. Trevor sits down on the chair that's in the hall, the making-telephone-calls chair that remembers when the mouthpieces were attached to the telephone base and couldn't walk about.

Trevor knows that the handset can work perfectly well even in the garden, but feels that the importance of this call demands an older formality.

"It's about the Choir that I'm ringing actually."

"Yes – I thought it might be."

"I just don't think that you realise what you're taking on."

"I'm playing at the session on Monday – Anna wants me to give it a go, as it were, see how I gel with the group."

Trevor takes a breath and plays his best card. "It's not really *you*, is it?

Small Town Choir, all very much amateurs. Most of them need molly-coddling, I used to have to write out all the individual parts – and not musically, mind – only a couple of them actually read music, so it's little diagrams of arrows ...."

He can hear Jonathan sighing, and is pretty sure he's heard a muttered "Oh God" at the other end of the line.

"Thing is, I spend half the week making sound-tapes for them to take home and memorise.. you know with me playing the melody and singing along with their particular part ... I spend a fortune in Smiths I can tell you because you never get the tapes back, they always say that they've lost them. They haven't, of course, probably recording last week's 'Woman's Hour' or....."

Jonathan's heard enough. "Yes, Trevor, I do understand. Thing is, a bit lumbered to do Monday, old son. Get your point though.

207

" Agree with you actually, but you know what Anna's like when she gets a bee in her bonnet."

Trevor makes to start on again. "You see most of the sopranos are, how can I put this, well a bit flat …"

"Tell you what I'll do Trevor – just between ourselves, man to man, I'll do Monday. See if the envelope gets posted as it were. Got to go right now, I'm late for the Abbey."

"Oh?"

"Dorchester. Just a fund-raising thing, but you know how these things are. I'll be in touch," and Jonathan hangs up.

Trevor does not know how these things are, he has never played in an Abbey, Witsham Methodist Church is his highest ecclesiastical achievement to date. Trust Jonathan to have to mention 'Abbeys' he couldn't have just said he had to go, oh no, had to rub it in didn't he; couldn't resist the one-upmanship.

Still, he felt a bit guilty at trashing the Choir, all that stuff about having to carry the unmusical, and then that lie about the 'sops'. Trevor actually liked it that some of them couldn't read music; he liked it that he could teach them something, that he could pass on his little skill. So, he'd planted a seed, if only he could overhear what happens on Monday… Trevor was going to work on that, there was that little room that Reg was always skulking in, he could always get the Caretaker on his side, another bit of that man-to-man stuff that Jonathan was so keen on. He had to hear what happened, he had to know.

Chapter 58

Diane's shoving her supermarket trolley around Waitrose. At every aisle she takes a surreptitious peep that Jo-Anne isn't there; last night's lies about a job interview at the Health Centre hang heavily about her shoulders. She stoops beneath the weight of the Good Luck card that had been slipped through her letterbox that morning – hand delivered, there would have been no time to post it – Jo-Anne was obviously one of those women that keep a drawer full of "All Occasions" cards, ready for action, just waiting for an unwary acquaintance to mention the death of a relative or the vague likelihood of an event in life that might just require the goodness of chance ...and wallop ! – there you go – the moment is sealed forever. You have been officially wished Good Luck and this seemingly innocent sentiment now dooms its recipient to further enquiries as to the duration and manner of said Interview, its expected outcomes and a steady flow of comments that will begin with the dreaded: *"Have you Heard Yet?"*

This, of course, all in the name of Caring, and even possibly Friendship. Diane feels bound by these silken threads; they're wrapping themselves around her chest – tight now with the suggestion of asthma - that hard pull in of breath against a thinning tube.

She's in front of the Ready Meals and looking at the Thai Lemongrass Chicken Curry with Jasmine Rice, and wondering when curry became green.

A couple stand beside her, classic Middle-England; he's wearing a woollen pullover that has leather patches on the elbows in the way that middle-class men wear their casual clothes, too conscious of the gesture they are making.

It's a relaxed informality that is careful to make sure that the garment is expensive, bought at one of those Country Fayre stalls that reassure with a price tag and the smell of horse.

She's wearing a skirt that'll sport a very good label, and a rather fine cashmere and silk scarf thrown negligently in a soft loop around a neck not unused to casually expensive jewellery.

Their voices are pitched just slightly too loud, they are generous with their lifestyle and perfectly happy to share it:

"Do you think Saint Agur this time?

"Well you know I prefer Brie, as long as it's creamy ripe."

"Some buffalo mozzarella just tossed among the baby tomatoes?"

Diane is gripping the ready meal, listening to them, she looks across at the man leaning as he stares into his trolley – it's full of the little white bags from the delicatessen counter, and organic strawberries and a couple of bottles of wine – why don't these people ever have toilet rolls in their trolley?

And they're going on and on about … cheese, the intricacies of cheese:

"That crumbly sour Goat's cheese was rather good."

"Or the Dolcelate that we brought back last year?"

"But it won't be as good here, will it ."

It's just bloody cheese, it's hard or it's soft – just buy the bloody cheese.

Diane knows that she has to move away from them and she twists her trolley sharply to one side to pass them. Leather-Elbows chooses that moment to push his trolley further out into the aisle; Diane jabs her shopping into his and the punnet of plums that she had so carefully laid on top of the kitchen-rolls tumbles down into the trolley, spilling the fruit amongst the cans of diet-cola and the plastic bottles of bleach and lavatory cleaner; the plums are squashing and bruising.

"Fuck! fucking fuck!" Diane's biting the words back into her mouth, she does not like to think of herself as someone who says this word, and she can feel the couple slide their eyes sideways to register her and then exchange a look between themselves.

She marches her trolley off down the aisle, and round the corner and off to the far side of the supermarket, she's knocking into other trolleys in her haste to get away from the moment, and her escape is accompanied by several outraged shouts:

"Excuse me!" …. "Watch what you're doing!"

Diane pushes her trolley up against the frozen foods and walks on without it, she's expecting to be hailed by some jobsworth in an overall, or arrested by that Assistant Manager with the boil on his neck. The further she walks from the trolley the more dangerous she feels; she's almost elated by a reckless energy as she brushes past the queue at the check-out. There's an old dear fumbling for the exact change in her small leather purse, she's sorting through the divided sections, arthritically slow:

"I know I've got a two pence piece here somewhere, dear."

Diane is behind her, stopped in her tracks by the woman who is now ferreting away in her handbag in her quest.

"Now just a minute, perhaps it was in my penny-wallet."

Diane tries to push past her and stares into the cloudy cataract eyes of the old woman.

"Oh get out of my way!" and Diane forces her way past. There's the tinkling sound of pennies being dropped and the hurt in those elderly eyes following her out into the street and lashing her into further fury.

Stupid, stupid; it was all that couple's fault, with their self-satisfied married-ness, and the cheese....their lives are so perfect that they have to discuss cheese!

The luxury of that conversation, it's soft trivia, and their shared knowledge that they can afford to debate the small details of their comfortable lives because there is nothing more serious or frightening in their lives than the choice of their cheese.

Diane's weaving her way through the car park, the words in her head a drum beat to her stumbling feet. That smug, oh so bloody smug acceptance of their happiness as if they're entitled to it, as if they've earned it and it will go on and on for ever ... and always, always as if they deserve it.

They're everywhere, walking together – just walking down a street, the bloody two-ness of them. And she has to keep seeing it and watching and smiling and she can't take it! The tears are streaming down Diane's face, her nose is running with a trail of mucus that runs over her top lip and into her mouth, she's coughing and snuffling at the wetness.

Her breathing is ragged, the wheezing breaths punishing her chest as it heaves. She leans against a parked car and notices the winking LED light of an alarm on the dashboard so she leans back away from the shinning metal. She can see her face reflected in the windscreen and she wipes at the snot and the tears with the back of her hand. She's fighting for her breath and for her sanity.

Across the car park, from inside his car, Tony watches her.
He recognises her, she was that nosy bitch who came round to talk to Lindsay, she was probably the one who put all those ideas in her head about her having to have a job. Interfering, always wanting to control you, telling you what to do and making you wait for it, he could see her now; she's gone over to the bench at the side of the car park and was sitting down, lazy bitch, just sitting there with her hand grabbing at her neck. She was undoing her blouse, pulling it open, pulling it down, showing off her cleavage.

Tony sits bolt upright in the seat of his car. He looks straight through the windscreen at the woman who is struggling to breathe.

Tony punches his dashboard and shouts with triumph at his sudden realisation. "She's doing it for me, she's showing me! "

Taunting him, teasing him; Lindsay's been talking to her, he'd left them together that day, what had they said? What women always talk about when they're alone together, slagging their men off to each other, giggling about what they don't do in bed, what they can't do... What had Lindsay told her about him? She must have mentioned the sex, why else would that tart be just sitting there flashing herself at him, showing him her tits !

Mocking him... Whore... Prick tease!

Tony's rocking himself, pushing his hands down onto his thighs; left, right, left, right, his shoulders jerking to the manic rhythm that might be a dance.

Across the car park, Diane leans back against the bench, dragging the air in through bared teeth; she pulls the hair grip out of the back of her hair and shakes the long blonde curls loose in an attempt to get rid of the bonds that are tying her chest.

Tony watches and understands, he has seen other women do this in the magazines that lie in the locked drawer of his den. She's throwing her head back for him, exposing her throat for him and still that pulling at her neck, revealing more of the soft curves of her breasts. He can see her reaching into her handbag but Tony cannot quite see what she's getting out. She's bringing her hand up to her mouth, opening her mouth, putting something into her mouth ...She's so obvious, so blatant ...

Diane is using her inhalers; first the blue one to open those tubes that are slowly closing and tightening against the air, then the brown one, the steroid, to medicate.

She throws them back into her bag and then leans down, doubled up.

Her blouse gapes across at the man in the car.

Tony rubs at his crotch and can feel a slight thickening against his hand. There, y'see, it just takes the right stimulus. Lindsay's so hopeless it's no wonder he can't get interested these days. He pushes his thumb hard against the flaccid flesh, working it, stroking it up and down and he's sure it's getting fatter, harder. The tight jeans reward his hopes by straining at the seam and he quickly unzips his fly. The soft whiteness bulges out between his fingers and lies quietly, bending limply in his hand.

"Bloody whore! ... I'll show you, you teasing bitch!"

212

Chapter 59

Trevor's at home. It's Monday, and he won't be there.

He standing in front of his Calendar – it's a 'Scenes of the Cotswolds'; because he thought it looked middle-class, last year's Beryl Cook one had been a mistake, he'd regretted it every time he went past it, he'd thought it would be fun, and make him smile, all those fat ladies doing inappropriate things, but it just depressed him because the women looked as if they were enjoying themselves more than he enjoyed laughing at them. No, this year's was a much better choice; he liked the way the days started on a Monday and he could write *Choir* in the little square on the left of the week; he writes the whole word, he doesn't just put a "C" or anything – at Christmas, when he's marking up his new Calendar for the new year he goes through writing the word on every Monday – he'd used a black felt tip this year and he liked the way the wedge of the felt made the 'C' look italic. These things matter to Trevor, he used to tell Zenata that they "kept him on track", but therapists never seem to understand that people *like* doing these things; they only ever seem to want to stop you – that and the elastic bands in pots.

Trevor looks at the word on the calendar, he's holding his 'correcting pen' – reading the label – "New Advanced Formula ! needle point precision corrector – no messy white overspill."

He should just remove the word – white over the black word – erase it, and then the next Monday and the next. He can't go on for months looking at that word; it's Warwickshire and the castle in November, and he'd been looking forward to that. This month's was just some high street with a Cotswold-stone war memorial and Trevor had hung onto Stow-on-the-Wold until the 4th because he didn't fancy looking at death for a whole month; it have been better to have that one for November, Poppy-Day and all that.

He's got to know what happens tonight, what Jonathan does, how Jonathan does, how the Choir react – they might even walk out? But Trevor is used to life not quite reaching his fantasies and visions of Lindsay and Diane striding manfully past a crestfallen Jonathan to stand outside in the playground remain stillborn.

Lindsay, he could ring Lindsay. He looks at his watch, eight a.m., bit early to ring people. He'd been awake half the night thinking about his calendar and what he was going to do about it, so he'd been up since six, but you have to be careful ringing people who aren't expecting it, he'd been caught like that before. He was pretty sure that Lindsay was the kind of woman who got up early to make her husband's breakfast. Tony looked like the sort of man who would require that. If he left it any later she might go out, and then she'd be out for the whole day and he wouldn't get her, he couldn't count on her going back to the house before choir – she might go straight on, after meeting somebody for an early supper – you could never depend on people behaving as you think they'll behave. No – he'd ring, anyway it was nearly five past eight now.

Lindsay jumps as the phone rings, she's standing by her sink and drops a knife and she coughs to cover the clattering. Tony is staring out of the dinning room window watching his neighbour leave the house opposite.
"Don't try and tell me he works in an Office … polo neck…"
Tony looks over at the phone.
"I hope that's not that woman who keeps coming round."
"She only came the once, Tony."
"It'll be a Hospital – this time of a morning – probably your Mother."

Tony and Lindsay are both watching the phone as it rings, just as Lindsay moves to answer it Tony reaches across and picks up the receiver.
"Hello? – yes she's here – who is that?" Tony is looking across at Lindsay who looks anxious.
"Is it the Hospital?"
"No… it's Trevor… for you"
"Trevor?"
"Yes – you know – Trevor." Tony is watching her keenly and he hands her the phone.
He then walks slowly out of the room into the hallway, where he stands, listening.

Chapter 60

The room felt dank, and Anna is pleased that she'd remembered to bring the air freshener, it was one of her 'bacterial' ones and she hoped that 'boys feet' came under the spray's 'micro-biotic elimination'

Anna looks at the room with Jonathan's eyes and sees the posters on the wall; she straightens the *'Macho isn't Mucho'* one to line up level with *'Racism Today'* and actually removes the very battered *'Achievements Week'* wall chart; she's walking around with it, wondering where to hide it when Jonathan arrives at the door. She's wrong-footed. "You're early!"
"Wanted to have a word before Middle-England arrived."

Anna's rolling up the wall chart in her hands; she waves it at the room:
"This is the snag of school accommodation" she's smiling weakly and hating it.
"Yes."
"We're moving on, of course, especially now that you are involved."
"Anna...."
"Look I know that this isn't very <u>you</u> – not now – but it will be. I have such plans for this Choir. Cheltenham is only the beginning; I'm going to throw them at every Competition there is ... then London. Oh Yes! – don't you see Jonathan that we're too big for Witsham, you and I, we need to breathe..."
She remembers the air freshener.
Anna walks over to her bag and is trying to get out the can without Jonathan actually seeing what it is.
"Look – Darling – Tonight is just a try out, you know."
"Oh I know, I know .. but you'll see the potential I know you will. I just so hope that my star choristers come tonight – you must listen out for Linda."
Jonathan wanders over to the piano and presses a few keys, a slight puckering around his mouth as he assesses the tone. Anna is using this moment to squirt a surreptitious "Spring Bouquet" and Jonathan coughs and waves his hand in front of his face.
This is not how she had planned it; Anna can feel the evening slipping away from her. Why did this always happen? everything within her grasp and it's slithering about, evading, she had to get it back or she'd lose him. She looks across at Jonathan, there's a peevish look about him and he's looking around the room again.

Anna moves swiftly over to him, she places her hands on his shoulders, looking up into his face.

"Jonathan…?"

Jonathan looks down at her, at the slash of lipstick on the rather tight little mouth; but it's red lipstick, red-yes-yes lipstick.

"Un-na… "

And Anna giggles. "Russian!"

He bends his face to hers and she moves a leg in against his crotch.

"They'll be here in a minute."

"That's why you're doing this – you're a tease, Un-na."

She's smiling up at him feeling her power over him against her leg, and he catches his breath.

"You wouldn't do this if you could follow through, would you."

"I might .." she's actually rubbing her thigh up into his hardness.

"One day, you little bitch," he's purring it at her, and she's loving the moment. She's got him back, he's stopped looking round that bloody room now, hasn't he …. it hasn't evaded her; she's got it back.

There's the sound of a car arriving outside and Anna peels away from him with a delicious reluctance.

The women are arriving. Jonathan sits down quickly onto the piano stool to hide his erection. He leans forward, laying his arms along the top of the piano, drumming his fingers against its stained wood as he watches Anna click straight back into choir mistress mode; all welcoming smiles and greetings. It's too quick, she's not aroused, she's playing him, the cold cow, he could bet himself that she wasn't even wet. He watches her handing out tonight's music and makes himself a promise.

Chapter 61

Trevor's looking at the clock in his sitting room. He'd promised himself he wouldn't do this, he wouldn't watch each minute and start imagining.

He'd planned to watch one of his videos, the 'Penguins' one he'd been saving for something special. He'd even put the video on top of the television, he could see it now, it had got one of his little post-it stickers on it with 'Save' biro'd across it and he'd drawn an outline of a penguin because they were easy to draw, penguins.

Chapter 62

Anna's decided upon a quick warm-up and then to throw them straight into "Rhythm of Life", they were good at that; she had to hit Jonathan with something impressive right at the start. She's excited; the moment with Jonathan had not aroused her, Anna was seldom sexually aroused, ambition was Anna's sex and it had fed this hunger.

The Choir were waiting for her command; Linda stood at the end of the soprano line and Anna allowed her a special smile. Susie was up for it tonight, even Grace, fat Grace, looked alert; despite their supposed loyalty to Trevor, these women were vain and that vanity meant that they would sing well, they would impress Jonathan. That was enough. Anna did not need their affection.

Jonathan was flashily accompanying them up and down the scales; he added lots of trills at the end of the basic chords, lifting his right hand high in the air at the end of the notes. Anna watched him, recognising.
"Rhythm of Life" went well; probably the best they'd ever done it.
Anna brought them off with a final raising of both her arms, flicking her palms toward the women and holding the final silence.
She looked across at Jonathan and he allowed her a slight nod.

At the break the talk drifted toward the Carnival; Susie was full of "What Stephen thought" and what exact size their 'float' should be.
Jonathan's eyes narrowed slightly at the word 'float' and when he looked across at Anna she avoided his eye.
"Thing is – it would be better if we had the Lorry – Stephen's very aware of health of safety, well he has to be, and it would be fatal to be all squashed around the edges if there was a jolt."
Rowena's nodding. "There's got to be some sort of railing to stop us falling off, only I'll have my drum and my hands will be involved musically as opposed to clinging on…"

Grace's main concern is the costumes: "I can't say often enough that I totally oppose any silly outfits .. it'll look demeaning if we're in anything scanty.."
Linda, of the very good body that goes topless in Marbella, is warming to any exposure. "Oh let's do basques and suspenders and stockings!"

A dull red flush is creeping up from Grace's neck; she's looking at Susie for support. Susie is aware of her own body, of the work she has done at the gym for the past couple of years. "Well it would be nice to be a bit daring for once, wouldn't it ..."

Grace actually jabs her with a fleshy elbow, and Susie turns to look at her friend, at the soft jowly face and the over-shirt that is meant to hide the bulk of her. "Well, Grace, honestly, I don't see why we should all have to cover up, I mean, some of us work really hard at our figures. Look, I'm sorry, but I don't allow myself treats.. and that's the price I pay .. so why can't I reap the reward for once."

Lindsay's feeling Grace's fear, the fear of being swept along with this, of a general decision that will force a terrible exposure.

"I have to say I agree with Grace on this one ... I mean ... some people have religious objections, don't they ..."

Susie's irritated by this. "You mean your husband wouldn't let you." This shuts Lindsay up and leaves Grace to seek other help.

"Jo-Anne, you don't want to be half naked do you?"

"Oh I don't know, it might frighten my daughter, so there's a plus."

Susie reaches out to touch Grace's arm. "It'd be fun."

There was that thin-women word again ...."No, it wouldn't."

"Look, we always dress in long black skirts for the Concerts, people only ever see us like that, so it would shake their pre-conceptions up a bit, show them we're not just a bunch of middle-aged past-its....you see it's all about perception isn't it...it's about challenging ...."

"Bollocks, it's about you and Linda showing off your spray-tans and it would not be 'fun' – oh yes it would be fun for you, for you with your body - but not for me ..." Grace's face is now a thick and livid red.

Paulette's trying to be helpful: "Well look what it did for the W.I."

"Bugger the W.I."

Grace grabs at her handbag and makes to leave the room.

"Oh for heaven's sake, Grace, don't leave. "

"I'm going to the loo."

Jonathan, realising that Anna is avoiding his look, goes over to her.

She's leafing quickly through a pile of music.

"Anna!"

"Sorry?" she is feigning distraction, and he snatches the music out of her hands..

"What the hell is this about a 'float' at the Carnival?"

"Oh? – oh it's just a thought really – to raise our profile."

"Along with the Morris Dancers and the Brownies dressed as tomatoes …I thank you, No."

Grace, squashed in beside the cricket bats and the footballs, has locked the lavatory door. She stands in front of the rust freckled mirror and twists at the elasticated-waist of her skirt that reaches the soft dough rolls of her ankles, and she hates herself.

Susie is not immune to Grace's pain, but she has had years of it, years of encouraging her and looking at the little weight loss charts, and she's eager to get her husband involved. "Stephen's offered to do the photos for us; he'll be on the float so that he can capture any close-ups along the route." Susie's smiling around at the others, confident of approval.

Jo-Anne's offering her husband too. "Mike can walk along the side of the float to collect the money."

"Oh yes, we'll need buckets."

Paulette - "Can I just say one thing; I think if everybody else is bringing somebody, then I want Harvey to have a role."

"Can he carry a bucket? – might look quite sweet."

Susie's dismissing this: "Hardly – he'd drop a bucket if he saw a 'smell' …"

Jonathan's looking at Anna in increasing horror.

Anna's explaining. "Her dog."

"Oh great … lovely … and where am I supposed to be?"

Susie's reassuring him. "Stephen can strap the piano up by the front, he's done it before for the Donkey Sanctuary."

Anna is keen to stop this.

"Well everybody – whatever we decide I think we should discuss this out of practice evenings."

"I could type out a list of members who would be keen to form a Committee."

Anna tries to smile at her: "At the end of the session please Paulette … let's get on, we made a marvellous start this evening…" and she hustles the women back into line.

Outside in that other room, Grace still stands looking at the large square that is her body; she sees the hollow hunger in her eyes and feels the emptiness inside her.

She'll go back to Weight Watchers, she's acutely aware of a mortifying prickle of how this will be. The crawling shame of facing Mrs. Pointer again, and all that sweet condescension. That this will be her ninth time, but this time she won't tell Geoffrey, she won't tell Susie either – she's seen her friend's look, that 'patient' look of the uncomprehending. All the reasonable: "Just cut down, Dear", "Eat salads". God, why does nobody understand.

Grace is always hungry, even on Christmas Day after a total blow out she could start over and eat it all again. Even at the end of the evening meal and she's clearing away the plates she'll look at a roast potato left on Geoffrey's plate and fold it quickly into her hand, she's always careful to make sure he's not watching though. She seems to be always hiding food. There's a cupboard in the dining room in the pine dresser that's supposed to be for the posh crockery, the wedding present cruet sets and the cocktail sticks brought home from hotels, and Grace has got a tupperware box in there that's shoved at the back behind the silver teapot they're never going to use, because that's where the Cadbury's flakes live. She's learned how to palm a chocolate button and put it into her mouth on the pretence of a cough, and she's had whole conversations with total strangers while melting a Malteser under her tongue.

Always hungry, only just sometimes after a bowl of midnight cereal, does she get that wonderful full feeling. That wholeness.

But now she has to punish herself again, she must ring up Mrs. Pointer, who, if there is a God, might even have left. But she must book herself in for the next meeting. She must.

Perhaps they'll give her a discount for being so regular. Perhaps this time it won't be so hard and she won't stand on the scales at the "weigh-in" tasting that flat metallic tang of humiliation as she reads those bloody little numbers that have remained the same.

Chapter 63

Trevor has not watched his penguins, he didn't want to waste them on this. His watch has told him that Choir must be over by now; he's staring down at his Radio Times and realises that he has doodled all over the article on Dolphin Watch that he'd meant to save.

Something outside his window makes him look up; the sun did this sometimes, flash a beam of light at the curtains if a tree was in the wind, but it was dark outside. It would have been headlights, but he hadn't heard a car.
Trevor moves over to put a finger where the curtains met and slightly, just very slightly lifts the material an inch out from the window so that he can see a thin small glimpse of his street.

Trevor always feels watched and often 'performs' for these unknown viewers of his life; he'll cross over to his piano and lift a piece of music up just a little too high in his hands so that they can see what he's doing, or he'll sit and read a book – if he's not ashamed of the title – and let the jacket and the title be readable from outside. He peers out into the puddled street and jumps at a spray of rain against the glass.

* *

Outside in that drizzle of wetness, Tony sits in his car and watches the thin line of yellow light widen as the curtains moved; he'd told Lindsay he wouldn't be back until late tonight, so now he waits.

* *

Trevor goes back over to his chair; he feels a heaviness pulling at him and he wants his bed. The lamp by the window will turn off automatically in a couple of hours but tonight he doesn't care what they think, and he turns it off at the plug. Upstairs in his bedroom he crosses to the window there and does not do his 'casual' look up at the night sky before closing the curtains; he was sick of pretending to know about the stars anyway.

* *

Lindsay, sitting on the edge of her bed, is dialling Trevor's number; he'd asked her to tell him about Jonathan playing at Choir. She won't tell him about the flashy bits and how Jonathan kept flicking his wrists into the air at the end of the numbers, she hadn't liked that. There was something about Jonathan that pulls her mind to Tony, something about his hands. She wants to help Trevor; Anna is a bully and Trevor's voice had had a crack in it when he had asked her to report back to him, and he'd said 'You'll probably think this is silly' but Lindsay had not thought that he was silly.

She remembered the meeting at the Corn Café and how he had fumbled with the zip on his little purse and she remembered the softness of those fingers, that slight trembling. But she's worried that Tony will come back at any minute. She hears a noise in the street and quickly puts the receiver down; she'll ring him tomorrow, after Tony has left for work. She'll ring when it's safe.

Chapter 64

It's last drinks at the" Crown and Anchor", Diane is staring into her gin and tonic, squashing the thin slice of lemon against the side of the glass so that the liquid is clouded with the fine shreds of pith. The ice has long since melted and there's a milky line along the rim that the dishwasher has failed to remove.

Paulette, chewing softly at a stray blonde hair, is in full flow.

"It's always the same, everybody gets to bring *the husbands,* like we've all got them there, on tap. It's all right for Susie and her precious Stephen and Jo-Anne going on and on about her bloody daughter…"

Diane is wondering whether it's too late to complain about her glass now that she's messed about with the lemon.

"No-body thinks about me, with Chris in Puerto Rico" Paulette's gulping her vodka breezer against the anger.. "I just don't see why the engineers need him to supervise them all the time anyway. I mean, they've got all the Plans and everything, I don't see why he can't just pop out there now and again to check on things every month or something…"

Diane looks across at the other woman, at the petulant mouth and the face greasy with temper. "Why don't you go out there with him?"

Paulette bangs her drink down "Oh God, why does everybody say that! As if that would solve everything … it's Puerto Rico! what am I going to do in Puerto Rico? and anyway what about Harvey! He's all settled now at the Obedience Training School and he's really calm about the new vet I discovered in Corn Street."

"But if you never see Chris ….?"

"So I'm supposed to just up-sticks and follow him round the world am I, it won't end there, they're talking about him transferring to Egypt in the Spring ..Egypt! – do you know how thick a spaniel's hair is, he'd fry!….so you see I think I should be allowed to have Harvey on the float, everybody's going to have somebody up there, even Jo-Anne's Mike is going to come and walk along beside us with a collecting tin, and he has never come to any of the Concerts…"

"Well if it's any consolation, I won't have an attendant male."

Paulette's quick to deny Diane's plight: "Oh it's all right for you; you're free now. I'm just neither one thing nor the other."

Diane's still staring into the warm dregs of her gin; she's weary of listening to Paulette's nonsense, at the stupid prisons people build for themselves, the endless discontent.

"No – look, I mean it, Diane – you should get a job! Or get away from here – get away from all the memories and being terrified of bumping into Paul at every corner."

"Yes! Yes – probably!" Diane's getting up, collecting her bag and coat from the back of the chair. She's looking down at Paulette and relents at the sheen of pale sweat on the small pointed face.
"Everybody thinks they can fix everybody else, don't they - go to Puerto Rico, move to Cornwall, change a job, change a life … I've a niggly little feeling that none of it matters at all, that nothing really changes anything; we're all just moving the deckchairs around on the Titanic."
"Well, if I can persuade Anna to let me have Harvey on the float I shall have changed something! …. Won't I!"

There's a moment between the women and Diane feels the thick, heavy weight of the pointlessness of this, of all of it.
"Yes, yes of course you will."

The barman is shouting at his customers to go home. The women reach the door and a fine drizzle of rain mists Paulette's glasses.
"I'm thinking of having that laser thing done, treat myself."
"Good idea."
"I mean, Chris had his teeth done; said he had to keep up the Corporate Face … he's practically got a whole new mouth now."
She's wiping her glasses with a tissue, trying to get rid of the smears.
"It's like looking though milk sometimes."
Diane looks up at the street lights and the rain angling silver lines across the yellow glow. "Yes, go for it."
Paulette's rammed the glasses back on and is squinting into the wetness.
"I mean it's a basic right, isn't it – seeing clearly."

Chapter 65

Tony is staring up at Trevor's bedroom window. What are they playing at? Trevor wasn't at Choir? – he's always at Choir. Lindsay's been lying to him; she's been trying to confuse him with some rigmarole about Anna getting a new Accompanist, and now those bedroom curtains are drawn … was he supposed to think that Trevor had just gone to bed? How stupid did they think he was? Lindsay hadn't turned up, so what was that phone call about?

He'd listened – he'd had to stand in his hallway and listen to her, to the murmurings.

He remembered the feeling as he'd stood there with his forehead pressed against that watercolour he'd bought for her and he'd looked at the watery trees in that thin brass frame - he'd spent so long choosing it for her, knowing she'd like it that the soft blue light in the painting echoed the egg-shell blue of the hallway – listening to her soft voice and smelling the betrayal.

He turns on the engine of the car and pushes the gear stick forward, he hasn't engaged the clutch and the metal screams its protest.
Tony looks down at the gear stick, not comprehending his mistake,
he is a meticulous driver and does not make mistakes, not these kind of silly women blunders that make him raise his eyebrows at traffic lights.

Inside the house, Trevor hears the scrunch of metal against metal and stirs in his sleep. He is dreaming of penguins, but they're very big penguins, larger than life, larger than him; he's trying to get the penguins to all stay together on an ice flow but they keep falling off into the water, they don't seem to notice him and they're all rocking the ice so that Trevor is terrified that he will fall into the deep cold around them.

As a car races off from outside his house the noise penetrates so that the dream whisks away from him and the images disappear so that in the morning all that he will feel is a resentment against wildlife in general … that, and a vague coldness.

* * * * * * * * * * * * * * * * * * * *

Anna sips de-caffeinated coffee and watches late-night television; she cannot sleep, Jonathan's comments after Choir remain in her head round and round on a hamster wheel of self-justification: his whining about the "Carnival Float", her trying to minimise the small town images. He'd got rather insistent about them having a 'meeting' at his flat during the week, and Anna was in no doubt about the nature of that. Jonathan wanted her to pay his Price. She knew that. It was all getting a bit out of hand; she just wanted a bit of flirtation, that's all, nothing wrong with that – everybody did it, didn't they.

Now he was pushing it, and he still hadn't committed himself to being the Accompanist. She's seen his face tonight as he watched her little Choir – why on earth had Paulette decided to wear that droopy cardigan and even Susie, ballsy attention-seeking Susie, had looked like a typical provincial housewife in that floral number and her red hair tied up away from her face in that clip.

They'd let her down. Linda had snuffled her way though her opening solo on "Down to the River to Pray" – why did she have to have a cold tonight ! – tonight, when it mattered so much that they looked professional and… shit it!

Why did everybody always let her down? She tried and tried and planned and thought things over and over and it didn't matter a damn. And now Roy was plodding downstairs …

"I thought I heard you down here – not like you to watch…"

Roy is peering at the television set: "....Ice Hockey?"

"Well I'm obviously not watching it as such, am I?"

"Couldn't sleep then?"

Anna is grinding her teeth. "No, apparently not."

Roy ambles through into the kitchen, and Anna can hear him fumbling about in the cupboards for tea bags.

She's listening to the slowness of him as he goes from cupboard to cupboard and she almost screeches at him:

"If you want de-caff' they're in the blue tin."

She can hear him humming to himself, and the creak of his knees as he bends down to rummage in another cupboard …

"Just wondered if there was a hobnob."

Anna can feel a sharp pain slicing into her forehead.

The television is telling her that there is live coverage of the Stanley Cup Finals tomorrow night and it flashes up a table of the Ice Hockey. Teams and the scores, and Anna wonders at the differences of other lives, that there are people actually watching this now, and caring about it; people who will tune in to the Final tomorrow and that they will Celebrate or mourn.

Roy is standing at the doorway to the sitting room; he's found his biscuit and Anna can sense rather than see the crumbs as they fall onto the carpet.

"We've never been to Italy, have we?"

"What are you on about – oh Roy, please use a plate!"

"Italy."

"What about it?"

"I was just thinking about it, what it would be like, you know."

Roy is leaning against the doorway, a dreamy look in his eyes, staring at the television and the padded men flying across the ice, and seeing pizza coloured dresses on dark curly haired girls.

"Go to bed, Roy."

Chapter 66

Tony is watching Lindsay as she prepares his breakfast. She is aware of his eyes following her and she is trying not to let him see her hands as she cracks the egg on the side of the bowl.

"You should use a knife."

"I always break the yolk if I do that."

"Let me show you," he moves across to stand behind her, and reach around her to hold the next egg. Lindsay is aware of every touch of his shirt against her, of a trousered leg brushing against hers; she is willing herself not to flinch or move away from him, she knows from a deep instinct that that will anger him and that it will prove something to him, something about guilt and about power. She is trying to breathe slowly against the fine trickle of sweat that is creeping down her neck onto the collar of her blouse.

Tony has cracked the egg with a small butter knife that lies beside the breadboard.

"You see – you should use the back of the knife."

"Yes. Right."

"What happened last night?" He's still standing close up behind her, his breath is against her neck.

"What do you mean?" She wants to move, she wants to move away from him, it is taking all her strength to remain still and not to run.

"What happened at Choir?"

"Oh – nothing – what do you mean?"

"Trevor wasn't there."

What did he mean, about Trevor, and how did he know he hadn't been there?

She tries to sound casual, light, to make it a nothing-comment, but it comes out on a breath of culpability.. "Well Anna's sort of fired him really."

"Really?"

"Yes – there's this Jonathan who's taken over – nobody likes him very much, he's one of those sneery sorts, you know."

Tony moves back away from her and Lindsay has to concentrate hard on standing; on not slipping down, sliding down onto the floor and staying there.

"What's naughty Trevor done then?"

"Nothing!" It's too quick, too defensive.

"Oh?" Tony is looking at her, and she flutters away from him.

229

He catches her wrist as she goes.

"What's the matter Lindsay?"

"Nothing. Nothing, Tony what are you <u>doing</u>?"

He spreads his arms wide. He's smiling at her, mocking her. "Not doing a thing, am I."

"Yes – you are, you're... I don't know.... you're thinking something..."

"And you are getting into one of your 'states' aren't you."

"No."

"I think you should go back to bed."

"I don't want to go back to bed, why should I go back to bed, I'm not ill."

Tony shrugs .. "Well, have it your own way, you always do."

Lindsay looks across at him "I don't have anything my own way" and it's a small bewildered voice. She moves out of the kitchen, careful to make her escape slow, careful not to draw attention to the fact that she is escaping and that she is afraid; if she once openly acknowledges that he is violent and that she is frightened, then there is no defence, she has to pretend that this is all nothing, some sort of silly misunderstanding, and then they can go back, they can go back to being normal again.

But he has hit her, and she knows that it is real, but she must push this down and away, for if this is real then this is chaos and she will never be able to undo it, she will never be able to return to that safe place where they had been before.

Chapter 67

Anna is in the choir room. She'd left the Rogers and Hammerstein's Medley books, she doesn't trust the choir to remember the phrasing for the Sound of Music melody so she's popped in to see if they're still on the piano, she can't remember leaving them there, and it angers her that she had forgotten to pick them up, she never forgets that kind of thing, but Jonathan has scrambled her up, she feels wrong footed and now makes the kind of mistakes that she used to despise. Of course, in the old days Trevor would have packed them away in his briefcase, but she can't rely on him now. Another Price paid. She's hoping that this is worth it, this difference.

The curtains move, a slight trembling. She turns to look at them and sees Tony standing just inside the door. He's scuffing the side of his heel against the leg of one of the desks. "Why did you tell her to cut her hair?"

"What?"

"My wife. You told her to cut her hair."

"Did I? – I really can't remember."

"Oh I'm sure you do, Anna, I'm sure you know exactly what you do and why you do it."

Anna is looking beyond him, to the school gates. "How did you get in here?"

It's a sneer. "That Caretaker doesn't really take care, does he?"

Anna can feel small pins of alarm pricking the back of her neck.

"Well, he'll be following me in here in a minute, he always does if it's not a choir night, I think he thinks I'm going to steal the pencils," and she's wondering why she's making lame jokes, and why she is so ill at ease.

Tony sits down at the nearest desk.

"Not like our day, are they? They used to be all little, with a hole in the top for the ink well," he's stroking the smooth veneer.

Anna gives a small tinkle of a laugh, it's a metallic sound. "Good God you're not that old! They haven't had desks like that since Dickens!" and she doesn't understand why she's talking like this because she never talks like this, this jovial laughing.

"Oh my school still had them, we never used the little holes though, apart from stuffing them with crisp packets."

"Well, the material I came for doesn't seem to be here. I'll have to ring Trevor or..." and she's moving over to the door, aware that she will have to pass him. And not wanting to.

"Things happen in a marriage sometimes... accidents... silly little things that don't really matter, but then it all takes a sort of turning."

He's stood up, and is between her and the door. Anna is not easily intimidated and is irritated by the power this man has seemed to bring into the room. Her room. Her choir room.

"I'm sorry Tony but your marriage is really none of my concern, now if you don't mind, I'm going to have to ask you to leave. This is the choir room, you see.."

"Oh I know what this room is. I've got a room like this. A room where I'm the boss." He's smiling at her, as if they have a bond, a similarity that he knows they share. "I've got something special in my room."

Anna thinks he means sordid and she curls a thin lip over perfect teeth.

Anna doesn't do sordid. "Yes, I'm sure that you do. Now if you don't mind."

He's still standing in her way. Not doing anything in particular, not threatening in any way, it's just that Anna feels a faint tugging of the carpet beneath her feet, that uncertainty.

Tony is looking at her. "I bet your Dad loved you."

And if he could have said anything to throw her it was that and Anna takes care to speak very calmly. "My father died when I was very young."

"Aah ! – there you are then!"

"Where, where are we?"

"I never had a father either" so Tony consigns all the hurt and the fear to an earlier grave.

"Who brought you up then?"

"If you must know, my Aunt." And Anna is forcing another one of her smiles.

"Aaah."

"We were very fond of each other. We still are."

"That's lucky then."

"Oh yes, she always encouraged me, supported me, you know.." Anna does not know why she is saying these things, and why she is saying them to Tony. She never talks to anybody about Aunt Jo, she used to talk to Roy, when they were first married, and couples care about these things.

It seemed important then to tell him how things were, and there was that small time in her life when Anna wanted to be Known.

To be understood.

Roy had been very sympathetic but she remembered now how he'd keep saying that it was a generation thing, and that she couldn't really expect her Aunt to understand ambitions when she herself had been denied any.

Anna had realised then that any ambitions that Aunt Jo had ever had, and there had been a few - mainly concerned with being the Manageress of the Florist's shop on the corner of Sydney Street – but these had been stifled by the death of her sister and the arrival of a rather thin eight-year-old with a case full of miniature china dolls, hard and easily broken.

Anna does not want to remember these things, and not now, facing this strange man who is looking at her as if he can see the thoughts in her mind and the rows and rows of little smiling dolls.

"My Dad was like that."
Like what? what was he saying?
"Mind you I think he'd rather that I'd joined the Army." Tony's looking over Anna's head, at the children's drawings pinned around the walls. There's a livid painting of a group of people who might just be a family, an older man with his hand on a child's shoulder.

Tony's laughing. "He used to say - Thing is your Mum and me would worry too much, spend all our time looking at the news on the telly and thinking that you might get hurt." (This memory of a man who had screamed at him that terrible Christmas, and all the other Christmases of pretending not to want a television, and being so afraid that his father would decide to touch that belt that hung behind the kitchen door.)

So why is he standing here talking to this woman and telling her that his father had.. what?… and he stalls even on the thought of the word.

His parents had never said that word and he could even remember the shock of hearing his father say that he "Loved marzipan" one day when they'd been down the shops and Tony was trying not to look at anything too much, and not to look as if he was whining for something.

So Anna and Tony face each other, each locked in their own pasts, each shackled by the tight bands of pain and regret that are hard against their chests.

Anna is first to break the moment, she has a future to build and many songs to sing.

"Yes. Now, as I said, I told Reg I'd only be a few minutes, I'm surprised he hasn't been in here to check."

"He couldn't give a bugger."

Anna walks towards the door, not pausing as she reaches him. Just as their clothes touch, Tony stands aside.

"My wife. She shouldn't stand at the front. It's too exposed; Lindsay doesn't like that, being noticed."

The curtains are swaying, billowing as if pushed into the room by a malevolent wind and Tony turns to look at them. Those shadowed walls, smeared with children's hands and careless biros stare at this man and his madness. Tony sniffs at the fetid smell of adolescent feet and his eyes dart with a swift awareness around the room and he feels its recognition, and the room watches Tony and it knows.

Anna looks at him as she pauses at the doorway, and, as he leaves and Anna reaches to turn off the lights, she wrinkles her nose against a new smell in the room. It's not the stale sweat of school- boys, it's a rich and acrid vapour and it makes her think of the butcher's window at Christmas and the rabbits hanging upside down with their little heads inside plastic bags and the blood puddling.

Chapter 68

The phone beside Anna's bed is ringing. Roy snuffles in his morning doze and nudges her to answer it. Anna was not asleep and she already knows who this will be; she has fought Jonathan off in her thoughts all night and she can feel his insistence through the harsh jangling ring-tone. She picks up the receiver. "Yes?"

Roy is listening, he's turned over onto his back.

"Is it the Care Worker?"

Anna holds her hand over the mouthpiece and snaps at Roy.

"Why do you always think it's your Mother?"

Roy's heaved himself up to look at the little clock on his bedside table.

"Well it's seven o'clock. You only get emergencies before nine."

Anna is listening furiously to Jonathan telling her that he has been thinking of her all night and that he must see her today.

"I don't know what my plans are, it's far too early … I'll call you back," and she actually hangs up on him.

Roy reaches a heavy hand over to lay it on her stomach.

"Who was that then?"

"Oh just bloody Choir, you know."

"At seven o'clock in the mor….."

"Yes!"

"Bit of a rum do."

"Yes, that's why I hung up."

"Was it Trevor?"

"No – Trevor wouldn't do that." .. No, he wouldn't, and Anna suddenly yearns for the dogged devotion and obedience of Trevor.

Roy has left his hand lying on Anna's stomach, she can feel the heavy heat of it through her nightdress. It's disturbing her; she can't work out whether this is one of Roy's bumbling attempts at intimacy or if he has just forgotten that he has put his hand there. It was difficult to tell with Roy, sometimes he'd start fiddling about in a vaguely intimate area and then sort of drift off and dreamily start that blessed humming.

Chapter 69

Trevor's coming out of his door, he turns the key in the lock and then turns it even further, once, twice, but then he has to turn the key back to get it out of the lock. He's standing there, worried that in turning it back on itself he's unlocked it again. He pushes against the door, feeling it resist, but he can't be sure. He can feel himself being watched from over the road, he knows that they always watch him when he goes out, he's seen their shadows against the net curtains – nobody has net curtains any more except in situation comedies on television – but They do. Trevor walks awkwardly down the path of his small front garden, towards his gate, and then, a pantomime of forgetfulness, he claps his hand to his forehead and spins round to march back to the front door again. Turns the lock and he's inside the door. He pushes the door "to" and stands in the hall for the requisite few minutes for him to have got what he's come back in for, then he's outside again and now he can check it properly; turn the lock twice, and then take the key out. Pushing and turning the handle at the same time to double-check. His hand is pressed against the door; it leaves a fine mist of sweat against the wood.

"Locked, locked." He's nodding.

He turns with studied casualness and strolls down to his front gate, careful not to acknowledge the net curtains, he's even whistling his boredom as he fixes his eyes upon the tree at the corner of the street, and then he sees it. There, watching him, waiting for him again. The Dog. The black dog. It's getting up as it sees him, stretching its front paws out in a long slide amongst the leaves. Standing, shaking itself, looking across at Trevor and waiting for what the man will do next. It's lunchtime, the animal must have been there all morning; Trevor had felt it, had felt its eyes against the walls of his house. He'd known.

Trevor is looking across at his car, he has to park on the other side of the street because that's where the street lamp is, that's where he always parks so that he can reverse into the lane and then be on the right side of the street for the town; it's just common sense. It's probably twenty feet to his car, and the dog is almost the same distance, just standing there by that tree, daring him to make a dash for it. It's flicking its back legs shooting sprays of leaves back against the tree trunk; Trevor's thinking of that bull on "Naturewatch", that's what it did before it charged – although the bull didn't actually charge because that idiot who used to be in Blue Peter was doing a piece to camera and the by the time the shot went back to the bull it had wandered off.

Bit of luck that, could have been nasty, could have gored the film crew ....stop it, stop it. Zenata would call this his circular-avoidance, going round and round to.... Oh God the dog's coming toward him.

Trevor sprints over to his car, scrambling to get the keys out of his pocket as he runs...

"Please God, please God..."

He sets the alarm off because he's fumbled the off button and re-set it, so with the alarm screaming, Trevor juggles alarm buttons and keys and finally falls into the driver's seat and slams the door. He presses down the door lock and leans over the steering wheel. Out of the corner of his eye he can see the net curtains billow softly against their window, he doesn't look at the dog – once it recognises that Trevor 'knows' then there can be no more pretence, there would be no reason for it not to attack.

The dog has sat down again by the tree; he's quite interested in the noise and the man jumping about by his car, but not interested enough to waddle over there. It's dry under the tree and the leaves are warm.

Trevor drives slowly along his road, past a parked car with a man reading a newspaper in the driving seat.

So Trevor, who has spent so many years performing for the watchers of his life, is now watched.

Tony lowers the newspaper and slowly follows Trevor's car, the mobile phone on the passenger seat is ringing, but Tony ignores it, he can see his Office number; they'll only be nagging, he was sick of it. It was his lunch break, he could do what he liked.

Trevor is driving into Witsham, he looks in his side mirror; part of him expects the black dog to be running alongside the car, tongue lolling out, teeth bared, and he instinctively picks up speed. He reckons that the dog will give up once he hits the roundabout, or maybe it'll try and follow him and get killed, it wouldn't be his fault, he hadn't asked the bloody dog to follow him, he'd pretend he'd never seen the thing before – he didn't think they'd caught him on any CCTV cameras. It was their fault; he shouldn't have to be harassed like this anyway.

Chapter 70

Anna is driving to Jonathan's flat. After that stupid phone call this morning she'd had to ring him back and agree to a meeting. He'd said that he had to discuss the Carnival and his role as New Accompanist, but Anna knew better, she knew that it was "pay day". She had been torn as to what to wear; she wanted to keep him at arm's length, so trousers and a top would be sensible, but Anna is vain, and Anna likes the idea of exciting Jonathan, so her tight skirt - the one that slides up as she walks - has won over caution. She can control him; she hasn't kept Roy on short rations for all these years to not know a few tricks.

* *

Jonathan is waiting for Anna to arrive at his flat. That phone call this morning had been inspired; it had flustered her into agreeing to this meeting. He's even made the bed – after spraying it with that "fresh linen" stuff – anyway she'd be in no mood to notice any stains, he'd done his best with a bit of wet kitchen roll, it would have to do.

He hears her car outside and goes to the window and watches her; Jonathan believes that he can tell a lot from how a woman prepares to meet him and he is pleased that she's sitting there looking in her make-up mirror, re-applying that slash of red – yes, yes, - lipstick. Now she's fiddling with her hair, pulling little strands around her chin. She's unsure, he likes that. She looks up at his window and Jonathan moves back into the room, he hears a car start up and thinks she's bottled it, she's going – he goes back to the window, but it wasn't her, she's getting out of her car - it's "on".

* *

Trevor has parked in the supermarket car park and is looking around, his frightened-little-rabbit face peering through the car windows, he's making sure that the black dog hasn't followed him.

Tony drives his car past Trevor and parks so that he can see him and he watches as Trevor gets out of his car and the lights flash as the alarm is set. Trevor looks into the car at the dashboard to check that the led-light is flashing and that the alarm is on.

Tony waits until Trevor has moved off towards the shops before he follows him. The mobile phone bleeps again and Tony snatches it to his ear.

"Yes, I know, I know what the time is. I'm following something up, I'll get back to the Office in.." and he's looking at his watch..

".. half an hour, yes I know, look, the signal's bad here, you're breaking up," and Tony punches the off button and throws the mobile back onto the passenger seat.

"Get off my back!"

Tony no longer knows why he is following Trevor; he has gone down this road and can see no way back. He knows he is being tricked, that they're all against him now, but he can't find a way to undo this, he can't find a return. Lindsay has gone all nervous on him and there must be a reason and the only reason he can think of is Trevor.

So Tony follows him into the shopping centre, the very following seeming to justify itself.

* *

Anna is perched on the edge of Jonathan's sofa, there's a glass of white wine in her hand and she's cradling it against the heat of her palm.

"I just want things to be clear, Jonathan, I really do need to have a commitment from you, you know, I've fired poor Trevor now...."

"Trevor's much more your local Choir sort of man really."

"But you said that you'd be..."

"I said I'd give it a go, Anna."

"Is it the Carnival? .. I know you think that's all pretty tacky, but..."

"It's not just that, you see Darling I just don't know where I stand with you?" and Jonathan is kneeling sweetly in front of her, taking the glass out of her hands and holding them in his own.

Anna smiling down at him. "You know I adore you, but ..."

"But?"

"Well I'm married, aren't I."

"And what's that got to do with anything?"

"I couldn't betray Roy."

She could, of course, but this moral high ground suits Anna's purpose perfectly, she even spreads helpless hands out, releasing them from Jonathan's rather damp clasp.

"What can I do?"

Jonathan gets up and walks away from her. "You're playing games Anna."

Anna can feel Cheltenham slipping away from her, all her ambitious dreams for the choir - the interviews, the articles in the press, the recognition at last for what she is - she's looking at Jonathan and wondering if it might just be worth it.

She gets up and stands behind him, slipping daring arms around his waist.

Jonathan spins round and pulls her to him, locking his mouth onto hers.

"Just a minute, just a minute…wait…"

This is going too fast; she's not ready yet, if he'd just take it a little slower she might, she might, but he's pulling at her skirt, sliding it up to her waist and backing her over towards the bedroom door. Anna is used to the humming slowness of Roy, of knowing each stage and being able to pace the speed of sex. Jonathan has been teased for too long and will not move at Anna's pace, he is used to getting women into his bed quickly, before they can think, before they can change their minds and do all that bloody talking thing.

Anna can feel the edge of his bed against the back of her legs, he's actually lifting her up and onto the top of the duvet. She tears her mouth away from his. "Jonathan, please, just a minute…I'm not ready ..I'm…."

"You're ready, and you've had me ready for weeks."

He's pressing down on top of her and she can feel his hand pulling at her knickers.

She's still fighting for control, to act the part of the femme fatale, she even giggles ..

"Take it steady.. Jonathan, we don't have to rush.."

Jonathan is beyond any playful reasoning, she owes him.

* *

Trevor is looking into the windows of the 99p Shop, he sees that That Woman is on the tills again today so he yawns hugely to show that he's not bothered and that he'd go in if he wanted to. Ultra casual, he saunters next door to the new stationers as if he'd always intended to go there.

Now he's there he'll have a mooch to see if they've got any reduced videos. Trevor hasn't got a DVD Player, and doesn't want one thank you very much, and they're selling off the BBC Boxed Sets cheap now that the video is passé, so Trevor's pleased to beat them at their own game and get some David Attenboroughs.

Tony's followed him to the door of the shop; he's beginning to think that this is a waste of time today. Lindsay's nowhere in sight.. oh they're clever.

Diane spots Trevor and wants to avoid him; she can't face any of his 'How did Choir go without me?' questions, she's sorry for him but she's got enough on her own plate. She walks over to the door and spots Tony.
Small Town life ! – Paulette's right, she should move to Cornwall, if she's not bumping into Paul it's some other man who's a shit to his wife.

Tony has seen Diane, seen her notice him, and seen the guilt on her face as she walks over to the magazines at the far left of the shop; she's avoiding him, why? what does she know?

Diane lingers at the racks of glossy faces promising unmissable
Celebrity gossip and quick-fixes for unattainable beauty. She's staring at a woman's grinning face – some nonentity from a reality-TV show, the woman is promising to 'bare all' and Diane remembers a softer, gentler time when her mother would show her how to make a knitted spiral through a cotton reel with four nails in the top and the magazine would have illustrations of hats made with these swirling ropes of wool. Whatever happened to that? Nobody did that any more.
The woman on the cover in front of her mocks her nostalgia, there's a tattoo on the breast that's falling out of her dress and the headline promises: 'My drunken night with Spang.'
Who is Spang? Who is that woman? Diane looks across at a girl who picks up a copy of the magazine; she obviously knows who these people are …
Diane isn't that old, why has everything happened so quickly, while she wasn't noticing.

Tony is watching Diane, she's skulking there, pretending to be interested in the glossies, but he knows what she's up to. All those chats she's been having with Lindsay, what has Lindsay told her? The woman wouldn't be avoiding him like this if there was nothing wrong, it stands to reason.

Diane looks down at her shoes, as if there's something on them, so that she can slide her eyes over to where Tony is standing. He's still there, damn him. She'll just have to march out quickly and hope he doesn't waylay her.

Tony recognises that bent-head thing, he's done it himself, he knows what she's up to. She's scuttling out of the shop looking down at the floor.
Nobody walks like that; you can crash into people walking like that. What's she hiding, what's going on?

Diane walks quickly down the high street, she's going back home.
Tony knows he's going to be in trouble at work, he can't just let this be a total waste for nothing. Diane knows something, he's sure of it, he's come too far into this now. So he follows her.

* * * * * * * * * * * * * * * * * * * *

Jonathan is inside her, she's sure of it, but it's all been such a scramble that she doesn't know whether it's fingers or something else. Anna has given up trying to pull away from him, she's got to try and make the best of this, she's actually holding onto him now. He mustn't think this is some sort of rape, and she mustn't think that.

This is two adults, that's all. It hasn't gone quite the way she wanted it but if she makes a fuss now he'll never agree to be the Accompanist. She can't live with knowing he's shamed her, and they can't continue together as professionals if they both know the truth of this. Anna's mind is racing, as Jonathan's body jerks at her and she can no longer pretend that this isn't happening. He's lunging and heaving at her and she looks up at his face mottled with red and his hair, greasy with sweat. Why did she ever think he was attractive?

* *

Diane is at her front door, and Tony stands quickly up beside her. She's so startled she drops her keys and he bends to pick them up.

"It's Diane, isn't it?"

"Yes."

"Tony – Lindsay's husband," and he's holding out his hand.

"Yes, look, I'm sorry but I'm in a bit of a rush."

"It's just that I need a word – about Lindsay."

Diane's opened her door and Tony has pushed it open and gone into the hall in front of her. She looks around, back out at the street. This is so stupid, he's in her house and she's outside. She wants him gone.

"Look Tony, I really can't talk now."

Tony, is walking down her hall, looking in at her kitchen: "These places are really well organised, aren't they, the kitchen leading through to..oh a little dining room.. oh that's perfect."

And he's off into her home, like a man viewing a house, like someone who's been sent by an Estate Agent. Diane feels stupid standing outside her own front door, she walks into the hall calling through to him:

"Tony, I'm sorry but what are you doing? I've told you I really don't have time…"

"Oh?" He's put his head around the kitchen door.

"Yes .. you see I have to get back to town."

"But you've only just come from town."

"Yes…. but…"

He's smiling at her, all sweet reason, and Diane can think of nothing to say to stop this. She sighs her defeat - "Tony what did you want?"

"Just a chat, shall we have some coffee?" and he's walking back into her kitchen again.

She strides past him, trying to claim back the control.

"Well, all right, just a quick cup – you see I really do have to go back into town. I'd forgotten, I've got to pick up a prescription."

"Are you ill?"

"No – it's just …. It's my asthma, I need some more inhalers."

"That's all psychosomatic, isn't it," and it's not a question.

"No! – I get it really badly."

"Lindsay thought she'd got that. She hadn't of course, it was just stress…. Shall I fill the kettle?"

Diane is angry and confused at this, she can't seem to think her way through it. She doesn't know whether she should be throwing him out and getting cross or whether she should just make the blessed coffee and be polite.

Don't make such a fuss, her mother would say, but then her mother never made a fuss. Even when they took her away in the ambulance she'd been apologising to the paramedics about wearing her slippers.

Tony is filling the kettle, plugging it in, and Diane is just standing there watching him and hating herself for it.
"Shall I tell you a little secret?" Tony's smiling at her; a schoolboy who's eaten all the chocolate.
"What?"
"I've got a gun."

* *

Lindsay is looking out at the little garden at the back of her house; she's standing there, a cup of tea cooling in her hands.   She's wondering, she's thinking of all those police appeals that tell you that "somebody knows. Somebody's husband, somebody's son …."
The police asking for people to ring in, for the women to ring in, because it's the women – they always know.

* *

Anna's trying to limit the damage, she's playing the coquette, rolling away from Jonathan and smiling at him.
"You've been very naughty, Jonathan."
Jonathan's regretting not taking his trousers off, the zip on his flies is digging into the side of his thigh .. why is she giggling? Christ she's even wagging her finger at him. What does she think he's done - raided the biscuit tin?
Anna's trying to smooth the skirt back down over her thighs, but it's sticky with sweat and is jammed in a tight roll about her waist.
She's pulling at the material, she's trying to make this look casual, as if it's nothing, but the strength of her fingers betrays her and the material tears.
"I didn't do that." Jonathan's looking at the torn skirt.
Anna's getting off the bed, trying to look calm and in control of the mess of tangled hair, the smudged mouth and the skirt, the bloody skirt still wedged around her waist like a great thick hoop. She makes to

walk to the bathroom and almost falls headlong as her feet tangle amongst the knickers that are wrapped around one ankle. Anna snatches off the knickers with a dignity that is almost heroic and throws them back onto the bed. She makes it to the bathroom, Jonathan's plastic "en-suite", and stares at the woman in the mirror.

* *

Diane's standing in her hall holding a mug of coffee that Tony has made her. She hasn't sat down at the table in the kitchen where Tony lounges; he's taking an aching age to drink that mug of coffee, he keeps taking what look like great gulps but the liquid never seems to go down. She's hovering, still with her coat on.

"Why don't you relax?"

"I told you – I've got to get back – the prescription"...

He's got a gun? – did he say he's got a gun?

"Lindsay talks to you, doesn't she."

"What?" She's looking at his face, at that quite ordinary face. A gun, he said a gun. "Well, yes ..we talk .."

"What does she say?"

"Oh - just the usual, you know."

"No, I don't know."

"About Choir and …"

"About men."

"No, not really."

"About me." Tony's nodding.

"No, no more than …"

"No more than what?"

"You know, just general stuff. Look I've got to go, I'm sorry, perhaps we can talk another time – on the phone."

Tony almost laughs at that.. "on the phone"

"Well, yes."

"So you don't have to have me here, in your kitchen."

"Tony, I don't want to be rude but I don't understand what all this is about, you seem to think that Lindsay has told me things. She hasn't."

Tony gets up from the table.

"That's how you want to play it, is it?"

"I'm not playing anything. Look … I just want you to go now."

There she's said it, she's stopped doing this polite cat and mouse routine, she's asked him to leave. But he doesn't. He just stands there,

245

in her kitchen, holding one of her funny-pigs coffee mugs in his large square hands, and he's laughing at her. "Women !"

She backs down the hall to the front door, and holds it open.
  "I'm sorry, but I'm asking you to leave now."
Tony ambles to the door, his sauntering walk insults her. At the door he hands her the coffee mug.
  "You should have real coffee, it's much nicer. Ask Lindsay."

And he's gone. Diane shuts the door behind him and leans back against it.
What was that? What was she supposed to think that was?
What was she supposed to do?
What would Paulette have done, or Susie, or Anna – but that wouldn't happen to them, would it. Did he actually say he'd got a gun? She lived so much in her head these days that her reality was slipping, sliding just out of sight into the grey corners.   When she'd hidden from Tony in the shop had he been following her? Really? .. Or was it all part of the mess in her mind, that confused thick darkness?

  It's her.
  She's got herself all wound up with Paul and the Choir and Witsham and whether to move or get a job or …she can't trust her self to know what's happening anymore. She had thought that she knew, that she knew Paul, and she was wrong. She thought that she had a happy marriage, that everything was fine, and it wasn't. Had she been in danger just now? with Tony?

  She's trying to put the last half hour in a box, a box with a label, but she doesn't know what label to put on the box; she doesn't know if her fears are real or if it was "just her". She's worried that she's exaggerating her fears again, but … but he said he'd got a gun, didn't he?
  She cannot think of this now, not now. She's got so much in her head, it wasn't fair. She didn't need this, it's not her problem. She'll talk to somebody about it later, maybe Jo-Anne would tell her that men always say these things. Do they?

* *

246

Anna's sitting back in her car. She throws the gear stick into first and pulls away from Jonathan's flat; she's trying not to look as if she's running away, and even manages a bored sort of yawn in case he's watching from that window.

As she moves her legs she can feel a hot, wet stickiness. Her knickers were still left on his bed, she'd wanted to stride out of the flat in one fluid movement, and scrambling to pull back on her underwear hadn't fitted in that scene. So the naked flesh of her crotch is sliding against her skirt and she can feel that terrible oozing. She can smell him on her, and she can still see his face, puffy with lust. She has to get home, have a bath, think about this.

She'd told Jonathan she had to meet Roy in Oxford; she'd have said anything to get away. She'd actually kissed him at his front door, she had to prove to herself that this was all right, that she'd intended this all along, that she could cope with this.

Back outside her house, when she gets out of her car she looks back down at the driver's seat and sees a small dark patch. It was all right, she could get that out with her "Stain-Away". She runs up the stairs of her house, screwing her face up against the hot trickling down her thighs.

Into the bathroom, and Roy is there, leaning back in the bath with his hand between his legs. The other hand holds a travel brochure, there's a picture of an Italian market, and a dark-haired girl holding out some fruit to the camera.

"What are you doing?" It's almost a shriek from Anna.
Roy drops the brochure into the bath and jolts upright, hastily shoving his face flannel over a penis that is losing its erection with remarkable swiftness.
He's floundering to retrieve the brochure and keep the flannel in place at the same time. "I'm having a bath, aren't I."
"You should be at work!"
"The computers went down."
Anna's staring at the flannel as if it's a personal affront.
"I was going to have a bath."
"Why?"

Anna is suddenly aware of the torn skirt, and the mouth burned red and sore from Jonathan's stubble. Roy's looking at her, seeing her now.
"What's happened to you?"

There's a moment. A total moment of silence between them.

"Paulette's dog – that runny-eyed spaniel – that Harvey."

"He attacked you?"

"Well obviously. He had me over, in the car park - he should be put down."

"How big is he?"

"Believe me, he's larger than he looks."

Anna marches out into her bedroom, she's peeling off her clothes, keeping a wary eye at the bathroom so that Roy will not see the lack of knickers.

She calls through to him. "What is it with you and Italy?"

There's a wet flop as Roy throws the brochure out of the bath and onto the floor… "Oh – just a thought."

Chapter 71

It's the morning of the Witsham Carnival. Anna is staring at the ceiling, at the patterns of muddy light filtering through the bedroom curtains. She can hear a suspicion of rain outside; the slush of passing tyres. The Carnival doesn't start until two, so there's just a chance it'll clear up, the image of that Float with a drizzled Choir and soggy crepe paper pinned round the side does not appeal.

It's been four days since... Anna shifts in her bed. She hasn't found the word for that yet. Four days of phone calls and careful scheming; oh she'd been good, she'd got him where she wanted him now. He was hooked, he wanted more. It hadn't been that bad, she told herself, the next time she'd be ready for him. She'd learnt that lesson; she wouldn't be swept away like that again. Now she knew, now she knew that he was - what had been his word? – 'addicted' to her. He was even going to be on the Float. If he turned up, if he did actually get up there behind the piano lashed to the lorry, if he actually did sit there in his tail suit, she'd know for sure. She'd know she'd won.

The alarm clock turns on, it's Radio Four and the words are punching their way into Roy's consciousness – slicing into his dream, pushing aside the soft sunshine and the dark curly hair. Roy moans as he turns over, it's a little lament of loss as he reaches out and finds Anna beside him.

"I'll get in the shower first, I've got that Old Times Music Hall Medley for the Day Centre this morning."
Roy grunts his reply, knowing what's expected. "What are you singing?"
"Oh the same as last time, you know: "When Father Papered the Parlour", "Daisy, Daisy" – they like to sing along to it, you see."
"Won't it feel funny – with Trevor?"
Anna gives a little shake of her head, dismissing Trevor's pain.
"We're Professionals, anyway I'm sure that Trevor has Moved On by now."
Roy looks his doubt at that but doesn't say anything.
As Anna gets out of their bed, Roy turns over and tries to push back into sunnier climes.

* * * * * * * * * * * * * * * * * * * *

Trevor's been awake for hours, his costume for the old folks show is laid across the chair in his bedroom and his funny-moustache is on the little table by his bed. He's been trying not to get up too early; he didn't want to get in a state. He's all too aware that he hasn't achieved very much vis-à-vis the Choir: Lindsay had proved a bit of a dead-end, that Tony had answered the phone when he'd called her yesterday and had actually hung up on him.

Perhaps this was all he was going to get now, the Musical Hall Do's; he couldn't see Jonathan dressing up in Edwardian gear and wearing a cap. He could always refuse to do it of course, leave Anna in the lurch, but Trevor was wise to compromise, so he would hold what he had.

* *

Tony's in his Den, there's a letter from his Office spread out on the desk before him. The letter had arrived this morning; he's been fired.

It was Saturday, the day of the Carnival in Town, the office was closed so he couldn't even ring them and explain, negotiate. By Monday the thing would have become a fact, would have solidified; a name plate removed from a door, the HR Department sorting out financials. If he'd got the letter yesterday he could have gone in and talked to Peter Norris – but they'd planned this – they'd planned it so that it would be over a week-end.

That Diane knew something, and Trevor – having the nerve to ring yesterday when he thought that Tony would be at work – but he'd put paid to that.

Lindsay had been avoiding him; she was always out these days,

Choir this and Choir that – extra rehearsals for the Carnival.

Diane, oh she'd been all promise and tease that day in the car park hadn't she, a bit of a different story when he'd gone round to her place. Keeping her coat on, lying about having to go back into town; why did everybody lie?

He opens the box with the gun in it and looks at the dull gleam of the metal, rubbing a finger along the barrel.

He can hear Lindsay scrabbling about. These days she moved like some small animal, darting through rooms and scuttling around behind the furniture.

* *

The Day Centre is filling up; walking frames clink against the chairs and a soft smell of pee rises gently from padded cushions. Trevor is angling the piano so that he's side-on to his audience, Anna is setting up her music stand; she doesn't need it, she knows this material backwards but it's a barrier between herself and the rows of gummy mouths. Anna is not overly fond of the aged and is always grateful that her elbow length gloves are a perfect match with the Edwardian dress. They always grab at her, wanting to squeeze her hand and tell her how they remember her from last year. They say it as if it is a feat of extreme memory, their lives packed with so many treats and Help-the-Aged Days Out, they tell her that they always enjoy her singing and she has to smile and pat the thin claws that tremble against her gloves.

Trevor never seems to mind all that, but of course all those years with his Mother would have made him think that it was normal to kiss sunken cheeks and breathe in that staleness.

Anna has been breezily jolly with Trevor, going through the programme suggesting that they do "Oh Dear What can the Matter Be?" as a finale.

Anna's looking at her watch and catching the eye of the Day Care Supervisor.

"Hello Everybody! We all know what today is don't we?"
There's a slightly less than enthusiastic "Music Hall" from a few
thin voices in the hall. Anna looks up sharply at her audience and actually catches a raised eyebrow exchange from a couple with deaf-aids.

She's rattled; they were supposed to be grateful for this, could they actually not want it? Was this possible? She looks at her 'front row' – her groupies as Trevor calls them – the hand grabbers, the ones who call her "Dear".. they're all watery-eyed enthusiasm, clutching the photocopied sheets with the words on that Trevor always brings.

Trevor looks across at Anna, waiting for her nod. Anna is watching the Supervisor settle two late-comers at the back, they're grinning at each other and giving rather 'knowing' looks toward the stage area, and as they sit they actually nod their approval at Anna for her to start. This was not right, this morning was going all wrong, already one old boy in the middle of the front row was nodding off; they get too much, this lot, all that bussing them about to the Garden Centres and Blenheim Palace,

251

they'd got spoiled; well she was buggered if she was going to do them a Christmas Concert again.

Anna launches into her first number, her consonants crisp and clear, her eyes hard and glittering, and she focuses on the exit sign at the back of the hall. Forty-five minutes, that's all, and she won't stay for the tea and biscuits.

* *

Paulette's tying a little paper "ruff" around Harvey's neck; the dog is not pleased with this activity but is enduring it, as he endures all things, in the hope of biscuits.

"Now you're going to <u>sit ...</u>"
Harvey sits, the biscuit is obviously imminent.

"Not now, you're going to sit on the <u>Float,</u> next to me."
Harvey does not know "Float", but it's not the vet word, so it can't be too bad. He wags an optimistic tail and lolls his tongue at her. Paulette stands back and looks at him. "Good Boy."
Great – now – where's the biscuit?

"I'm wearing this," she's holding up her costume, "we're supposed to be nuns – because we're singing the Sound of Music Medley – I'm not sure why really, it was all because that Linda wanted to be all sexy and revealing and Grace got in a flap because she's overweight."
Harvey's concentrating hard on this, and Paulette bends down to share a whisper with him. "Well actually she's quite fat, but we don't say that word."
Harvey's ears are beginning to ache, his ears often ache and she never seems to notice. He gives them a waggle, that does it sometimes.

"So I'm the sort of cheeky novice nun and Linda and Susie are the sexy nuns, habits slit up the side and garters sort of thing ... why are you waggling your ears?"

Paulette's lifting up the great spaniel flaps.

"I hope you won't have to go back to the vet's again …. Harvey!"
He's off, round the back of the sofa, nose on paws, eyes closed.

* *

Trevor's sipping his tea and enjoying his talk with Mrs. Gorringe; he likes her, she reminds him of Mother – the nicer bits – the gratefulness and the soft holding of his hand.

Anna has left early on the excuse of getting ready for the Carnival. She's Mother Superior apparently, but with make-up, and she'll do the "Climb Every Mountain" Solo even though she'd given it to Linda last week. Anna had gone on bit about 'Deserving Something for All This Ingratitude' and had said that since Linda didn't ever do any charity work she didn't really deserve any glory anyway. Trevor had just listened, as he had always listened, he found it was best with women to just do that nodding thing.

* * * * * * * * * * * * * * * * * * * *

Grace is holding up her nun's costume. It does say XL on the tab but she's been here before. One woman's XL is another's Medium in her experience. She not sure whether it's supposed to be worn <u>over</u> anything; it was all very well for Linda and Susie to be hoiking up their habits to reveal Marbella tans and thighs as thin as a tube of Smarties, but she wasn't going to have her draperies flying up as she scrambled onto that float and risk showing her varicose tree trunks. She'll wear a long black skirt underneath, that would do it. Unless it was too tight when she had to climb onto the float...why was she always punished? She'd tried, she really had. She'd lost half a stone last year and got her Weight Watchers Certificate; she'd blue-tacked it to the fridge so that Geoffrey would see it, but he hadn't commented. She had been going to join again, last month, but she couldn't face ringing Mrs. Pointer and have to do all that explaining again. She should have rung, she should have joined ... again. Over and over, the wretched cycle of it, the precious pounds lost and then the miserable inevitability of the thickness creeping back. Grace pulls the black habit over her skirt, it's a tight fit and she has to yank it down over her not inconsiderable thighs; she's flushed with the effort and the panic that it won't fit and as she looks in the mirror she sees a large black wrinkled sausage-shape. She pulls at the material to make it longer, but it's stuck mid-calf and her skirt hangs beneath.

She looks at the clock, it's gone one, she should have left by now; they were rendezvousing at the church hall, Stephen was bringing the float there. Grace is panting with panic; she's got to wear this thing and it Doesn't Fit – she'd told them it wouldn't – they never understand, XL isn't enough when you're size 22, it's no good Susie saying 'Oh it'll fit, just breathe in a bit' she's never had to stand in front of a mirror and pray, and know that she's going to look like a hippo.

It doesn't fit !

She won't go. She'll say that she was sick, that Geoffrey was taken into Hospital, anything. She can't go like this, she can't look like this.

This was worse than his Masonic Do when she'd hired that floaty green number, at least that had had a scarf to drape over the tear in the front, and she'd been able to safety-pin the waist band so that it didn't have to be zipped right up ... but this is hopeless!

She's going through her wardrobe, taking out anything that's black, throwing it onto the bed behind her.

"Please God....please...there must be something..."

There's a mounting pile of black skirts and blouses tumbling off the side of the bed onto the floor. Grace is rummaging through them: "Anything... anything...please..." She's coughing back tears of panic and screwing the clothes in her hands, hating them.

* * * * * * * * * * * * * * * * * * * *

Rowena looks frighteningly convincing in her habit; she's put on an old pair of reading glasses with small round nun-ish frames and pulled the wimple low over her forehead.   She can't actually see too well because her prescription has changed a couple of times, but she's too impressed by the effect to wear her new 'frameless' pair; Rowena is often meticulous if required to don fancy dress, an aspect of her personality that her husband has had cause to celebrate.

Their marriage is a delicate balance between compromise and a determination not to see the cracks: she ignores his frequent week-end fishing trips when waterproofs are brought back home as dry and as neatly folded as they left, and he pretends not to notice that she prefers the choir meetings to attending his Wine Circle evenings. They both like being married, that anchor that allows their ships to sway sometimes away into a rougher sea. The safety of returning to the tried and tested, the familiarity of a shared appetite.

They are young enough to enjoy each other's bodies and the little games they have invented employing Colin's purchases from the 'Intimate & Fun' site on the internet, and while this lasts the fragility of their union is disguised beneath a vigorous lust.

Rowena's got her drum and beats a steady rhythm on it as she descends her stairs to the hallway. Colin is waiting to take her to town, and he smiles at his wife. "Can you keep that costume, for later, you know."

"Oh yes."

"You will wear suspenders underneath, won't you?"

"As long as you do the chanting first."

"Right." Colin watches her trot demurely to the car and has to start thinking quite intently about Ann Widdecombe and the European Union.

Chapter 72

The embarkation point for the floats has not been well chosen.

The church hall is teeming with Witsham toddlers dressed as flowers, their faces ringed with paper petals, their mothers debating coats on or off because of the weather. Witsham Primary School are using last year's costumes and are tomatoes again, round and red, they bounce around the hall knocking over the boxes of plastic masks; there's half a dozen Margaret Thatchers and a couple of Ronald Reagans, old stock that the Council had got on the cheap.

The Brass Band, second runners up at the Festival, are trying to change into their military frogging and complaining about the lack of space on the rails that have been lent by the Oxfam Shop. As they're hanging up their sweaters and coats, the shop owner is running a practiced and proprietorial eye over the garments.

"Excuse me...these aren't for your shop, we've got to go home in these."

The second trumpet's warning the trombone player. "She'll grab anything for that shop – nothing's safe – she cleared out the cloakroom at the 'Spring Bingo' last year. My mum spotted her 'Cotton Traders' fleece on Madam's 'Push for Africa' Rail."

The Hepton Village Majorettes are practicing their marching routine, a rather shambolic affair but much enlivened by twirling pom-poms and the fact that their skirts barely brush their thighs and the steps seem to require a lot of high knee jerks.

"One for the Dads then." Susie's nudging Linda as she watches them.

Linda has totally abandoned the wimple part of her costume and has created a false low neckline to her habit, Susie wishes she had had the nerve to do the same but as her hair is now greasy and flat under the headdress she's stuck with it, but she's hoisting her hem up and tucking the right side under the rope round her waist to further display her garter. They spot Grace trudging towards them.

"What is she wearing!?"

"Don't say anything, we'll have a fat-moment otherwise... Grace! – over here!"

Grace joins the other women. Nobody comments on anybody else's costume. Grace's Kaftan is dark blue with white embroidery around the neck only partially covered by a black pashmina shawl topped by a red scarf tied round her head. There are lions on the scarf.

"I'm an African Nun."

"Right."

"Absolutely."

Anna, stately in her Mother Superior costume, is making her way past men in gorilla suits. The gorillas wave their hands under their armpits at her and make grunting noises.

"I assume they're with the Young Farmers' Float." She joins the other nuns. She looks at Grace, opens her mouth but Susie jumps in.

"Stephen's just backing the Float round now. I told him you'd want to check it."

Two other nuns are approaching them, Diane and Lindsay, they're carrying their wimples and are wearing track suit tops over their habits.

"You two haven't made much of an effort."

Diane's pointing to the door. "It's freezing out there, and it's started to rain again."

"We thought we'd take our tops off once we were on the Float" Lindsay's face is pinched tight .. "Paulette's outside but she doesn't want to bring Harvey in here because she said he's having one of His Days and she wants to keep him calm."

Linda's peering over their shoulders at the church hall door.

"What's he supposed to be anyway?"

Diane shrugs: "Some sort of religious mascot, Cardinal Wolsey had one apparently."

"I don't think he had a spaniel."

"Oh she's tied his ears back... he doesn't look very happy about it."

Anna's sticking to her lies. "That blasted dog's a menace."

Stephen appears at the door and shouts across to the women.

"It's here! – we've got the piano up – you'd better see if it's in the right position, Anna."

Anna moves regally over to the door. One of the gorillas is making its way towards her again and she manages to scrunch a hairy foot under her stiletto heel. The other nuns step round the gorilla who is now hopping about and making screaming noises through his mask.

The Float is festooned with balloons and several posters of Austria from the local Travel Agent. The Sound of Music theme is further advanced by a dummy dressed in lederhosen from Bartlett's Men's

Outfitters and a rather ill-advised swastika. The piano has been strapped to the front of the lorry and Anna is testing the ropes as if she spends her life ascertaining safety standards.

Jo-Anne's husband Mike is standing on the float bouncing up and down on the little wooden platform beside the piano.

"You'll be all right up here, safe as houses, hold an elephant", and no-one seems bothered that this remark is accompanied by a series of creaks and a slight splintering sound.

Jo-Anne's coming round the side of the lorry. "Where's Jonathan?"

Anna looks at her. "You've got your wimple on inside out."

Diane goes over to Jo-Anne. "It says wash at 40 degrees on the front."

Jo-Anne takes it off and Diane helps her to get it sorted.

"Haven't seen you much lately?"

"No – sorry – I've been a bit, you know."

Jo-Anne thinks she does. "Yes I heard, about the pregnancy."

"The what?"

"Oh – I thought that's what you meant."

"What pregnancy?"

"Oh God – not now, Diane – you don't need this now."

"What are you talking about?"

"I'll tell you when we're on the Float."

Jo-Anne's daughter who looks as if she has just risen from the dead is standing beside the cab of the lorry as if rooted to the spot, a mammoth sulking figure of malevolent spite. The purple lips part enough to snap at her father. "You said I could drive the lorry."

"I said you could help – you haven't got a HGV."

"Yes – we got them through 'Go-Malaysia' for the gap year."

Mike's unconvinced but has long since given up against the strength of his daughter's will. He'd held out against boyfriends in her room with the door shut for three months, and she'd worn him down, day after day with the reasoning and the nagging and the shouting, and he's been eroded.

Three years ago he'd have held out; of course she shouldn't drive the lorry, she'll probably kill somebody, but he's tired, he's tired of all the battles and the conversations. He can hear the other women discussing his daughter and he reminds himself why he never usually takes part in these Choir things.

"Who's that? – why is she dressed like a vampire?"

"Oh she always looks like that."

Jo-Anne reaches across to her husband. "Oh let her drive it, we'll only be crawling along anyway."

Mike shrugs at Jo-Anne. "This is a mistake."
Jo-Anne's persuading. "Well at least she's Taking Part."
Susie's signalling to Stephen.

"That girl isn't seriously taking the wheel is she?"

"She looks murderous."
Diane agrees but sees Jo-Anne's face. "Oh I think that's sort of her usual expression. I think they're all like that at her age."

The Steam Engines arrive at that moment, and the debate is forgotten as the majorettes squeal and jump at the noise, watched with not a little joy by the Young Farmers. The Brass Band add their tuning-up to the row, and the two local Councillors who have been lumbered with the buggins-turn of marshalling this event raise their loudspeaker hailers to shout the company into further confusion.

"Will the Young Farmers and the Witsham Singers please get on their Floats."

"We are a Choir!" Anna is shouting across at Councillor Peters..

"And have you seen my husband? He's supposed to be in charge of Loading the Floats."
Amid the chaos, Faye climbs into the cab of the lorry and a look of sheer delighted venom briefly crosses the chalk-white face.

Rowena, clutching her drum to her chest, is struggling to climb up the back of the lorry.

"Put the drum down for a minute, I'll pass it up to you."

Rowena looks back at Paulette, decides to trust her, and heaves herself onto the wooden platform. Paulette is handing up a dog bowl and a large bottle of mineral water.

"He'll get de-hydrated with his ears back."
Harvey is on the end of his lead and at the end of his tether. His ears hurt; she's got them tied back behind his head where he can't see them. He's heard the 'vet' word and now he's being lifted up onto a big road thing that isn't his car. This is obviously another horrible way of taking him to that white-coated person and she's trying to confuse him with all this other stuff. There have been no biscuits for some considerable time and now he can smell that woman he doesn't like.

Anna has spotted Harvey. "That dog is baring his teeth at me ... Paulette, you should have a muzzle on that thing if it's on the float – health and safety – his mouth will be too near everybody's ankles up there. Anything could happen."

Paulette who does not know about Anna's lies and the Incident of the Attack in the Car Park is understandably confused. She shakes her head at Rowena. "I think Anna's losing it. There's no sign of Jonathan, is there. She'll have to eat humble pie and ask Trevor if it gets any later."

Anna is well aware that Jonathan has yet to turn up; she is trying not to keep looking for him as she supervises Linda and Susie up onto the lorry.

They turn to help haul Grace up, and Mike and Stephen are called into play, all gallantly pretending that she isn't heavy and that it's the angle of the climb.

Other nuns are appearing and as each one climbs onto the lorry there is another creak from the wooden platform.

Diane and Lindsay have positioned themselves at the back of the lorry, furthest from the piano and Anna's musical ear.

Across the room Anna can see Roy, in Councillor mode, sheep-dogging the children into lines beside the floats.

"Roy! Did you bring the small bottles of mineral water?"
Roy walks over to the Choir float followed by a dozen giggling tomatoes.

"I thought you'd got them – it's all right, I'll get some from the shop on the way round – pass them up to you."
Roy spots Harvey. "I should keep that animal on a tight lead if I were you."
Paulette actually looks behind her as if to see another animal.

"That dog... Harvey isn't it .. you should have seen the state of Anna when she got home the other day!"
Roy is pleased with himself for this, the animal is safely up on the lorry and can't get at him, and Anna can see that he is defending her and remembering what she says to him all in one comment. Anna purrs slightly at Roy's attention, that and the fact that her subterfuge has worked so well.
Paulette is totally confused and Harvey does not like being called an 'animal' and he does not like standing on this wooden thing, he is planning something, something horrible.

Diane is beckoning Jo-Anne to join her and Lindsay, and Jo-Anne is wishing she'd kept her mouth shut about Paul's girlfriend's pregnancy.

"I'd better stay here with the sopranos."
Diane hisses across at her. "Who's pregnant?"

The lorry lurches forward and the nuns cling to the wooden rails that have been erected around the lorry. The wood creaks beneath their feet as the Choir lorry moves out into the road. Anna's shouting down at Roy:

"We can't go without our Accompanist - he's not here yet!"

Diane's calling across to Jo-Anne again. "It's That Woman, isn't it ... Paul's girlfriend..."

"I'm not sure – well yes – my neighbour works at the Health Centre and she just happened to mention..."

"Is it His?"

"What?"

"Is it Paul's baby?"

Other nuns are joining in:

"Whose baby?"

"Paul was her husband."

"So who's pregnant?"

Lindsay is holding onto Diane's arm and trying to calm her down.

"Leave it for now, Diane."

"I'll kill him."

Anna can feel everything slipping out of control, nobody can seem to keep their balance on this lorry, it's jerking about all over the place, and Where Is Jonathan?

Roy's at the side of the float, looking up at her. "Shall I try and find Trevor?"

Later in the day, Anna thought that there should have been trumpets, a fanfare, something, as Jonathan appeared. Just as she was about to capitulate, just as she was about to admit that all her plotting and her scheming had been in vain, he arrived. And how he arrived! In his tailcoat suit and looking fabulous.

She wanted to shout "There, I told you! I was right!"

He had marched straight up to the lorry and climbed on board, and all the nuns had cheered and Anna had thought that this was her finest hour.

* * * * * * * * * * * * * * * * * *

Tony can hear the noise as he approaches the high street; the squealing children, the chuffing and hissing of the steam engines. The brass band is striking up with Colonel Bogey; they're off rhythm, the trumpets in the front can't really hear those behind them and their conductor hasn't really mastered walking-backwards-and-beating-time.

Tony arrives at the corner of Church Green and he can see the first float appearing round the corner of the war memorial. The Witsham Dramatic Society has surpassed itself, its members actually performing "The Importance of Being Earnest" as their lorry trundles over the speed bumps.

Dozens of small walking tomatoes are milling about bumping into each other and the teacher leading them, her face pallid with exhaustion, is waving with a leaden arm to the rows of digital cameras focussed upon their darlings.

Tony can see his father, taking that picture at the school play, shouting at him to "Look up Tony"; but he had been wearing his Herod's crown, and the sequins and the pins holding it together had got caught up in his hair and he had been trying to free it. His father had gone on shouting "Tony you're a cretin…put your head up". Tony had not known what a cretin was, but Herod's Attendants had, and they'd all started giggling at him. Tony had never had a leading role in the school plays before; he was usually a sheep or someone with a tea towel on his head. Miss Johnson told him afterwards that he had let everybody down and she wouldn't listen to him even when he showed her the crown and the pins that had been sticking into his head.

Now as he watched the tomatoes giggle and wave at their parents, he tried to remember when he had ever done that: that grinning, that splitting the whole face apart.

He was leaning back against the wall by the Oxfam Shop and his hand had found a rough bit of brickwork to rub against and he could feel the comfort of the beginning of the soreness.

Trevor is standing at the opposite corner. He hasn't brought his camera along this year. He wasn't going to come, he was going to watch that Penguins video, the one he's been saving for special and he'd reckoned that this was justified today. Then he'd got sniffy with Radio Three again this morning and he'd tuned to local radio – he'd had a good snigger at the rubbish presenter with the speech impediment who couldn't say her 'r's and wondered not for the first time at whether this was a requisite now at the BBC, and then she'd started on about What's On Around Oxfordshire this morning, and he'd been sitting on the toilet and hadn't made it over to the radio to turn it off before he'd heard her trailing the Witsham Carnival, and how there were twice as many "Floats" as last year .. Trevor had started humming loudly at that, sitting with his pyjama trousers around his ankles and his hands over his ears, but he'd still heard it - even though the woman had called it the Witsham Co*ww*al Society.

So now he's moving over to stand in front of the Men's Outfitters and Hire Shop because they've got a large receded doorway and he's going to stand back inside there when the floats go past, that's why he's chosen this corner. He should have brought his cap from this morning; he could have pulled that down over his face.   He can see Tony across the road, the man's got a bulky anorak on and his right hand is jammed down inside the front pocket, and Trevor hopes he's not doing anything disgusting in front of all those tomatoes.

Roy is holding a box of mineral waters and wondering where it will be best to stand. The first floats have come to a halt beside the war memorial so that the belly dancers can catch up; there's only five of them and they're dancing 'All The Way Round for Cancer' and two husbands who are determinedly not looking embarrassed, are rattling hopeful tins and trying not to look at their wives.

Roy is trying to remember how they do this on the Marathon, giving drinks to the participants, he knows that he will get it wrong and that Anna will be furious, at moments like this he has an uncanny ability to actually *hear* her: "Roy, all you had to do was hold the box up."
So he's standing there, doomed to failure, hoping that the bottom of the box won't fall through when he tries to get it up on the float.
"A handbag!!" is being shouted from the Dramatic Float, and the crowd cheer. The cheer gets less spontaneous as the actors repeat this scene several times; they had tried to time it so that the Big Scene would occur when they drew level with the Channel-7-for-the-Cotswolds Film Unit.
"I can't do it again" is being hissed out of the mouth of Lady Bracknell and there's a rather awkward silence as the actors wait for the float to get on the move again.

A gorilla is limping painfully along beside the Young Farmers' Float whose theme is 'Animals and Enemies' with lots of foxes with chickens in their mouths, and a pretty young girl in a gingham frock blowing a hunting horn at the crowd...Roy thought that that was a bit political and was annoyed, he'd had "Young Farmers' : Oklahoma" on his Floats List, and the float had started off with a few cowboys and the gingham'd piece, he hadn't noticed the foxes climbing aboard at the crossroads.

Trust them to spoil it, he'd be blamed of course, could see the headline now: "Political Demonstration Ruins Carnival – Councillor blamed."

Anna will go mad, she'll say he was trying to upstage Her Day.

Jonathan is praying that all those cameras and videos aren't going to capture this humiliation. Anna had been delighted at his costume but hadn't realised that the top hat – several sizes too big and borrowed with a last minute's inspiration from the Hire Shop - was so low over his eyes that he'd hoped to pass unrecognised. Every time a camera flashes at the float Jonathan bows his head low over the keys and hunches his shoulders in what he hopes is a Trevor-like flinch.

Last night he wasn't going to come, he'd decided that during a sleepless night of tangled sheets, damp with the sweat of his indecision. But he wanted her, he wanted her again, God help him, and he knew that this was her price. Her price for entry into that tight little part of her.

Their float is approaching the speed bumps, they're following the majorettes and the brass band is behind them - not good positioning for a Choir that's half way into the Musicals Medley. At the first speed bump the piano lurches alarmingly and there's a cracking noise under his piano stool.

Anna is looking at Jonathan, she's remembering how he jumped onto the float with his coat-tails flying just as she had begun to despair, but now she is jubilant. She's done it. Cheltenham is as good as won.

Lindsay and Diane don't know the words of "My Favourite Things."

Diane has sung the 'whiskers on kittens' bit twice and Lindsay is repeating 'when the dog bites' because she's forgotten about the 'bees stinging'.

They're at the back of the float, with the brass band only feet away, and what with their trumpets doing 'Memories' from 'Cats' and the lorry jumping forward whenever there's a gear change, it's been quite difficult to hold the alto line.

"Who's driving?"

"I think it's Jo-Anne's husband."

"It is Mike driving, isn't it?"

Jo-Anne bumps against Diane, she's holding her wimple on with one hand and clutching at the side of the lorry with the other, but she's smiling hugely.

"Actually it's Faye – my daughter – I'm so pleased she's Joining In with all the fun. She's been so distant you see, they are at This Stage. You've got to admire her, Having a Go."

Susie's leaning over. "As long as Faye's Having a Go doesn't mean we all end up having an accident."

The Lorry jolts forward and Rowena's drum topples over.

"I'm going to sit down and play it from here, I'm not going to take any chances with this, it's genuine goatskin you know, I can't get it repaired in Europe."

Harvey is slithering about on the wooden stage, his paws can't get a grip, and his water bowl had fallen over at the first crossroads and now his ears are wet.

Paulette has tied his lead to one piano leg because she had to volunteer to hold Anna's music stand, and Grace's African turban-scarf has slipped down around her neck.

"Can you shove this back on my head?" she's shouting across at Linda.

"I can't let go of the sides, I can't fall. I won't be able to get up."

Linda reaches across to pull Grace's scarf up and treads on something soft and hairy.

"Mind Harvey!" Paulette's heard his yelp.

Harvey is trying to lick his paw and remember who it is he is going to bite. He is going to bite somebody, he's fixed on that.

The Choir Float jolts on, and Anna has begun her solo and the "Hills Are Alive" in Witsham High Street. She's resting one hand on the lid of the piano and Jonathan is looking at that hand, at the possessive triumph of it. He can smell that the dog at his feet has disgraced itself and can feel thick sweat puddling under the rim of his hat and knows that no sex is worth this, nothing is worth this.

* * * * * * * * * * * * * * * * * *

Trevor's left the shelter of the Men's Outfitters doorway and is now walking slowly back to the car park. He'd twigged that the Choir were behind the Majorettes. So when the yobs watching from the roof of the building opposite had set up a cheer for the short skirts, he knew to turn away and face the window and stare at the "Back to School!" banner, he'd read the "Reductions on all Uniforms" sign three times while the Choir Float went by. He knew that Jonathan was there, even though he was screwing his eyes up not to see reflections, but the window had betrayed him and he'd seen a flash of a tailcoat. Typical.

The Steam Engines were going past him as he walked and Trevor would have normally liked them, but he hasn't the heart for it, he's going to go home to his penguins.

* * * * * * * * * * * * * * * * * * * *

Roy is walking back down the line of the Parade; the Steam Engines have got themselves into a bit of bother with the back end of the Diamond-Year's-Club lorry, the theme of which, 'Gambling Through The Ages', has dictated that a rather ill-advised matron dressed as a roulette wheel has managed to wedge her furry dice down the funnel of the steam tractor. The good lady's explanation: "I thought the steam would throw them up in the air," is not endearing her to the irate driver, there's much shouting to the effect that this tractor is a work of engineering art and furry dice belong hanging in car windscreens.

Roy is used to conflict and relishes the opportunity to use his ambassadorial skills. He may fail Anna on a fairly daily basis but he prides himself on being able to mediate the larger issues in life. The roulette wheel turns on him.
"Are you a Marshal? – aren't you supposed to make sure that consecutive Floats interact."
The tractor driver is having none of this.
"I'm not interacting with fluffy dice. I'll have you know there's Dignity in Steam."
Roy is at his most soothing. "Let's not spoil the day folks."
There's an acrid smell of burning fluff, and black smoke is now curling from the tractor's funnel. The Diamond-Years Ladies are beginning to panic.

Roy hates panic, he gets enough of that elsewhere, and he throws two bottles of Anna's mineral water up to the row of matronly playing cards that line the Gambling Float.

"Pour it down the funnel."
The four of spades is reaching over to comply just as the tractor driver reverses his darling out of this danger into the following majorettes, who, although unhurt, feel obliged to scream with satisfying volume.

"Roy!"
He can see his Mother Superior glaring at him from the front of the Choir Float.

The majorettes have upset Harvey; he's never liked screaming, She doesn't do much of that at home, and apart from the sniffing after the Man goes off again, Harvey hasn't had much to do with emotional noise. Today has been a very traumatic event for a dog, and he's still got his ears tied back and they still hurt. That man in the long black coat is waving his feet around again, he's already knocked over the water bowl twice and now that black foot is coming near his ears again. His ears hurt. The foot is right by his mouth, this is Harvey's moment. Jonathan yells as slightly yellowing teeth just penetrate his sock. Paulette is straight into denial. "It wasn't him, he's never bitten anyone."
Roy's quick to disagree. "He savaged Anna only last week"
Harvey is totally traumatised by his action and now buries his head pathetically into Paulette's skirt. "It's all right Harvey; I'm not having you Put Down."
A slight stirring on the dog's tail confirms that Harvey is thus reassured.

Roy, Marshal of the day, is taking charge.
He turns on the majorettes: "Stop screaming!"
Jonathan's agreeing. "Yes, you're not bleeding are you?!"
A couple of the more stalwart baton-twirlers are peering up at the choir float and at the slight smudge of red on Jonathan's sock.

"Well neither are you, really."
The nuns have all gathered around to share in the moment.
Susie's keen to display that she is au-fait with all things medical. "You'll need a tetanus for that, Jonathan."
Paulette's affronted. "No he won't. Harvey is regularly wormed!"
and Grace's getting one in for all the times she's watched that flaming red hair being tossed around and has had to hold Susie's dresses while

267

she tries on yet another size 10 in a changing room. "I'm afraid that watching 'Casualty' doesn't qualify you to advise medical intervention, Susie. Whereas I've done CPR training, remember?, the Council sent me on that two-day Course in Basingstoke."

"He doesn't need CPR!"

"I'm not saying he does, I'm just saying….."

"Enough!" It's Roy again, who seems to have risen to this occasion as something for which he has waited for a long time.

"Come along, let's get this Parade going again…Choir Float, Forward!"

Anna is looking at Roy with something rather akin to pride.
Another Parade Marshal runs up to help sort out the chaos, and Anna is moved to snap at him. "Oh, you took your time, well Roy has sorted everything out, and don't tell me he couldn't be Mayor."

With a look to her husband that he could perhaps interpret as a smile, Anna returns to the task of regaining her composure for her next solo.

Her determination to ignore the fiasco around her is fuelled by her ambition and her longing for this moment of glory. She smiles her tight and brittle smile at the crowds and breaths deeply into her fantasy of this day.

Order is restored, the Parade continues.

Bright red and shiny, a couple of the tomatoes are paying the price for their earlier enthusiasm of all that hopping up and down and the ill-advised consumption of hot-dogs. The tears and vomiting have alerted the mothers who have bustled to the rescue with baby-wipes.

One of the tomatoes is bending double and hawking onto his mother's shoes, and his little round friend is copying him and trying very hard to make the same noise. The mothers watch them, weary with a concerned apathy:

"…. I don't know why they always have to be vegetables."

Tony sees the Choir float jerking towards him, the majorettes are in front of it, leaping about, raising their knees, flashing their silly frilly knickers at him, one of the girls looks a bit like that stroppy typist from work…work..he mustn't get confused. He's so sick of being lied to, and ignored. He'd asked that typist to do his Analysis Sheet last month, he'd asked her twice, really politely, telling her that he knew that she was 'up to her ears' because he knew that she was always saying that. They sit there, those girls, giggling and sending silly jokes to each other on their e-mails but they're always 'up to their ears' if you want anything done. If *he* wants anything done. Oh yes, they're all over Miss Johnson, no, that was school, he mustn't get confused, they were always trying to confuse him. And the lies, Lindsay and that Diane, it's always lies.

It was the Choir; everything had been fine until she'd joined that Choir. Lindsay and that solo, and the drumming, why hadn't that cow Anna got back to him about the drumming?

Now Lindsay was going cold on him; well just wait until she found out about the job. She'd leave him. Women did that when you got the sack. Why was everybody screaming? All those silly tomatoes squealing at their parents. "Take a photo, Daddy."

Why was everybody laughing? What was funny?
There were a couple of thugs in masks bearing down on him, waving their collecting tins. Margaret Thatcher and Ronald Reagan, but they were dead weren't they? The plastic faces grinning hugely and the muffled voices beneath.. "Come on, it's for Charity!"
Tony can feel the hard piece of metal in his pocket, it was warm now from the holding.

Another masked face is leering at him; it's a cowboy from the Young Farmers' float, walking along squirting the crowd with his plastic water pistol. He halts in front of Tony and points the weapon at him There's a bubble of water trickling from the plastic barrel.
"Hands up mate! – your money or your life."
Tony's eyes are gleaming with pure joy and his hand closes around the handle of the gun in his pocket.

Margaret Thatcher has come back to grab hold of the cowboy.
"Come on, let's squirt the majorettes!" and they bound away.

The Choir float draws level with Tony and he looks up and at first is confused that they're all nuns. Then he sees them, Lindsay and Diane, together, side by side. Lindsay's actually got her arm around Diane's shoulders.
"I just can't get over it … pregnant … after all he said."

Tony can't hear what they're saying, but he knows, Diane is telling Lindsay about him going round to her house. He can see from Lindsay's face – she's angry. Diane is waving her arm about and Lindsay is nodding, she's agreeing with her!

Anna is signalling for the next number. She reaches over to rub Jonathan's shoulder, leaning down to murmur into his face. Tony watches her straighten up, a great stupid smile all over her face, She looks down at the crowd – straight at Tony – and that red mouth is flashing at him, laughing.

It was the Choir, it had started all that nonsense, Lindsay blaming him for crushing her hand in the car door, and then going on and on about how he had hit her, and then all that dodging about and the phone calls. Wearing that bloody great bandage around town. Getting the Choir on her side, talking to Diane and Trevor and God knows who else.

That bloody choir, it's ruined everything. Lindsay wouldn't have met Trevor, wouldn't have got all stupid about that solo, that stupid solo, why couldn't she have just sung it instead of making such a fool of him.

Anna is looking down at the crowd; they're all looking up at her, waiting for her to sing. Jonathan is playing that piano, she'd done it, she'd got him, and now everybody is waiting for her solo, her face is pure joy as she hears the cheering all around her.

She'll send Miss Etch the Witsham Gazette, there'll be a picture of Anna by the piano, singing, and the usual three-page-spread about the Carnival, so she'll know now, she'll see she was wrong.

Anna closes her eyes and she is at the front of the crowd at Cheltenham, and Aunt Jo is sitting in the front row. Aunt Jo is clapping and clapping and smiling up at Anna, and Anna is full of the noise and the shouts from the crowd.

Tony stares up at her. Anna. She'd made him tell her about his father, he'd stood in that choir room and he'd had to tell her all those lies. She'd made him audition, she'd humiliated him and he can taste the shame in his mouth, it's an old taste, a remembered taste, and it takes him back – back to being small and having to pretend he wasn't hurt.

Anna is actually laughing, throwing her head back and laughing, and Tony can see his father, laughing as the kid from next door blows out the candles on his Birthday Cake. Laughing because the candles fell over and the little flames sizzled into the fat white icing.

Roy is holding up the box of mineral water, Linda has seen him and is reaching down to get it as one of the bottles slides off the top and bounces onto the ground; it splits open and the water splashes onto the roadway.

Anna does not hear the shot that kills her; there is a quick hard push against her chest and then oblivion.

She lands on Harvey and her blood wells thick onto the wooden platform beside the piano.

Linda with a misplaced sense of "professionalism" goes straight into her solo and belts out "Doh, a deer, a female deer" at the crowds who are understandably paying more attention to the fact that a gorilla has rugby-tackled the man with the gun.

The gorilla – feeling immune from bullets because of the barrier of his costume – is fuelled as much by the pain in his foot as by any heroism, although The Witsham Gazette will later be moved to write that ...

"Young Farmer prevents further bloodshed at Carnival Massacre"

The gun skitters across the pavement to come to rest at the feet of a tomato, who picks it up and points it at the video camera that has lovingly followed his progress along the route.

There is much screaming at the child, and Tony, as he lies beneath the gorilla, hears a man's voice shouting: "It's not a toy!" and remembers Christmases of clothing and school shoes, and his father telling him not to get excited at the parcels under the tree because they weren't things to play with.

The child is now waving the gun at the Gorilla....

And the moment is enough..... enough for Tony to wrench himself free and run off between the floats.

The crowd parts before him, they've seen the shooting and the blood and brave men are scrambling to move out of the way of the fleeing man, and later telling each other that they would have tackled him if not for having to pull their wives away from the danger.

Roy cannot understand what he has seen. His wife is not really a nun, the children are not really tomatoes, and the masks on the revellers around him are leering with huge grins that hide the shock and fear beneath, and into his mind he sees the adverts for Disney World and the fact that nothing is real.

So too Rowena, hindered by last year's prescription glasses, is not really sure that she has seen correctly as she stares down at Anna who looks as if she's singing because her mouth is open, but as she focuses hard upon that gape of red lipstick, she sees that it is full of blood.

Susie screams down the side of the lorry into the cab that Anna's been shot and that they must get a doctor, and Faye – wild child with attitude – comes into her own, she drives the float straight across Church Green, scattering tomatoes and parents, and buggies with babies snatched out of the way of her wheels, and makes it up Walsh Way to the Medical Centre in four minutes, which was later agreed to be a record, and young, new Dr. Kinsala was able to add an emergency gunshot wound to his CV and also a 'Death At Scene'.

Faye gets out of the lorry and kneels quickly down on the pavement, vomiting quite carefully into the gutter. Her mother, momentarily forgetting the cause of her daughter's actions, and the dead woman lying in the lorry, is quite overcome with pride as she kneels down beside her child and tissues vomit and mucus from that purple mouth and cries tears of relief that – as she will later recount – Faye has become a valuable member of Society.

Jonathan has stepped away from the piano into a puddle of thick blood, and as he stands beside the lorry he wipes the side of his shoes against the grass verge.
The nuns stand around the lorry and watch as Roy runs puffingly up the road towards the float; the crepe paper banners are trailing loose from the little wooden stage and the dummy dressed in lederhosen has toppled sideways to lie beside Anna.

Lindsay and Diane are standing a little apart.
When the shot had rung out Diane had known immediately who had fired the gun and as she had crouched down in the float she had met Lindsay's eyes and saw that she too knew.
Because they always knew, the women.

Chapter 73

The door to the Choir Room finally gives way under the smashing of Tony's fists against the wooden frame.

He stumbles into the room and throws himself back onto the door to close it against the madness.

The sound of the squealing steam engines echoes around the room and the curtains billow softly against the watching windows.

Tony staggers across to the piano, and leans hard against it so that a single note escapes. He pushes his hands down onto the lid to silence the keys, he's gibbering with panic, pushing his hands over his mouth to silence the fearful noise as he tries to gasp hot air between fingers slithering with sweat, each breath is a jagged knife against his chest.

He'd run away once, after that birthday party and the candles he hadn't been allowed to blow out, he'd run out to the garden shed and hidden behind the lawn mower, hunkering down amongst the wet grass clippings and the cans of stuff that killed the moss. He'd looked at that, the vile blue liquid with the little black skull on the can to tell you it was poison.

He'd thought about drinking it, he remembered that, tracing his finger round the words that told him not to, and he'd seen the nails on that finger bitten down to their quick and he'd known that he wouldn't dare.

Today he had dared.

A lifetime of wanting to do it. To show them. So many years of hating, and being hurt, over and over, but never doing it.

So he'd done it, and now he can hear the wailing of sirens and the shouts of "He's in there!" and the stamping, pounding noise of pursuit from shoes heavy with power.

Tony can feel the hot piss trickling down his leg.

This has gone beyond his idea of how this would be, he is in a foreign country and he does not have the language.

This is Big Boys' Games and he doesn't want to play any more.

The Room will not protect him; it has waited for this moment and it can smell the blood on him.

Chapter 74

The room is waiting; it is holding its breath. It knows what is to follow, and it waits for the voices and for the music.

Trevor gets there early, as he always does these days, and sets out the sheets of music that he has photocopied that morning.

The choir arrive, there have been some who have left, but many more have joined. Trevor thinks that perhaps there really must be no such thing as bad publicity.

Outside, Diane and Grace are walking together towards the school, their choir folders under their arms, they pass "Annaroy" House, beneath the "Sold" sign attached to the Estate Agent's board.
Roy has moved to Oxford, not quite Italy.

Many miles away, in a town called Gravesend, a retired History teacher is reading her newspaper, "Woman killed at Carnival" about a nun who was singing as she died, and Miss Etch looks at the picture of a woman called the Choir Mistress, and does not recognise nor understand as she casually turns the page.

In the Room, Trevor has angled the piano so that he can now conduct his choir from the piano stool: "We'll warm up with 'Ah Poor Dove.....' Ladies. Lindsay, Dear, if you could lead us in....."

The women's song drifts outside, their voices hanging damply in the darkening air of the car park where a black dog sits patiently beside Trevor's car. It is watching the door to the choir room, and it waits.

Lightning Source UK Ltd.
Milton Keynes UK
UKOW04f1537051113

220464UK00002B/16/P